The bronze giant, who with his five aides became world famous, whose name was as well known in the far regions of China and the jungles of Africa as in the skyscrapers of New York.

There were stories of Doc Savage's almost incredible strength; of his amazing scientific discoveries of strange weapons and dangerous exploits.

Doc had dedicated his life to aiding those faced by dangers with which they could not cope.

His name brought fear to those who sought to prey upon the unsuspecting. His name was praised by thousands he had saved.

DOC SAVAGE'S AMAZING CREW

"Ham," Brigadier General Theodore Marley Brooks, was never without his ominous, black sword cane.

"Monk," Lieutenant Colonel Andrew Blodgett Mayfair, just over five feet tall, yet over 260 pounds. His brutish exterior concealed the mind of a great scientist.

"Renny," Colonel John Renwick, his favorite sport was pounding his massive fists through heavy, paneled doors.

"Long Tom," Major Thomas J. Roberts, was the physical weakling of the crowd, but a genius at electricity.

"Johnny," William Harper Littlejohn, the scientist and greatest living expert on geology and archaeology.

**WITH THEIR LEADER, THEY WOULD
GO ANYWHERE, FIGHT ANYONE,
DARE EVERYTHING—SEEKING EXCITEMENT
AND PERILOUS ADVENTURE!**

Bantam Books by Kenneth Robeson
Ask your bookseller for the books you have missed

(Coming in January 1987 is Doc Savage Omnibus #2)

Four Complete Adventures in One Volume

THE ALL-WHITE ELF, THE RUNNING SKELETONS, THE ANGRY CANARY, and THE SWOONING LADY

Kenneth Robeson

BANTAM BOOKS

TORONTO • NEW YORK • LONDON • SYDNEY • AUCKLAND

THE ALL-WHITE ELF, THE RUNNING SKELETONS,
THE ANGRY CANARY, and THE SWOONING LADY

*A Bantam Book / published by arrangement with
The Condé Nast Publications Inc.*

PRINTING HISTORY

The All-White Elf *was originally published in* Doc Savage *magazine,
March 1941 Vol. 17 — #1. Copyright 1941 by Street & Smith
Publications, Inc. Copyright © renewed 1968 by The Condé Nast
Publications Inc.*

The Running Skeletons *was originally published in* Doc Savage
*magazine, June 1943 Vol. 21 — #4. Copyright 1943 by Street
& Smith Publications, Inc. Copyright © renewed 1970 by
The Condé Nast Publications, Inc.*

The Angry Canary *was originally published in* Doc Savage
*magazine, July 1948. Copyright 1948 by Street & Smith
Publications, Inc.
Copyright © renewed 1976 by The Condé Nast Publications, Inc.*

The Swooning Lady *was originally published in* Doc Savage
*magazine September-October 1948. Copyright 1948 by Street
& Smith Publications, Inc. Copyright © renewed 1976 by
The Condé Nast Publications, Inc.*

Bantam edition / August 1986

ISBN 0-553-25947-4

Published simultaneously in the United States and Canada

*Bantam Books are published by Bantam Books, Inc. Its trade-
mark, consisting of the words "Bantam Books" and the por-
trayal of a rooster, is Registered in U.S. Patent and Trademark
Office and in other countries. Marca Registrada. Bantam
Books, Inc., 666 Fifth Avenue, New York, New York 10103.*

PRINTED IN THE UNITED STATES OF AMERICA

O   0 9 8 7 6 5 4 3 2 1

Contents

THE ALL-WHITE ELF

Contents

I

THE OGRE

The man stopped his black coupé in the street in front of the apartment house. He looked at the apartment house, then glanced up and down the street, looking particularly for a policeman. There was no cop. Relieved, the man wiped his mouth on the back of his hand.

He felt of his hip pocket.

Then he got out of the coupé and headed purposefully for the apartment-house entrance.

He was a man made of bones and dry, brownish hide. His suit was dark and new, apparently being worn for the first time. He had made a mess when he tied the knot of his dark tie. He had eyes like a tiger.

He ran a finger up and down the doorbells until he located one—*Arnold Haatz, Apartment 4F.*

To get into the apartment house, the man used an old gag. He pressed several buttons at once. He did not ring Arnold Haatz's bell, however. When the lock release buzzed, he entered.

The elevator was a self-service type—there was no operator. The man rode it to the fourth floor, pulled off his overcoat and rolled it into a ball, used the ball to block the elevator door so it would not close. The elevator would remain there as long as the door was blocked open.

He felt of his hip pocket again. He stood with his hand on the pocket for a while after he reached the door of Apartment 4F.

He was perspiring. His face was white. His chest felt heavy, as if his lungs were made of lead.

He was afraid to kill Arnold Haatz here, he realized. It was too public. The sensible thing to do, and the only alternative he saw, was to decoy the man into the country.

He knocked on the door.

"Mr. Arnold Haatz?"

"Yes."

"You are the Haatz who works for the government—you are in Russel Kinner's office, connected with the superintendent of prisons?"

"That's right."

Arnold Haatz was a placid-looking goose of a man. His skin was pink, his eyes were as pale and pleasant as August sky. His body was thick, and his hands were small hams.

"I've got a message for you, Mr. Haatz."

"Message?"

"From Audine Million. You know her, don't you?"

"If it's Jerry Million's sister you mean—yes, I know her."

"That's the one. She's in a jam. She wants you to help her."

Haatz narrowed his blue eyes. "Where is she?"

The man who was made of bones and dry brown hide hesitated for a grim instant.

"She's at a tourist camp north of town," he said.

Haatz did not answer immediately. He was puzzled. "I don't understand why she should send for me," he said.

"I was just around handy, so she sent me."

"What is this trouble?"

"Don't know. She didn't tell me."

"Is it her brother who is in trouble?"

"I don't know."

Haatz said coldly, "I wouldn't give that brother of hers a drink of ice water if he was in hell. Jerry Million is no good. I would rather help a snake."

"It ain't her brother."

"Jerry Million is as low as they come." Harshness was in Haatz's voice. "A man who would do what he did should be hung."

"It ain't her brother."

"I thought you said you didn't know what it was," Haatz said.

"I just know it ain't her brother."

The puzzled frown left Haatz's forehead. He looked at the other man. "What did you say your name was?" he inquired.

The other hesitated.

"Smitty," he said. "Call me Smitty."

"Well, wait a minute, Smitty," Haatz said, "and I'll get my hat and coat."

Haatz stepped back and shut the door. The moment he was alone in his apartment, he flung to the telephone, riffled through the directory, found a number, and called it, dialing with nervous jerks of his stubby forefinger.

"Hello. Miss Audine Million's home?... Can you tell if Miss Million is there?... Oh, it is! You are Miss Audine Million?"

"Yes, this is Audine," the young woman said. She had a throaty, pleasant, earnest voice.

Haatz scowled at the hall door. "Have you been home all evening?" he asked.

"Yes."

"Are you in trouble? Do you want help?"

"No. Why, of course not." The girl sounded completely amazed. "What... what on earth is this, anyway. Who... who are you."

"Arnold Haatz. You remember me?" Haatz considered, frowning. Then he said suddenly, "Listen, where is that brother of yours?"

The change in Audine Million's voice was stark. Terror came rushing with her words.

"Oh, mother of mercy! Has Jerry been— Did they find him, and— *What has happened to him?*"

"Were you expecting something to happen to your brother?" Haatz countered.

"I don't know. Something strange is going on, and I was afraid—" She stopped with that, and was silent a moment. Then she said, "Oh, I shouldn't have said that." She laughed, but it was not a hearty sound of mirth. "I was just kidding."

Haatz was puzzled enough to nibble at his lower lip.

"You say something strange is going on?" he asked.

"No, no, I was just—well, being facetious," the girl said swiftly.

She's a very poor liar, Haatz thought. And very upset.

He said, "I like for people to tell me the truth."

Audine Million's answer was slow coming.

"Really, Mr. Haatz, aren't you presuming a little?" she said finally. "After all, we hardly know each other."

"Yes, we hardly know each other," Haatz agreed dryly. "As a matter of fact, that's why I called you."

"I don't understand."

"And I," said Haatz, "don't understand that remark about your brother and something strange going on."

Again, there was a silence. This time, the girl did not reply. She hung up. The click was a slow one, as if she had placed the receiver on the hook very thoughtfully.

Haatz stood and bit at a thumbnail for a time. Then he went into his bedroom, and got two heavy woolen socks. He put one sock inside the other. Then he entered the kitchenette, poured a box of common salt into the socks, and smacked the result against the palm of one hand. He had a very good blackjack.

He opened the hall door. Smitty was standing there. Haatz hit Smitty with the salt-filled socks. He tried to land the blow on Smitty's temple, but the man ducked. The blackjack, glancing off the top of Smitty's head, knocked the fellow to his knees.

Haatz grabbed the socks with both hands and wound up like a baseball pitcher and did his best to brain the other man. More by accident than design, Smitty got his head out of the way and the socks hit his shoulders, so that there was a loud report and a white spurting of salt as the socks split. Smitty flattened out on the floor. He pulled a gun out of his clothing.

The gun made a deafening noise. The bullet made cold the left side of Haatz's face, went on up and made a neat round hole in the ceiling plaster, and, on the floor above, started a woman screaming.

Haatz jumped back, slammed the door. The only gun he had was a .30-06 caliber big-game rifle. There is a Federal regulation about the ownership of a gun with a barrel less than sixteen inches long, but this one certainly didn't come under that prohibition.

He got the rifle, clipped some of the cartridges—they were almost the size of fountain pens—into the magazine. He tossed a chair against the door. The man outside promptly fired a bullet through the panel. With the .30-06, Haatz proceeded to blow channels through door and wall.

The man outside ran.

Haatz heard the man's feet rapping the corridor floor, and peered through a hole he had blown in the door. He saw

Smitty scoop up his balled topcoat, which had been holding the elevator door open, leap into the cage, close the door.

Lunging down the hall, Haatz reached the elevator door. He lifted his rifle. For a moment, he calculated where he should aim; then the rifle blasted flame and lead against the sliding metal door.

The one-hundred-and-eighty-grain bullet had a muzzle energy of twenty-nine hundred and fifteen foot-pounds. It tore through the sheet metal and ripped the safety switch off the inside, opening the circuit. The opening of the safety circuit instantly cut the current out of the motors at the top of the shaft, and the cage stopped.

The moment he was sure the elevator had halted, Haatz ran for the stairway. He took the steps in a series of downward jumps, holding the rifle ready.

The elevator had stopped between two floors, in such a position that, when the doors were opened, there was a crack at the top through which a man could crawl to freedom, although the crack was very narrow and difficult to reach.

Haatz saw the man crawling out of the elevator. He saw this without being noticed. He hesitated, half lifting the rifle. Then he changed his mind.

Running down another flight of stairs, and out of the door, Haatz looked about for a hiding place. There was only one car parked in the block, a black coupé. Haatz started to climb into the machine; then it occurred to him that the car might belong to his quarry. Smitty had said he had a car waiting.

Haatz tried the baggage compartment in the back. It was open, and it was roomy. He climbed in with his rifle, and lowered the lid. To keep it from locking, he jammed his handkerchief into the slot which the lock tongue normally entered. This not only kept the lid from locking, but caused it to remain open a crack, through which he could keep a watch.

Grim curiosity was causing Haatz to do what he was doing. A stranger had come to him and lied to him, apparently in hopes of decoying him into the country. Haatz was going to trail him.

Haatz wanted to know why. What was going on? At heart, he was a man who liked excitement, although he looked meek and, he well knew, a little like a pink pig. His fondest memories were of his army days, the war, of a hitch he had served with the Villa revolutionists in Mexico. These things were in his youth, and he did not talk about them much any more. People did not believe him. No one could think, after looking at him, that he had done deeds of daring and peril, and would like to do them again.

It was luck that put him in hiding in the back of Smitty's car.

Smitty dashed out of the apartment house a moment later, dived into the machine and drove it away.

The car went fast. The bouncing made dust rise up and get in Haatz's soft pink nostrils. He ground a finger against his upper lip desperately, but in spite of that remedy, he had to sneeze twice. Luckily, the car made so much noise that he was not hear.

Soon the car traveled at a more leisurely pace. And eventually it stopped. Through the crack around the edge of the lid, Haatz watched Smitty cross the sidewalk with nervous haste and enter a drugstore.

The drugstore had a side door. Haatz reached that. He held the rifle straight up and down at his side, so that it was as inconspicuous as possible, and eased inside the door.

Smitty was in one of a bank of three telephone booths.

Haatz stepped into the adjacent booth without being noticed. He could hear some of what was said.

"—and I got into the apartment house all right," Smitty was saying. "I knocked on the door, and this Haatz opened it. I had me a story all ready. I told him Audine Million was in trouble, and wanted him to help her."

Smitty sounded whining and uncertain. Obviously, he was making explanations to someone he feared.

"I couldn't just fill him full of lead when he opened the door," he wailed. "There was a cop in front of the place a minute before. I knew the cop was somewhere in the neighborhood. And how was I to know the guy wouldn't fall for the story about the girl wanting his help? . . . What's that you're saying? Oh, why didn't he fall? I don't know. He said he was gonna get his coat and hat, but when he came back, he cut loose on me with a club. I was damned lucky to get away from there alive. That Haatz guy may look soft and pink, but he's hell on wheels."

Haatz was warmed by this praise of his ability. He had

been thinking about calling the police. But now he changed his mind.

He would enjoy some excitement. His daily employment, the hunched-over-a-desk job which he had held during recent years, was monotonous. For a long time, his life had been dull to the point of despair. Now he felt a sudden consuming desire to take another whirl at the kind of life he had once led.

He heard the man in the adjacent booth say, "What do you want me to do now?"

Haatz strained his ears.

"What about my car?" Smitty asked. "But that jellopy cost me—Oh, sure. Sure. I wasn't trying to argue. Sure. I'll let the car set where it is. But what if the cops find it?"

The other lowered his voice, and it was more difficult to catch what he said. But Haatz gathered that the man at the other end of the wire, who was Smitty's boss, was going to send a third man, a man who had an air-tight alibi for the time of the excitement at the apartment house. This third man would pick up the car and see that it was run into the river in an obscure spot, where it would not be found.

Haatz grinned thinly. These men were clever. If he was going to take a whirl at excitement once more, Haatz thought, these men would be worthy foes.

Haatz slipped out of the telephone booth. He left his rifle behind, because it was too conspicuous. He wished he had a pistol.

Smitty was not difficult to follow. He used a bus, changed to another bus, then walked. After a time, he joined a tall, cadaverous, bushy-haired man.

Haatz stared at the man whom Smitty had met.

"What a horrible thing!" he muttered.

He was so shocked that he felt a little sick.

The man whom Smitty had met had the general aspect of an emaciated crow, and he attempted to overcome this handicap by wearing bright clothing—his garb just now was gay tweeds, ox-blood shirt, with emerald tie, handkerchief and socks—with the result that the effect was even more macabre. His face was long, had the complexion of deceased fish; his nose was large and hooked; his eyes were piercing black demons that roosted back in the caverns under the black caterpillars that were his eyebrows.

He could have played the lead in a horror picture without much make-up.

Smitty met him in front of a house. The two turned, sauntered idly to a tobacco store a few yards away, where they bought cigars. Then they returned to the house, and entered.

The pair had seemed well known in the store, so Haatz entered and made a check.

He bought a cigar. "Thought I knew those fellows who were just in here," he said. "Haven't seen either one of them for years, so I was a little bashful about walking up to them. It always embarrasses me to make mistakes in identity." He looked at the clerk. "Happen to know them?"

"Oh, sure," said the unsuspicious clerk. "The tall one, the skinny one in the dark suit, is called Smitty. I never heard him called anything else."

Haatz was a little surprised that Smitty had given his right name.

"It's the other one I was really interested in," Haatz said. "You see, if he's the man I think he is, he was blind when I knew him."

"He's the man you think he is, mister," the clerk said. "Milan Zinn used to be blind."

Haatz masked his excitement.

"Then that cadaverous man in the loud clothes is Milan Zinn?" he asked.

"Sure. Known him for years."

Haatz hesitated, then leaned over the counter. "What do you know about his character?" he asked. "He looks like a sinister master mind out of some bloodcurdling thriller. Is he that type?"

The clerk scowled. "Thought *you* knew him, mister," he said suspiciously.

Haatz straightened up. He shrugged. "Skip it," he said. He smiled at the clerk. He did not want to attract notice to himself by arguing with the fellow. "You see, I was just wondering what kind of a guy old Zinn turned out to be after he was no longer blind."

"Oh, I get it." The clerk moved his shoulders. "I couldn't tell you, mister. I don't know a thing about him except that he's been living in this neighborhood for years, and he always comes in and buys a Fantesto fifteen-cent cigar at this time every evening. Always says the same thing to me, too. He'll walk in, and he'll say, 'What's good news today?' He always says that."

"Thanks," Haatz said. "I guess I'll look him up." He hesitated, then turned and left the cigar store.

The cigar-store clerk stepped from behind his counter and went to the door, where he watched Arnold Haatz going down the street. Haatz was not heading toward Milan Zinn's home. The clerk's suspicions were aroused. They were not quieted at all when he saw Haatz begin running from the vicinity.

The clerk used the telephone.

"Mr. Zinn," he said. "This is Ernie Meeks. Quite probably you don't know me by name, but I'm the clerk down at the store where you buy your Fantesto cigars. I may be making a dope out of myself, but you've been a customer of mine for a long time, and I want to show you that I appreciate it. . . . A minute ago, some bird was in here asking about you, and acting funny while he did it. He just ran away."

Milan Zinn was much interested. He asked several questions.

Arnold Haatz ran four blocks, his head back, breathing easily—he was in good physical trim—until he found a drugstore which had telephone booths. He had not wanted to telephone from the cigar stand, because there had been no booth and the clerk would have overheard.

Haatz got his boss on the wire.

Haatz had no great degree of respect for his boss, Russel Kinner. But he felt he owed the man a warning. Kinner was flighty, possessed of delusions of grandeur, inclined to be a bit short on scruples, Haatz suspected.

"Listen, Kinner," Haatz said bluntly. "If you're half smart, you'll throw some clothes in a suitcase, sneak out of the back door of your place, and catch a plane for Florida or the Maine woods or somewhere."

After a startled silence, Russel Kinner said, "Haatz, are you drunk?"

Haatz said, "Less than an hour ago, a man came to my apartment and tried to decoy me away and kill me. I think you will be next."

"Me?" Kinner's voice, ordinarily deep and pleasant, became shrill. "Why would anybody want to kill me?"

"For the same reason they tried to knock me off."

"Why is that?"

"To shut our mouths."

"Huh?"

"I think," Haatz said coolly, "that we are the only two people in the world who know one certain fact, and that very thing is going to get us killed."

Kinner was silent a minute. Then he began to laugh. "You sound like you had gone completely crazy," he said.

Haatz's voice was like something made by steel.

"You remember Milan Zinn?" he asked.

Kinner stopped laughing. "You mean the old duffer that looked like Frankenstein's monster—the one who said he had been blind for so many years?"

"I see you remember him," Haatz said grimly. "Well, get this through your head. That stuff he was talking about that day he came to see us—he wasn't crazy. *You remember what he said that day,* don't you?"

"Yes... but... but it's so incredible."

"Zinn isn't crazy, and the thing isn't incredible," Haatz snapped. "The thing may be frightful, hideous and astounding."

Kinner made gurgling sounds of astonished stupefaction.

"But—great grief! Haatz, you must be mistaken about this."

Haatz said, "If you're half smart, you'll get out of town, where you'll be safe."

"I'll do nothing of the kind," Kinner snapped. "I'm no coward."

"It isn't a case of being a coward. It's a matter of having good sense."

"I don't like your brusque tone, Haatz," Kinner said sharply. "After all, I'm your boss."

Haatz lost his temper.

"Listen, you stupid braggart," he said, "you're no longer my boss, because I quit! I resign. If the government is dope enough to let you work for it much longer, I'm badly mistaken, too. I'm doing you a favor, calling you up and trying to save your life. And what do you do? You get officious about it, and start telling me who is boss."

To Haatz's astonishment, the other man took this meekly.

"Now, now, let's don't fall out about it," Kinner said ingratiatingly. "After all, the thing is something of a shock. It just kind of knocked me loose from my wits."

Personally, Haatz believed it would be very hard to knock Kinner loose from his wits. However, he agreed, "Well, it is fantastic, all right."

"Zinn must be insane!" Kinner exclaimed.

"He may be a little abnormal. Being blind all your life, then suddenly being able to see, is liable to do something to your balance." Kinner swore grimly. "It's too bad the old reprobate didn't stay blind. That damned surgeon who brought back the old man's eyesight should be shot."

Haatz started. A look of intense thought overspread his face. His lips shaped, "The surgeon who operated on old Zinn," thoughtfully.

Aloud, he said, "Say, it was a man named Doc Savage who operated on Zinn, wasn't it?"

Haatz sounded a little excited in spite of his effort at control.

Kinner said, "I don't know."

Haatz, suddenly anxious to end the conversation, said, "You better get out of town until I get this cleared up."

Then he hung up.

Haatz went to the cashier of the drugstore and changed two five-dollar bills into quarters, dimes and nickels—coins which would go into a pay telephone. He went back to the telephone. He dialed the zero for the operator.

"I want to get in touch with a man known as Doc Savage," he said. "It is very important. How do you go about doing it?"

II

THE ELF

The telephone operator said in a mechanical voice, "Just a minute, sir. I will give you the information operator."

There was a delay. Haatz compressed his lips in thought. He was in a dilemma—he had unexpectedly found a menace, a ghastly danger, threatening not only himself but many others. It was hard to estimate the scope of the peril, but it was great. His dilemma sprang from the fact that the thing was so fantastic. He could hardly make the police believe him. They would probably laugh at him. If they did not laugh, they would hardly be likely to give the situation the intense action it needed. All in all, this was a job for someone with more agility and capacity for coping with the unusual than the police possessed.

"Information," a friendly voice said.

"Operator, this is Arnold Haatz calling from"—Haatz looked up and got the number of the phone—"Arling 9-9-100. I want to get in touch with a man named Clark Savage, Jr."

After a moment, the operator said, "We have no Clark Savage listed."

"He probably doesn't live in Washington," Haatz said hastily. "You see, I don't know *where* he can be found. But I've got to locate him. It is very important."

"I am sorry, but I am afraid we can not—"

"This is a matter of life or death for quite a number of people," Haatz said seriously. "I wish you would understand that. It is very serious."

The information operator hesitated. "Can you give me any further information about this person?"

"He happens to be one of the greatest surgeons in the world, although he does not have a practice," Haatz explained. "He is also a scientist, a chemist, an electrical wizard, and a man of all-around marvelous mental ability."

Haatz pondered a moment.

"But Doc Savage," he continued, "is best known because of an unusual career he follows, a career of righting wrongs and punishing evildoers in the far corners of the earth. I understand that he was trained from childhood for this strange profession.

"Savage," he finished, "maintains a corps of five assistants, all of whom are trained specialists, and they have a headquarters somewhere. I do not know just where. Probably it is in a city. . . . Does that help you any?"

The operator asked, "Did you say Doc Savage?"

"Yes."

"Simply call New York City, and ask for Doc Savage."

Haatz was impressed. He said, "Thank you." He had heard of Doc Savage at various times, but always in the back of his mind there had been an impression that the man was overrated.

When Haatz heard Doc Savage's voice—the long-distance phone connection went through quickly—he was even more affected. It was a controlled, modulated voice that was as full of latent ability as dynamite.

Haatz came directly to the point.

"I have just discovered a devilish thing," he said. "I need help."

"Who are you?" Doc Savage asked.

"Arnold Haatz. Employed by the government. The office of superintendent of prisons. I'm a minor assistant executive. It would be a miracle if you had ever heard of me."

"What is your trouble?"

"An hour or so ago, a man tried to kill me," Haatz said steadily. "I was puzzled, so I followed the fellow.... And I found out that I was to be killed because of something I happened to know. One other man has that same information. He is Russel Kinner, my immediate superior in the office."

Doc Savage said, "Warn the other man, Kinner."

"I just did."

The man who had called himself Smitty entered the drugstore. He came in cautiously, hat low over his face, eyes roving. He spotted the figure in the telephone booth. The clothing told him the man was Haatz, but he maneuvered and got a look to be sure.

Haatz did not see him.

Smitty eased back out of the store. He glued his elbows to his side, and ran until he reached another store, and another telephone. He put in a call.

"Smitty calling, boss," he said.

"Yes?"

"I had luck. I spotted Haatz. He is in a telephone booth, in a drugstore.... What do you want to do about that?"

"What drugstore?"

Smitty told him.

"Trail him," the voice ordered. "Report as often as you can."

"What about finding out who he telephoned?"

"I'll send a man to the drugstore after he leaves to do that."

Smitty said uneasily, "Something should be done about this Haatz fellow."

"It will be."

In the drugstore phone booth, Haatz said, "I do not think it would be a good idea if I went into details over the telephone. But I can tell you this thing is fantastic to the point of being unbelievable. That is why I hesitate about going to the police."

"Can you come to New York to talk to me about it?" Doc Savage asked.

"It might be better if you came down here."

"It will be impossible for me to leave for twelve hours," Doc Savage said. "I have important laboratory experiments under way."

"Then I'll come to New York."

"Good."

Haatz said, "Do you know a man named Milan Zinn?"

"There is a very brilliant man by that name," Doc Savage replied. "He was blind until two years ago, when a surgeon was fortunate enough to be able to return the man's sight."

"Did *you* operate on Zinn?"

"No. A technique of optical surgery was used by the surgeon who did operate, however. That is how I happen to know of the case."

"Have you ever met Zinn personally?"

"No. Why?"

"I better let that part of it go until I talk to you personally," Haatz said.

Doc Savage did not argue. He said quietly, "Give me an exact outline of your plans for the next few hours."

Haatz told Doc Savage where he was, what he intended to do between now and the time he caught a plane for New York. He finished, "That's a good idea—in case anything happens to me."

When the conversation ended, Haatz hung up and stepped out of the booth. He felt relieved. He knew that he had just talked to a man of unusual ability, a man who was quite possibly the remarkable combination of physical and mental genius which rumor claimed him to be.

Grimly, Haatz returned to the place where he had left his rifle. It was still standing behind a showcase where he had left it, and he tucked the heavy weapon in the crook of his arm and sauntered out.

He took a taxicab.

"Going hunting?" the cab driver asked.

"Figuring on it," Haatz said. He gave the address of his apartment.

The ride was without incident. Before entering, Haatz searched the vicinity thoroughly, but saw no sign of an enemy "Wait for me," he directed.

The cab driver nodded, gave him a strange look. It had dawned on the driver that something was wrong.

Haatz packed a light bag with shirts, socks, a spare suit, and adjusted the sheath of a long-bladed dagger inside his trouser waistband. The dagger was a relic of his old days; he had taken it from a hashish crazed brown maniac on a Cristobal street.

He carried the bag out to the cab.

"Hey, bud," the driver said.

"Yes."

"Guy trailed you here, I think," the cab pilot explained. "He cruised past and looked us over. Then he went around the block, and parked."

"Was he a bony, brown, dried-out man?" Haatz asked.

"Yeah. Mean eyes, too."

No flicker of expression changed Haatz's round pink face.

"An old pal of mine," he said. "Take me out to the airport. And thanks."

The cab was of the fresh-air type, with a sliding hatch in the ceiling which, when shoved back, gave the passenger air and light. Haatz eyed the hatch, then shoved it back.

He waited until they were on the outskirts of the city. By that time, he had gotten a good glimpse of the man in the car behind, and was sure it was Smitty.

He pushed up through the hatch with the rifle and put a hundred and eighty grains of jacketed lead through— he tried to put it through Smitty, but the cab hit a bump—the windshield and seat cushions of the following car.

The other car angled off the road, dived into a shallow ditch and stood on its nose. It remained that way briefly, upended on the radiator, as if undecided whether to go on over. Then it fell back on all four wheels.

Smitty got out and ran. Haatz dusted off the ground under Smitty's feet. But Smitty got behind a low stone building to which was attached a stone fence. He was safe.

Haatz wriggled back down into the cab.

"You tried to kill that guy," the driver said. His voice was full of horror.

"Yes, and it was the second time," Haatz said. "The third time I'll get him."

The driver made a terrified noise.

Haatz said, "You seem nervous. Maybe you had better let me drive."

The driver nodded frantically. "If you don't mind, I'll get out and walk."

"No need of that," Haatz said. "You can ride in the back seat, or the front seat, whichever you want."

"No. I'll walk."

Haatz said, "I'll leave your cab at the airport."

The driver alighted, and he was very glad to get ground under his feet, even more pleased when the cab taillight vanished down the road. The cab belonged to the company, so he didn't care about that.

"That guy ain't afraid of anything," he muttered.

The statement was in error. Haatz *was* scared. In fact, he was as terrified as he had ever been in his life, which, considering the kind of a life Haatz had once led, was strong tribute to the danger which now menaced him.

During the ride to the airport gate, Haatz spoke only once to himself, and that was grimly.

"I should have told Doc Savage the whole thing," he growled.

The rest of the time he wondered how Smitty had gotten on his trail. Checking back in his mind, he thought he saw how it had happened. The cigar-store clerk. The fellow must have called Milan Zinn, and Zinn had put Smitty on the trail. That was what Haatz concluded.

He was wrong. But, unfortunately, he never knew that. There were ramifications to it that he never imagined. He had believed that the thing was fantastic, extensive, charged with peril, yet his wildest guess never encompassed the full extent of the matter.

For instance, he had not imagined there was such a thing as the very white elf.

He saw the elf almost as soon as he parked the cab. He drove into the parking area, stopped the machine in a remote spot, alighted—and saw the thing.

His eyes popped a little. It was a weird figure. It was some distance away, so he never did know for sure just how large it was. He was not even sure it walked upright, because it was on all fours when he saw it. It was creeping through a mass of shadow, as furtive as a big white dog prowling. It was very, very white.

Haatz opened and closed his mouth, then he shuddered. He lunged back into the cab, snatched out the rifle, and raced forward. The white elf had disappeared for the moment, having either gone into a small hangar, or ducked among the parked cars, machines belonging to the airport employees.

Holding the rifle with both hands and moving like a charging soldier, Haatz kept going. He thought he saw a flash of white.

"Hey!" he yelled. "Halt!"

The flash of white was the elf of a figure, all right. It halted, turned toward Haatz. It seemed to stare at him. Then it advanced. It seemed to be curious, a hideous kind of curiosity.

The world began to turn white then. The phenomena was exactly that. Whiteness. It came slowly, evidenced at first by the fact that the night seemed to lose its blackness, become gray. The grayness increased, and simultaneously the sharpness of objects decreased. The brighter it became, the more blurred everything got.

In coming, the whiteness took no more than three or four seconds. It was sudden, really. And it seemed never to stop increasing. It became like match flame, then white, like an electric lamp, then bluish with the incredible brilliance of an electric arc. By that time, it was unbearable.

Haatz was screaming in agony.

A car, one of the airline machines bringing passengers from the city, angled off the road beside the airport, rooted into the ditch and turned over.

A plane, a giant airsleeper, trying to land, crashed down on the field, wiping off its undercarriage and bending its propellers and sliding along on its belly.

The confusion spread.

III

DEATH RAN AWAY

The two persons who probably reacted most strangely to what had happened were standing in the waiting room, in a remote corner, where they had been watching unobtrusively.

One of the pair narrowly missed being as wide as he was tall, and had arms of remarkable length, a growth of hair on hands, arms and head that was like rusty shingle nails, and a face that was mostly mouth.

The other man was slender, had the body of a movie idol, the mouth of an orator, and the clothes of a modern Disraeli. His garb was sartorial perfection.

What rendered these two gentlemen startling was the fact that they were accompanied by two pets.

The apish man's pet was a pig. The shote had long legs built for running, a body that was nothing much, and ears that were like wings.

The well-dressed man's pet was some species of chimpanzee, monkey or dwarf ape. This animal was surprising because of the startling resemblance it bore to the apish man.

The apish man was Andrew Blodgett Mayfair, one-time lieutenant colonel in the army, now world-renowned chemist. The dapper man was Major General Theodore Marley Brooks, eminent lawyer, always at the head of any list of best-dressed men. The pig was Habeas Corpus, hog of Arabian extraction and unusual accomplishments. The ape was Chemistry, South American in nationality, doubtful of ancestry.

These four were associates of Doc Savage, the remarkable individual known as the Man of Bronze, who made a career of righting wrongs and punishing evildoers.

The four of them were notable for one other fact. They had managed to keep an almost continuous quarrel going for some years.

To the present situation, they reacted about as could be expected.

Ham Brooks, the dapper man, carried an innocent-looking black cane. He poked around with this—his eyes were completely useless, and he did not feel at all good—until he found his companion. Then he gave the homely Monk a whack over the head with the cane.

"Ow!" Monk yelled. "Somethin' hit me!"

"I hit you," Ham said. He took another cut with the cane, but missed. "I'll teach you to throw some of your infernal chemicals in my face!"

After that, they were both so very ill that they felt they needed to sit down. They did so, remained there a while. They felt worse by the moment. Not only was the world one intense blaze—they could see nothing but white-hot light—but they were becoming quite ill.

To make it worse, something else happened.

"Great grief!" Monk croaked. "The earth is rockin'."

Ham snapped, "Do *you* feel it?"

"Sure. Why not?"

"I thought," Ham said, "you had used some kind of tear gas on me, or something."

"Why would I do that?" Monk asked in an ill voice.

Confused, Ham said, "I didn't know but what you had found out who told that little Finnish girl you were a Russian commissar. Say—is this an earthquake?"

"Dizzy."

"Eh?"

"Dizzy." Monk said. "Things keep turning over and over, and they don't do that in earthquakes. We're dizzy."

The universe came back to its normal condition again.

Not completely normal, however. They hauled themselves to their feet—they discovered they had to hang on to some object to keep from upsetting—and peered over the edge of the balcony. Turmoil, tumult and confusion were rampant in the waiting room below. A few persons were trying to stand, but having great difficulty.

Monk peered at Ham.

"Blazes!" he said. "What happened? What *was* that, anyway?"

Ham was rubbing his face, feeling of his eyes. "How would I know?"

"You reckon it had anything to do with the reason we were here?"

"How would I know?"

"Ham, what did Doc say to you on the telephone?"

"He said," the dapper lawyer explained, "that some fellow named Arnold Haatz had called him and talked rather strangely. He described Haatz. Doc said that, inasmuch as we happened to be in Washington, he thought it might be a good idea if we got on the trail of Haatz."

"Did the idea seem to be that Haatz might be setting some kind of a trap for Doc?"

Ham shrugged. "You know the precautions Doc takes. My guess would be that this Arnold Haatz's story sounded so queer that Doc thought it should be checked into."

"Doc just wanted us to trail Haatz?"

"Yes. He was to catch a plane for New York at this airport in"—Ham consulted his watch—"about ten minutes. Doc suggested that we pick up his trail here."

Monk tested his ability to stand. He managed to do so.

"Let's hunt this Haatz," he said.

Ham started to walk, and after the first two steps went reeling until he collided with a wall. Monk, in spite of the way he felt—he was weak and nauseated—managed to grin. Any discomfort that befell Ham always pleased him. He professed to dislike Ham intensely, and the sentiment was returned by Ham. Contrarily enough, each of them occasionally risked his life to save the other.

They managed to get down the stairs and onto the waiting-room floor. At close hand, the confusion seemed greater.

A fat man stumbled up to them, grabbed Monk's coat lapels and bleated, "The world is coming to an end! The reckoning day is here!" He was frightened to a glassy-eyed, drooling condition. "You better be praying, brother," he added.

Monk watched him rush off. The man looked like a prosperous politician.

Monk grinned. "He don't act as if he was ready for his reckoning day."

They moved outside.

"Look!" Ham ejaculated.

He meant the big plane. A small crowd had already collected around the skysleeper, and there was an ambulance siren wailing somewhere.

Monk said, "You wait here."

He disappeared for a moment, trailed by his pet pig. He used the telephone, then came back.

"Whatever that blindness was, it didn't affect the city," he said. "It seems to have been local, just around the airport, here. I talked to the telephone operator in town about it."

Ham was watching the pets, Habeas Corpus and Chemistry. It was obvious that both animals had been victims of the thing.

"Let's look for this Haatz," he said.

The man who was screaming was locked in a small room in the right wing of the new depot building. Actually, Ham's pet chimp found him. The animal came scampering back, made an excited clattering, and otherwise showed excitement.

Ham frowned. "Take us to it, Chemistry," he directed.

The man was not letting out scared screams. They were shrieks of rage, and yells intended to attract attention. Monk and Ham exchanged glances.

Ham tried the door. It was locked. Monk said, "We should have Renny here to bop that door with his fist." Renny was Colonel John Renwick, noted for his feats as an engineer and the size of his fists. "Stand back," Monk added.

The homely chemist took a run and jump, hit the door with both feet, and the panel came to pieces. Monk and the splinters landed in a naked-looking room in which was a stack of discarded paper and boxes, the latter of cardboard and wood.

The man inside lifted one of the wooden boxes, then stared at them.

"Where'd Million go?" he growled.

He was a long crow of a man, a crow who was wearing canary feathers. His tweeds were loud, his shirt an ox-blood hue, and tie, socks and handkerchief were matching emerald green.

Monk misunderstood the man. He thought there had been a robbery. He thought someone had stolen a million dollars.

"Where was the money?" Monk yelled. "Who got it? Which way'd they go? Great grief! A million-dollar robbery!"

"The Million I meant is a man," the other said. "Jerry Million."

"Oh." Monk stared at him.

"I'm Milan Zinn," the cadaverous man explained.

"And there's no robbery?" Monk muttered.

"No."

"What happened? What was that light?"

The man hesitated. An expression crossed his face.

"I have no idea," he said.

The homely Monk's head did not look as if it contained much room for brains, but his appearance was deceptive. The ungainly chemist was clever and able to read character. He was positive this Milan Zinn was lying.

"You better tell us what it was, brother," Monk said levelly.

Milan Zinn scowled at him. "I don't know what you are talking about."

"That kind of blinding sickness that hit us a minute ago," Monk said.

Zinn hesitated.

"I don't know anything about it," he said.

Monk's most dominant trait was love of action, preferably the two-fisted kind.

He reached out suddenly and got Milan Zinn by the neck. He was promptly kicked on the shins and walloped in the stomach. Monk grinned fiercely.

"Which wall shall I bounce this guy off of?" he asked.

A new voice, one from the door, asked, "While you're at it, you might pick which wall you want your brains splattered on—if you don't turn that old man loose!"

The most noticeable feature about the young man in the door was, naturally, his gun. It was a very big gun, and it was blue.

He was a very big young man, too, and he was brown. He looked healthy, competent, and as reckless as a boulder rolling down a mountain. His eyes were as blue as a gun barrel, his nose was flattened as if by pushing against things, and he had a protruding jaw of the pushing-through type.

Milan Zinn wrenched away from the astounded Monk.

"They just got here, Jerry," Zinn said.

Monk asked, "You Jerry Million?" of the capable young man.

"Yeah," the young man said. He moved his gun suggestively. "Go over there and rub your face against that wall, pal. You, too, pretty pants." This last at Ham.

Ham snapped, "Put that gun away, you fool!"

The young man's voice became a roar.

"Get your face against that wall, pretty pants!" he bellowed.

Ham and Monk hastily complied. They could tell that the young man was violent.

Jerry Million asked, "Who are these guys, Zinn? Are they airport cops?" The wailing of the siren on a police car caused him to decide not to wait for an answer. "We better blow," he said. "They must belong around the airport here."

Jerry Million gestured with his gun. Monk and Ham could not tell whether he was ordering Zinn out of the room, but Zinn went. It seemed that Zinn looked at Jerry Million fearfully.

When the two had gone, Monk and Ham stared at each other.

"Pretty pants!" Ham said fiercely.

Monk grinned without much humor. "He sure sized you up in a hurry."

They moved to the door and looked out. Jerry Million was still backing away. He lifted his gun. They ducked back in haste.

Once more, they got the impression that Milan Zinn was a prisoner of Jerry Million.

"Did that Zinn *want* to go with that loud mouth who had the gun?" Monk asked.

"I couldn't tell," Ham admitted.

"Well, let's get on the trail of them guys," Monk said.

The window of the room was small, opened readily. They dropped their two pets to the ground outside, then followed.

Without a word, Ham went one direction, Monk the other. They were accustomed to working with each other, and they rarely discussed a course of action. As a matter of fact, they had learned from experience that any kind of a discussion would turn into a heated argument. It was painful for either one of them to admit that the other ever had a good idea.

Monk made an ungainly figure, racing around the operations office trailed by his pig.

The excitement at the airport had, if possible, increased. The crowd had thickened around the big plane that had crashed. And airport attendants were dashing here and there, trying to ascertain what had caused the weird thing that had happened to everyone.

When Monk reached the other side of the building, he halted and searched with his eyes. He saw no sign of Zinn and Million. But he did discover, off near the parked cars to the right, a prone figure, another man kneeling over it, and several curious spectators.

Monk ran to that spot.

The kneeling man was shaking the one on the ground, as if trying to revive him.

"Haatz! Haatz!" he was exclaiming. "What's wrong with you? What happened?"

Hearing the name Haatz, Monk became very interested

in the man on the ground. He studied Haatz's round, soft-
looking body and rather harmless general appearance. Monk
had seen plenty of men of nerve and action, and he was not
deceived by Haatz's roly-poly body.

"Haatz!" barked the kneeling man. "Answer me?"

"You knew him?" Monk answered. The kneeling man
ignored the inquiry, so Monk gripped his shoulder and put on
a little pressure. Monk could take walnuts in his hands and
crush them without much difficulty. "Know him?" Monk
repeated.

"I . . . Yes." The other gasped under Monk's grip. "I . . . he's
one of my assistants. Works in the same office."

Monk said, "Now, you might tell me who *you* are."

"Russel Kinner," gasped the kneeling man.

Russel Kinner was a square, compact man with an
aquiline nose and very small ears. He had alert eyes, a rather
thin mouth. He was handsome, rather than pleasant-looking.
When he shook off Monk's hand and stood erect, he did it
rather arrogantly.

"Just who are you?" he asked sharply.

Monk ignored the query. "What's wrong with him?"

"If you'll keep your hands off me, I'll find out."

Monk said, "You won't learn anything by shaking the
gizzard out of him, the way you were doing."

The homely chemist got down beside Haatz, and felt of
the man's wrist. "Call a doctor," he ordered.

There was pulse in Arnold Haatz's wrist, but there was
something wrong with it. Monk stared at the man's face. The
color was wrong, too. Paleness would have been understandable.
But there was a bluish cast to the features, a marked green-
ness about the mouth. Monk lifted the lids and looked at the
eyeballs, then dropped the lids hastily. He didn't like the
expression on the eyeballs.

He glanced up at Kinner.

"Didn't you hear me tell you to get a doctor?" he
snapped.

Kinner glowered at him. "Really, I think you have no
right to give me orders."

Monk said, "You get a doctor, and get him quick, if you
don't want to be a patient yourself."

Monk had a small, childlike voice which was usually
comical to strangers. It could change, and become as ominous

as the gritting of a sharp knife against bone—which was something like its present tone.

Kinner backed away hastily, turned and walked toward the operations office.

An idea hit Monk. He sprang up, ran and caught Kinner. He whirled the man.

"What were you doing here at the airport?" Monk asked.

"I . . . I—" Kinner paled.

"Out with it!"

"I . . . I was going to catch a plane," Kinner said nervously.

"Yeah?" Monk said suspiciously.

Kinner bristled. "I'm not lying to you." He whipped an envelope out of his pocket, and flourished it. "Here are my tickets."

Monk, not taking the envelope, glanced at the outside and saw that it was the type which airlines handed out to customers, containing the tickets.

"O.K.," Monk said impatiently. "Get that doctor and get back here."

Kinner scowled, whirled and stalked away. He jammed the envelope in his pocket hastily, but did not get it securely inside, so that after he had taken a few paces, the night breeze whipped the envelope out of his pocket.

Not noticing that he had lost the airline ticket envelope, Kinner went on. He began running, as if he had finally realized the necessity for haste.

Monk saw the envelope drop. He walked over, picked it up, and thrust it in his own pocket. His intention was to return the thing to Kinner when he came back.

The shooting over on the west edge of the parking lot began suddenly, and did not last long. It was impossible to tell just how many shots there were, since the reports were crowded together, more than one gun going at once. These shots were followed by a sound as if a bull had bellowed.

The bellow could not have been made by a bull. It was mechanical, and also no masculine bovine could have made such an uproar.

The sound was enlightening to Monk. He recognized it. Ham's machine pistol. These little weapons, no larger than oversized automatics, had been developed by Doc Savage, and they could pour out an astounding number of slugs per minute.

Monk ran toward the sound, elbows glued to his ribs, head back. He was scared.

A car appeared and streaked toward the exit from the parking area. The windows were down, and two men leaned from the machine, holding revolvers. Monk braked to a stop, feet scattering gravel, and hauled out his own machine pistol. They carried the weapons in padded under-arm holsters where their presence was not conspicuous.

Powder flame and sparks jumped from the car. Monk heard a sound like brittle sticks breaking close by, knew it was bullet noise, and hastily changed his course. Before he could get under cover, the car was turning onto the highway.

The machine rocketed past the airline limousine which had upset in the ditch, and got away.

Monk said several words which he had not learned in church.

Then, racing toward the spot where he had heard Ham's machine pistol, he roared, "Ham! Did they hit you?"

His anxiety, considering the fact that he habitually professed the intention of some day taking Ham apart and seeing what made him tick, was remarkable.

Ham came out from behind a car.

Monk looked him over and saw he was unharmed.

"Well, well," Monk said. "I was hoping they broke a leg for you, or something. What happened?"

"They recognized me," Ham explained.

"Eh?"

"I was looking through these cars for Zinn and Million, and some kind of a sound drew my attention over this way. I didn't know what the sound was, so I came over to investigate. And what do you think I found?"

"Don't be kittenish," Monk suggested. "What did you find when you investigated?"

"Milan Zinn and Jerry Million and four other men," Ham said, "having an argument."

"An argument?"

"A violent one."

"Who was arguing with who?"

"Jerry Million seemed to be doing most of it, although it was hard to tell."

"What was Milan Zinn doing?"

"He was standing there, looking kind of horrified."

Monk snorted. "How could you tell if he was horrified? He looks kind of like a horror to begin with."

"Well, maybe Zinn was looking natural, then."

"What happened to you? How did you get mixed up in it?"

Ham sighed. "That was when they recognized me. One of the four men—it wasn't Zinn or Million—let out a yell. He yelled, 'There's one of Doc Savage's men!' Then he cussed a blue streak. And guns began going off."

"Who were the other four men?"

"I had never seen them before."

"How did they look?"

"About like guys who start shooting at us on sight generally look."

"Mean, eh?"

"Extra-special mean."

"Then they ran to their car?"

"Yes. They got away while I was jumping behind a car, and ducking from there to another car, to keep from being shot. When I got to a safe place, and got set, they had piled into their car, and gone."

"Did Jerry Million and Milan Zinn go with the four men in the car?"

"I suppose so."

"Are you sure?"

"No. I tell you, they shot at me, and I was too busy getting behind some parked machine to pay any attention to who got in that car, and who didn't."

"And you say it was not Zinn or Million who yelled that you were one of Doc's men?"

"No. Zinn and Million didn't seem to know who we were."

Monk pondered for a moment. "What do you make of it?" he asked.

"Why, I happened onto a gang, and they tried to kill me, then got away."

"I mean—what do you make of the quarrel they were having?"

"Oh, that. I didn't hear enough of the quarrel to make anything out of it."

Monk rubbed his jaw. As far as he could tell, Ham had not accomplished anything, except get embroiled in some excitement. He mentioned this casually.

"Listen, you homely missing link!" Ham said in answer. "I haven't seen you accomplishing so much."

"I found Haatz."

"The dickens you did!"

"Yeah, and I found his boss, a guy named Russel Kinner," Monk added. "This Kinner is a guy who is inclined to act a little snooty. He said he was out here to catch a plane, and I guess he was telling the truth."

"What makes you think Kinner told the truth?"

"Why, he had his airplane ticket. He showed it to me, then put it in his pocket, and it fell out. I got it here."

Monk drew the airline ticket envelope from his pocket, opened it, and peered inside, his intent being to show Ham the ticket and allay all argument on that point.

"Blazes!" he exploded.

"What's wrong?"

"This envelope ain't got no ticket in it," Monk growled.

"That's funny."

"Yeah, and what's more funny, the envelope is dated to show that it was issued more'n a week ago."

A small crowd had gathered around the prone form of Arnold Haatz.

Monk and Ham stopped on the outskirts of the crowd, and looked the gathering over closely. Then they exchanged glances.

"Kinner ain't here," Monk said.

"What does he look like?"

"He looks kind of like a mink. Got the small ears and bright eyes of a mink, and kind of a muscular body."

"There's something funny about that lad."

"You're telling me."

They approached Haatz, shouldering the crowd away from the man. Haatz lay about as they had left him, except that his eyes were open, so that it was not necessary to peel back his eyelids to see that something rather weird was wrong with him.

Monk went to his knees beside Haatz.

"You feeling better?" the homely chemist asked.

The sound that Haatz made was half hiss and half animal scream as he lunged up and got hold of Monk's throat with one hand. Ham's bark of warning was half submerged in

Haatz's noise. Haatz had been lying on a long-bladed knife and he now had it in his free hand.

IV

THE ELF AND A GIRL

Bright sunlight was streaming across the steps in front of the hospital when the taxicab arrived.

Ham Brooks, looking worried—he was wearing the same clothes he had worn the night before, which indicated how bothered he was—ran down the steps to the cab.

"Doc, I'm glad you got here," he exclaimed.

Making no comment—he was habitually sparing with words—Doc Savage got out of the cab, and paid the fare.

The cab driver, coming up with a piece of paper which he had hastily unearthed, said: "You're Doc Savage, aren't you? How about autographing this for my kid?"

Doc Savage complied. He was a giant bronze man who was so symmetrically proportioned that, standing alone, there was nothing particularly remarkable about him, except the bars of tendons in the backs of his hands, and the cabled sinews that sprang out whenever he moved his neck, together with a few other indications of tremendous physical strength.

The cab driver, grinning at the signature on the piece of paper, drove away.

"How is he, Ham?"

The bronze man's voice was low, deeply timbred, but controlled.

"Not so good," Ham confessed. "In fact, all the doctors say he will not live." He turned. "I'll take you to his room. They have him in a private room."

The interior of the hospital did not look like a hospital. There was no odor of antiseptic, no atmosphere of suffering. They rode up in a gay, modernistic elevator.

Ham's face was grim.

"I should have telephoned you earlier," he said. "But to tell the truth, the doctors thought they could save him up until about two hours and a half ago. You sure made a quick trip down here."

The cage let them out, and they moved down a hall that might have been in an expensive apartment house.

Monk met them at the door. The homely chemist wore a strip of adhesive tape across the back of his right hand.

"This guy is violent, Doc," Monk explained. He exhibited his taped hand. "Out at the airport, he came up at me with a knife, and darned near put the sticker into me."

Ham said, "Why don't you tell the rest of it?"

"What rest?"

"That I kicked the knife out of Haatz's hand, or he would have slit you wide open."

Monk snorted. "If you hadn't kicked him, he wouldn't have given me a scratch." Monk looked indignant. "The way it was, he almost cut my hand off."

The two glared at each other.

Doc Savage, apparently not noticing their angry manner, stepped into the room. Three doctors stood near Haatz's bed, and two nurses were at the window. It was a large room.

The three doctors looked at the bronze man with obvious awe. One of them, after a hesitation, stepped forward. "I believe I was at a lecture which you gave on the inferior cervical ganglion," he said. He turned to his companions. "These are Drs. Steiner and Laughline."

Doc Savage acknowledged the introduction, then turned to Arnold Haatz, who was confined to the neat white bed with wide webbing straps. He made a brief examination, then looked up, asked for the records of diagnosis. One of the doctors got them, and the bronze man worked for a while.

Then Doc Savage stepped back. He named a poison. And he told what antidotes and counteractives he needed. The doctors hurried to get them.

When they were alone in the hall, the three medicos exchanged sheepish looks. Two of them were dumfounded; the third, who had met Doc Savage once before, was not as surprised.

"That knocks me cold," said one of the two astounded ones. "He didn't take over five minutes to make that diagnosis, and we had been working on the case all night."

"Maybe he's wrong," said the other.

"I'll bet my month's salary against a pleasant grin that he's *not* wrong," offered the third medico.

* * *

It was eleven o'clock, and Monk and Ham were listening to a news commentator on the radio when a nurse arrived with the information that Doc Savage wanted to see them.

Doc met them at the door of the hospital room.

"He was poisoned," the bronze man explained. "It was an unusual type of poison, producing some of the symptoms of hyoscyamus, or henbane, but with a stronger tendency toward hallucination."

"Can he talk yet?"

"Only in delirium," Doc said. "I called you to listen to what he keeps repeating."

They bent over Arnold Haatz. The poisoned man lay quite motionless, as stark as a corpse. His lips moved from time to time, very faintly.

Doc Savage swung a sensitive velocity microphone stand so that the mike was close to the man's lips. The microphone was connected to a power amplifier, from which a flexible cord extended to a loud-speaker that had been placed in the other room, where feed-back would not interfere with the mike.

"Keep the microphone close to his lips," Doc told the nurse.

The bronze man moved into the adjacent room, with Monk and Ham, and they gathered about the loudspeaker. The sensitivity of the apparatus was enormous; the breathing of the poisoned man came out of the loud-speaker with the volume of steam escaping from a locomotive.

They listened to words, half whispered, half mumbled, not all of them understandable, as Haatz formed them.

"Sounds like he keeps talking about someone named Dean," Monk suggested.

"No, there's another part of the name," Ham said.

Finally Haatz spoke one sentence that was coherent and distinct.

"Audine Million wanted me to come and help her, and that was a trap to get me to a place where they could kill me," Haatz said.

Monk exclaimed, "That's what he's been saying over and over. Somebody named Audine Million tried to kill him, sounds as if."

The loud-speaker went silent, as far as mumbling was concerned.

Doc Savage took a morning paper from his pocket and

handed it to Monk and Ham. Without comment, he indicated what he wanted them to read.

A great deal had naturally been printed about the weird incident at the airport the night before. The item Doc wished them to note was in a box on an inside page. Evidently the editors considered it one of the goofy aspects of the mystery.

It read:

> Another man from Mars?
>
> Bill Smith thinks so. Bill is a grease monkey (mechanic to you) at the airport where the excitement occurred last night.
>
> Bill Smith says he saw an elf. A white elf. Bill says he saw it skulking furtively through the shadows at the airport. It was behind a hangar. Bill says the creature was white, and strangely shaped.
>
> Our dictionary says an elf is a small mythological being, the female members of which are of dazzling beauty.
>
> Bill says this elf was no beauty.

When Monk and Ham had read the item, they exchanged puzzled glances.

Doc Savage asked, "Did you see such a creature?"

"No." Monk grinned. "I wonder if Bill Smith was packing a bottle."

Ham also chuckled. Like Monk, they did not place any more credence in the story about an elf than had the newspaper reporter who had written up the yarn in a facetious vein.

They got a shock when Arnold Haatz's incoherent mumbling came out of the loud-speaker, and finally formed an understandable sentence.

"The all-white elf," Haatz croaked. "Keep it away from me! Keep it—Oh, my eyes . . . my—"

There was nothing after that but the whistling breath of the poisoned man, until Doc Savage moved to the door.

Doc said, "Obviously an attempt was made to kill Haatz. There is no reason to believe his life is not still in danger. You two men guard him. I am going to look into that elf matter."

The bronze man went out.

Monk and Ham gazed at each other with startled expressions. The pig and the chimp—both animals had been in the other room with Haatz—entered. Monk frowned, and took another look at the newspaper which Doc had handed them.

"There's a story in here about Haatz being brought to this hospital," Monk said.

"That is not good," Ham suggested.

"No. If anybody *is* out to kill him, they'll know where to find him."

"We better move him."

"You said it." Monk rubbed his jaw. "The guy is in bad shape, though. I would hate to move him, and then have him croak."

Ham pondered. "We don't necessarily have to move *him*."

One of Monk's small eyes narrowed appreciatively as he stared at Ham.

"I get it," he said.

They moved through the hospital until they found a fat man who was built somewhat the same as Haatz. They talked to him, and some money changed hands.

With the contents of a bottle of harmless white medicine, they made the fat janitor pale. Ham penciled a few lines about his eyes and created suitable shadows. They found a stretcher.

They managed to make arrangements to go through the motions of taking Haatz out of the hospital—actually taking the janitor instead—with only one doctor in the institution knowing of the fact.

Haatz they transferred to another hospital room, under a different name.

The operation of checking the fake Haatz out of the hospital was carried out without hitch, and with a great deal of ostentatious display. It was Ham who located a pair of newspaper reporters, and gave them a sensational story about Haatz being poisoned mysteriously during the excitement at the airport the night before. He added casually that Haatz was being transferred to a place of safety.

The reporters naturally wanted to question Haatz, but Ham assured them the man was far too ill for that, and pointed to the patient's paleness—a part of the fake Haatz's plump cheek was uncovered on the stretcher—as convincing evidence.

"That smoke screen ought to work," Ham whispered to Monk.

"It's perfect," Monk agreed.

It was, too. They found how perfect it was when they reached the hotel where they had decided to take the decoy, and were unloading the stretcher from the ambulance, with a great show of seriousness, in front of the hostelry.

Monk let out the first yell.

"Blazes!" squalled the homely chemist. "Have a look!"

It was hardly necessary for him to point. The figure moving down the sidewalk was noticeable enough. Pedestrians were turning to stare at it, fascinated by the weird aspect of the form, and the grim, silent and purposeful manner with which it strode forward.

"The white elf!" Ham grunted.

If an elf is supposed to be a little creature, the name did not fit this thing. The figure was hard to define as to size, for none of the pedestrians were close enough to compare sizes. It was wider than a man. Not as tall, possibly, although the grotesque shape made it hard to tell.

In general, the figure was rather shapeless, although it was more human than not. The color was unusual. Startling. It was white, and yet a strange kind of white. Not the hue of white in the sense that a sheet or a piece of canvas is white, but white with a brilliant, intense, mirrorlike quality. White almost as a frosted electric-light bulb is white when lighted, although there was no definitely luminous quality about the figure.

Monk made his best growling noise.

"I'm gonna collar that what-is-it," he declared. He started forward.

Ham grabbed his shoulder. "Don't be a fool! Let's get this stretcher inside."

Monk hesitated. And while he was undecided, the surroundings began to turn white. Everything, it seemed to Monk, rapidly took on the same glistening white quality that characterized the "elf" of a figure.

"Quick!" Monk roared.

With Ham, he seized the stretcher. They dashed with it into the hotel entrance. The whiteness was worse. Their eyes ached. They could distinguish objects in the hotel lobby only with difficulty.

The janitor suddenly gave up the job of acting as patient. He sat erect on the stretcher.

"What the hell is this, anyhow?" he barked.

Monk gave him a shove.

"Run for it!" the homely chemist shouted. As an afterthought, as the janitor started away, Monk roared, "And take that sheet and wipe the white stuff off your face!"

The janitor complied with the suggestion as he dashed across the hotel lobby. He tried to make it to a rear door, but fell over a chair, sprawled on the floor, and lay there a moment before springing to his feet. Once more, he set out for what he thought was the rear door, but it turned out to be the entrance to the dining room. He passed through that, and began knocking over tables.

Monk, straining his eyes, distinguished a figure coming into the hotel. It was the elf figure, and it was as if the thing walked through white-hot fire. After that, Monk could see nothing whatever.

"The stairs!" Monk gasped. "Maybe we can fight the thing off!"

V

TWO TO DIE

The little man with the cheerful eyes and the quid of tobacco in his cheek grinned and wiped his hands on a piece of waste. He shut off the airplane motor on which he had been working.

"Yeah, I'm Bill Smith, a grease monkey here at the airport," he said.

He shook hands with Doc Savage.

After looking at the bronze man, he added, "Say, aren't you Doc Savage?"

The bronze man admitted that.

"I saw that new chemical-cooled motor you designed," Bill Smith said admiringly. "That thing is a whiz-ding. You know what I said to myself when I saw that motor? I said, 'I'd sure like to meet the fellow who had brains enough to think up a honey like that.' That's what I said."

Doc Savage looked a little embarrassed, said, "I understand you saw something strange at the airport here last night."

Bill Smith got rid of his quid of tobacco. "They don't let you smoke around here, so I chew," he explained. Then he grinned sheepishly. "You saw that thing they put in the newspaper about it, I guess?" he asked.

Doc nodded.

"Well, there ain't much more to tell about it," said Bill Smith. "I was working overtime last night, and had finished my job and was starting out to the road. There is a bus goes past here, and I usually catch it and ride home. I was going around behind No. 6 hangar when I saw this white thing. It looked like kind of a goblin or an elf, if there was such things. I thought at first it was somebody dressed up in a masquerade suit. But somehow this didn't look like that."

"Will you describe it?"

"Not as tall as a man, wider, shaped something like a man, but without a man's features. And it was white. The color was kind of a funny white. It was like—well, it was *so* white. That's all I can say. It was just about the whitest thing I ever saw."

"Was it a man wearing a disguise?"

Bill Smith hesitated. "It would sound crazy if I said what I think."

"Say exactly what you think."

"Well— How could it have been a man? It didn't have any face at all. It wasn't wearing goggles. Where the face should have been, there were no features—no nose, mouth, eyes or ears. It was just blank."

"What else?"

"That's all."

"Where did this white goblin of a thing go?"

"I don't know," Bill Smith explained. "You see, right after I saw the thing, I had this spell where everything turned to white fire, and I was dizzy and sick. I thought the world was turning over and over. Matter of fact, I thought the end of the world must be coming."

"How did you feel afterward?"

"Not very good," the mechanic admitted. "I felt like hell, in fact. My stomach ain't the same yet."

Doc Savage extended his hand in a warm grip of thanks. "You have been a distinct help," he said.

Bill Smith looked doubtful. "You don't think I'm crazy?"

"Not at all. Would you mind showing me exactly where you saw this white thing?"

Bill Smith conducted the bronze man to a spot beside No. 6 hangar. The place was bathed in midday sunlight.

"It was kind of dark here last night," the mechanic explained. He consulted his watch. "I'm supposed to be working. I better get back on the job. Like I said, I'm mighty glad to have met you."

Doc Savage watched the mechanic go back to his job. Then the bronze man gave close attention to the surrounding ground. It was covered with gravel, did not retain footprints. The gravel was new, sharp.

The bronze man had brought along a small metal case containing various apparatus. He opened this, produced a kind of overgrown atomizer, filled this with fluid from a bottle that was labeled only with a number, and began spreading a thin spray over the gravel.

When that spray had no effect, he changed to the contents of still another bottle, and finally a third, and a fourth.

The fourth liquid caused some few of the sharp pieces of gravel to take on the faintest of spots of a greenish discoloration.

He carefully gathered up the discolored bits of gravel and placed them in the metal case.

A girl came out of the office portion of a nearby hangar, carrying a bird cage. There was a dead canary in the cage.

Doc stopped her. "What happened to the bird?"

The girl was grim. "It was my pet. It . . . died last night."

"Was the bird here in the hangar when it died?"

"Yes." She bit her lower lip. "I was going to bury it."

"Would you allow me to examine it?"

"Of course."

Doc Savage worked with the carcass of the bird for a while. Becoming more interested, he moved into the privacy of an empty office, and there used various chemicals, and a powerful portable microscope.

The bronze man was working intently when the sound came into existence. It was a weird sound, a trilling that was low and exotic, a note that was without tune, yet not unmusical, and which seemed to come from the very air itself. When Doc became aware of the trilling, he looked guilty, and the sound stopped. The trilling was a small unconscious thing which he did in moments of intense mental or physical stress, or when he was making a discovery.

As he was on the point of returning the canary, Bill Smith appeared. There was a small glint of excitement in Bill Smith's eyes.

"Just wondered if you would be interested in knowing another guy is curious about that white elf, or goblin," Bill Smith said.

"Another man?"

"Yeah. Young. Big as an ox. Sunburned brown. Blue eyes, flat nose, and a jaw like the front end of a truck."

"Did he give you a name?" Doc asked.

Bill Smith grinned. "Said his name was Smith."

"Did not say his name was Jerry Million, then?"

"No." The mechanic shook his head. "Say—I seem to remember reading about a man named Jerry Million. Got into some kind of trouble, if I recall."

Doc Savage made no comment, except to nod very slightly.

Five minutes later, Doc Savage stood outside a window and used a long, thin tube of a device, a telescoping periscope of mirrors and prisms and good lenses—no larger than a pencil when closed, capable of being stretched to more than arm's length—to examine a room.

The sunburned young ox of a man with the jaw was inside the room, giving it a quick search.

The reason for the search did not puzzle Doc. The room was the one in which Monk and Ham had found old Milan Zinn locked. The young man in there now seemed to be making sure there were no clues to indicate his presence the night before. And possibly he was getting rid of traces of Zinn having been there, as well.

He had gotten around to using a handkerchief to carefully wipe the knob and edges of the door for fingerprints.

Doc Savage took from a pocket a small metal case which proved to be lined with cotton padding, and contained some objects which looked like bilious-tinted marbles filled with liquid.

The window was open a crack, and Doc pegged two of the "marbles" inside. They broke with about the same sounds that bird eggs would have made.

Doc left the spot under the window, sauntered around to the entrance, and made his way to the door of the room.

The sunburned young man with the jaw was lying on the floor. Judging from his breathing, he slept. Doc shoved his body to one side, and closed the door.

The bronze man's first act was to test the victim's pulse and respiration. The anaesthetic gas contained in the "marbles" was—as its sudden action indicated—powerful stuff, so that there was always some slight danger that a victim with an abnormally weak heart, or some chronic physical difficulty, might succumb. There was no danger of this fellow dying, however. His body was functioning like a machine.

Doc gave attention to the young man's pockets.

His name was Jerry Million—his driver's license bore that name and his description, and he had a belt buckle, a handkerchief, initialed JM.

The young man's inside coat pocket held a packet—a long cardboard box, snapped around with rubber bands—which Doc Savage opened. It contained newspaper clippings.

The clipping on top read:

JUDGE SCOURGES JERRY
MILLION IN ACQUITTAL

In acquitting Jerry Million of charges of manslaughter today in district court, Judge Melvin Reynolds gave the young man a blistering verbal lashing.

Jerry Million, former laboratory manager of the Kesta Photographic Products Corp., was charged with manslaughter in connection with the death of six persons at the Kesta plant a month ago.

"You are being acquitted," Judge Reynolds told the defendant in a regretful voice, "on a legal technicality, although there is no doubt in my mind, and no doubt in the mind of any person in this courtroom, I'll wager, but that you are guilty."

The attitude of Jerry Million was defiantly silent throughout the harangue. It was the same defiant silence he had maintained during the entire trial.

"You are unquestionably the lowest form of

human life I have ever seen," the judge said bluntly.
"I know it is not judicial procedure for a presiding
court officer to make such a statement. But on this
occasion I am sickened by the thing that you did,
and nauseated by your insolent silence and refusal
to once open your mouth. It is to my everlasting
regret that I must order your acquittal on the charge
of manslaughter.

"However, I sentence you to the maximum
penalty on the other charge, destruction of property.
I sentence you to one year in jail, with the added
recommendation that you not be paroled."

The item was worn and stained, as if it had been handled
a great deal. Doc Savage riffled through the other clips, most
of which were about the trial. He came to several items
concerning the crime itself.

One of these, more concise and comprehensive than the
others, read:

SIX DEAD IN FLAMES; LABORATORY MANAGER JAILED

Death toll in the fire which swept the Kesta
Photographic Products plant last night now stands at
six.

Jerry Million, laboratory manager of the plant,
has been placed under arrest. It is alleged that
Million was in charge of the laboratory where the
fire started, and could have checked the flames at
their beginning, but failed to do so.

Police Chief Carter says, "There is unimpeach-
able testimony that this man's rank carelessness and
cowardice allowed the flames to get headway and
reach highly inflammable chemicals and explosives."

Doc ran through the rest of the clippings. All of them
bore on the fire in the photographic plant, the trial that
followed, and Jerry Million's sentence to jail for a year on a
minor charge. The bottom clipping was one that indicated
Jerry Million had been released from jail six months previously.

In the bottom of the box, there was a tight bundle of
letters. Doc studied them. They were curious documents.

They were letters from persons to whom Jerry Million had applied for a job after his release from jail. They were bitter missives. They did more, most of them, than refuse Jerry Million employment; they condemned him as a coward, a cur.

Doc Savage replaced the stuff in the young man's pocket. For a moment, he contemplated Jerry Million thoughtfully. The bronze man's eyes, of flake gold, seemed strangely animated and concerned.

Jerry Million did not look like the kind of man which he was branded to be by the clippings and letters.

Fifteen minutes later, from outside the window, Doc Savage watched the young man with the jaw regain consciousness. Jerry Million sat up, looked around foolishly—the anaesthetic had the unusual property of causing no noticeable aftereffects other than a slight weakness and dizziness—and finally got to his feet. His lips moved. Doc, watching, was sufficiently skilled at lip-reading to tell what he said.

"Hell, I forgot to eat last night and this morning," he muttered. "It must have made me weak."

He left the airport then. He had a small roadster of the convertible type, and he drove this.

Doc trailed him in a car which he had rented.

Jerry Million stopped at a restaurant, where he wolfed down a substantial meal. After that, he strode back to his car. His manner was purposeful.

Doc followed him again. This time, Jerry Million drove to a residential part of the city, a section where there were substantial middle-class homes located in wide grounds. An old part of town.

Jerry Million parked the car in a side street, walked two blocks, entered an alley, suddenly became furtive. He crept into some brush, flattened out in the weeds of a vacant lot, and finally took a position in some shrubbery.

He began watching a house with binoculars.

After it became evident that Jerry Million was going to watch the place for some time, Doc Savage retreated, and maneuvered to a spot where he could get the house number and street name without being observed.

He made a personal visit to the head office of the telephone company to get the information he wanted.

Jerry Million was watching the home of Milan Zinn.

*   *   *

Doc Savage returned to his rented car. He had placed several cases of equipment in the back of the machine, and one of these was a portable radio telephone, a short-wave outfit with a surprising range for its size. He switched it on, picked up the microphone.

"Renny," he said. "Renny, or Johnny. Come on the air, if you are tuned in."

A few moments later, the carrier wave of another transmitter became audible.

"Holy cow," said a voice that might have been the product of a large bear in a deep cave. "What is it, Doc?"

The voice—it was as unmistakable as the foghorn of the *Queen Mary*—belonged to Colonel John Renwick. Renny was famous for two things—his engineering ability, and the size of his fists. Like Monk and Ham, he was a Doc Savage assistant.

"Is Johnny there?" the bronze man asked.

"Yeah, he's right here, big words and all," Renny rumbled.

Johnny was William Harper Littlejohn, noted archaeologist and geologist and eminent user of big words. He was another associate.

Doc said quietly, "Renny, you and Johnny had better come to Washington by plane at once."

"Something breaking down there?"

Renny's rumble was excited.

"It appears so," Doc admitted.

There was a brief exchange of words away from the other transmitter.

"We'll be down there in two hours, Johnny says," Renny announced.

Doc said, "Very well. I shall be expecting you." He gave them a hotel address where they could make contact in Washington, then switched off the radio.

The bronze man drove to the hospital. He was advised there that Monk and Ham had moved Arnold Haatz to a hotel for safekeeping. They furnished him the address of the hotel.

VI

THE DEVIL FEARS FIRE

While he was still some blocks from the hotel, he knew something was wrong. A traffic officer stepped in his path, waved for a detour.

"Sorry," the cop explained. "All traffic is being detoured."

Doc said, "But I am going to the Capitol Lawn Hotel."

The officer stared at him. "Nothing doing."

"But it is important."

"You a newspaperman?"

"No."

"Every newspaperman in town is trying to get to that hotel," the cop said. "You'll have to drive on, brother. My orders are to allow no traffic in that direction."

"What is happening?"

"Drive on, drive on," the policeman said impatiently. "You'll have to read about it in your newspapers."

Doc let in the clutch and the car moved ahead. In the middle of the next block, he pulled into a parking lot, left the machine and headed for the Capitol Lawn.

He ran.

Two ambulances passed him, coming from the direction of the hotel. A sedan followed them, and there were white-uniformed interns and patients in bloodsoaked bandages in the back of the car.

There were fire engines. Police reserve cars were thick. A uniformed patrolman barred the bronze man's path.

"You can't go any farther," the cop said.

Doc Savage did not argue. He produced a document which he carried for such emergencies—an honorary police commission. He held such commissions in most of the large cities.

The policeman was satisfied.

"What is going on?" Doc asked.

"I can't tell you, exactly," the officer admitted. "It seems it must have been the same kind of thing that occurred out to the airport last night. Maybe you read about *that* in the papers?"

47

Doc said, "Thanks," quietly and went on.

The Capitol Lawn Hotel was in as much of an uproar as such a dignified hostelry could manage. The lobby was crowded with police, and the manager was wringing his hands, thinking of the publicity, and practically sobbing.

Doc Savage paused in the door, and his flake-gold eyes went over the crowd quietly. He singled out the officer who was obviously in charge, and introduced himself.

The man stared at Doc, surprised.

"This is a pleasure," he said with genuine admiration. "You know, our department laboratory uses some blood-test methods, and processes of bringing out latent prints, developed by you. What can I do for you?"

Doc repeated his inquiry as to what was happening.

"We don't know for sure," the police official explained. "All of a sudden, everyone in the hotel and in the neighborhood seemed to have some kind of a spell. The world seemed to turn a blinding white, and nobody seemed able to stand up or move around."

"Similar to what happened at the airport last night?" Doc inquired.

"Yes."

"What else?"

"Well, this happened all of three quarters of an hour ago. There was so much confusion that no one could do anything. The reports that came in to police headquarters were completely crazy. People reported seeing the strangest things."

A small stir of bright interest appeared in the bronze man's flake-gold eyes.

He asked, "Did anyone report seeing a white goblin of a figure?"

The other gaped. "How did you guess that?"

There was a sudden uproar from high up in the hotel somewhere—shouting and loud thumpings—and a squad of emergency policemen entered the lobby with fire axes, gas containers, bulletproof vests, sawed-off shotguns, ropes and scaling ladders.

"We have somebody cornered on the fourth floor," the police official explained. "There are two of them, and they refuse to let anyone in."

"Who are they?"

"Two fellows who ran in here with a runt ape and a pig."

*   *   *

Two minutes later, Doc Savage was pounding on the fourth-floor door.

"Monk," he called. "Ham."

From inside the room, Monk's ridiculously childlike voice came, asking a question in the ancient Mayan tongue, a language which the bronze man and his aids used when they did not wish outsiders to understand. The Mayan language was spoken by very few persons in the civilized world, other than themselves.

Monk asked, "Is it sure enough safe to come out?"

"Yes."

There was noise of a quantity of furniture being moved from the other side of the door, and the panel opened. Monk and Ham, machine pistols in hand, peered out.

"These are policemen," Doc explained.

Monk looked over the cops.

"Yeah, they said they were," he admitted. "But me and Ham wasn't takin' any chances."

Doc drew the homely chemist and the dapper lawyer aside, listened to an explanation of what had happened. "You see, we figured it was a bright idea to fake that business about taking Arnold Haatz away from the hospital," Monk declared.

He completed his story by advising, "When everything went white, and we knew that infernal elf was after us, me and Ham made a break for the stairs. We got up to this floor, and found a room unlocked. We dived in, shut the door, and have been here since."

"We could have come out earlier," Ham said.

"But we were playing safe," Monk added.

"What became of the janitor you hired to pretend to be Haatz?" Doc asked.

"Oh, he got away. He lit out like a rabbit."

"Did this elf, as you call it, see him?"

Ham and Monk exchanged glances.

"Afraid so," Ham said.

Doc Savage made, quite suddenly, the small trilling sound that was his peculiarity in moments of mental stress. The sound had an anxious quality.

"Come on," he said.

There was just enough excitement—he rarely showed any emotion—that Monk and Ham realized that something serious was wrong. They scooped up their pets and trailed him.

"What's up?" Monk asked uneasily.

"As soon as the janitor turned out not to be Haatz," Doc said, "it must have been apparent that you had left Haatz in the hospital."

They borrowed a police sedan for the ride to the hospital.

The police machine was long and black, with red lights and a noisy siren under the hood. Doc kept the siren on steadily, kept the speedometer needle on the high numbers of the dial throughout the drive.

Nearing the hospital, Doc cut the siren. He coasted in under the marquee of the ambulance entrance, cut the engine, and the abrupt halt of the car seemed to fling him out.

"Third-floor," Monk barked, and started forward.

"Wait," Doc said.

The bronze man confronted the checker at the hospital door. "Any emergency stretcher cases been brought in during the last half-hour?" he asked.

The man nodded. "One."

"Was the fellow bandaged?"

"From head to foot, yes."

"Face covered?"

"Yes."

"What kind of looking men brought the case in?"

"Now that you mention it," the attendant confessed, "they were kind of tough-looking guys."

"What floor was the case taken to?"

"The third."

Monk and Ham got it then. Their faces became stark. Ham growled, "You think the thing on the stretcher was that elf?"

Doc Savage nodded briefly. Then, as Monk started forward, the bronze man flung out an arm and stopped him.

"I saw a grocery store across the street on the corner," Doc said. "They probably sell bottled soft drinks. Monk, you and Ham go to that store. Buy a dozen or so bottles of soft drinks. Empty the bottles, fill them with gasoline, and cork them. Wrap rags around the bottles, tie them on with string, and soak the rags in gasoline."

"What'll we use for rags?" Monk demanded.

"Your shirt," Ham suggested. "It's practically a rag to begin with."

Doc said, "Hurry. Meet me on the third floor. But be careful when you come up."

Monk and Ham raced away.

Doc turned to the attendant. "There is a dangerous criminal loose in the hospital," he said. "Get this door locked. Stop all the elevators. Close the front doors and lock them."

The attendant stared blankly. "I...uh...I ain't got no authority to do any of that."

Instead of arguing, Doc Savage ran through the corridors, located the office. He found the superintendent inside. Doc identified himself—he had not met the superintendent earlier—and repeated the instruction he had given the attendant.

"Can you get hold of gasoline in any quantity?" the bronze man demanded.

"I... I don't know," said the astonished superintendent. "Y-yes, there is a tank which we use to refuel the ambulances."

"Run gasoline on the sidewalk outside, under all the windows," Doc ordered. "Run it in the gutters. At the first sign of excitement, set it afire."

The superintendent, pop-eyed, made a bewildered noise.

Doc gripped his arm. "Do as I tell you," he said urgently. "The lives of a great many people may depend on it."

He left the superintendent then, and went to the third floor, climbing the stairs with long leaps. He had the number of the room in which Monk and Ham had placed Arnold Haatz.

He flung open the door, took a pace inside, and stopped.

There was no need to look more closely at the form that lay on the bed with legs spread-eagled and arms outflung, shoulders twisted a little so that the left was higher than the right, and the head flung back, flung farther back than it could ever have been normally. The neck was practically severed, the mouth stood widely open, and the red flood had stopped flowing from the mouth, and no longer came, except for a trickle, from the neck. The red was dripping from the bed to the floor.

Except for the frightfully dead body of Haatz, the room was empty.

Doc whipped back into the corridor, closed the door. There was a presiding nurse in charge on each floor. He went to her desk.

"Where is the emergency case that came in half an hour ago?" he asked.

She nodded at a door. "There."

"Has he been out?"

"Why, yes. His nurse took him into the room where you just were. They remained there a few minutes, then came out again, and went back into his own room. The nurse said he was an old friend of the man in the room where you were, and wanted to see him."

"When did that happen?"

"Fifteen minutes ago."

Doc Savage's metallic features did not change expression, but he felt better. At least, Haatz had not been murdered while he was giving instructions downstairs. He had been killed fifteen minutes earlier—before Doc and his two men reached the hospital.

Doc addressed the presiding nurse.

"Leave this floor," he directed. "Get down to the superintendent. Tell him to spread that gasoline on the sidewalks and under the windows in a hurry. Tell him to set fire to it at the first sound of alarm. *Set fire to the gasoline.* You understand!"

The compelling urgency, the power in his voice sent the presiding nurse flying for the stairs.

Doc went to the door of the room into which the emergency case had been taken. He did not enter. He waited. It was hard to wait. The nurse was in there with an inhuman monster. But it was essential for Monk and Ham to return with their gasoline-filled bottles.

It must have been three or four minutes later—the seconds were like years—when Doc heard a faint sound. It was a strangled noise, full of tearing meaning. A woman made the noise. The nurse! It must be the nurse!

Doc knocked the door open.

The grotesque figure of the elf, dazzling in its whiteness, was standing in front of the window. A sheet had been twisted into a long rope, and this rope was being used to strangle the nurse. She fought weakly, but it was obvious that she had lost most of her consciousness.

The white thing whirled. It started to make some kind of a gesture, the nature of the movement indefinite. Probably it expressed surprise.

Doc took a running leap, landed with both feet against

the middle of the white apparition. It was hard under his feet; felt as hard as metal. And when the thing upset, it made a distinct rattling noise.

Not wasting time, Doc started to spring upon the fallen figure. But the whiteness came. It came suddenly. Monk and the others had said that it had come slowly, with everything taking on a gradual luminosity that gradually increased. But this was abrupt.

Doc abandoned his plan to attack the white figure. Instead, he scooped up the nurse, whirled, and dived out through the door, carrying her. He banged the door behind him, raced down the corridor, following the wall with one hand.

Vision was completely gone. There was nothing in his eyes but searing white agony.

"Monk!" he shouted. "Monk! Ham!"

Monk's squeaky voice came from the stairs. "Coming, Doc."

The bronze man found them by the sounds they made. With his hands, he first located Ham.

He shoved the limp nurse into Ham's hands.

"Get her downstairs," he rapped. "Find a room, and lock yourself inside it with the nurse."

Ham departed with the nurse.

There was a grim silence in the hall. Downstairs, and out on the street, there was noise, confusion, shouting and rushing about, the screaming of a voice that had started crying out a moment after a metallic crashing that was probably a car colliding with some object.

Then, listening closely, the bronze man's trained ears detected a rock-hard, grinding tread on the corridor floor.

"Hand me one of those bottles of gasoline, Monk," Doc said.

The soft-drink bottle was small in his hands, the gasoline-soaked rag wrapped around it cool to the touch. Doc said, "Stay back, Monk. I am going to spread burning gasoline in the hall."

"But the fire danger!" Monk exploded.

"The building is fireproof."

Doc struck a match. Flame heat rushed over his hands, singeing them. He flung the bottle, throwing it hard, standing on tiptoes to do so. The bottle slanted down and struck the floor a few yards away, shattered.

The flames made a noise like a sudden wind.

And the white elf of a figure emitted a sound, too. It was a stifled noise, a bark and whine that was horrifying. The footsteps of the thing, like rocks striking the tiled floor, went away rapidly.

Doc applied a match to another bottle, threw it at the sound of the footsteps. He missed. Moreover, the bottle hit the far end of the hall, and did not shatter.

A door banged.

Doc said, "There is another set of stairs at the opposite end of the hall. It went down those."

Monk emitted a roar—he liked to yell when he was in action—and started forward. Then he emitted another yell that was louder and agonized, and came rushing back. The loud slappings—they were still completely blind—were probably made by his hands beating at his clothing.

"There's fire all over the hall," the homely chemist howled.

Doc felt his way along the wall to the elevator doors. He had noted a fire-alarm box there. He found it, and dragged down the lever.

He went back to the stairs, took them as fast as he could manage without the help of sight. He kept going to the ground floor. It was not likely their quarry would stop in the building.

VII

THE SILENT GIRL

Thirty minutes later, the superintendent of the hospital was very apologetic. He was also ill. But he was more apologetic than ill, for the police had given him their opinion of his intelligence, or, as they stated with trimmings, complete lack of any.

"I did not see any reason for spreading gasoline around the hospital and setting it afire," the superintendent said miserably. "It seemed like a completely insane thing to do."

"But Savage told you to do it," the police official told him angrily.

"I know."

"Then why didn't you?"

"Because I... it seemed crazy."

"Yeah," the cop said disgustedly, "and because you didn't do as you were instructed, that white goblin of a thing was able to walk right out of here."

"What good would the fire have done?" the superintendent muttered.

"For some reason or other, the white thing is deathly afraid of fire," the cop told him. "Of all the stupid boobs, you take the prize!"

Doc Savage had taken no part in the condemnation of the hospital official. The man was actually not to blame. He had followed the dictates of his common sense, a natural thing to do. The bronze man spoke quietly.

"I believe we will have to agree," he said, "that the superintendent did what was sensible from his point of view. My orders to set a fire around the hospital, given without an explanation, for I had no time for one, did seem mad."

The superintendent looked grateful.

The battalion chief of the fire department which had answered the alarm reported that the fire on the third floor had been extinguished, and that the damage seemed to be negligible.

Doc Savage joined Monk, who had been searching.

Monk reported, "I found one guy who saw that white elf leaving this part of the woods. He saw the elf about six blocks away."

"Did he know which way it went?"

"No." Monk shook his head. "The man was about half blind, and leaning against a lamp-post. He saw the figure pass him. He just got a glimpse of it. Couldn't tell which way it was going."

"I see."

"That thing is afraid of fire. Fire scares the devil out of it."

"Yes."

"How did you figure that out, Doc?"

The bronze man seemed not to hear the question. Monk did not repeat the query. He knew Doc Savage's small habit of not seeming to hear questions which he did not wish, usually for good reasons, to commit himself by answering.

A nurse came up.

"Two gentlemen to see you," she said.

"Has one of them got big fists?"

"Yes." The nurse smiled slightly. "And the other one has big words."

"Renny and Johnny," Monk declared.

Renny Renwick towered alongside Doc Savage, but he lacked the bronze man's symmetrical physical build, and his strength, while remarkable, did not compare with that of his chief. Renny's face wore a perpetual expression of gloom, and, contrarily, the sadder he looked, the more he was usually enjoying himself. His fists were the outstanding thing about him. A quart pail would hardly have contained either of them.

In greeting them, Renny used his pet ejaculation.

"Holy cow!" he said. "Whatever you fellows have stirred up, it seems to be causing plenty of excitement."

Johnny Littlejohn was tall, very tall, and thinner than it seemed any man could be, and still live. He was as thin as a strip of rawhide, and as durable. Suspended from his coat lapel he wore a monocle which—long ago, the sight in one of his eyes had been bad, and he had affected a monocle—was a magnifying glass.

Johnny said, "I'll be superamalgamated! An unparagoned bit of suscitation."

Which meant roughly that there was indeed some excitement, and that he approved of it.

An attendant approached and advised that the nurse who had been the victim of the white elf was now able to talk. They found Ham with the nurse, who was on the attractive side.

The young woman's voice was clear, but rather weak.

"That horrible thing forced me to take it into the room down the hall, where that poor Mr. Haatz was killed," she said. She shuddered. "I . . . I was there while—" She bit her lips.

"What was the murder instrument?" Doc asked.

"A knife. The . . . the thing carried one."

"Why do you call it a *thing*?"

"Because I don't believe it was human," the girl explained swiftly. "It did not once speak to me, and its actions were not human. They were awkward, rather stiff."

Doc studied the girl. "How did the creature instruct you to take it to the room which Haatz occupied?"

"The instructions were on a piece of paper. It grabbed me, showed me the paper and—well, I had no other choice. The paper said I would be killed if I did not obey."

"Were the instructions handwritten?"

"No. Typed."

Monk said, "What I don't understand is how the thing happened to have typed instructions all ready."

"That's not so hard to figure out, Ignatz," Ham told him. "That thing was carried in here on a stretcher by four men. The four men probably made inquiries, and found out where Haatz actually was." The dapper lawyer glanced at Doc Savage. "We might make inquiries, Doc, and find out if that is what happened."

"I have already done so," the bronze man said. "And that is what occurred."

Monk was studying the nurse with appreciation. "It's your idea that this thing wasn't human?" he asked her.

She smiled at him shakily. Monk's homely face, instead of frightening young women, as Ham insisted it should, usually had an opposite effect. Monk was so ugly that he was pleasant.

"I'm not quite insane enough to stand here and tell you a mysterious monster from another world had me prisoner," the nurse said dryly. "But I will say this: There wasn't anything human about the thing."

That seemed about the extent of the information which the young woman was able to give them.

Doc Savage, with his four associates and their two pets, found a private room where they could hold a consultation—and give Renny and Johnny a brief outline of what had happened. Renny and Johnny listened to the story intently.

When Doc finished the recital, Renny nodded soberly.

"Holy cow! The thing shapes up so that it makes some sense," declared the big-fisted engineer. "What happened is this: Arnold Haatz found out something. Probably he found out about this white-elf thing. Haatz was coming to Doc with the story. He was killed to prevent him doing so, and to stop him from telling what he knew."

Monk snorted. "Very brainy, as far as it goes."

Renny asked indignantly, "What's wrong with my reasoning?"

"It's about the speed of a two-year-old."

Renny narrowed one eye at Monk and said, "Listen, Brother Mayfair, when you start insulting me, just remember it's not Ham you are riding."

Monk snorted again. He enjoyed irritating people.

"You're overlooking Milan Zinn, Russel Kinner, Jerry Million and his sister, Audine," the homely chemist reminded. "All of them except the girl were out at the airport last night."

"Yes," Ham said, "it was a strange set-up out at the airport. We found Milan Zinn locked in a room, and apparently Jerry Million had locked him there, or at least the first thing Zinn asked after we found him was where had Jerry Million gone."

"But right after that," Monk pointed out, "you said you found Milan Zinn and Jerry Million and four other guys quarreling. Say, by jinks!" Monk stared at the others. "The four men at the airport! They answer the description of the four birds who brought that—whatever it is—here to the hospital on a stretcher."

Ham nodded solemnly. "Those four were in with the white elf. Since Jerry Million and Milan Zinn were associating with them, it shows Million and Zinn are in with the elf, too."

Renny rumbled, "You two guys are doing some tall guessing now."

"Well, it's more of an idea than you had," Monk said.

Doc Savage interposed. Speaking quietly, the bronze man gave the location of Milan Zinn's home.

"Jerry Million was watching the house when I last saw him," Doc told Monk and Ham. "Suppose you two get on Jerry's trail, and see what develops."

Monk and Ham, entirely agreeable, hurried out to their car—a rented machine, a small coupé—and placed their pets in the rumble seat, climbed in front themselves, and drove off.

As their machine started to move, big-fisted Renny sauntered over to it casually, and, unobserved, dipped into the rumble seat. Renny came back with Monk's pet pig, Habeas Corpus, in one of his huge hands. He held the porker so it couldn't squeal.

"Monk won't miss the hog for a while," Renny chuckled. "When he does find the hog is gone, he'll lay striped eggs."

Northland Street was a pleasant thoroughfare of homes

across the river, and, out at its far end where the signposts no longer labeled it as a street, it turned into a country lane bordered by delightful small farms.

The afternoon sunlight was an amiable brilliance over everything when Doc Savage turned into the driveway. He was alone in his rented car. He parked.

The doorway was clean, white, and gave out a firm drumming sound under his knuckles.

"Yes?" said the man who opened the door.

He was a man who would be easily forgotten. He had no outstanding characteristics, and the only thing that distinguished him was the fact that he wore a chauffeur's uniform that was rather new.

"I would like to speak with Miss Audine Million," Doc said.

The chauffeur did not look pleasant.

"She's not seeing anybody," he said curtly.

Doc Savage did not say anything for some moments, but he kept his flake-gold eyes on the chauffeur steadily, and soon the man began to squirm.

"What's your name?" the fellow asked finally.

Doc told him.

The chauffeur's eyes batted. He stepped back quickly, closed the door. There was a wait of three or four minutes, during which there was no sound other than the birds in the adjacent bushes. The man came back.

"This way," he said.

He led Doc to a door, then went away. The bronze man entered the room.

Audine Million had her brother's height. Character was stamped on her face, as on his. She was rather severe in dark serge, but there were little touches—the sprightly do of her ravishing mass of copper hair, the touch of color that a flower gave to her hair, gay trim on her frock—that showed she knew how to wear clothes. Her voice was modulated.

"I understood Charles to say your name is Savage," she said.

"Yes. Doc Savage."

"Oh, oh, *that* is who you are." She was impressed, but she did not extend her hand. "What can I do for you?"

The bronze man got to the point immediately.

"I believe you can help us with some information," he

said. "We are trying to get to the bottom of a rather incredible mystery, and I think that you can be of material help."

"I don't understand."

"What do you know about Arnold Haatz?" Doc asked.

Her face tightened.

"Nothing," she said.

"You know him, I believe."

"Yes. Just barely, however. To tell the truth, the only time I ever saw him was once when he was having lunch with my brother, and I happened to enter the same restaurant, and sat with them."

"Where is your brother?"

She became quite tense, did not meet his eyes. "I don't know," she said.

"What can you tell me about the thing the newspapers call the white elf? It is a figure of unusual shape, somewhat human, but not quite, and very, very white. So far, whenever it has been seen, a kind of fantastic white blindness strikes everyone."

The girl looked at the floor. "I never heard of such a thing," she said.

Doc Savage's flame-gold eyes had been taking in the room without appearing to do so. He noted, in one corner of the room, where picture moldings met, a small loop of tiny wire that showed.

His eyes moved to a picture on the wall.

"That is a nice picture," he said.

He got up and went to the picture, looked closely at it, and while doing that, took it in his hands and examined the back. He returned to his seat.

"I thought, for a moment, it was a copy," he said. "But it seems to be original. Rather valuable, isn't it?"

The girl nodded. "Yes," she said, rather grimly. "Once we were quite wealthy. That is—one of the souvenirs."

She was silent then.

Doc said, "I presume you know there is a microphone on the back of that picture?"

She stared at him. "A what?"

"A microphone. So someone can hear what is said in this room." He indicated the tiny loop of wire he had noticed. "The wire seemed out of place there, and it suggested a microphone."

The stark expression on the girl's face showed him that she had not known the mike was there.

Doc leaped erect. He said loudly, "It would be a good idea if we seized the person listening in at that microphone."

The bronze man, however, made no effort to follow the wires, that led from the mike to a listening post somewhere. He went up on tiptoes, moved to the window, slid it up, and landed on the grass outside. There was plenty of shrubbery; he kept in it, veered right, and stopped when he could see—and reach, if anybody tried to leave in a car—the driveway.

It was no more than thirty seconds later when Charles, the chauffeur, burst out of the side door of the house and took to the brush, moving fast.

Doc pursed his lips, made the call of a mockingbird—a mockingbird imitating a succession of three birds common to the region.

A moment after, a bird call came back from some distance away.

Doc followed Charles. The man had found a path, put his head back, and was making speed. He mounted a hill, took the right path of a fork, and moved down the slope beyond.

Twice, Doc gave his bird whistle, imitating the same three birds. Each time, he was answered.

There was a little-used road, not much more than a lane, and a car stood parked in the lane. A man sat on the running board, smoking. He stood up suddenly when Charles appeared.

Doc Savage, moving very fast himself, and keeping under cover, was close enough to hear what was said between the two. Charles was excited, his voice loud.

"Doc Savage showed up at the house," Charles barked. "He found one of my microphones right away."

The other man said, "Not so loud, damn it! You want to tell the whole country about it!"

Charles dropped his voice. He repeated what Doc had asked Audine Million, and her answers. He had a good memory, for he managed to relay the conversation almost verbatim.

"The girl didn't tell him anything more than that?" the listener demanded.

"That was all."

"Why'd you skip out?"

"Savage said something about grabbing whoever was listening in. He'd 've caught me, sure."

"You idiot! You could have denied knowing anything about the microphones."

Charles gulped stupidly. "I never thought of that." Then he added brightly, "But he'd 've found my fingerprints on the headsets."

"You could have wiped off the prints." The other man cursed Charles for his stupidity. Then he shrugged. "Well, the damage is done. You won't learn anything more there. I ought to fire you!"

Charles muttered that he was sorry.

"Get in the car," the other snapped. "Let's get going away from here."

Doc Savage came out of the brush then, and they had a fight.

The fight was not long, but it was full of flashing speed, grunts, blows, the sound of ripping cloth. The cloth-ripping noise was made when Doc tore the pockets out of their clothing to save time in making sure they had no weapons.

Having rapped Charles on the jaw, Doc straightened with the other man, who was square, compact, with small ears, alert eyes and a sulky mouth.

Doc said, "You are Russel Kinner, aren't you?"

The man spluttered, started to answer with profanity. Doc shook him until his teeth clicked like castanets.

"Y-yes," the man gasped. "I'm Kinner."

"What are you doing here?"

"None of your damn—"

Kinner did not withstand the next shaking so well. When it ended, he was so disorganized that he would have fallen, only for the bronze man's supporting grip on his collar.

"The thing for you to do," Doc Savage said, "is answer questions."

The bronze man's methods were not excessively rough, normally, but he had decided from Kinner's appearance and manner that violence was the thing that would disturb the man the most, have the greatest likelihood of getting answers out of him.

"What ... you ... want ... to know?" Kinner puffed.

"What were you doing here?"

"I ... I—" Kinner swallowed, panted for breath. "I was

trying to find Jerry Million. I had a detective"—he pointed at Charles—"hired to eavesdrop on Audine and find out where her brother was, if he could. The detective usually reports to me here at about this time every afternoon."

Charles had revived enough to sit up. Doc whirled on him. "Are you a detective?"

"I sure am," the man said. "I got a license. And where do you get off, jumping on us and—" He went silent, apparently deciding not to be belligerent about it. He felt of his bruises.

"Why didn't you take the reports over the telephone?" Doc asked Kinner.

"I work for the government," Kinner said promptly, "and I don't want those telephone girls prying into my private business. I made arrangements with the detective here to report personally and not over the telephone."

Doc studied them.

"Why are you so anxious to find Jerry Million?" he asked more quietly.

Kinner, somewhat reassured by the bronze man's calmer tone, straightened his coat.

"You are Doc Savage, aren't you?" he asked.

"You can answer my question."

"About Jerry Million, you mean?" Kinner rubbed his jaw tenderly. "I've got a darned good reason for wanting to find that big devil. He took a shot at me."

"How do you mean?"

"How does a man shoot at another man? With a pistol. If I hadn't jumped when I did, he would have killed me."

"When did this happen?"

"Two days ago. It was when I was coming home from work one night. I didn't tell anybody about it at the time, because I was sure it must be some kind of a mix-up. And I wanted to help Jerry Million what little I could. Telling the police about his attempt to shoot me wouldn't have been so good for Jerry. Although, damn him, he doesn't deserve any breaks."

Kinner looked righteous and indignant after he finished his speech.

"Why did Jerry Million shoot at you?"

"That's what I wanted to find him for. I wanted to ask him why."

"You know of no reason?"

"None whatever."

"Was it dark?"

"You mean when he shot at me? I'll say it was. That helped me get away."

"Are you sure it was Jerry Million?"

"Of course."

"Did you see his face?"

"Well—no. No, I didn't. But what the hell! It was Jerry, all right. He said it was. He said: 'This is Jerry Million, you so-and-so. Kinner, I'm going to blow a hole in you, you dirty so-and-so.' And then he shot."

"But you didn't see his face?"

"No."

A breeze stirred the leaves of the trees that overhung the lane, and the sunlight sloping down on the short grass was shaped into moving patterns without stable shape or position. From nearby, a bird called softly. It was the same kind of call that had answered the bronze man's mockingbird imitation.

Doc said, "One more question. What were you doing at the airport last night?"

Russel Kinner seemed uncomfortable.

"Well— To tell the truth, I was scared. I had come out there to get a plane and fly to Florida."

"What scared you?"

"A telephone call I got from poor old Arnold Haatz." Russel Kinner peered at Doc Savage. "That was a strange call. Haatz said that a man named Milan Zinn had tried to kill him, and was probably going to try to kill me. Haatz said it would be smart for me to get out of town. I—well, I was going to do it."

Doc asked, "Did Haatz say why Zinn tried to kill him?"

"No-o-o. Well, not exactly. He asked me if I remembered Zinn. I did. The old duffer came to our office. I'm an official in the Federal prison department, and old Zinn came in with some kind of a wild story about something horrible he had found and that he was willing to sell to the government."

"What had Zinn found?"

"I never asked. I threw him out. He was a nut, I thought at the time."

What was probably Russel Kinner's normal manner was returning. He was becoming supercilious, overimportant, and rather curt.

Doc said, "Have you any idea what Zinn wanted to sell the government?"

"I told you I hadn't."

"But when Haatz called you, you were scared enough to take flight."

Kinner said curtly, "I told you that, too."

"Where did you go last night?"

"To the airport."

"I mean after my two men found you there."

"Was that ape one of your men?"

"Yes."

"I went home," Kinner replied shortly. "After what had happened—that silly spell of blindness everybody had—I didn't want to get mixed up in any mess." He drew himself up. "I have an important position to think of."

Doc happened to know that Russel Kinner's position in the government was of a minor variety, but he made no comment. The man was obviously somewhat of a fourflushing politician type.

"Just what," the bronze man inquired, "changed your mind about flight?"

"Seeing poor Haatz lying there dead," Kinner retorted. "I am not a coward. I decided to stay and find his killer."

"Have you any ideas about who the killer might be?"

"It might be Jerry Million."

"You sure?"

"No."

"Are you even positive it was Jerry Million who shot at you?"

"I certainly am!" Kinner took out a handkerchief and wiped his hands neatly. "Jerry Million has been proven to be a rat. A fire started in the laboratory of the photographic company where he was employed. It started through Jerry Million's criminal carelessness, and he let it spread. It was proven in court and by witnesses that he could have stopped the fire. But he didn't. He ran. He should have gone to prison for it."

Doc Savage did not answer. Instead, he bent over and began picking up the contents of Russel Kinner's pockets, which had scattered when the pockets were ripped open. There was a gun, a revolver which Doc emptied of cartridges, and money, penknife and keys.

While he was making a business of picking up the stuff,

Doc identified the car key on the ring, and slipped it off. He pocketed it, and gave the rest of the keys back to Kinner, along with the other articles.

Kinner was examining his torn clothing, and was too angry to notice the absence of his car key.

"You'll have to buy me another suit!" he snapped. "This is a very good suit, too! It cost eighty dollars."

Doc had decided the suit had cost, at the most, thirty-two fifty. He reached out suddenly, opened the coat and looked at the label. It was a chain-store label.

"Have them send me the bill for an exact duplicate to that suit," he said, "and I'll pay it."

He walked away while Kinner stood there red-faced with rage.

Beside a clump of bushes fifty yards away, Doc paused. His voice was very low as he bent over and pretended to tie his shoes.

"Johnny with you?" he asked.

"Yes," said Renny's deep whisper.

"Trail those two."

"Who are they?"

"Russel Kinner and a man he says is a detective. Check on the detective and see if he is genuine, when you have time."

"Right," Renny whispered from the bush. "Any other instructions?"

"That is all."

"How was my bird imitating?" Renny asked.

"Good."

Renny whispered, "How about taking this hog of Monk's off my hands? The darned insect bit me."

Doc said, "You stole him from Monk, so you are stuck with him. Take him along."

"Holy cow!"

"I took the key to Kinner's car," Doc said. "It will require a few minutes for him to wire around the ignition switch. That will give you time to get your own car, and be ready to trail him."

Doc went on.

VIII

THE WRONGED MAN

Audine Million came forward and gripped Doc Savage's hand. Her fingers were warm and tight about his. Her manner was suddenly genuine.

"I'm afraid I made a mistake," she said.

Doc Savage entered what seemed to be the living room of the home—not the room where they had had their first interview; that had been the library—and looked for a hidden microphone. It was inside the bowl of one of the wall-bracket lights. He tore it out.

He said, "The eavesdropper on these microphones was the chauffeur, the man you called Charles."

She nodded. "I got to wondering who it could be. And Charles seemed the logical one."

"Has he been with you long?"

"No. I just hired him yesterday."

"Do you know Russel Kinner?"

"Very slightly. I met him once with my brother—Jerry."

"You know Kinner no better than you knew Haatz, then?"

"About the same. Both of them worked in the same office for the government. In some department that has to do with Federal prisons."

The bronze man took a chair, stretched his legs and relaxed. Audine Million also seated herself, her manner showing that she was reassured and at ease. It was evident, too, that she was not unimpressed by the bronze man's handsomeness.

Doc could tell that she was worried.

He asked, "What is wrong?"

She bothered her lower lip with even white teeth, and twisted her hands uneasily.

"It's my brother," she said. "Jerry Million—" She hesitated.

"What about him?"

"Someone is trying to kill him."

67

"Who?"

"Jerry said it was Russel Kinner."

"Do you think Jerry is right about that?"

She was uncertain for a moment. "I am not sure. We were riding in the car day before yesterday afternoon, and someone shot at us with a rifle. It was a high-powered rifle, and the bullet passed completely through our car, narrowly missing us. Jerry was very angry."

"What was your brother's reaction?"

"He said he would *get* Kinner, and break up the whole devilish plan."

"Those were his exact words?"

"Yes."

"What was the whole devilish plan he referred to?"

"I don't know. He wouldn't tell me when I asked."

"When did you last see your brother?"

"Yesterday, about noon."

Doc Savage said slowly, "I just talked to Russel Kinner. He said he hired Charles to watch you in order to find Jerry. Kinner says Jerry tried to kill him."

Her hands flew to her lips. "When?"

"Two days ago, Kinner said. It was at night."

She said tensely, "That might make it the evening of the day that Jerry thought Kinner shot at us." She got a little pale. "Maybe Jerry rushed out and tried to kill Kinner. But no! No, no, Jerry wouldn't do that!"

"Perhaps we should talk to Jerry," Doc said.

She stared at him eagerly. "That would be a good idea."

Audine Million disappeared for a moment, was back with hat and coat. "I have a car," she said.

Doc shook his head slightly. "We will use my machine."

They got in the rented car, and the bronze man drove. He took a roundabout route to skirt the spot that led to the lane where he had left Russel Kinner and Charles.

Audine looked at Doc earnestly.

"I wish you wouldn't get the wrong idea about Jerry," she pleaded.

"What idea is that?"

"That he is a kind of double-dyed villain who would rob widows and strangle babies." Her hands knotted and unknotted. "I do not know what happened that day at the factory. But I do know this: It wasn't what people think happened."

"Did Jerry ever tell you exactly what happened at the factory the day of the fire?"

She shook her head. "No—and that was strange, too. He never told anyone. Not even Lucille Gavett."

"Who is Lucille Gavett?"

"The girl Jerry was engaged to marry. He met her through her brother, Dennis, who worked at the laboratory with Jerry." Audine was silent for some time, staring fixedly at the concrete road that crawled toward them like a gray snake. "The girl broke off with Jerry."

"Miss Gavett broke their engagement?"

"Yes. There was not much else she could do, because her family was bitterly opposed to Jerry after the trial and—Jerry going to jail and everything. But I think Lucille Gavett still loves him. I know Jerry still loves her."

Doc Savage reached back and lifted the little radio transmitter-receiver onto the seat. He adjusted the knobs, threw a switch, and picked up the microphone.

"Renny?" he asked.

"This is Johnny," came a voice out of the speaker. "Renny is in the back seat trying to control Monk's hog. I'll be superamalgamated if I ever saw one hog make so much trouble."

"Are you on Kinner's trail?"

"His car is about half a mile ahead. You were right about it taking him a little time to wire around the ignition switch of his car."

"Is there any indication that Kinner knows you are following him?"

"No."

"Is Charles with him?"

"The detective? Yes."

Johnny, for some reason or other, never used his big words in conversation with Doc Savage, although Doc was one of the few individuals who probably understood the meaning of most of the jawbreakers.

"What does his destination seem to be?" Doc asked.

"Can't tell yet. He's just heading for town."

"Call me if anything develops."

IX

TWO AND TROUBLE

Johnny—William Harper Littlejohn—switched off the transmitter of his radio, ending the conversation with Doc Savage, but left the receiver apparatus turned on in case the bronze man should call. Johnny had been driving and using the radio at the same time.

They were traversing a boulevard where there was considerable traffic, and Johnny had driven terrifically to decrease the distance between themselves and the car ahead.

In the back seat, Renny rumbled plaintively.

"Holy cow!" complained the big-fisted, big-voiced engineer. "How about you getting back here and trying your hand at controlling this hog, while I drive?"

"An innavigable machination," Johnny announced.

"Eh?"

"No!" Johnny said.

"What ever possessed me to steal this hog, I don't know," Renny grumbled. "Talk about a joke backfiring!"

There were no more remarks, because the car ahead turned sharply to the right, and headed toward the waterfront. Johnny drove carefully, keeping well back, so that his machine was as unobtrusive as possible.

Kinner drove into a sandwich stand, where he and Charles had soft drinks and sandwiches. Johnny circled the block and parked at an intersection which was a favorable vantage point.

"Looks like they might be heading for the yacht basin," Renny hazarded.

The guess proved good. A few minutes later, Kinner had driven to a spot near the yacht harbor, parked, and alighted. Charles joined him. They conversed for a while, and Charles gestured slightly. Then the two men stepped back behind the line of parked cars, moved along those, and got behind a building.

"They sneaking up on something?" Renny rumbled.

70

Johnny nodded. "Looks like it," he said, so interested he forgot to use a big word.

Kinner and the other man moved slowly, using caution with elaborate pains to make it seem they were not doing so.

"Interested in one of those boats," Renny muttered.

The big-fisted engineer doubled over, took shelter behind a truck. Johnny crouched beside him. Habeas Corpus kept close at their heels. The pig was well trained, and, although he showed no preference whatever for the company of Johnny and Renny, the shote took their orders readily.

Kinner and his companion finally moved out on a short dock, and gave their attention to a boat.

"They sneaked up on that bugeye," Renny said.

He added an explanation of what he knew about bugeye boats, explaining the craft were peculiar to Chesapeake Bay, having been developed originally for the special needs of the oyster-dredging business, before the days of power. The boats were very shallow draft, drawing only a few inches of water, but with their slanting clipper-type bows and masts which raked back in streamlined fashion, they were among the most attractive sailboats in the world. Originally, Renny explained, the bottoms of the bugeyes had been made with three or five logs drifted together with Swedish iron, an unusual type of construction, and one which would at first seem to be clumsy, but that was actually of deceptive speed.

Renny went back still further in the history of bugeye boats, telling about the log canoes which were really the first craft of the type—when Kinner and Charles disappeared into the bugeye which they had been inspecting cautiously.

Almost instantly, Kinner and Charles popped into view again. To all appearances, they were running for their lives.

Renny and Johnny were astounded. But not half as surprised as they were when the whiteness came.

They had not experienced the whiteness before, and the thing had been so fantastic that, when they had been told about it previously, they had hardly conceived the thing as an actuality.

Now Renny even mistook it, at first, for the work of the sun. "Holy cow, the sun is getting bright!" he remarked, and glanced upward.

The next instant, Johnny clamped a hand on his arm.

Johnny's bony fingers were like steel rods, for he was excited. He used small words.

"The white elf!" he exploded.

"Where?"

"There"—Johnny pointed—"coming out of the bugeye." Then the gaunt archaeologist and geologist whirled Renny, and tried to bustle away from the vicinity.

Renny resisted, tugging at the armpit holster where he kept his supermachine pistol. "I ain't gonna run from that thing," he growled.

"But Doc's orders were to keep away from it!"

Renny grunted, got his machine pistol out. By now, however, he could not distinguish the figure on the dock. The air seemed to have turned to white heat.

The agony in their eyes was intolerable. Somewhere near, a woman began screaming, and there was a loud splash as someone fell off a boat.

Renny boomed, "Make a break for it, Johnny! I'm gonna turn loose on that dock with explosive bullets!"

He threw himself flat, his idea being to shoot over the edge of a timber at the dock. But the moment he was prone, he found that he had lost all sense of direction, all idea of what was right or left, up or down. The entire universe seemed to be going over and over, and around in circles.

He changed his mind. "Johnny!" he yelled.

"Here," gasped the gaunt archaeologist.

"Which direction is the car?"

"I don't know. I'm all whirly."

"Whirly" was a mild word for it. Renny groped around, found the timber behind which he had been going to take shelter. He remembered which way it pointed. He yelled, "Get hold of this beam. We can follow that, and get going in the right direction."

They were following the timber, helplessly blind, when blows on their heads made them unconscious. Johnny was the first one struck, then Renny, and they flattened out on their faces, unconscious.

The pig, Habeas Corpus, running and squealing, fell over the edge of the quay into the water and sank.

X

BLITZKRIEG

Doc Savage was standing in the office of an advertising agency when he became aware of a brightness that seemed to suffuse his surroundings.

The manager of the advertising agency—it was an inside office and the electric lights were on—glanced at the ceiling, said, "The current must have gotten stronger."

Doc wheeled.

"You stay here," he told Audine Million. To the advertising-agency manager, he said, "Keep this girl here. Keep her here by force, if necessary."

The bronze man then flung out of the agency.

The manager came over, said, "Won't you be seated?" to Audine. She stared at him, then made a move toward the door. The manager grasped her arm. "Sorry," he said.

Astonished, Audine demanded, "You mean you *would* keep me here by force?"

He nodded. "I most assuredly would. You see, I happen to have known of Doc Savage, and the kind of work he does, for a long time. If he wants you to stay here, you will stay, if I can manage it."

She hesitated, then took a chair. The manager peered at the electric fixture in the ceiling. "A little too bright for me," he said.

He went over to the wall switch and flicked it.

"Great grief!" he yelled. "Where is that light coming from, anyhow?"

Down in the street, Doc Savage was inside his car. He switched the radio on, snatched the microphone.

"Renny!" he called. "Johnny!"

There was no answer. He repeated the summons in a continuous urgent voice.

Eventually another transmitter cut into the wave length, and Monk's small, squeaky voice said, "What goes on, Doc?"

"Where are you now?" Doc Savage asked.

"Watching Jerry Million," Monk explained. "And Million is still keeping an eye on Milan Zinn's place. Ham is here with me. Say, I've lost my hog."

Doc asked, "Do you notice any brightness?"

Monk made a startled noise. "Say, I have, at that. It started just a minute ago. I thought the sun had gotten brighter, or something."

"Close your eyes," Doc suggested.

Monk evidently did so, because he growled, "Closing your eyes, you can still see it. Hey! Blazes, Doc! Are Renny and Johnny in trouble?"

"They were trailing Russel Kinner, who was head of the office where Arnold Haatz worked," Doc said. "I do not know any more than that."

The bronze man resumed calling Renny and Johnny on the radio. After a few moments of growing apprehension, he switched to the ancient Mayan tongue, which Renny and Johnny also spoke, and did his calling in that, not using their names. He took that precaution in case someone should get hold of the radio which Renny and Johnny were carrying.

The brightness went away. Its departure was slow, like the fading of dusk. Several times, while using the radio, Doc had swung slowly, trying to ascertain from what direction the whiteness came, but it was difficult to tell. A general southerly direction, it seemed. From anywhere on the southern horizon would be a guess. And that was too indefinite for a search.

Doc said, "Monk, you and Ham stay on Million's trail. One of you take Zinn, the other trail Million, if they leave the place. *And be careful.*"

"Right," Monk agreed. "And, Doc, if you see any sign of my hog, let me know."

Doc Savage went back to the advertising office, took pencil and paper, and quickly drafted an advertisement. It read:

WARNING!

Anyone seeing a weird and strange all-white "elf" of a figure should throw fire upon the thing. Their lives may depend upon it. Any kind of fire

will do—a lighted match, a piece of flaming paper,
but better still, balls of cloth soaked in gasoline or
kerosene and lighted.

IF SURROUNDED BY FIRE, THE
"ELF"CAN BE MADE TO
SURRENDER.
*$20,000 REWARD FOR ITS CAPTURE
ALIVE.*

Doc passed the advertisement to the manager of the
agency. "Run that in every newspaper in the city, and in
Richmond, Annapolis and Baltimore," he directed.

"How big?"

"A full page."

"What!"

Doc said grimly, "Run it full page, and put the expense
on my account."

It was twenty minutes by automobile—it would not have
taken so long, but Doc Savage drove slowly and called repeatedly for Renny and Johnny over the radio, without results—
and then it was probably five minutes by creeping and crawling to the spot where Monk was watching Milan Zinn's home.

"Where is Ham?" Doc inquired.

"On the other side," Monk explained. "You know what? I
think that blasted shyster did something with my hog."

The bronze man's flake-gold eyes searched the vicinity
and located Jerry Million. He asked, "Has Jerry done anything but watch the house?"

"No."

Audine's hands flew to her lips. "My—is Jerry here?"

Doc pointed out the spot where the young man with the
jaw was lying, using a pair of binoculars on first one window
of the Zinn home, then another.

"Oh!" The girl stared at the bronze man. "What is he
doing?"

"Watching Milan Zinn's home."

"But why?"

She seemed genuinely surprised, bewildered. At least that
was the bronze man's impression, and he watched her closely. He did not depend too much on his judgment of women,
however, having learned in the past that it was anything but

reliable. The character of a man, he could read. But not a woman, and particularly one as attractive as this girl.

"You might ask your brother why," he suggested quietly.

"Good idea," Monk agreed. "This watching may go on and on."

The homely chemist came half erect in the weeds, with the idea of hurrying forward. Instantly, there was the ugly sound that a high-powered bullet makes, the cloth on the back of Monk's coat flew open, and he dived forward on his face.

"What happened?" the girl gasped, half rising.

Doc pulled her down. "He was shot."

Jerry Million had whirled to face them. His hands were empty; he had not fired the shot.

Monk's legs made the movements of a sick frog, and his hands opened and shut.

Doc went down beside Monk, felt for the homely chemist's machine pistol. Monk rolled over, began coughing.

"Can you run?" Doc asked.

"Show me the guy who done that," Monk gritted, "and I can chase him."

The girl looked utterly astounded, as if she thought Monk must be bulletproof. There was no time to explain that Monk, like Doc and the others, wore a chain-mesh undergarment of special alloy metal which would stop anything less than a specially jacketed army-rifle bullet.

Jerry Million suddenly emitted a yell.

"Get down!" he howled. "They've spotted us!"

He said more, but it could not be understood. There was noise like an outboard motor, only immensely greater, and mixed with that gobble another noise that was not unlike a mowing machine in tough grass. The tops broke off weeds. Dirt geysered over them.

"Submachine gun," Monk said, and went away through the weeds like a mole.

Doc sent the girl after Monk, followed after them and a moment later, they encountered Jerry Million, who was crawling very fast on his stomach.

Jerry Million seemed to recognize Monk, for he scowled. He demanded of his sister, "What the devil you doing here? Who is this big guy?" all in one breath. Then he added, "We gotta get out of here."

Loud crashing caused Doc to lift his head briefly. What he saw was not reassuring. A huge vehicle, painted the color of a green olive, had vaulted the sidewalk and was smashing through a wooden fence which surrounded that part of the vacant lot. Gun ports in the thing lipped powder flame.

Jerry Million said, "An armored truck! I wonder where they stole that."

Doc said, "Try to get to Zinn's house." The bronze man's voice, without rising, had an imperative force.

"May be more of them in there," Jerry Million barked.

Doc said nothing. The house was their only chance. They crawled fast. Doc saw they could not make it, scooped up the girl, and leaped erect. The others followed. They rounded the house corner with lead gnawing off large pieces of the weatherboarding.

Ham met them. He had come running from the other direction.

"What's going on?" he yelled.

Doc veered for the back door of the house, hit it with his shoulder. The lock tore out, leaving a hole as if something had taken an ample bite out of the wood. They plunged through into a gloomy hall. Behind them, the armored truck roared like an angry juggernaut. They kept going down the hall, turned left into a room. In the hall, an instant after they quitted it, something that must have been a hand grenade exploded, deafening them, knocking them off balance. Plaster loosened from the ceiling and caved down upon them, giving for an instant the impression that the whole house was falling.

"A blitzkrieg, maybe," Monk said, answering Ham's question about what was going on.

Milan Zinn came down a stairway then, and stood looking at them. The stairway was majestic—this place had once been a mansion—with walnut and velour as darkly red as the lifeblood of the dragons that were woven into its design.

Milan Zinn himself wore colors. He looked as garish as an organ grinder's monkey, and there was something of an organ grinder's monkey in his general aspect. His trousers were red-brown, his shirt pine-green, his sport coat a mixture of those two colors. The pistol in his hand was larger than anything, and it was rusty, but not rusty enough.

Monk mentioned a description of the pistol, under his breath. "As horse pistols go," Monk said, "that thing is a stallion."

Milan Zinn spoke with remarkable calm, considering

that plaster was still dropping off the ceiling and the air was full of swirling lime dust.

"What is going on?" he asked.

Another grenade exploded immediately, and the floor gave a jump, what plaster was left on the ceiling came down, a chandelier in the ceiling let go and hung by its wires.

Ham said, "We can't have that," and unlimbered his machine pistol. He moved back to the door, poked the gun out into the corridor, and raked back on the firing lever. The noise of the grenades was a cricket chirp beside the uproar that ensued. The machine pistol was charged with explosive pellets that were probably as destructive for their size as anything ever created.

Ham's gun suddenly stopped stuttering. The dapper lawyer gaped at it. He peered into the mechanism.

"I thought that ammo drum was full," he muttered. He wheeled on Monk. "You better use yours."

"I haven't got any explosives in mine," Monk said.

Doc Savage moved suddenly then. He had not seemed to have been watching Milan Zinn, but now, after the old man had come down the stairs and advanced two steps across the floor, Doc Savage reached him and had the gun with blinding speed. Zinn stared at his empty hand rather foolishly.

Doc broke open the enormous pistol. It was empty.

Zinn said, "I do not understand this."

Monk, who was rather proud of his association with the Man of Bronze, said, "This is Doc Savage, and we're investigating the mystery behind this so-called white elf."

Zinn stared at them.

"In that case," he said, "you need not have taken my gun."

The ring of truth, or relief, in his voice was startling. Doc Savage's flake-gold eyes studied the man.

"You know who is behind this mystery about a white elf?" the bronze man asked.

"Yes," Zinn said promptly. "I do."

"Who is it?"

"Russel Kinner."

"The man who was manager of the government office in which Arnold Haatz worked?"

"Yes. And Haatz was killed because he had unwittingly learned the truth," Zinn added grimly. "Russel Kinner had him killed."

Doc Savage, in a tone equally sober, asked, "You are *sure* about that?"

"Absolutely," Zinn said with a violent nod. "Here is what happened and it proves—"

Zinn never did get to explain what had occurred and what it proved, because a grenade blew in the west wall of the room at that point.

The blast upset them all. Doc landed on all fours, came up quickly, and his voice drove powerfully into the clatter of falling wreckage. "Get into the upstairs rooms," he ordered. He scooped up Jerry Million and his sister then, and moved out of the room. Monk and Ham, grabbing elderly Zinn, followed.

In the hall, Doc countermanded his order to go upstairs. He did it by gestures, indicating the basement. Monk showed his teeth grimly, realizing that Doc had given the upstairs order in a loud voice to mislead the attackers.

Unfortunately, the ruse was futile. Another grenade popped into the place, exploded with a dull noise, and became a spreading cloud of dense smoke. Ham started into the cloud of sepia vapor with the idea of kicking the chemical contents out of the place before it could cause more smoke. But he backed away, grimacing, squinting.

"Tear gas," he gasped.

Doc and his men frequently used gas themselves, and they carried hoods of transparent plastic material, rather like cellophane but tougher, which took little pocket space. They yanked these over their heads.

A man rushed them. He was a wiry, vicious shape in the spreading smoke. He wore a gas mask. Monk and Ham dropped old Milan Zinn, lunged at the attacker. Monk swung a fist, and the assailant doubled over it, hung there long enough for Monk to hook an arm around his neck. Monk kept the grip.

The smoke bomb turned their surroundings a midnight black. There was noise of pounding feet. It came from all directions, from the halls, and the hole that had been blasted in the side of the adjacent room.

Doc drove a hand inside his clothing, brought out a metal cylinder that resembled a bicycle pump. He twisted a small valve on the end, and the thing whistled like a peanut wagon, threw a stream of liquid a little thinner than a darning needle. Doc swung the nozzle as if he were wetting down a lawn with a hose.

A man screamed, the scream starting as a howl of pain and rising to a throat-ripping crescendo of agony. Doc himself set his teeth as stinging pain leaped across his hands.

He had developed this gas recently. This was his first attempt to use it, and he was not too confident of its effect. It was tricky stuff, a fiercely agonizing irritant that acted upon the skin. It had the unusual quality of being almost instantaneously nullified upon coming in contact with cloth or other porous material which had been impregnated with a chemical mixture.

Preparing for use of the new gas, days previously, Doc and his aids had soaked their clothing repeatedly in the nullifying chemical mixture, which left no outward evidence except a slight stiffening of the fabric and a fading of some dye colors. The fabric rendered the gas impotent before it reached their skin. Thus a common suit of clothes, if treated with the proper chemicals, became effective protection.

The gas exceeded expectations. A voice, evidently belonging to the leader of the assailants—Doc had never heard it before—roared out a wild guess that the gas was poison. It ordered flight.

Doc moved backward, found a door, and entered a room that had windows. He threw the window up, went out through it. He pulled off the transparent hood as he hit the ground. There was no oxygen supply inside it, so he had been getting short on air.

His idea was to cut off the retreat, if possible. But they had worked more rapidly than he had expected. Already, they were piling into the armored car.

Furthermore, they had seized Milan Zinn and Audine Million.

Doc saw both the girl and Zinn clearly. The pair were being dumped into the rear of the armored machine.

At about the same moment, a man saw Doc and yelled a warning. From one of the gun ports protruded the snout of an automatic gun—either rifle or submachine—and the muzzle angled toward Doc.

The bronze man rolled into the handiest shelter, which was a basement window. The window was closed, but he knocked out sash and pane and landed on a concrete floor.

The armored car, the motor laboring noisily to get the

machine across the soft turf of the lawn, passed the window a moment later, and a man tossed another hand grenade. Fortunately, it did not roll into the basement. But it did kick a dozen concrete blocks of the basement wall down on top of Doc Savage, and one of these landed on his head, so that he lay there, very still, for long enough that the armored car got away.

Three or four minutes later, Doc Savage made his way upstairs. He was still dizzy. Monk and Ham were searching the house angrily.

"They got away!" the homely chemist shouted. "They took Milan Zinn and Audine with them!"

Monk was wrong to some extent. Two of the assailants, felled in the fight, had been left behind.

Doc boosted them out of the window to Monk and Ham.

Jerry Million was incoherent with agony from the gas. Doc was interested in his reactions. The gas seemed to have rendered him quite helpless. That was understandable. His own hands felt as if they were in fire. He made a mental note to add chemical-treated gloves to their equipment before they used the gas again.

Doc finally managed to steer Jerry Million outside.

"I believe it would be wise to leave the vicinity," the bronze man advised. "Take these two prisoners and Jerry Million, and get to our car."

Doc went back into the house, after pulling on the transparent hood. He searched. His hunt was hurried, very brief.

He devoted most of the search to the library which he found. It was an unusual library, because it was all in Braille, the system of lettering by upraised dots used by the blind. It was not truly a library—it was more of a file of notes made in Braille. There was a machine, on the order of a typewriter, for printing Braille letters.

Since there was no time to study the notes closely, Doc stuffed a few sheets in his pockets, selecting them at random.

He found his men waiting in the car. Doc got behind the wheel, and drove rapidly.

"There is a chance," the bronze man explained quietly, "that the so-called white elf may come hunting for us. It would be better if it did not find us. At present, we are not equipped to deal with it."

Monk peered at him. "*It?* You don't talk as if it was—well, anything human."

Doc did not answer. On the seat, Jerry Million twisted and made faces and groaned. The tires whistled complaints as they took corners, and bumps made the machine take long leaps through space.

Finally Ham said, "Well, we learned one thing, anyhow."

"What's that?" Monk eyed him.

"Russel Kinner is the brains behind this."

XI

TRAILS GOING NOWHERE

Ham Brooks was the first to notice the weird whiteness, and he demonstrated his discovery by letting out a howl—he was much impressed by the eerie nature of the white elf and the fantastic thing that happened to people who saw it—and snatched at the car-door handle, preparatory to leaping out and dashing away in flight. However, when the glow did not increase in intensity, Ham remained where he was, in the car with Doc Savage, Monk, Jerry, the two prisoners. Doc Savage stopped the machine, alighted, and covered his eyes with both hands, then turned slowly in a complete circle. Ham was puzzled until he did the same thing, then he realized the reason for the maneuver. The hands over the eyes made no appreciable difference in the quality of the strange whiteness, but covering the eyes did keep out the sunlight, so that it was possible to tell that the whiteness was stronger in one direction than in another. The strength was back in the direction from which they had come, back toward Milan Zinn's home.

Ham said, "I guess the white elf *did* come to Milan Zinn's home, hunting us."

Doc Savage made no comment.

Monk and Ham were surprised at the spot where Doc Savage finally stopped their car, but they made no comment. Jerry Million was not as controlled.

"This is a hell of a place!" he exclaimed.

He meant the appearance. It was river front, and not in a

populated neighborhood. Only structures nearby were a long shed on the bank, a substantial and plain dock that thrust out into the stream. A barge, old and large, but neat, was tied to the dock. In the distance, the crimson sun of late evening made the surface of the Chesapeake like salmon-colored corduroy.

Doc went aboard the barge. He met the only men who seemed to be in the vicinity, two rangy fellows who were sunburned and healthy.

"Why, I remember those guys!" Monk ejaculated.

"Who are they?" asked Jerry Million.

Monk opened his mouth, then hesitated. It flashed through the homely chemist's mind that he couldn't very well give the correct answer. Not the whole truth. Those two rangy men had once been violent criminals, and Doc had captured them, sent them to his "college" for curing crime. The world was not supposed to know of the existence of that "college," because its curing methods were unorthodox. The criminals consigned to the place first underwent a complicated, unusual brain operation which wiped out all memory of past; following this, they were trained to hate crime, and taught a trade. When graduated from the place, the men had no knowledge that they had once been criminals.

"Oh, they're Alec and Joe, a couple of friends of Doc's," Monk told Jerry Million casually.

Alec and Joe, it was obvious, were making a success out of the oyster-farming business.

Doc left them, came back to the car.

"Alec and Joe will let you use their place here for the night," the bronze man said. "Monk, you and Ham will take these two prisoners and get the truth out of them. Mr. Million, you will stay with them."

Jerry Million scowled. "Listen, where do you get off, giving me orders?"

Doc looked at him. "You can consider yourself a prisoner in charge of Monk and Ham," he said.

When they had transferred the two captives to the interior of the barge on which Alec and Joe had living quarters, Doc Savage touched Jerry Million's elbow, explained, "We had better get your story. So far, you have not volunteered any information."

Jerry Million looked startled. "I haven't, at that." He put fire to a cigarette. "What do you want to know?"

"One thing," the bronze man replied.

"And that is?"

"Exactly what we are involved in."

"That covers a lot of ground, and I wish I could give it to you," Jerry Million said frankly. "But the truth is that I was trying to find out the same thing myself."

Monk took a step forward and doubled his fists. "Listen, bud, that kind of an answer won't do the job. We want the truth."

Jerry Million shrugged. "I can't tell you what is going on."

Monk looked at him.

"Those men got your sister, remember," the homely chemist growled.

Jerry Million turned slightly white. "And you fellows are holding me here, instead of letting me see if I can find her."

After the young man was calmer, Doc took him onto the afterdeck, "You might tell us some kind of a story," Doc said.

"Damn it, I'm anxious to tell you the truth," Jerry Million said angrily. "If that big ape would have kept his mouth shut! Well, anyhow, here is what happened: About a week ago, Russel Kinner telephoned me. I had known Kinner a few years ago when he was on the sales force of the photographic supply manufacturing company I worked for. Kinner sold for them a while, then got fired. I happen to know he was canned for being crooked. To get back to the story, Kinner called me, and he seemed to know I was down and out."

Jerry Million paused to clench his jaw and glare at Doc Savage defiantly. "You've got no idea how many people kick you after you get down. Talk about *me* being a rat, will they! I tell you, this thing I've gone through has sure educated me in human nature."

Doc asked, "Do your personal troubles have a bearing on this?"

The other shrugged. "Only to the extent that they account for Russel Kinner calling on me. He knew I was broke, and that nobody would give me a job."

"You went to see Kinner?"

"Yes. And I found out right away he wanted me to do some dirty work. Something crooked."

"What was it?"

"I don't know. I didn't wait to find out. I could tell it was dirty work from his manner, from his insinuations. So I walked out. Then I came back; I got mad, and I decided to punch Mr. Kinner's snobbish nose for him, so I came back. And stepped right into the mess."

"How?"

"I stopped on the sidewalk in front of Kinner's office and lighted a cigarette. I wanted to consult myself and be sure the satisfaction of punching Kinner's nose would be worth being arrested for assault and battery. I had just decided it would be, when Kinner stuck his head out of the car against which I had been leaning. It was a pure accident. I had leaned against a car in which Kinner and old Milan Zinn were talking."

"Zinn was in the car with Kinner?"

"Yes."

"What happened?"

"Kinner had a fit. Mad! Boy, oh, boy! He thought I had been eavesdropping. He started calling me names. So I did what I had come back for. I hung one on his kisser."

"Kinner was mad because he thought you had overheard a conversation he and Zinn were having in the car?"

"Yeah. And mad was a mild word for it."

"Did you overhear?"

"Not a word."

"Then what happened?"

"Day before yesterday, someone took a shot at me while I was riding with Audine. I got a glimpse of the guy with the gun, and I think it was Kinner. So I started to work on him."

"How did you work on Kinner?"

"I started off tough. That night, I caught him in a dark alley, and threw the fear of Old Nick into him. I even took a shot at him. I was going to grab him after I got him scared, and make him talk. But he got away from me."

"Why were you at the airport last night?"

"I had trailed Kinner there. I saw him meet Milan Zinn. The two of them separated, and I grabbed Zinn. The old fellow seemed puzzled, and I locked him in an empty room and went hunting for Kinner. I didn't find him, so I went back to get Zinn out of the room where I had locked him, and your two men were there. I took Zinn away from them at the point of a gun, and we started to leave the airport. We met some guys. I think now the guys had been trailing me. Anyhow, they took Zinn away from me, and there was some shooting when your man, Ham Brooks, turned up. After the shooting started, I cleared out. I went back to the airport this morning to see what I could dig up, but found nothing, and went to watch Milan Zinn's house. I was still at that when you showed up."

Doc Savage was silent for a while in the darkness. The young man's story checked with the one his sister had told, and with Monk and Ham's explanation of how they had met him at the airport.

Jerry Million seemed astonished when Doc Savage shook his hand.

"For the love of mud!" he said. "You believe my story?"

"Yes," Doc Savage said soberly.

Jerry wrung the bronze man's hand. "I want you to know I appreciate that. I think this is the first time in two years that anybody besides Audine has believed anything I said."

Doc went back into the cabin. "Jerry will stay here with you," he told Monk and Ham.

During the ride to the airport—it was an army field, where the presence of his unusually fast ship would not be so noticeable—Doc tried repeatedly to raise Renny and Johnny on the radio. He got no response.

The bronze man took with him in the plane a small package containing the stuff he had picked up at the airport that morning—the discolored bits of gravel, the vital organs of the girl's dead canary.

The plane made the flight to New York in close to record time. It was an amphibian ship which would operate from land or water, and he set it down on the Hudson River, taxied along the piers that stuck out into the river like huge fingers, then headed for a looming structure.

The doors of the building—the structure resembled a warehouse, but it extended out into the river some distance—opened when he actuated a radio control. The doors closed again when he was inside.

Ten minutes later he was in his headquarters laboratory on the eighty-sixth floor of a midtown skyscraper. The laboratory was vast, occupying the major part of the floor space, and its equipment had been rated by experts as probably the most advanced in existence.

He went at once to the department devoted to analyzing apparatus. He worked there for a few hours. Then he went to the telephone, began making urgent calls to the managers of houses supplying chemicals and rare metals.

It was past midnight by then.

At three o'clock in the morning, Ham awakened Monk by dumping a glass of water in the homely chemist's widely gaping mouth, jumping clear of the resulting upheaval.

"Look out, the boat's sinking!" gasped the befuddled Monk. Then, getting his wits together, he outlined Ham's ancestry in sulphur-tinged detail.

"I believe our prisoners are about ripe to be questioned," Ham said.

"Humph." Monk sleepily stuffed his feet in his shoes. "Is that Jerry Million still here?"

"Yes."

"I favor working on him first. I don't trust him."

"Doc seemed to," Ham reminded.

That silenced Monk's objections for a moment. Then he ventured, "Yeah, but you can't tell about Doc. His methods are devious. Try to figure Doc out, and you have about as much luck as a monkey taking apart a watch."

They put their heads together and held what, for them, was an amiable consultation. They were looking forward with pleasure to working on their captives. "That ought to do the job," Monk agreed finally.

A bit later, Monk and Ham walked into the main cabin. The two prisoners were lashed to chairs, and Jerry Million was pacing back and forth. They ignored Jerry.

Ham went over to a captive. He freed the man from the chair, but the fellow's wrists and ankles remained bound.

Ham said, "We've asked you before to answer some questions."

"And I told you where you could go!" the man snarled.

Ham's expression was fierce. "You know that your only chance is to talk, don't you?"

Jerry Million said, "He's tough, that baby. He keeps telling his pal here that they're safe, because Doc Savage and his gang never kill anybody."

"Oh, he's heard that, has he?" Monk said ominously. The homely chemist wheeled on the prisoner who had the courage. "You might be mistaken, wise guy. There's a difference between doing a thing and getting *caught* at it. To stick you for a murder, they got to prove what they call a corpus delicti. And we don't leave any corpus delicti around."

The other prisoner spoke for the first time. "Bushwah," he said. "Bunk."

Monk wheeled on the fellow. "Tough guy," he said.

Ham nodded. "He'll be a hard one to make talk. Why waste time on him?"

Monk said, "Who said anything about wasting time on him?"

The homely chemist stepped forward, and as he did so, brought a knife of startling size out of his clothing. He flung a hand to the bound prisoner's collar, jerked him erect and whirled him toward Ham, saying, "You hold him."

Ham grabbed the captive. Monk leaped upon the fellow from behind. They went to the floor. Monk lifted the knife and brought it down. A grinding sound that might have been the grit of edged steel against bone, and a hair-raising scream came out of the melee.

Monk and Ham got to their feet.

The prisoner went through weakening throes on the floor. The knife hilt protruded from his back. A red flood poured out of his chest, spread on the floor. His gasping, his scream—there was just one more shriek, and it was like a file on a saw—brought a spray of red from his mouth, and the red also crawled from the corners of his mouth. The struggling went out of his body and it was without much shape on the floor.

Jerry Million had stood there, struck dumb and motionless by the unexpectedness of the deed.

"You murderers!" Jerry croaked suddenly.

He made a leap, then, trying to reach Ham. But Jerry acted without planned reasoning, and he came too close to Monk, so that the hairy chemist was able to reach his jaw with a fist that could open a horseshoe. Jerry sprawled out on the floor, remained there, and Monk picked a piece of loosened skin off his knuckles.

Ham jerked his head at the other prisoner. "What about this one?"

Monk got down beside the man on the floor. When he straightened, he was holding the knife, and its blade was dripping red.

"We might as well give him the same dose," Monk said.

Ham nodded. "Of course," he suggested, "if he could

talk enough to make it worth while, it might be we could let him get on a boat for South America."

It did not take the captive long to make his decision. He ogled the body on the floor, his eyes mostly white. For a while, he looked as if he was trying to faint.

When he started talking, his voice was so incoherent that at first they could not understand him.

Jerry Million had been hit hard on the jaw. When he awakened, his head hurt and he was dizzy. He peered vacantly at Monk and Ham, and astonishment overspread his face.

The two prisoners were back in the chairs, tied. Neither seemed to have been harmed.

"But—you stabbed that one!" Jerry said.

Monk grinned, then picked up a knife handle and exhibited it. The handle was attached to a bit of blade no more than half an inch long. Monk also showed a block of wood.

"Put the wood inside his coat, then stuck the knife handle through the cloth onto it," Monk explained. He picked up a bottle which had contained red ink. "This was the blood."

"But the man went through the motions of dying," Jerry said blankly.

"That was practically genuine," Monk admitted. "You see, when Ham jumped on him, he gave the fellow a hypodermic shot. It knocked him out. We had the gag all fixed up ahead of time."

Jerry rubbed his jaw. He decided that, involuntarily, he had played a helping part in the ruse.

"What did you get out of them?" he asked.

Monk shrugged. "Not enough to pay for the trouble."

Ham said, "Oh, I don't know. We learned something, if we can figure out what it is."

Monk snorted. "Listen, both these lugs"—he gestured at the bound prisoners—"were hired by a fellow named Smitty. They are common crooks, these two birds are. Smitty had worked with them in the past, and they knew him. So when he offered them two hundred dollars a day—"

"How much a day?" Jerry exploded.

"Two hundred. Somebody is putting out real money."

"Who?"

"Whoever is hiring Smitty. They don't know who it is."

Monk scowled at the captives. "Anyhow, here is what they did tell us: They were hired three days ago by Smitty, and their first job was to steal an armored truck this afternoon, take it to Zinn's house, and pick up Zinn. When they got to Zinn's house, we were watching the place, and you know what happened. That was as far as these two got."

Jerry Million was puzzled.

"But why did they need an armored truck to pick up Milan Zinn at his house?"

Monk grinned. "My guess is that they didn't need the truck for that, but for something else. Just what, these rats don't know."

"What do they know about the white elf?"

Monk shrugged again. "Nothing. It's connected with the mystery, all right." The big chemist strode over to the prisoner who had done the talking. "What was that you said about the elf? Repeat it."

The man said resignedly, "All I know is I heard Smitty talking to somebody on the telephone, and Smitty said that nobody would ever catch on to what this white thing is. At the same time, Smitty got his orders to steal the armored truck and pick up Zinn."

Monk nodded. "What else did you hear mentioned?"

"An island," the man said. "Royal Island, as near as I could overhear it. There was something said about getting on it tomorrow—that would be today."

"You ever hear of Royal Island?" Monk asked Jerry Million.

"Nope."

"What do you figure it means?"

"I don't figure anything," said Jerry, "except that Russel Kinner is behind this mess."

XII

THE N. E. LIGHT

Doc Savage came back at ten o'clock. The bronze man, never a demonstrative personality, was stoic, wordless, as he listened to Monk relate what they had learned from the two captives.

"Royal Island?" the bronze man said finally.

"The guy told us that was what he overheard," Monk explained.

Doc Savage had a newspaper under his arm, and he unfolded it, indicated an item.

Monk read it, and yelled, "Great grief!"

The newspaper was a small daily published in a town on the eastern shore of Chesapeake Bay, some distance from Washington. The item Doc had pointed out was short, humorous, and about a remarkable pig that had been found wandering, and created a turmoil when the local police department tried to collect him. The hog, said the item, now occupied a police-station cell.

Monk grabbed his hat. "Let's go."

Doc Savage explained to Alec and Joe that an ambulance would arrive later in the day for the two prisoners, but the bronze man did not add that the ambulance would take the pair to the criminal-curing "college" for treatment. Although Alec and Joe had graduated from the "college," they had no knowledge of its real nature.

An hour and a half later, they were in the small-town police station, exhibiting the newspaper and claiming the hog. The desk sergeant was relieved. "Friends, you're welcome to that animal," he declared.

Habeas squealed, stuck out his large ears, and ran circles around Monk.

They left the police station.

"Message?" Doc asked.

Monk nodded. The pig's neck was encircled by what appeared to be a solid metal collar of bright chrome. Monk pressed this, and it flew open. It still looked innocent, merely a hinge and lock. But Monk worked upon the seemingly solid metal, and the hinge portion suddenly separated so that a hollow tube was disclosed. The contents of this seemed to be a rolled sheet of thin paper bearing a message, and a bit of pencil lead which had been used to scribble the message.

Monk shook the tube, then looked in it. He said, "The little capsules are gone."

"What did the capsules contain?" Ham demanded.

"Some stuff that you could put on a knife blade, on a thorn, or even on your fingernails, and scratch a man and make him unconscious," Monk explained. He shook the tube again. "There was also a capsule or two of chemical to stupefy and dull pain."

"To what?"

"You take one of them, and you become kind of semiconscious and insensible to pain." Monk looked grim. "They're handy in case you know you're going to be tortured. If Renny and Johnny took them—"

Ham snapped, "Well, what is in the message, stumble wit? Does it say where they are?"

The missive that had been in the collar had no wasted words.

> Elf got us at yacht basin.
> N. E. light blinks two five seconds three minute.
> Whole mystery centers on Isle Royal tomorrow
> five.

The writing was erratic, as if it had been executed in the dark, or by a person who was blindfolded.

"Renny wrote that," Monk decided.

"But it doesn't mean a thing," declared Jerry Million.

The building before which Doc Savage stopped their car—the bronze man had surprised Monk, Ham and Jerry Million by driving on to Norfolk, Virginia, instead of back to Washington—was a ponderous brick structure, impressive for nothing but its rather ancient, somewhat decrepit appearance. Smoke had darkened the outer walls, and usage had worn pits in the stone steps. A sign said "U. S. Coast Guard."

Doc said, "Ham, get marine charts of Chesapeake Bay, and of the Atlantic coastline from Sandy Hook to Cape Hatteras."

Jerry Million interposed, "There isn't any Isle Royal in the Chesapeake, or nearby on the Atlantic coast. I happen to know."

Monk nudged him to admonish silence. A moment later, the bronze man left the car and entered a nearby store. The arrangement of the store was such that they could see the telephone booths from where they sat, and they saw Doc enter one of these.

"There's no Isle Royal around here," Jerry repeated.

Monk said, "Keep your shirt on, and your eyes open.

Doc isn't trying to find any island. He's looking for Renny and Johnny."

"But we haven't a chance of finding them. We don't know where they are."

"Want to lay a bet on that?"

Jerry peered at the homely chemist, then grinned faintly. "I don't think so," he said. "I've been seeing enough of this Doc Savage lately that I wouldn't want to bet against him."

Ham returned with a roll of charts. He explained, "I added some charts to Doc's order. In the coast guard office there, they said if we needed any help, to let out a yell."

Doc came out of the telephone booth. Getting into their car, the bronze man seemed somewhat more confident than he had been, although his expression was normally inscrutable enough that it was hard for Monk to tell.

"You learn something good, Doc?" Monk inquired.

Instead of answering, the bronze man unrolled the charts and began following shipping lanes with a fingertip, starting in the vicinity of Washington and progressing in all possible directions.

"Here," he said.

They looked.

Jerry Million, reading from the chart, said, "Gp Fl (2) ev 5 sec ev 20 sec 146 ft vis 18 mi." He scratched his head. "That sounds as complicated as a chemical formula. What in the dickens is it?"

Monk looked blank, then explained: "This designation on the chart means a lighthouse which signals with a group flash of two flashes every five seconds at intervals of twenty seconds. The lighthouse is one hundred and forty-six feet high, and the light is normally visible a distance of eighteen miles."

Ham got it then. "Somewhere in that eighteen miles, Renny can see the lighthouse from where he is being held prisoner."

Monk nodded. "According to his message, the light is northeast of him."

Ham, examining the chart, muttered, "That includes a lot of land and water."

"Water only," Doc Savage said.

"Eh?"

"Examine Monk's hog," the bronze man suggested.

Ham did so, and decided from the condition of the pig

that the animal had been in water some time previously for a long interval. He announced his surmise, and Doc Savage nodded slightly.

"Habeas apparently swam ashore from a boat," the bronze man said.

"Then Russel Kinner is holding Renny and Johnny on a boat near that lighthouse!" Monk ejaculated.

Doc asked, somewhat strangely, "You are sure Kinner is the villain at the bottom of this?"

"Who else could it be?" Monk countered.

A uniformed coast guard officer dashed out of the headquarters building, peered about, saw their car, and raced toward them. He arrived breathless.

"Mr. Savage, an urgent call for you from Washington. Telephone call."

Doc went back with the officer, both of them running. In something over three minutes, he was back. The bronze man's explanation was cryptic.

"Russel Kinner. Turned up at police station in Washington. Wants us. Says he has the whole story about the white elf."

Ham's jaw fell, and he turned to stare at Monk. "You're a darned poor clairvoyant. You just said Kinner was behind this."

Monk was blank. He scratched his head. Then he climbed into the car and turned on the ignition switch. He said, "I got to see it to believe it. I wonder how fast this thing will take us back to Washington."

The answer was an average of around eighty miles an hour, it developed.

The normally placid Washington street was full of fire equipment—four pumpers, three ladder trucks, five emergency trucks—and hose lines, fat with water, were gray snakes everywhere on the pavement. Through treetops, and between two buildings, the illuminated dome of the Capitol was visible whenever not obscured by climbing black smoke.

Doc and his men eventually worked their way through the cordons of police. The police were not in a favorable humor, for it was a precinct station that was burning.

They found the captain in charge, and Doc identified himself.

"That's fine," said the captain grimly. "Maybe you can identify the body."

"What body?"

"Russel Kinner. They are getting the body out now. It's badly burned."

"Did he burn to death?"

"No, he was shot." The officer scowled. "It was the most brazen damned thing that ever happened. A man walked in and said he wanted to see Kinner. When he confronted Kinner, he pulled out a gun and shot Kinner between the eyes."

The captain paused to snap an order at a subordinate, then continued, "I know the bullet got Kinner between the eyes, because he clapped both hands to his forehead, fell backward, and blood shot out of his nose and mouth. Then everything seemed to turn to white fire. I was blinded. Everybody was blinded. It was that infernal white elf again."

"Did anybody see the elf?" Doc asked.

"Nobody saw anything," the police official growled. "The blindness lasted for a little while, and when anybody could see again, the whole place was afire. We barely got out."

A man in white came up, spoke to the official in a low voice, and the other turned to Doc again. "They've got the body. Want to see it?"

Looking at the body did them no good as far as identification was concerned. Looking at it proved nothing, really, except that a man was dead, and that there were handcuffs on the cooked wrists.

"Kinner," the police captain said.

The strange golden flakes in the bronze man's eyes seemed to swirl. "You are sure?"

The official pointed.

"Those are my handcuffs," he said. "I know them positively. They were on Kinner's wrists. Kinner was shot between the eyes. You can see the bullet hole."

"Maybe," Monk suggested, "the man wasn't Kinner in the first place."

The official produced a fingerprint card from his pocket. "These are the prints of the man. I took them myself. I checked them with Kinner's record in the government files. Employees in his governmental department are fingerprinted. He was Kinner, all right. And he is dead."

As they left the vicinity, firemen were raking the ruins. At least one policeman was missing in the blaze, and possibly more, the official in charge of the precinct had announced.

Newspaper and newsreel cameramen were thick, and Doc and his men had some trouble evading them.

XIII

SINISTER SHIP

That night there was a ceiling of mouse-colored clouds hanging uniformly at eight thousand feet. Below there was darkness, and above there was silver moonlight. In the east, almost continuous thunder grumbled.

Doc watched the altitude needle register twenty thousand, then held it there, and cut in the robot pilot which flew the plane without further assistance. He manipulated the radio direction finder, located directional beams from radio lighthouse stations, and drew lines on a chart.

Finally he stood, thrust his arms and legs into parachute harness, and strapped on a garment resembling a hunter's vest, except that the pockets were larger, more numerous, and crammed with gadgets of the peculiar type which he preferred to use.

He said, "Open the floor trap, Monk."

Monk, much concerned, growled, "But just because Renny was on a boat down there when he turned my hog loose with a message—that's no sign he's still there. The boat could have moved."

"In that case, you can land and pick me up."

Because air pressure normally made use of the cabin doors awkward, the escape trap had been built into the plane floor for dropping either an object or a man by parachute.

Doc went out headfirst. He did not pull the cord, but kicked and waved his arms until he was descending feetfirst through space.

Overhead, the plane banked, began circling. It would circle until further orders were received. The motors were silenced, the pitch of the propellers turned to make the least noise, so that supersensitive listening devices of the army type would not register the ship at that height.

Out of sight in the cloud mass, Doc jerked the ripcord, and the big mushroom of silk leaped up overhead, wrenched at him. Its distinctive white flash as it opened would not be noticed there, should a plane be in the vicinity. He kept his eyes downward.

His guess had been good. There was an island below, where the chart had said it should be.

Doc hauled down on one set of shrouds, spilling air from the 'chute and sending it to the left, toward the end of the island where, according to the chart, there was a harbor with water deep enough for a boat of some size. After a while, he released the shrouds. Air currents were not only drifting him toward the harbor; they would carry him beyond it, well out into the water, past a headland which would obstruct the view of any lookout in the vicinity of the harbor.

A few hundred feet above the water, Doc twisted out of the harness, hung by one hand. He freed his grip the moment he plunged into the surface, then stroked back to the top. The 'chute had spilled wind and lay flat on the water. He hastily gathered it and pushed the folds beneath the surface.

For the next fifteen minutes, he made no commotion and no noise, but during the interval, carefully crowded the parachute silk into a compact waterlogged bundle. Eventually, when he swam ashore, he carried the bundle with him. He concealed it in a bush.

The bugeye schooner was tied to the end of a long and rickety dock, where it was like a black bug with its antenna laid back.

It took Doc Savage another seven minutes to locate the guard. Because it was infinitely dark, he used a gadget to locate the guard. He pulled the cork out of a small vial, and tossed it away from him, toward the bugeye. The wind was also blowing toward the bugeye. The vial contained an irritant type of gas which, in extremely small quantities such as this, caused no effect except an inclination to sneeze. It was not even noticeable as an odor. In a closed room, however, or crushed in a handkerchief and held to a man's nostrils, it would cause violent agony and nausea.

After a while, the guard sneezed twice, and Doc located him.

The bronze man then retreated a few yards and unlimbered his portable radio. The set was very small. The microphone and some of the apparatus was built into a cup-shaped container which was edged with sponge rubber and fitted over the lips and nostrils, so that a conversation could be carried on without being audible more than a few inches away.

Doc said, "Monk, Ham, you on the air?"

He held the small receiver to his ear, and Monk's small-child voice answered, "We are circling at twenty thousand."

"Continue doing that. I have landed, found black bugeye on which guard is posted. Intend to board it. Listen for further instructions."

He returned the portable radio to the vest affair to which his equipment was attached. The rank salt grass was wet, and as rough as rattail files against his face as he crawled toward the bugeye.

The guard was at the shore end of the dock, and when Doc Savage was quite close to him, there was an interruption. A man climbed up the bugeye main cabin companionway and approached. He had a flashlight that made a white ghost race here and there.

It was Smitty.

He said, "That you sneezing a minute ago?"

"Yeah. Must be catching cold." The guard bummed a cigarette, and blaze of a match when he lighted it splashed yellow light over a rifle he was holding. "Any news?" he asked.

"Just listened to the news over the radio," Smitty said. "Everything came out all right at that police station."

"How do you mean?"

"Russel Kinner was burned to death in the police station. They have identified his body."

The guard laughed, and sounded a little like a witch.

"Any sign of the boss yet?" he asked.

"Not yet," Smitty said.

"We ain't got much time left. Should be sailing, or we'll never contact Isle Royal."

"Orders were to wait here until the boss showed up," reminded Smitty.

"Sure, I know. You know something?"

"What?"

"Maybe the boss is still with Doc Savage."

"Maybe. I wouldn't be surprised." Smitty chuckled.

"On the other hand, maybe there has been some trouble

getting back here with the white elf." The guard sounded uneasy.

"I wouldn't worry about that," Smitty said.

Smitty went back aboard the bugeye.

Doc Savage came aboard the bugeye at the bow, using the heavy chain bobstay for a handhold, and hanging there until water ceased dripping from his body. He climbed up then, gripping the safety basket, and finally landing in a crouch beside the anchor-chain winches.

The bugeye was big for that type of vessel, well over a hundred feet, and she was shipshape, well made. The bright-work varnish felt smooth, lines were neatly coiled. Small waves made licking sounds against the hull.

Some faint light came from the forecastle hatch. Doc looked down, saw six men gathered around a table. There was money and dice on the table.

Doc went aft, found a companionway. He peered into it and listened, and there was silence, the blackness of an octopus cave and faint odor of incense. He went down the steps, following a brass rail that was slick and cool, like an eel. It led downward into the low whispering of voices.

The bronze man listened. The words were not distinguishable. Doc waited. It must have been five minutes before he heard a grunt that was easily identified.

Johnny's voice asked, "Something wrong, Renny?"

"Huh-uh," said the voice that had grunted.

Doc Savage unlimbered the radio transmitter-receiver, put the receiver to his ear and buried his mouth in the transmitter cup.

"Monk, Ham," he said. "I am on board the boat. It is a bugeye schooner, over a hundred feet long. Smitty is here. They are waiting for their leader. They plan to sail, as soon as their leader returns with the white elf, to Isle Royal."

In the receiver, Monk's voice was an anxious squeak. "Any sign of Renny or Johnny?"

"That is why I'm calling you," Doc said. "Renny and Johnny are here in the hold of the bugeye, a little beyond the midship section. I have not talked to them, but I have heard them. Listen—look in the map compartment and you will find—"

That was as far as he got. His words had been hardly a breath into the microphone. He had not thought he could be

heard. Probably he was not. The person who found him in
the darkness must have come upon him by accident.

The first warning was a terrific blow which Doc instinctively
dodged, so that it shaved his head. But the blow struck the
radio apparatus, and it fell to the floor. Then, as the bronze
man closed with his assailant, they trampled back and forth
only a few times before the apparatus was crushed underfoot.

In the plane at twenty thousand, Monk and Ham stared
at each other in horror. Enough sound had come through
the radio before it was smashed to give them some idea of
what had happened.

Jerry Million breathed inward hoarsely. "They grabbed
Doc," he said.

Monk faced him. "Get back in the cabin," he ordered.

"Aren't you going to help him?" Jerry barked. "He must
be fighting them now!"

"Get back in the cabin," Monk repeated.

Ham clutched Jerry Million's arm, forced him back. The
young man went reluctantly. Then Ham returned to the
control compartment.

"What was that Doc was saying about the map compartment?" the dapper lawyer demanded.

"Look and see."

There was an envelope. They opened it, found one sheet
of paper, and stared at that. They exchanged surprised looks.

Immediately, Monk straightened the plane out of its
monotonous banking circle and headed north and east.

Three or four minutes later, Jerry Million came dashing
forward.

"You're *leaving!*" he yelled.

"Sit down!" Monk rapped. "We're running this show."

Jerry Million did not argue. Not with words. His right
hand grabbed at his clothing and came out with a flat
automatic.

"I know you wear bulletproof vests," he said grimly, "so
any shooting I do won't be vest shooting."

Monk and Ham looked at him and wondered where he
had gotten the gun. The expression on Jerry's face was not
pleasant. Ham put his hands up. Monk released the controls,
started to get up.

"You fly this thing," Jerry rapped. "You know more about

it than I do. But, for your information, I can fly it, if I have to."

"Where'd you get that cannon?" Monk asked.

"Picked it up at the police station." Jerry moved the gun menacingly. "Land this thing close to that island."

"They'll hear us."

"Land it so they won't," Jerry grated.

Monk was impulsive himself, and he knew reckless frenzy when he saw it. He had better land this plane, or something unpleasant would happen to him.

He landed the ship on the sea half a mile from the island, making a dead-stick landing, all motors shut off, and splashing the ship down cautiously so that there was as little noise as possible.

The breeze began carrying them toward the shore.

"That was good," Jerry Million said. Then, when Monk tried to stand up, he shoved the homely chemist back with the gun muzzle. "Sit down!"

"You better use your head before—"

"Shut up. I'm running this."

Ham said, "They'll sure hear the plane land."

Jerry waved his gun. "Get one of the rubber boats in the water. Ham, you do that. How do you inflate the thing?"

Ham unrolled a rubber boat. A small cylinder containing chemicals was attached, and when he turned petcocks on this, there was a hissing commotion and the boat became fat. They pushed it out through the cabin door.

When they rowed ashore, Jerry Million sat in the stern, facing them with his gun. As soon as the bow bumped mud, he stepped out and waded onto the beach.

What followed was quick and simple. Flashlight beams jumped out of the bushes. A gun exploded, and Jerry Million yelled involuntarily and sat down, holding his arm, which had acquired an extra joint. It was his left arm.

Men came out of the bushes. Monk and Ham tried to throw themselves into the water, but it was not a foot deep, and the mud bogged them down when they tried to run, so there was nothing to do but stand there and get hit on the head. They were not hit lightly.

Someone kicking Monk in the face brought the homely chemist back to awareness of his surroundings. As soon as he was mentally organized, he grabbed the kicking foot, and

endeavored to twist it off the leg to which it was attached.
From the agonized howls that resulted, he concluded the foot
belonged to Ham, who was himself floundering around trying
to regain his senses.

"Where've they got us?" Ham demanded dazedly.

A voice—such a rumble undoubtedly belonged to Renny—
said, "On the boat. You better take a look at that fellow's
arm."

The boat was moving, too, Monk judged. "What fellow's
arm?" he asked.

"The one who was with you."

"Why don't you look at him?" Monk suggested. "My
head is going to fall off if I stand up."

"Turn on that light," Renny boomed, "and you'll find
out."

Monk stood and fumbled around in the darkness. He
found a light switch, and brought momentarily blinding illumination to the cabin.

His left ankle was chained to a floor timber. Ham was
also chained. The cabin was long, a part of the floor had been
ripped up to expose the floor timbers, and they were fastened
to these. Renny, Johnny, and Jerry Million were nearby. Jerry
was very pale, clutching a bandage about his broken arm. His
agony was so evident that it aroused Monk's pity.

"How's the arm?" Monk asked him.

Jerry showed his teeth, which were only slightly more
white than his face.

"Let me look at it," Monk said. The homely chemist
worked over the arm for a while. He had some skill at first
aid, but this arm needed more than first aid. He muttered, "I
wish Doc were here."

Ham demanded, "Renny, what became of Doc?"

Renny spoke hurriedly and in Mayan, the tongue which
only Doc's associates understood.

"Don't ever let on Doc was aboard this boat," Renny said
in Mayan. "He got aboard, and I bumped into him in the
darkness. I thought he was one of the guards, so I took a
swing at him and grabbed him. Doc was using the portable
radio at the time. The radio got busted before we found out
who we were fighting."

In Mayan, Ham demanded anxiously, "What happened?"

"The noise of the fight attracted attention," Renny
explained, still using the Mayan tongue. "Doc had to skip.

There was no time to turn us loose. We pretended we had gotten in a fight among ourselves. I chucked the smashed radio through a porthole."

"The same porthole through which you chucked the hog?" Ham inquired.

"Yes. Did the hog get ashore? Is that how you found us?"

"Yes. What became of Doc?"

"I don't know." Renny looked distressed. "Say, there's a guard on deck who can understand this. We better mislead him about this conversation."

In English, Monk demanded loudly, "Say, what are you guys talking about? Why don't you speak somethin' I can savvy."

Ham, also in English, said, "I was just telling Renny that we have no idea where Doc Savage is. I wish we had brought him along."

"Oh," said Monk, who understood Mayan as well as any of them.

A few minutes later, two guards descended the companionway from the deck. They carefully unlocked the chain from about Jerry Million's ankle, then lifted him and helped him up the steep companionway stairs to the deck. The three of them disappeared, the companion hatch slamming.

The schooner was plowing through a seaway now. They heard the rattle of spray across the deck planking, like the sound of rabbits running, and the creaking of frames and planking. The quick response of the craft to the seas told them she was not using sail, even if there had not been the drone of powerful motors somewhere aft to indicate the motive power.

Monk said, "Renny?"

"Yes."

"You found out what this is about?"

"They're going after something named the Isle Royal," Renny said. "What that is, I'm not sure."

"It's an ocean liner," Monk said. "It's making a secret trip to America from Europe, and it's due in New York tomorrow evening."

Renny demanded, "How did you find that out?"

"Doc dug it up. Had it written down in a message he left for us in the map compartment of the plane. We were to do what we could to stop the attack on the *Isle Royal*."

"Why didn't you carry out instructions? What made you
land on the island?"

"Jerry Million had a gun."

"Oh."

Monk added, "Here's another fact that was in Doc's
message. The *Isle Royal* is bringing a shipment of gold. One
of the biggest that ever came over in one lump."

"Holy cow! That explains what they're after, then. Do
you know what that white elf is?"

"No, but I do know one thing." Monk's tone was fierce.
"The guy back of this has got to be one of two people. It's
either old Milan Zinn—"

"Not Zinn," Renny said quickly. "He's a prisoner aboard
here."

"Then," said Monk flatly, "it's that bird they just took out
of here, Jerry Million."

Ham snorted at this. "Jerry was shot through the arm by
these men, you homely dope."

"A guy as slick as the guy at the head of this," Monk said,
"would go as far as to pull something like that to make us
think he was innocent. It'd give him a better chance to get
Doc. Make us trust him."

Ham asked, "Where is his sister?"

"Audine? She's aboard here, too."

"A prisoner?"

"Sure. They got her when they got old Zinn, remember?"

Monk said, "I'll bet one thing. I'll bet the girl isn't mixed
up in this."

Ham snorted again.

"You'll always bet on a pretty girl, won't you?" he said.

XIV

DISASTER IS A WHISTLE

It was the darkest part of the night—just prior to three
o'clock in the morning—when Doc Savage crawled out of the
sail locker in which he had been concealed. The locker was
situated just aft of the forecastle, and it was stacked with sails
in neat canvas sacks, behind which the bronze man had

burrowed deeply, although the precaution had not been necessary, because they were using the motors alone.

The motors were very big, and they were laboring hard. The sound, and the nervous racing progress of the boat told him that. This bugeye type schooner—it was not genuine bugeye, in that the hull was not made of logs—was of flat-bottomed, streamlined shape, so that it probably had as much speed as could be built into a craft without putting on a special modern hydroplane hull.

Now and then a wave hit the bow planking with the noise of a shotgun. Past the hull there was the steady boiling, like a waterfall sound, of seas rushing past. Once, much earlier, Doc had heard a sea buoy that had passed, mooing like a cow, close to starboard, and the speed of its going had given him an idea that their own pace must be surprising.

This boat, obviously, was a hybrid of the sea. It was built to look like a graceful sailing bugeye, most picturesque of American ship designs. But it had hull lines and a big engine for speed. Millionaires who were always in a hurry liked their boats built that way.

Inside the sail locker there were certain packages. Doc Savage had put them there. He had gone to Monk and Ham's plane, after their capture, and gotten the stuff. He left the packages in the sail locker, and worked aft.

In the radio room, the operator was wearing a headset and standing slowly rotating the dial of a radio compass. He picked up a monotonous signal—the letters "IR" repeated over and over in continental code—and got the volume to its highest point by rotating the aërial loop, then to the lowest.

He snapped on an intercommunicator loud-speaker, said into it, "Boss, I still get Dave's signal from the *Isle Royal*. It's about north-northeast from our course."

"The boss isn't here," Smitty's voice replied from the intercommunicator. "But I'll tell him."

"Listen," said the radioman. "Those messages to the *Isle Royal* are still being broadcast, and signed Doc Savage."

"The messages ordering the *Isle Royal* to change course?"

"Yes."

"Has the *Isle Royal* answered them?"

"No. But she's received them, and changed her course."

"Fat lot of good that will do. They don't know we've got a man aboard with a secret transmitter, so we can locate the hooker, no matter how many times she changes course."

They both laughed.

Doc Savage did not feel like laughing. He had gone to pains—telling no one about it, because he often kept his actions to himself—to have several powerful commercial radio stations begin calling the steamship *Isle Royal* and transmitting a warning to the vessel to alter its course. He had hoped to get the *Isle Royal* out of danger. Apparently it wasn't working.

He eased back into the darkness. It was with the greatest difficulty that he had learned anything about the *Isle Royal* in the first place. To find that the name *Isle Royal* belonged to a steamer was simple, but first inquiry had indicated the ship was bound for Africa with a cargo of manufactured cloth. But persistent inquiry, and contact with the Federal government, had brought out the truth. The *Isle Royal* was en route to New York with a fabulous cargo of gold. And the ship had orders not to use its radio from the time of sailing, since a prize of such size might easily interest one of the predatory European nations.

This thing had been carefully planned. It was strange that these men had known in the first place that a treasure ship was bound for New York. It had been kept such a secret.

Still, the Federal government had known. And Arnold Haatz and Russel Kinner were both connected with the government. The information must have leaked.

The bugeye intercepted the *Isle Royal* exactly at dawn.

The *Isle Royal* was a new liner, as dark and streamlined as a Bali maiden. She was not half the size of such seagoing Gargantuas as the *Queen Mary*, but she had speed and comfort and, best of all, she was the right size to operate at a profit. She was not so huge that she could only run the high-pay transatlantic routes and make money; she could be shifted to South America, to the Pacific, to a world cruise, and still turn a penny.

The bugeye came to a standstill. The crew heaved barrels of steel onto deck. Into these they stuffed cotton waste and chemicals. They applied matches. Smoke climbed off the decks of the craft in great billows.

A man ran the flag aloft, upside down. A flag upside down at sea is the signal of distress.

A vessel was burning, apparently, in the path of the *Isle*

Royal. There was but one thing she could do. Heave to, and offer a rescue.

The *Isle Royal* lost headway, and blew a reassuring blast or two from her whistle. The sea was very calm.

There was a small porthole in the sail locker. That, and his sensitive ears, had given Doc Savage a good idea of what was going on.

He dug into the sail bags, got out the packages he had brought—five of them—and opened one. The garment he removed from the package was like a suit of coveralls, with an all-enveloping head hood added, made of an utterly white substance.

The white garment was heavy. It gave out a sound like chain mail as he unrolled it. He took off his shoes, coat, and worked into the thing. It fastened with a double zipper, the zippers being made out of the same metal as the garment. He closed these.

Carrying the other four packages, he stepped out boldly and made his way to the empty hold, a little forward of amidships, where the prisoners were held.

There was a guard outside the door. He glanced at Doc Savage.

"You supposed to relieve me while I get my suit?" the guard demanded.

Doc kept his face averted, made his voice gruff. "Go ahead," he said.

The guard departed, completely unsuspicious, not having glimpsed the bronze man's features.

The door had no lock, but there was a heavy bar. The moment the guard was out of sight, Doc threw the bar, pushed the door inward. He snapped on the lights.

"Doc!" Monk exploded.

The bronze man dropped the packages on the floor. "Get into those suits," he directed.

He sank to a knee and went to work on the padlocks that secured the leg irons, using a metal pick. His unusual education had included lock picking, so that he was able to make the metal probe function with almost the speed of a key. Fortunately, the padlocks were simple.

Monk, the first released, wrenched open a package. He exploded. "What the dickens!" He whirled on Doc. "Is this what the white elf is?"

Doc said, "Get them on."

"*Is the all-white elf just a man dressed in a coverall garment made of this stuff?*" Monk demanded.

The bronze man nodded. He had Renny free. He went to work on Ham's leg irons, then tackled gaunt Johnny. The motors of the big schooner were silent. Some of the smoke from the smudges on deck had penetrated below, and a man was coughing violently near the stern.

"Close the hoods of these things," Doc ordered.

Doc left the four liberated and white-garbed men in the cabin, went out alone, closed the door, and stood there. Three or four minutes later, the guard came back. He wore a white garment, somewhat more crudely made than that of the bronze man, one that gave the fellow a misshapen, hobgoblin aspect.

"Say, you got a better outfit than mine," the guard said. "Where'd you get it?"

"It's one of the new suits," Doc said, keeping his face turned. "When is it going to happen?"

"Huh?"

"When are they going to turn the machine on?" Doc asked.

The guard had strapped a wrist watch around one paw of his strange garment, tying it there with string because the regular band was too short. He consulted the timepiece.

"In two minutes and twenty seconds," he said.

Doc hit him then. He struck hard, landing on the jaw which was exposed—the guard's suit was also a closed coverall with zipper fastenings—and dropping the man without any sound other than the single smacking report of the blow. Opening the door into the hold, Doc thrust the unconscious shape into the arms of the astonished Monk who unzipped his hood in wild haste.

"Keep him there," Doc said. "Ham, you are about his build. You take up the job of pretending to be the guard. And all of you be ready to act."

"What goes on?" Ham asked lazily, opening his own hood.

"They have intercepted a steamer, the *Isle Royal*, loaded with a bullion shipment," Doc said. "The idea is obviously to get the bullion."

"Why these suits?"

"That blindness," Doc said, "is made by some kind of a machine. The suits are a shield. I hope so, anyway. I worked out an analysis of the metal from some of the stuff I found on sharp rocks at the Washington airport where the white elf first appeared. I made the suits up in a hurry in my laboratory. If they protect us, we may be able to stop this."

The light came. There were three loud reports, evidently shots from some kind of a signal gun, a moment ahead of the light. They could hear the concussions through their suits.

It was intensely black inside the suits, then it became light. Not light, exactly, for it was sensation of brightness, not any light that enabled them to observe objects. It lasted not more than two minutes, then went off.

Doc stripped open his hood. He got his aids to do likewise.

"The attack on the liner will start now," the bronze man said. "Everyone on the ship will be blinded."

He flung open the door, went out into the passage. "Try the stern part of the boat," he said. "Look everywhere."

"The machine?" Ham demanded.

"Yes."

"What will it be like?"

"Complicated. A little like a radio transmitter, perhaps. Vacuum tubes and coils. Probably a radiating antenna. Small enough to be portable by automobile. A machine that generates an ultrashort wave, either of hertzian or sonic type, possibly of both. A wave that travels through most substances, and causes a paralyzing effect on the visual nerves."

Monk growled, "Let's don't get technical. I'll know the thing if I see it."

As they started down the corridor, Doc gave one last warning.

"Keep away from fire," he ordered. "These suits are as inflammable as thermit, the stuff they put in incendiary bombs."

Monk nodded. He was chemist enough to see that Doc's feat in analyzing the metal of which the protective armor was made was not superhuman—the bronze man had had several clues to follow in his research.

Doc swerved to the left, mounted a few steps up a companionway and looked out. The bugeye was warping up alongside the steamer.

The *Isle Royal* had come to a complete stop. A landing stage had been put out from a cargo port for greater facility in taking the supposed rescued victims out of the lifeboats. The bugeye was making for this.

As the bugeye came alongside the landing stage, a man leaped the gap to the stage, carrying a light line. Another followed, and a third. They were clumsy in their white suits. The light line was attached to a heavier, and they hauled this into the liner and made fast somewhere inside. Other lines followed.

Doc said, "We will have to work fast. Find that infernal machine."

What they found, instead, was an alert guard. They were charging down a dark corridor when the lights came on brightly. A man, evidently a watchman, stood at the far end of the passage.

The lookout was holding a rifle. He did not try to use it. Instead, he whirled, scrambled out on deck.

Renny rumbled, "I can catch that guy!" and lunged forward.

A whistle blew. A whistle on the boat, and it blasted three times, then three times again. Its gobbling echoes, crashing back from the wall-like hull of the steamer, made an uproar.

Doc shouted, "Close the hoods of these suits!" But he was not heard. His men were running. Monk was yelling something inarticulate and fierce, the way he liked to yell during excitement, and that, with the roaring whistle, drowned out the bronze man's instructions, or at least made them go unnoticed.

So that when the light came on, they were trapped. All but Doc. He got his hood closed.

The blinding light came quickly, lasted about a minute, then went off. The bronze man stripped open his hood. His four men were reeling in the corridor, Ham down on his knees, so that all were quite helpless.

Doc deserted them.

His desertion was not complete. He did retreat, but it was only to the nearest cabin door. He went through it, waited. In his right palm, which was cupped, there were half a dozen of the little anaesthetic grenades which, when thrown, would break and release a vapor that would bring quick unconsciousness to anyone who breathed the stuff.

He pegged two of the anaesthetic grenades into the

corridor. Through the crack of the partially opened door, he saw Monk, Ham, Renny, Johnny, all go down.

Motionless on the floor, they would be less likely to be shot when found, Doc hoped. Certainly, they would be spared the misery that was caused by the blinding emanation from the machine, electrical or sonic, or whatever it was.

The illness that the thing caused undoubtedly came from the distressing effect upon the sensitive nerve centers of the ears and eyes. It was something akin to seasickness.

After some shouting on deck, and cautious bellowing down a companionway, a man descended with a rifle. He was followed by others, including Smitty.

Smitty swore. "Damn them, they must have broken out of the hold where we had 'em locked. But where'd they get these suits?"

"What'll we do with them?"

"Throw them in with the girl, old Zinn and the girl's brother," Smitty ordered.

A door—the same door in which had stood the guard who had discovered them and brought disaster—was opened. Doc's four aids were tossed inside.

Smitty indicated a white-robed man.

"You stay in there with 'em," he ordered. "I'll be back later."

The designated man entered the cabin, closing and locking the door. The others went away, hurrying out on deck to take part in the boarding and rifling of the *Isle Royal*.

Doc Savage left his cabin and ran to the cabin which held the prisoners.

"Open up," he growled, imitating Smitty's voice.

"What's matter?" asked the guard.

Still using a remarkable likeness of Smitty's tone, Doc said, "Open the door, damn it. I've got another prisoner for you to watch."

As soon as the door started to swing, Doc hit it, flinging the panel back and following it. He landed upon the startled guard. He used both fists, very hard, for a while. Then he looked about the cabin.

His four men were there.

Jerry Million, his arm bandaged, was handcuffed by his left wrist to the stanchion of a bunk. In the adjacent bunk, her wrist fastened to the same stanchion by chain and padlocks, was his sister.

Old Milan Zinn was fastened, by the simple expedient of having wrists handcuffed to ankles, around a bunk leg. His position was twisted, cramped.

Doc dropped beside Zinn. "Can you hear me?"

The bizarre old man—his red-brown trousers and pine-green shirt had lost none of their loud color by being bedraggled—spoke in a perfectly rational voice.

"I'm not sick," he said. "The vibratory wave does not affect me as much as the others, because I have experimented a lot with it."

"You invented the thing?" Doc demanded.

"Yes, that's right. I started working on it years ago, when I was as blind as a bat. I hoped to develop a kind of ultrastrong light which would enable me, and people afflicted with my kind of eye trouble, to see. After I got my vision back, I continued—"

Doc interrupted, "Where do they keep the machine that makes the wave?"

"In my laboratory."

"This bugeye is your boat?"

Zinn nodded. "The laboratory is aft. The whole back part of the boat. The door at the end of this corridor. It leads into a cabin. In the back of the cabin is the door to the laboratory."

Doc flung out into the corridor, raced along it, and shoved open the door at the end. The cabin was shabby. A locker door hung open, and the interior bulged with Milan Zinn's garish clothing. One bulkhead was lined with bookcases gorged with scientific tomes. There was a gun cabinet opposite, but it contained nothing but an automatic shotgun and several boxes of shells.

Doc crossed to the other door. It was locked. He banged on it.

"Yeah?" said a muffled voice from within.

Doc imitated Smitty again, said, "Let me in."

"What's the idea?"

"Let me in, blast you! This is important!"

"Orders were that nobody was to come in here," the voice said.

Doc, making his voice as angry as he could and still hold the Smitty imitation, snarled, "The boss sent me! Open up!"

That was a mistake. A small slip, but it was almost fatal.

A rifle crashed in the other cabin, the lead clouting a palm-sized fragment out of the door panel.

Lunging backward and to the side, Doc realized what his error had been. The boss couldn't have sent anyone. The boss was in that cabin.

He veered left, got to the gun cabinet and scooped out the shotgun and a box of cartridges. He stuffed shells in the iron rump of the piece as he ran. He gained the door, then the corridor, a little ahead of the rifle bullets that were ripping into the cabin, searching.

There was a fire ax on the corridor bulkhead. He scooped that off, reached a companionway and went up on deck.

An instant later, the signal whistle began blaring out its three short blasts, repeating them in succession.

That time, the blinding light lasted for fully three minutes. Doc had the hood of the protective suit over his face, and his objective was definitely in mind. He found the rail, shoved along it, keeping against the smooth varnish.

When he came to a rope, he slashed with the fire ax. He could tell, from the force with which the rope parted, that it was a mooring line.

The blinding light went off. He wrenched open his hood, got the two other mooring lines in rapid succession.

A man yelled at him and started to use a rifle. Doc fired the shotgun. The man doubled over, grabbed his ankles.

Whirling, Doc vaulted over the deck house, got down low, and dived for the nearest hatch. There was a long flight of steep steps that were greasy and ended in the engine room.

He started the motors, shoved the clutches into full speed ahead. The bugeye surged ahead. Immediately, the engine room telegraph began jangling. Doc ignored it. He battened the hatch from below. He locked the doors in the fore and aft bulkhead.

He judged that no more than half a dozen men had been on the bugeye when he chopped the mooring lines free of the *Isle Royal* landing stage.

Later, when they began to drive rifle bullets at the locks of the engine-room doors, the bronze man made a statement. He made it in a voice that was probably audible all over the vessel.

"In ten minutes," he said, "I am going to set fire to the

boat—unless that infernal machine is put in a lifeboat and cast adrift, where I can see it through a porthole."

He was cursed roundly, but the profanity was uneasy.

Milan Zinn and Jerry Million were lying, blinded and entirely helpless, in the cabin where Doc had left them, when the door was slammed open and men entered.

"Bring them into the laboratory," a voice growled.

The voice shocked Jerry Million. He cupped his hands around his eyes in a vain, painful effort to get some kind of vision.

"I...I thought you were dead," he gulped.

Someone kicked him.

"Bring them both," the voice said. It was ugly.

Milan Zinn and Jerry Million were unlocked from the steel that held them, and hauled into the laboratory.

Smitty's voice asked, "Which one would be best, boss?"

The ugly voice, the one that had surprised Jerry, said, "I think Zinn. Savage would probably come nearer trusting him."

"You think he knows Zinn isn't behind this?" Smitty inquired.

"Sure he knows it," the other snapped. "He knows more than we ever thought he did. He figured out the whole thing, and even made a chemical-and-metal shield that was effective. If you don't think he knows I'm back of it, you're crazy."

"But that was a neat trick you pulled to fool him, chief."

The leader swore. He grabbed Milan Zinn's shoulder.

"Listen, old man," he snarled. "Ten minutes ago, you didn't have a chance of getting out of this alive. But now you have. You do one thing for us, and we'll turn you loose."

Milan Zinn stood very still. Then he put out his hand, and found a table. His fingers moved, apparently caressing the edge of the table nervously. He had been blind for many years of his life, and he still retained the extremely developed senses that blindness had created. He knew where he stood. Knew the exact spot in the laboratory.

"I don't understand," he said.

"Savage is holed up in the engine room, and is going to set the boat afire if we don't give up," the other said fiercely.

Milan Zinn showed his teeth. "From what I have heard of Doc Savage, he will do exactly what he says."

The other cursed. "I know it. Here is what you do. I've

got a gun, and I'll give it to you. You go to the engine-room door. Tell Savage who you are. He'll let you in when you pretend we are about to find you."

Milan Zinn stiffened.

"You mean," he said, "that I am to get in the engine room, then kill Doc Savage?"

"That's it."

For an interval, fully a minute, there was silence. Milan Zinn's breathing was distinctly audible.

"Come on, old man," the leader said. "You do this, and we'll let you live."

Milan Zinn slowly put his hands to his eyes.

"For more than twenty years," he said, "I was completely blind. Blindness that comes at birth is bearable. But when a man has seen all that is beautiful in the world, then has to step into blackness, it is a thing more awful than death. But to see again afterward—there is nothing quite as wonderful as that."

"What the hell? Why the speech?" The other man was irritated. "What's that got to do with it?"

Milan Zinn said, "The sight was returned to my eyes through the wizardry of a great surgeon who had developed a new operative method. I am not the only blind man who has been able to see again because of that surgeon."

"Come on, old man. We're wasting time," the leader growled.

"That surgeon's life is worth many of mine," Milan Zinn said. His voice lifted desperately. "And the surgeon happens to be Doc Savage."

Old Milan Zinn took his desperate chance then, and lunged for the platform which held his machine. He knew instinctively that the machine would be there—not only was there no other place for it, but he could hear the humming of the apparatus.

The leader yelled a warning. And as he yelled, Jerry Million was upon him. Jerry had taken a chance, realizing that old Milan Zinn was going to do something desperate. He flung toward the leader's voice, and got hold of the fellow.

They careened, the two of them tightly locked, to the right, and landed against a switchboard. They fought there, grinding their weight against meters and switches.

Jerry heard the snarl of sparks, felt the convulsing leap of electricity through his uninjured arm. Then his foe became suddenly convulsed, began screaming.

Heat, utterly searing heat, smashed like something solid against Jerry's face. He lunged backward, letting the man in his arms drop.

The arcing sparks from short-circuited switches had evidently ignited the highly inflammable metal of the suit the leader had been wearing.

By that time, old Milan Zinn had turned the machine on, and there was whining and spluttering, and the light that was utterly sickening in its violence—it lasted a long time, at least four minutes—and afterward they could hear the screaming of the men on deck, but there was no more sound from the leader in the laboratory, only awful heat.

Milan Zinn said, " The floor and walls and ceiling of this place are shielded with steel. I guess there is not much danger that he set the boat afire when he burned."

He sounded satisfied.

Jerry said, "That man—the leader—was Russel Kinner."

"Yes, Russel Kinner," Milan Zinn agreed.

"But Kinner burned to death in a police-station fire in Washington yesterday."

Milan Zinn snorted.

"Kinner," he said, "was clever."

XV

BREAD ON THE WATERS

The United States coast guard plane landed on the sea at ten o'clock. A newspaper plane that had been trailing landed almost immediately afterward, and cameramen scrambled out on deck and began taking pictures of the *Isle Royal*.

Monk said, "Wait until they see Audine. They'll have something to take pictures of."

Doc asked, "She is all right?"

"Sure. Worried about her brother, is all. But she needn't worry. That guy is too tough for a broken arm to do him any harm."

The bronze man frowned at the newspaper plane. He did not like publicity.

"Are the prisoners all tied up?" he asked.

"Yep. Renny and Johnny are watching them."

Doc nodded. "And did you find the man who used the radio to direct the bugeye to the steamer?"

Monk grinned. "One of the crew. I got him."

"How did you find him?"

"I asked questions," Monk said, "of that bird, Smitty."

Doc Savage eyed Monk's large set of knuckles. There was not much skin left on them. "I hope Smitty is not seriously damaged," he said.

"He'll live long enough to get electrocuted," Monk said cheerfully.

Doc's gaze moved to the newspaper plane, and he frowned.

"Before the newspapermen get aboard," he said, "we had better get the rest of the story from Milan Zinn."

Milan Zinn had the facility of telling much with few words. He had developed the light—it was not light, but a combination of mircrolength radio waves and sonic vibration in ultrashort wave lengths, as Doc had surmised—while experimenting in hopes of finding some method of bringing sight to certain types of blind. He had continued his experiment after the operation had returned his own sight.

"I did not see any particular value that the 'light' might have, at first," he explained. "Then it occurred to me that the thing might be good for quelling riots in prisons. It would beat tear gas. It would make the convicts as sick as dogs. So I went to the Federal prison department with the idea of selling it."

"That is where you met Russel Kinner?"

"He was the man I talked to," Zinn said. He paused thoughtfully. "I should have known from his manner that he was a crook."

Jerry Million said, "Kinner was a slick devil."

"Yes, he decided to grab the 'light' and turn crook on a big scale," Zinn agreed. "He got a gang together. He kept consulting me, and visited me on this boat. He seemed very interested, but I thought he was only considering buying the 'light' for the government. Then, when he had his gang together, he grabbed me, my boat and everything."

"And killed Haatz," Jerry added.

"Yes, Haatz worked in the same government office," Zinn said. "Kinner thought Haatz suspected what was afoot. Anyway, Haatz knew about the 'light,' and he had to be killed for that reason."

Jerry Million said, "That's why Kinner tried to kill me, too. When he called me to his office that time about a job, he thought I was a crook who would make a good member of his gang. When he found out different, he got rid of me."

Doc said, "Kinner discovered you leaning against a car in which he was sitting with Mr. Zinn, did he not?"

"Yeah. Must have thought I was spying on him. That's probably when he decided to kill me."

Milan Zinn finished, "The government had been informed that this shipload of gold was to come to America, and Kinner must have had methods of learning of the fact. Probably he thought something of the sort would be just the kind of a haul he wanted, so he made deliberate plans."

Monk scratched his head.

"What gets me," said the homely chemist, "is who died in that police-station fire? The body was identified as that of Kinner, but it wasn't, obviously."

Doc said, "There was a policeman missing after the fire."

Monk's jaw fell. "Oh! So they arranged the identification, did they? That poor cop!"

Doc Savage held a consultation with his four men before they received the newspaper reporters and cameramen. He began with a flat statement.

"We do not want publicity," he said.

Ham nodded, but added, "I fail to see how we are going to avoid it."

"Milan Zinn and Jerry," Doc suggested.

"Eh?" Ham was puzzled.

"Give Zinn and Jerry all the credit," Doc suggested. "Keep in the background ourselves."

Monk, who was distinctly the extrovert type, and who furthermore liked to see credit go where it was due, particularly when it was due him, emitted a groan.

"But, Doc, we cracked this thing," the homely chemist said. "You solved it. You made those suits. You had them in a crack when you threatened to set the boat afire. All Zinn and Jerry did was save them the trouble of surrendering."

The bronze man seemed not to hear the interruption.

"We do not need publicity," he said. "And Jerry Million can use it. It may help him get a job."

"But can we keep out of it?"

Doc said, "I will talk the matter over with the coast guard, and see if it cannot be arranged."

To Monk's disgust, it could be arranged, and was.

Jerry Million got a job the next Friday. It was a good job, appropriate for the hero who shared honors with Milan Zinn for having thwarted the robbery of a bullion ship at sea and solved the mystery of the all-white elf.

His sister visited Doc Savage in the New York skyscraper headquarters. She was elated.

"I'm delighted for Jerry." She took the bronze man's hands impulsively. "He's terribly embarrassed, though. He feels that he accomplished nothing, actually."

"Jerry is actually doing us a favor, bearing the brunt of the publicity," Doc assured her.

"Well, he's doing himself one, too," Audine said earnestly. "Here, look. He doesn't know this yet, but read it. I think it explains itself."

The newspaper item was a confession. A confession by a young man named Earl Graves, stating that his own cowardice had been responsible for the laboratory fire which had disgraced Jerry Million. Jerry, said Earl Graves in the confession, had not even been present in the laboratory at the inception of the trouble, but had appeared later.

In the confession, Earl Graves said:

> I was Jerry Million's close friend, and we were both in love with the same girl. The girl, Jerry believed, loved me. So he took the blame and disgrace for the fire, for my cowardice. I was coward enough to let him do it.

Audine took the newspaper back and folded it and said, "Human nature is a strange thing, isn't it? Here is that young fellow, Earl Graves, who kept back and let Jerry sacrifice his life and self-respect as long as Jerry was an object of public contempt. But the moment Jerry becomes a hero, Earl Graves confesses the truth."

Doc asked, "How will Jerry and the girl come out?"

"She is Lucille Gavett. Remember I told you about her?"

Audine smiled quickly. "She is in love with Jerry. She had told him so, I've just discovered. But Jerry kept away from her while he was in disgrace."

"That seems to make everything end very favorably," the bronze man suggested.

Probably everybody was pleased but Ham, and he was not displeased until that evening, when he discovered Monk had dated Audine, practically snatching her from under his nose.

THE RUNNING SKELETONS

Contents

I

DARK AND SCARED

Lincoln Wilson Washington Smith was an amiable colored gentleman who was baggage attendant and porter on a passenger train running from Chicago to New York.

He had a kind heart.

He liked dogs.

He didn't scare easy, this last being a part of his character which contributed no little to the subsequent mystery which came out of the first-of-the-week run of the limited train.

The train was one that left Chicago late in the evening and got into New York City the following afternoon, making about a twenty-hour schedule, which was good time. The train carried two lounge cars, coaches, sleepers, drawing-room cars, baggage coaches—and Lincoln Wilson Washington Smith, who was porter.

Duty of the porter was to put bags aboard, generally "butter up" the passengers so they felt good toward the railroad and shelled out fancy tips, and kid along with the soldiers who were crowding the trains these days, as well as occasionally rescue a girl passenger from a sailor.

Feeding dogs was not among his duties.

He put the dog-carrying case aboard, himself, in Chicago, and he noticed it particularly at the time because carrying large animals, even in cases, was against the rules in the coaches.

A dollar fixed up everything, though, as far as getting the dog-carrying case aboard the train. The young man who had brought the case contributed the dollar, together with a wink, and that fixed that. Anyway, the young man had a drawing-room ticket, and drawing-room passengers get a little extra consideration.

There was a dog in the case—at least there was a dog's weight in the case, and a couple of disgruntled dog barks.

The case was about Airedale-dog size. It was covered with black leatherette and had ventilation apertures covered with black wire screen. The construction of the dog-carrying case was such that it was impossible to tell anything much about what kind of an animal was inside, even by putting an eye to the ventilating grills.

The case was not locked.

The young man carrying the case was a tall young man with a tan overcoat and tan hat, the latter yanked down over his eyes. The porter accidentally rubbed against him and felt something hard in the young man's pocket which he—the porter—took to be a flask or a pint; but this proved to be a bad guess as to the nature of the hard object, as was afterward evident.

For a young man who was as terrified and puzzled as he later proved to be, he showed very little of the emotion which was lashing him.

The young man sat, white-faced, in his compartment for some time, then got up and went back to the bar. But he stopped and spoke to the porter.

"Porter," he said. "Porter, for five dollars could you start watching something and not stop watching it?"

"For how long, suh?"

"For long enough for me to go to the bar and get to the stage where I can flap my wings."

"I sho' could," said the porter.

So Lincoln Wilson Washington Smith sat in the compartment and began to feel sorry for the dog in the case.

The unseen dog in the case, from the beginning, had shown signs of uneasiness and discomfort, stirring around a great deal and giving small, complaining barks now and then. Now that the man was gone this grew worse.

The dog jumped about, barked, whined, made plaintive noises, pitiful noises. Noises that soon began to wring the heart of Smith, the porter.

This went on for some time. "Nice doggie," Smith said, and wondered if the dog wanted water, and looked around for a dish in which to give him some water, but there was none.

The train had been booming along on its way for some

time now and it had reached the first of the infrequent stops which it made between Chicago and New York.

"A hamburger!" yelled Smith, the porter.

That was the answer. The dog was hungry, and a hamburger would shut him up, and there was a lunch "quickie" near the railroad platform in the next town, where the porter could dash over and get a hot one. After all he'd have to pay for the hamburger, of course; but then he was making five dollars out of this deal and he couldn't stand the whining and carrying-on the dog was doing.

Lincoln Wilson Washington Smith got off and secured the hamburger without incident, except that he got stuck fifteen cents for it, and he did some squawking about that.

He made a quick trip and got back in the car before the train began moving again. The train started just as he was entering the compartment and, taking the dog case off the floor, where it had been resting, and placing it on one of the seats.

He opened the dog case.

His idea was to stick the hamburger inside with a quick gesture. One could never tell when a dog might bite, particularly a discontented pooch, and this one certainly sounded discontented.

But there was a little accident—the engineer goosed the throttle and gave the train a hell of a yank at just that point—and the case toppled off the seat, the lid fell open, and the dog tumbled out.

Or what had been in the case making the sounds and movements, and having the weight of a dog—*it* tumbled out.

The scream of Lincoln Wilson Washington Smith was heard all through the car, where it made everyone jump and started three babies to bawling. Heads turned toward that end of the car. Due to the construction of the car, only a few passengers saw Smith break out of the room. The compartments were at the far end of the car, with an aisle on what happened to be the north side of the car the direction the train was traveling.

Those passengers who saw could tell that Smith had had a little accident.

Smith had tried to leave the compartment like a bullet, his coat pocket had got caught on the door handle, it had yanked the door shut, and the closing door had pinched

Smith's coat and held him hung. It didn't hold him long. He tore half the tail out of his coat and took wings.

No movie director staging a comedy exit of a scared man out of a graveyard ever got more action. If Smith's feet touched the car floor at all they didn't remain there long enough to be visible.

He reached the car door and left the train with a blind, flying leap.

The train was traveling fairly fast now, and Smith hit the roadbed hard and broke a leg and was knocked senseless.

II

ABOUT A BRONZE MAN

In stopping the train to pick up Smith, the engineer did the halting job with another of those terrific examples of slam-bang carelessness which had started the whole thing. The train halted as if it had run into something as solid as Gibraltar.

The young man who had brought the dog-carrying case aboard was sitting in the bar, at a round table only slightly larger than his hat, and the shock dumped his Scotch and soda in his lap.

He stood up and cursed the engineer, the railroad and Scotch whiskey. Everyone else was cursing, so his maledictions got no special attention. He sat down again.

Some of the passengers climbed off the train to see what had happened.

The young man remained where he was.

There was some shouting, then those who had got off jumped back on. The engineer got the train started again, trying to break everybody's necks in the act.

A passenger who had got off sat down beside the young man.

"What," asked the young man, "was it? An earthquake?"

"A man."

"He must have been braced to stop the train like that."

"It didn't hit him."

"No?"

"He jumped off."

"Remembered he'd forgot something, I suppose?"

"He was the porter." The passenger scratched his head. "Poor devil has a broken leg and a fractured skull, or something. Anyway, he was incoherent. Kept muttering about a dog—"

The young man jumped. He looked as if he'd found he was sitting in some water. "Dog?" he said.

"Yes."

"And it was a porter off this train?"

"That's right He—"

"A tall, kind of hungry-looking porter?"

"That's him. He—"

"Excuse me," the young man said, and got up and headed for the compartment where the dog-carrying case had been placed.

The young man was wearing composure on his face like a mask, just as he had been wearing it all along, to hide inner terror; but now the mask was made of thinner stuff and a little of what he felt showed through.

He took a gun out of his pocket. The gun was the object the porter had thought was a flask or a pint. He carried the gun under his hat, and held his hat close to his chest. He walked with care and tried to look all directions at once.

Without trouble he reached the compartment. The porter's coat tail was wedged in the door and he had a little trouble forcing the door open for that reason. People in the car stared at him curiously—those who knew the porter had popped out of this compartment—but no one did anything.

The young man got into the compartment in a hurry, quickly, ducking inside.

He was there three or four minutes.

Coming out, he was carrying the dog case, holding it down at arm-length, casually. A coat was over his other arm, covering the gun that was still in his hand.

He worked his way forward slowly and carefully until he came to the office car.

The office car was a special idea on the limited, one of the reasons the railroad soaked you twenty dollars extra fare for riding the train from Chicago to New York. Here, for the use of passengers, there were desks, typewriters and stenographers, all free. There was an information clerk, a young woman, to give you data on time tables, hotels, plane reservations, shows and so on.

The young man with the dog-carrying case went on through the car. At the opposite end he encountered a locked door.

"Mail coach and baggage cars ahead," said the young woman information clerk.

The young man nodded.

He looked as if he were ill.

Plainly, because he could not think of anything else to do, he sank in the chair beside the information girl's desk.

"Look," he said. "Look, I've got to get to a man named Doc Savage."

There was interest and curiosity in the reception girl's eyes. She was not a fool; she could see there was something amiss. And she began to realize, slowly, that the young man was full of writhing terror. Fear was in him like snakes.

"In New York," the girl said. "Yes, his address is in New York City. The tallest building in the midtown section. The eighty-sixth floor."

The young man looked at her. He wet his lips. "You don't know me. My name is Tom Lewis—Thomas Maurice Lewis, and I'm a traveling salesman for the Admiration Radio Cabinet Co., manufacturers of snazzy cabinets for radios. Around the Admiration Radio Cabinet Co. office they would tell you I'm the office humorist, and very funny."

"Tom Lewis," the girl said. "Yes?"

Tom Lewis licked his lips grimly. "Funny man, that's me. Fired five times by old Walt Buxton because of my practical jokes, and then hired back because I'm a good salesman." He showed his teeth fiercely. "A good, loud-mouthed salesman, that's me. But don't forget that name—Tom Lewis. And the company—Admiration Radio Cabinets."

"Chicago?"

"Gosh, no! Way south of there in the Ozarks. Sort of an unusual factory out in the country with a little town of its own called Admiration City."

He went silent. The words seemed to have stuck in his throat.

The girl, to break him loose from his tension, pointed at the dog-carrying case and said, "Is that one of your samples?"

Tom Lewis seemed to shake a little at all his joints.

"What do you know about Doc Savage?" he asked.

The girl watched him intently. "So you're in trouble?"

"I—"

"Don't," said the girl, "start telling me about it. I don't want to hear it because I've got troubles of my own dealing with the pot-stomached Romeos and big butter-and-egg men who seem to think a train secretary should swoon on their necks."

Tom Lewis complained, "All I wanted was to ask you about Savage."

"O. K. Ask!"

"You know him?"

"Of course not!"

"You knew where he could be found?"

"I didn't say he could be found there. That was the location of his headquarters that I gave you. A lot of people know that. It's part of my business to know such things."

Tom Lewis sat biting his lips for a while. "Look, you seem to have sense," he said. "What do you know about Savage?"

"I saw him once from a distance," the girl said. "I dreamed about him for about a week after that. He affects you that way."

"I don't care if he is a woman-killer. I want to know—"

"You've got the wrong idea—at least, partly wrong. I understand the girls have to take it out in looking."

"I want to know—"

"You want to know whether his business is righting wrongs and punishing evildoers in the far corners of the earth? Correct; that's what they say. It sounds screwy, and probably it is screwy, or maybe it just sounds crazy when you call it a business. Anyway, that's right."

Tom Lewis bit his lips some more. "How do you contact him?"

"Just contact him," the girl said. "That's all I know."

For a moment Tom Lewis looked down at the dog-carrying case.

"I want you," he said, "to fix up a shipping tag I can put on this case."

"Who to?"

"I want this case to get into the hands of Doc Savage," Tom Lewis explained.

The girl riffled through the contents of her desk and came up with a regulation shipping tag which she filled out. She started to tie it to the case, but Tom Lewis hurriedly picked it from her fingers and tied it on himself. The girl undoubtedly realized he didn't want her to touch the case, but she made no comment.

She leaned back and watched the young man curiously. Tom Lewis wasn't hard to look at, but the terror so obviously within him made him a little repellent, as if he had warts.

Because she was watching him she saw his reaction when the redheaded man went past.

The red-haired man was well-dressed, but not sufficiently overdressed to be conspicuous. His hair was not a spectacular red, his suit was a discreet dark-blue, his tie and shirt subdued. He was not outstanding.

The redheaded man walked past without apparently noticing Tom Lewis.

Without moving a muscle, without stirring anything but his eyes, and those only slightly, Tom Lewis managed to look as if he had been stabbed dead.

The redheaded man came to the locked door, tried it, looked disappointed, said "Where is the dining car, please?"

"The other direction," the firl said. "Seven cars back."

The redheaded man went away. Tom Lewis sat there more dead than alive from terror.

The train secretary-information clerk tried to think of something. She was getting a little scared herself. She didn't know what was afoot, but she wanted no part of it.

"Look," she said, "why don't you telephone him?"

Tom Lewis stared at her wordlessly.

"Telephone Doc Savage from the train," the girl explained patiently. "You can do that, you know."

Four or five times Tom Lewis moved his lips soundlessly, then he managed to ask, "How?"

"Radio," the girl said. "Radio and telephone. Regular service."

Tom Lewis, shaking a little, said thickly, "Get Doc Savage on the telephone for me, and quick, because I don't think I'm going to be alive ten minutes from now."

III

THE INDIGNANT MAN

The radio contact from train to land-line station, and thence by regulation long distance to New York City, was made, and the telephone rang in the eighty-sixth-floor Doc Savage headquarters.

Lieutenant Colonel Andrew Blodgett—Monk—Mayfair took the call.

There were two outstanding things about Monk Mayfair. First, he was one of the world's industrial chemists, although his head did not look as if it contained room enough for a spoonful of brains; and he was also a man who would be a sure bet in any homely-man contest.

Second, today Monk Mayfair was very indignant.

"Yah?" he said into the telephone. "What you bothering us for?"

"This," said a distant voice, "is a limited en route from Chicago to New York, and we have a call from a passenger to Doc Savage."

The voice was feminine, and ordinarily Monk was a push-over for anything in skirts. But today his temper was very bad.

"Yah?" he said. "Can'tcha call some other time?"

"This," said the girl on the train, "is important."

"Yah."

The girl on the train now became indignant herself and shouted, "Yah, you little shrimp! Yah, yah, yah, it's important! Now get a civil tongue in your head and put Doc Savage on the wire."

Startled, Monk stared at the telephone. He hadn't been called a little shrimp before. He'd been called many things, but not that. Although not a tall man, Monk was a very big one, being almost as tall as he was wide. His small, childlike voice had doubtless led the girl to deduce he was a little shrimp.

"I'll take the call," Monk growled.

"We want Mr. Savage—"

"*I'll take the call!*" said Monk in a voice that must have scared the birds off the telephone wires. "Now put your party on."

"Who are you?"

"I'm the guy who is talking—"

"Listen, simple-wits, if you—"

"O. K.," Monk said. "O. K., sister. I'm one of Doc Savage's associates and my name is Monk Mayfair. Now, if—"

"Hold the wire, please," said the girl. She evidently

consulted Tom Lewis, because he took over the other end of
the conversation.

He got to the point.

"My name," he said, "is Tom Lewis, and I'm in trouble. I
want to talk to Doc Savage."

"Everybody is in trouble. I've got plenty of my own," said
Monk disagreeably. "And why don't you talk to the police?
They get paid nice fat salaries for taking care of the citizens.
Why not let them earn it?"

"This," said Tom Lewis, "is a little beyond the police."

The grimness, the terror in Tom Lewis' voice took some
of the acid out of Monk.

"What's the hitch?" Monk asked.

"I must talk to Mr. Savage—"

In a much more patient and reasonable tone, Monk said,
"That is out of the question right at this point, I am afraid.
Doc is working in his laboratory on some special government
stuff and can't be interrupted. The experiments he's doing
will go to pot if he's interrupted in the next hour, and the
president himself couldn't get a telephone connection. I'm
one of his assistants. You'll have to talk to me or make an
appointment for later—and then you'll have to talk to me,
anyway because I'm the guy who decides who shall talk to
Doc."

"All right," Tom Lewis said. "Listen!"

Apparently he did not quite have his words organized, or
wanted to hold back some—and wished to decide what to
hold back—because he was talking to a subordinate of Doc
Savage rather than Doc himself.

"I'm coming to New York right now," Tom Lewis said, "to
see Doc Savage."

"Yes?"

"But," said Lewis, "they've followed me."

"Who followed you?"

"I don't know their names. But they are the men who are
after the dog."

"What dog?"

"The dog in the carrying case I have with me."

"This is making sense," Monk told him, "about as fast as a
woodpecker drills a hole through a rock."

"The men," said Tom Lewis, "are trying to keep me from
reaching Savage."

"Why?"

"Because the dog is—well, rather incredible."

"What do you mean, incredible?"

"The porter on the train just took a look at him and was so horrified he leaped off the moving train. That's how incredible the dog is."

Monk eyed the telephone sourly. "Say, you! Is this a gag?"

"It certainly is not."

"Then make sense out of it."

"I'll make sense when I see you," Tom Lewis said. "Now, listen to this: I will meet you at the station exactly ten hours from now." He named one of the terminals in New York. "I will be wearing a white raincoat. Understand, a white raincoat."

"A white raincoat," Monk said. "O. K."

"And the dog-carrying case will be with me if I can manage. But if it isn't, don't get alarmed. I'm a tall man and I'll have a tan hat and tan gloves. I'm wearing a tan overcoat now, but I'll put on the white raincoat I have in my suitcase."

"What," asked Monk, "does this dog-carrying case look like?"

"A black case, leatherette-covered, with ventilating holes covered with black wire screen. You've seen a hundred like it. It's just a carrying case for travelers to use when they take their dogs with them. This one would hold a shepherd or an Airedale dog."

"What kind of a dog is in it?"

"The damnedest dog you ever saw," said Tom Lewis. "I'll be seeing you in ten hours, exactly!"

This ended the conversation. Monk's bad humor came back because he had started getting interested. "Always something!" he snarled.

He turned around and for once in his life spoke a civil and polite sentence to Brigadier General Theodore Marley—Ham—Brooks.

"What do you think of that call, Ham?" he asked.

Ordinarily, Monk would also never have asked Ham's opinion on anything.

Ham Brooks had picked up the receiver on the extension telephone as a matter of course, and had made shorthand notes of the conversation. This was a regular procedure on a call of the sort.

Ham Brooks was a lean, dapper man with a thin waist

and the wide, flexible mouth of a man who made his living by talking. He was a lawyer, and Harvard Law School considered him its leading product. He was wonderfully dressed and was always immaculately dressed, being as famous for his clothing as he was for his legal ability. He carried, as he habitually did, an innocent-looking black cane that was a sword cane.

"Well, Ham," said Monk, "what did you think of the call?"

"There might be something to it," Ham admitted. "And again it might be some feather-wits with some new breed of dog, or a dog with two tails, or something like that."

Monk nodded. "Yeah, you can't tell. People's idea of the importance of things varies a little."

"It certainly does. He may have a dog he's taught a few tricks, and think he's got something world-shaking."

"He might have."

"We better see him when he comes in, though."

"Yes, we'd better."

This was probably the longest harmonious conversation that Monk and Ham had conducted in years.

Anyone knowing them well would have known something was stridently wrong.

They sat in silence for a while.

Then Ham absently fished in his coat pocket for a handkerchief with which to wipe his perspiring palms. When he dragged the handkerchief out a small square of cardboard was dislodged from its folds and fell to the floor. Ham picked the cardboard up, read:

PEACE IS WONDERFUL!

The effect of reading this on Ham was pronounced. His neck got red. He slammed the table with his sword cane.

"That's fifty or sixty of them cards I've found!" he shrieked.

Monk pounded the table with him. "Me, too!" Monk shouted. "I get up this morning and there it is painted on my ceiling!"

"Somebody," said Ham, "had written it on the breakfast plate on which my scrambled eggs were served."

"The taxi driver who brought me to the office sang it over and over," Monk contributed.

"It isn't funny."

"You're danged right it isn't funny any longer," Monk said.

"Let's tell them so."

"Why not?"

Monk and Ham had taken the telephone call in the reception room, which was equipped with a large safe, comfortable chairs, a remarkable inland desk, and not much else that met the eye outwardly, although there were quite a few gadgets in concealed spots.

The adjoining room was the library, and into this Monk and Ham stamped.

The library was very large, crowded with bookcases containing one of the most complete, purely scientific book collections in existence.

Three men were in the library—the other three members of Doc Savage's group of five assistants—checking over the parts of the library in which they specialized. This was a periodic procedure.

William Harper—Johnny—Littlejohn was checking the tomes on archaeology and geology. Johnny, who was taller and thinner than it seemed any man could be and still live, was one of the world's eminent men in archaeology and geology, and also capable of using words of stunning size.

Major Thomas J.—Long Tom—Roberts, an undersized man with a mushroom-cellar complexion, was going over the electrical-engineering section. He had just returned from England, where he had been doing advanced work in electronic airplane detection.

Colonel John—Renny—Renwick, big fists and all, was poking around the engineering section. He'd found an engineering book lately published by a rival and was reading it, disagreeing heartily, and muttering his favorite expression, "Holy cow!" about every third paragraph.

Monk and Ham advanced on these three gentlemen.

"Holy cow!" said Renny loudly in alarm.

"A nonultraadvantageous adventation," remarked Johnny Littlejohn.

"We," announced Monk, "are going to break bones."

"We're going to peel you from head to foot," agreed Ham. "All three of you."

"Like bananas," Monk added.

Long Tom Roberts said, "Now, wait a minute, you two! There is no reason—"

"It's not," said Ham, "a joke. It's not any part of a joke. We're tired of it."

"We're awfully tired," said Monk.

Renny Renwick looked extremely alarmed.

"Holy cow, they're agreeing with each other!" he said. "Our lives are in danger!"

"Peace is wonderful!" Monk snarled. "I'll show you how wonderful peace is!"

"Several pieces," said Ham. "The ones we're going to separate each of you into."

In a moment the place was in an uproar. Someone upset a bookcase in front of Monk and he fell over it. Ham beaned Renny Renwick with a large law book, flooring 'enny. Long Tom Roberts, who looked to be the most ineffec've fighter of any of them, proceeded to tie into Monk and begin trying to remove a leg.

The laboratory door opened, Doc Savage came in and asked, "What kind of a civil war is this, anyway?"

The fight stopped and there was sheepish silence except for the breath sounds that were like escaping steam.

Doc Savage was a big man with such symmetrical proportions that he seemed big only when he stood close to some object to which his size could be compared. Tropical suns had made his skin a deep bronze, and his hair was only a slightly darker bronze, his eyes a strange golden color, like pools of flake-gold always stirred by tiny winds. There was no quality of coarseness about him, nor any of physical weakness. The whole effect of him was arresting.

"What," he repeated, "is this?"

Monk tried to get the two halves of his necktie to fit together, foolishly. "We're teaching them what's a joke and what ain't," he said.

Ham said, "That's it."

"They have," explained Monk, "been riding us."

"Wrongly."

"Putting signs in our pockets."

"And painting them on our plates."

"And our ceilings," added Monk.

"Insulting signs," said Ham.

"Signs," said Monk, "telling us peace is wonderful!"

Doc Savage's bronze features did not change expression as he turned to Johnny, Long Tom and Renny and asked, "What is your side of it?"

"We just," said Renny, "ran out of patience."

"Enough," said Long Tom, "is enough."

"Enough," said Johnny, "is a supermalagorgeous abundance."

Renny said, "We mean their quarreling."

"Monk and Ham have conducted a perpetual quarrel between themselves that has lasted for years," Long Tom explained.

"Until today," said Johnny, using small words in his vehemence, "no one has ever heard them say a civil word to each other."

"They've enjoyed it," said Renny.

"But nobody else has," said Long Tom.

"Only a sesquipedalian ambagious inveteberate lacks convulition," said Johnny.

"He means," translated Renny, "that it's a mighty long

Doc Savage's expression became slightly thoughtful and he said, "Monk and Ham have entertained themselves with a perpetual quarrel for years and you fellows have gotten tired of it."

"As who hasn't got tired of it!" said Renny.

"And now," continued Doc, "you are conducting a campaign to reduce the nuisance of this quarreling."

"That's right."

"That," Doc said, "is fine. I hope no one gets fatally killed."

He turned around and went back into the laboratory.

Monk and Ham, their feelings hurt, retired from the premises. They left the building and got into a cab and headed for their apartments to change clothes. The bout in the library had done their garments no good.

"Doc," said Monk, "let us down."

"He certainly jerked it out from under us," Ham agreed.

They were silently and mutually indignant.

The quarreling in which they had indulged for so long had actually become a part of their character, of themselves; and to think of giving it up was worse than the idea of surrendering their money, or even an arm apiece.

"We can't," said Ham, "do any such thing."

"Naturally not," Monk agreed.

"You see how we're getting along now?" said Ham. "Very polite. Agreeing with each other. There's no fun in it."

"It's sickening," Monk said.

"We might," Ham suggested after some thought, "do an

about face. Be so goody-goody nice to each other that it would turn their stomachs. Alfonse-and-Gaston stuff."

"That wouldn't be any fun. And I'd hate to give them the satisfaction."

"Yes, you're right. We can't do that."

Monk sat up straight. "We can do something, though."

"What?"

"They're sitting around up there," Monk pointed out, "itching for some excitement to come along. They think they're checking over the books in the library, and Doc thinks he's making something out of chemicals in the laboratory. But, actually, they're waiting with baited breath for some excitement."

"What's your idea?"

"We'll gyp them out of their excitement," Monk declared. "That'll get even with them."

Ham began looking very cheerful. "Starting with this Tom Lewis and his fantastic dog. That your suggestion?"

"What do you think of it?"

"I think it's fine," said Ham.

"What do you say we get in touch with Tom Lewis on the train and ask him for more details?"

"I think that's a swell idea," Ham said.

Monk Mayfair occupied a penthouse apartment-laboratory on top of a very high building in the financial district on the lower end of Manhattan Island. The place was about as modernistic as a penthouse could be made, looking like an overdone movie set. Ham considered the place gaudy and in very bad taste, and invariably told Monk so. Today, though, he uttered not a word of criticism of the apartment.

Monk had installed in the place, before war days, an expensive arrangement for his pet pig, Habeas Corpus. The pig was an Arabian runt hog of unknown species, very long of leg, enormous of ear, scrawny of body, with the disposition of a bumblebee, yet very intelligent. The hog apartment included a mud bath with perfumed mud and other luxuries.

Hitherto, Ham had not cared for Habeas, the pig.

Monk likewise professed no love for Ham's pet, an undersized chimpanzee named Chemistry, which bore a remarkable likeness, in miniature, to Monk himself.

Monk and Ham were so upset by their current trouble that they had done something they would never have done ordinarily. They had left the two pets at Monk's place together.

And the two pets, which usually fought as enthusiastically as their owners, were behaving like lovebirds.

Ham got on the telephone and started contacting the limited train.

Monk checked over his automatic telephone recorder to see how many of his girl friends had called him. This apparatus was an affair which, when a telephone call came in, automatically asked the caller for name and business, then recorded the answers, together with the explanation that Monk was absent.

"*Ps-s-t!*" Ham said. "Got the train."

Monk hurriedly plugged another telephone instrument into the circuit. "Don't hear anybody," he said.

"The girl has gone to page Tom Lewis," Ham explained.

Monk frowned. "The guy sounded as if he was scared or worried."

"That's right."

"Maybe," Monk said, "the girl shouldn't be going through the train paging him by name. He might not want his identity known."

"She's not."

"How's she going to find him?"

"It's the girl who is the information clerk on the train," Ham explained. "She knows him by sight. She is going to find him, and—Hello? Hello?"

It was the information clerk on the train.

"About Tom Lewis," she said. "A strange thing happened."

"Yes?"

"The train slowed up for a small town a few minutes ago," the girl explained, "and Tom Lewis jumped off. I just happened to see him."

"Was he," Monk asked, "carrying a leatherette case of the type used for transporting animals, a case about large enough to contain a shepherd or an Airedale dog?"

"Why, yes—he was!"

IV

TROUBLE HERE AND THERE

The train secretary was an experienced young woman and capable of taking care of herself. One of the best ways of taking care of herself in her present job, she had found, was not to get unduly excited about anything that happened, and she had made a practice of this.

So, at the end of the telephone conversation with Monk Mayfair in New York, she replaced the receiver on its prong and picked up the detective thriller she was reading. That was the way she relaxed.

The system collapsed violently when she looked up and found a gun under her nose.

The man back of the gun had red hair and wore a quiet blue suit and looked as if he was not fooling.

"Sis," he said softly, "I shot a woman one time, believe it or not, right through the pretty mush. It made a hell of a mess out of what had once been a nice baby-blond face, and it kept me awake for a while. But it didn't bother me as much as I thought it would, so I might do it again with the right provocation."

The girl believed him. She sat perfectly still.

"Tom Lewis," the man said. "That name mean anything to you?"

"He was talking to me," the girl said, genuinely afraid to lie.

"What was the talk about?"

"He made," said the girl, "a telephone call to New York."

"That," said the man, "is the way I want you to talk to me. Open and frank. The blonde would have been all right if she had done that. What did he talk about?"

"He called—"

"What else did he talk about to you, I mean?"

"Oh. He asked me if I had heard of a man named Doc Savage, and where he could find Doc Savage. I told him Savage was a rather remarkable man who is supposed to make a business of righting wrongs and punishing evildoers, and he could find Savage in New York."

"Savage?" the man said. "Doc Savage?"

"Yes."

The redheaded man looked as if a dull sickness had suddenly come inside him. He fought the feeling, the greenish tint around his mouth, for a few moments.

"He telephoned Doc Savage?" he asked.

"Yes."

"Who's telephone operator?"

"On the train here? I am."

"You hear the conversation?"

"I—yes."

"Repeat it."

The girl grimaced. "Good gracious, how do you expect me to remember—"

"Remember, sis!" the man said grimly. "Remember, or this gun will start making holes. And it makes big ones."

The girl closed her eyes. She was trembling.

"Ten hours," she said. "In ten hours he was going to meet a man named Monk Mayfair, an associate of Doc Savage, in a railroad terminal in New York. He was going to be wearing a white raincoat and carrying a dog-carrying case. I do not remember the exact words of the conversation, but that was the general sense of it."

"Ten hours from when?"

"The call," said the girl, "was made one hour and forty minutes ago. Ten hours from then."

"What else was said?"

"Tom Lewis said, or gave the idea, that the dog in the case was the cause of some rather fantastic mystery, and it was about that mystery which he wished to interview Doc Savage."

"That all?"

"All I remember. All that's important, I'm sure."

The redheaded man slid a hand into his coat pocket and brought out a pair of small white pills. He placed them on the desk beside the girl. He indicated the pills, then a glass of water which was standing on the back of the desk.

"Take the pills," he said. "Use the water for a chaser."

The girl got white and showed signs of fainting.

"They'll just put you to sleep for a few hours, sis," the man said. "Of course, if you'd rather get shut up by getting shot, I can accommodate you there, too."

She took the tablets.

The man sat down and smiled at her, his hand holding the gun thrust into his pocket until the girl began to sway and her eyes closed. This did not take more than ten minutes. Finally, the young woman toppled out of her chair.

The redheaded man called the car attendant.

"Fainted or something." He indicated the girl.

The man then walked back through the train and entered

a double bedroom. The bedroom, very small, was full of men with guns and uneasy expressions. Four of them.

"Want a good scare?" asked the redheaded man.

They obviously didn't, but one of them nodded foolishly in response to the query.

"Tom Lewis," the man said, "is headed for help from Doc Savage."

The silence was stark.

The redheaded man laughed, said, "I see you've heard of Savage."

He took out his gun and contemplated it obviously, not because he was interested in the condition of the gun, but in order to show them that he had it and to impress a point on their minds.

"Nobody," he said, "is backing out because of Savage."

No words from the others.

"Tom Lewis," said the man, "has hopped off the train. He got wise that we were following him."

They nodded. They had known that.

"The information girl, who is also the train telephone operator, tells me Tom Lewis made an appointment to meet one of Doc Savage's men in a railroad station in New York in"—he consulted his wrist watch, named the station—"seven hours and fifty minutes."

He tucked the gun away in a hidden holster.

"We better be there," he said, "to take care of that meeting."

They nodded. They were glad to agree with him.

"We want Tom Lewis," the redheaded man said.

More nods.

"But we want that case and the dog more than that," the man added.

"What about the telephone operator who gave you the dope?" a man asked.

"I gave her a pill. She won't tell anybody anything that makes sense for two days."

V

WHITE RAINCOAT

The more they had thought about it, the more pleasant Monk Mayfair and Ham Brooks felt about the prospect of cutting Doc and Renny and Long Tom and Johnny out of a bit of excitement. This struck them as a very just kind of vengeance for the ribbing they had been taking. Nobody would be harmed, actually, and Monk and Ham considered themselves, not without reason, perfectly capable of taking care of any mystery about a dog in a box.

Missing a little excitement would hurt Doc and Renny and the others more than anything else that was harmless. Doc and the others liked excitement, although Doc himself had never admitted it. But it was entirely plain that excitement was the glue which held the bronze man and his group of five associates together.

Monk and Ham had changed clothes, eaten a good dinner, fed their pets, had a nap, and taken a subway up to the railroad terminal. Riding in a subway was a little beneath Ham's dignity, but what the Japanese had done to the rubber supply in the current war made a little matter like dignity not so important.

Now they stood in the station, in the great domed room of the upper level, and were jostled by soldiers, sailors, marines and commuters.

"Gate 69," Monk said. "The limited comes in at Gate 69."

"Yes, and there comes its passengers," Ham pointed out.

"Watch for a white raincoat," Monk urged. "It would be a shame if we didn't meet this guy and he went ahead and got in contact with Doc and the others. Then they'd have the sneer on us. And, boy, would they lay it on!"

A river of passengers flowed up the sloping ramp and through the metal doors. Monk and Ham craned their necks and dodged this way and that. As the river of people flowed its fullest and then began to get thin, they exchanged dumfounded looks.

"Missed him!" Monk bleated.

"Couldn't have. He wasn't aboard."

"Blazes!" Monk wailed. "Now he'll contact Doc and the others and they'll laugh us out of six years' growth! I wish—" A strange voice said, "Doc? You mean Doc Savage?"

Monk and Ham wheeled.

"A white raincoat!" Monk exploded. "Brother, are *we* glad to see you!"

Ham looked at the large leatherette case the man was carrying. "Not to mention," he said, "a dog-carrying case. I guess you are Tom Lewis?"

"Tom Lewis, that's me," the other said. "Best damned salesman that ever sold a man something he didn't want."

"Salesman?" Monk scowled.

"Oh, don't get excited," said the other briskly. "I'm not selling anything right now but trouble. The strangest kind of trouble you ever heard about. Where can we go and talk?"

"Let's go up on the balcony," Monk said. "There's never anybody around there."

"Nobody around, that's fine," the man said.

They climbed the steps, turned to the right, and stopped in the lonely marble nakedness of the balcony.

The man in the white raincoat set down the dog case and unbuttoned his white raincoat, saying, "Here, I'll show you what this is all about." He took two flat, blue automatic pistols out of his clothing, showed Monk and Ham the noisy end of the weapons and said, "If you guys want to see a nice double murder, just dance around."

The man with the gun made a gesture and two more men joined him. These had lumps in their coat pockets which were probably guns.

"So these are the kind of guys the famous Doc Savage has workin' for him," one of them said.

"Yeah. Not so tough, eh?"

"No, pretty soft. What do we do with them?"

The man in the white raincoat looked around and made sure no one was passing. "Give them a quick frisk," he said. "Look for guns or anything they could use on us."

The quick frisk turned up a pair of remarkable-looking weapons resembling oversized automatics, but with curled drum magazines. The leader fiddled with one of these, examining it.

Monk said, "Go ahead and pull the trigger," hopefully. "You'll see more fireworks than you ever saw before."

The man hastily ceased fooling with the supermachine pistol.

"The fireworks," he said, "wouldn't be anything to the ones you'll be inspecting before long."

"Meaning," asked Monk, "that you figure on knocking us off?"

"I might be meaning something like that."

Monk, watching the man's face, decided that the fellow did mean something that drastic. The fellow might be planning to murder them in cold blood, an entirely feasible act, here on the deserted balcony. If they did not plan to kill Monk and Ham they had something else in mind that was not pleasant.

"A gun," said Monk, "makes a lot of noise. Somebody might hear."

The leader snorted. "Walk," he ordered. "Walk out and get in the sedan that you'll find parked in the drive."

The sedan really wasn't parked in the drive, but in a section assigned to the machines of a rent-a-car firm which had one of the station concessions.

There was a driver in the sedan who belonged to the gang, and three men in the back seat, one of these being Tom Lewis.

Monk knew his captor with the gun was not Tom Lewis, having by now realized that the man's voice was not the voice they had heard over the telephone from the train. Tom Lewis sat in the back of the sedan with two men pointing revolvers at him.

"They're not going to kill you," Tom Lewis said quietly to Monk and Ham. "But what they are going to do is worse than that."

Tom Lewis, all right, because Monk recognized the voice of the train telephone call.

"That's too bad," Monk said deceitfully, "because we can't do a thing to help ourselves."

He then hit one man in the stomach and kicked the feet out from another. He intended to start a first-class fight. He and Ham were wearing bulletproof undershirts of chain mesh, which the searchers had evidently mistaken for stiff underwear of some sort. These would stop revolver bullets.

A man hit Monk over the head unexpectedly and knocked him flat and helpless.

Another man clubbed Ham down.

"That's right," said the first man. "You can't do a thing."

Neither Monk nor Ham were completely unconscious, so they were both able to watch Doc Savage appear on the spot and start work.

Doc Savage was the last sight they expected to see, and yet they were not too surprised. It was touches of magic which made Doc the unusual individual he was.

Doc had been behind a nearby parked car, apparently observing proceedings.

He came from behind the car, came forward and threw a gas grenade.

His luck with the gas grenade was unusually bad for it hit the car window and did not break for some reason, probably because the impact on the window was a glancing one. The grenade consisted of an egg affair, shell of brittle plastic resembling glass, contents a liquid anaesthetic gas which vaporized and became effective quickly, but which could be avoided by holding the breath. The grenade hit twenty feet away and burst harmlessly.

Doc never even reached the car.

Sight of the bronze man had an electrifying effect on the occupants of the machine and those standing outside. Everyone piled into the car and simultaneously the driver let out the clutch and gave the engine all it would take.

The sedan rocketed out into the street, made the corner traffic cop jump for his life, and was gone.

Monk and Ham crawled around on the concrete pavement trying to get organized and on their feet.

Doc Savage ran out into the street but ran back again when a small flurry of bullets arrived from the sedan, which was just rounding another corner to disappear.

"One can never tell," said the bronze man, apparently explaining his race for cover, "when a wild bullet might catch one in the face."

He wore the same type of bulletproof undergarment which Monk and Ham wore.

Monk and Ham had an embarrassed nothing to say.

Doc Savage listened to the distant howl of the fleeing car and his metallic features showed no particular excitement. When he glanced at Monk and Ham there was no special expression, no noticeable disapproval on his bronze face.

Monk and Ham were far from reassured. When you could tell the least by looking at Doc's face, then was when you'd better look out.

"They got away," Monk muttered finally, "with the dog-carrying case."

"Yes," said Ham hastily. "We'd better catch them."

"Am I," asked Doc quietly, "supposed to know what you are talking about?"

Ham looked at Monk and Monk shuddered.

"O. K., it was my idea," Monk said gloomily.

"It was both our ideas," Ham corrected. "How were we to know it would blow out from under us?"

Monk stared at Doc Savage. "Doc, how'd you know about it? How'd you happen to come here?"

"Have you forgotten," the bronze man said, "that we have recording apparatus on the telephone circuits leading into headquarters?"

Monk looked blank. The recorder in Doc's headquarters was the same type which Monk himself employed to retain the calls of his girl friends.

"I forgot," Monk admitted. "So you played the record back and got all the information we have."

"All you know is what Tom Lewis told you in that telephone call from the train?"

"Well, yes. That is, we tried to contact Tom Lewis on the train later, but he'd gotten off."

"Did you find out anything from those men?"

"Nothing except that we had better learn to keep our eyes open. That fellow in the white raincoat just walked up to us and showed us a gun and said to come along."

Ham said, "Doc, just as we were about to start fighting, Tom Lewis said something to us. He said they weren't going to kill us, but what they would do to us would be a lot worse."

"He did not explain that?"

"He didn't have a chance."

"What gets me," Monk said, "is what went wrong."

Doc Savage made no comment and no guesses. He listened again for the car, which by now had entirely gone from hearing. He listened to the loud complaining of the cop on the corner, who had nearly been run over. The cop was excited and telling everybody in hearing what he thought of motorists in general, his thoughts not being very flattering.

"Are your heads clear enough," asked Doc, "to remember a license number?"

"Doc," Monk said, "I'm afraid we made a little mistake. We were going to take this thing over and handle it ourselves, by way of getting revenge for this 'peace is wonderful' stuff."

"Can you remember the number?"

"Sure."

Doc gave them a New York State car-license number. "Taxicab," he said. "Private machine, not belonging to a fleet."

"Yes?"

"Repeat the number."

Monk repeated it.

"Now," Doc said, "find the driver of that cab. Hand him a ten-dollar bill. Say to him, 'The redheaded man sent me.'"

"'The redheaded man sent me,'" Monk muttered. "Is that supposed to make sense?"

"It might," Doc Savage said, "It might!"

VI

SHE WASN'T FOOLING

Doc Savage left Monk and Ham headed for the subway, bound downtown to the bureau of licenses and the police department, where they could trace the taxicab license number.

Entering the station, Doc located an assistant passenger agent whom he knew and asked if anything out of the ordinary had occurred on the limited, just arrived from Chicago.

The answer he received gave him a good idea of how Tom Lewis, as well as Monk and Ham, had come to meet misfortune.

The girl who served as telephone operator and information clerk on the train had collapsed, and a doctor had diagnosed her trouble as an overdose of a strong hypnotic. But the doctor had also mentioned that his attention had been called to the young woman by a redheaded man.

One of the assailants of Monk and Ham had been a redheaded man, so that made that fairly clear.

Doc Savage then left the station, walked up a side street and entered a car. It was a sedate machine, not a large one, and belied the armor plate and bulletproof glass in its construction.

From a compartment Doc removed a loop antenna and plugged it into a jack. He switched on the radio, changed some connections with a jack to make it highly directional, and began experimenting.

He had a little trouble picking up the note of the transmitter, which he had attached to the sedan driven by the men who had seized Tom Lewis. He got it, finally, an endless series of tiny dots that sounded very much like interference from some nearby electrical system.

The signal was coming from either the north or the south, and the north seemed a more logical guess. He drove north.

The trick transmitter which he had attached to the sedan the men were driving was quite small, powered by a dry battery, and would give this continuous signal over a period of ten hours or so.

Using a radio direction-finder and a planted transmitter to trace individuals in a case of this kind was not a new method for Doc Savage. This particular transmitter, however, was a new type. It was held in place by a powerful, permanent magnet of the new type of metal which held several hundred times the magnetism that ordinary steel would retain. The transmitter, itself, was extremely sturdy, containing metal tubes and everything specially reinforced.

It was possible to apply the transmitter to a car, for instance, by merely tossing the gadget against the machine in passing. The magnet would hold it in place and also served as part of the transmitter entrails.

North was the right direction.

The trail led up into suburban Westchester County, finally ended in a section—or rather came to a stop—in a section of rather impressive estates.

Loudness of the transmitter note warned Doc and he scooted down in the seat, kept his hat over his eyes and watched right and left.

It was not hard to locate the house. It stood alone on a wide sweep of somewhat untended lawn, that was so thickly furred with untrimmed shrubbery that it was a jungle. Somewhere in there was the car.

Doc drove on a quarter of a mile, turned right, found a secluded spot and parked. He headed for the house with caution, carrying a small case of equipment.

The shrubbery was even larger, more overgrown than it had seemed from the road. The stuff was expensive, or had been expensive in the beginning, fifteen or so years ago; but for at least seven or eight years it had been permitted to grow rank and unguided and practically unattended, so that it towered and the branches interlaced.

Doc went from one patch of shadow to another, rarely sinking to all fours, but always silent.

The dog came around the corner of the house when he was about fifty feet away.

The bronze man stopped instantly, stood very still. The dog was no different from a wild animal in not having the ability to immediately distinguish an object that was not moving. The animal sniffed a time or two, seemed about to bark, then moved a little, passing behind a bush.

The moment the dog was out of sight, Doc Savage dived into the small equipment case. He brought out a glass phial, uncorked it, sprinkled a few drops of the contents on himself, then flipped the remainder out into the air around him.

He waited.

The chemical mixture was one that was in the experimental stage. If it functioned as it should it would arouse a desire for self-preservation in the animal, an emotion akin to fear, and yet *not* fear. The chemical had grown out of earlier experiments aimed at developing a substance which would keep dogs and animals away from expensive shrubbery.

The thing might have worked on this dog, and it might not have had any effect at all.

Because a man opened the door, stood there smoking, and finally called the dog inside.

The dog, Doc noted, was a police dog and too large to have been in the dog-carrying case.

Doc went immediately to the side of the house, eased into the thick undergrowth that had once been a neat foundation planting.

He soon found a basement areaway, used a glass cutter on the window, kept the cut panel from falling out by the use of chewing gum, removed it, unlocked the window, went inside.

He found a stoneware laundry tub under the window which could be reached easily, and from there to the floor was a silent matter. The laundry was none too clean. From a drying rack hung two pairs of overalls, a work shirt, some underwear.

Voices were distinct enough to be a little startling, and he located the source in a moment. A laundry chute, evidently leading to a bathroom where men were having a drink.

He could hear the squeak of a cork, clink of glasses, rush of water into glasses. A man coughed explosively.

"Where'd you get that panther sweat?" demanded the man who'd coughed.

"That's good stuff, Joe."

"They drained it off some corpse," Joe said disagreeably. "Have another?"

"Well, that one didn't kill me, so O.K."

There was more cork-squeaking, gurgling, glass-clinking, water, and appreciative coughing.

"I don't like Savage being mixed up in this," said a man unexpectedly.

"Oh, hell! Do you have to keep harping on that?" demanded another.

A third man, a more educated voice, said, "That's all right. We're all worried about Doc Savage. And it's not a bad idea to sweat a little, at that. Savage isn't anything to fool around with. We know that, and nobody but a fool would shut his eyes to the danger."

"You sound," said the man called Joe, "like a guy I used to know named Crying Thomas."

The other laughed. "Matter of fact, I don't think Savage will bother us now."

"How come?"

"We got Tom Lewis before he was able to tell Savage or Savage's men anything. We got the case and the dog."

"We didn't get Savage's two men, though."

"A damned good thing," said the man with the educated voice. "In grabbing them we were just pulling a hornets' nest down around our ears. It wasn't my idea."

"Too bad," said Joe sarcastically, "that you aren't running the thing."

"I've thought so a time or two myself," the other agreed.

"Maybe the boss'd like to hear that," said Joe.

In a voice just as pleasant and educated, the other man said, "Joseph, I'll bet they would give you a big funeral. One of those whoppers with lots of flowers, the way they used to send off the boys back in the good old prohibition days."

Joe said, "Huh! Say, are you—"

"Put your head back on your shoulders, Joe," someone said in a cold, warning voice.

Joe had nothing more to say.

"Another round?" asked the man with the bottle.

They didn't mind if they did, and a man said, "It was nice of old Dirty Chin to have this place lying around for us to use."

"How'd old Dirty get a place like this?" someone asked.

"Oh, he heired it. Uncle or something. Poor old Dirty. He's wanted for knocking over a bank in this State, and he doesn't dare come here and live. Doesn't dare try to sell the place. Just has to leave it here with a caretaker."

"So that's why it's gone to seed. How's old Dirty pay the caretaker?"

"Oh, there's a farm connected with it, and he rents that for enough to pay expenses. Can't keep up the place the way it should be, though. Shame, too."

"How long you reckon we'll be here?"

"No longer than necessary, I imagine," said the man with the educated voice. He was in a little better humor. "I expect we will receive orders to get the blazes back to the Ozarks with Tom Lewis and the dog."

"Hell, I wanted to see a little night life while I was here!" one man muttered.

They got to discussing the various kinds of night life the city offered.

Doc's interest in the conversation lagged and vanished completely when he discovered a young woman standing in the door with a gun pointed at him.

"Quiet," she said, "like a mouse." Her tone was very low.

She was a theatrically spectacular girl who was not gaudy, an unusual combination. She was something that might have stepped off a magazine cover, preferably, the cover of a men's magazine which doted on interesting figures. Blond, with tawny eyes and humorous lips, and a face that had more character than doll beauty; a face that lent itself well to laughter, you could tell. And her clothes hadn't been bought on any stenographer's twenty-five a week.

She waggled the gun at Doc.

"Nice day to get shot," she said. "I hope you don't think—"

Doc gestured slightly at the upper part of the house. "Suppose they hear you?"

"I'd be awfully sorry," she said. "But not as sorry as you would be."

Doc said, "You do not want them to hear?"

"No."

"Would you believe me," he asked her, "if I told you I do not want them to discover me, either?"

She shook her head instantly. And then she looked doubtful, concerned, curious. "How did you get down here? I thought I was watching the stairs."

"Window."

"Yes?" She moved a little, saw the window from which Doc had removed the glass. "Why did you come in that way?"

"The obvious reason."

"Didn't want them to know you were here, eh? Who are you, anyway?" She moved a little to give him a closer inspection. "You know, there *is* something familiar about you. I'm having trouble placing you, though. Ever been connected with the stage?"

"The theater?"

"Don't be silly. Theater is the highbrow end of it. Just say stage, and you measure me. No burlesque, though. Not that I wouldn't have taken a burley job if one came along. Say, who are you, anyway?"

"Clark Savage," Doc admitted.

"Well, I don't know any—" She stopped. "Wait a minute! You're kidding. You *couldn't* be!"

Doc said nothing.

"Wow!" the young woman yelled. "You *are* that Savage!"

"Sh-h-h," Doc warned. "They can hear you in the next county."

The young woman stared at him unbelievingly. "Well, nail me down and call me floored." Then she clapped a hand over her lips. "You suppose they heard me?"

Doc Savage listened for a while. He heard no alarming sound from above.

After a while, in a low voice, the young woman said, "Say, overlook my astonishment, will you? I never met you before, but up until about a year ago I kept your pictures thumbtacked all over the wall of my dressing room and in the lid of my trunk. Pal, did I have a crush on you!"

Doc's face lost its calmness. He looked very embarrassed.

"This," he muttered, "is no time to be facetious."

"You think I'm kidding?" said the young woman. "Oh, oh, brother!"

Still more uncomfortable, Doc asked, "Do you have a name?"

"Willie," she said. "And don't call me Billie. Ten chorus girls out of every dozen are called Billie, and I resent being one of the mob."

"Do you," Doc inquired, "have a more reserved name?"

"Who wants a reserved name? I wouldn't have any use for one."

"Ah—"

"Willie Stevens," said Willie. "And that much name will have to do you."

Doc was satisfied.

"What," he inquired, "are you doing here?"

Willie Stevens shrugged. "Checking up on a man. What else?"

"What man?"

"Boy friend. Name of Tom Lewis."

Doc Savage, beginning to recover his composure, said, "'Checking up' is a rather broad term. Would you care to be more specific?"

"If it was anybody but you I'd tell you to go roll your hoop," the rather eye-filling Willie Stevens informed him. "But considering it's you, and in memory of old loves—and, brother, I wasn't doing bad, I see now—I'll tell you all about it—"

That ended the tale for the time being because there was a rumbling rush of men down the stairs and glass-breaking as they kicked in the basement windows.

"Oh, oh!" said Willie. "They heard me yelling at you."

VII

WHO HAS THE DOG?

Doc Savage was not taken entirely by surprise, having heard the men moving about upstairs in such a way that he had been fairly sure they were preparing to raid the basement. Doc had not moved then because they would be watching the yard, and would stand an excellent chance of shooting him down if he ran for it. Nor did there seem to be any place in the basement where it was worth hiding. Now that the men had started their rush, he spoke quietly.

"Get behind this," he said.

He seized the heavy, stoneware laundry tub and yanked it off its stand so that it fell heavily on the floor. The copper water-piping broke and water, hot and cold, spouted out.

The calmness of the bronze man's voice shocked Willie, apparently. But she got behind the tub.

"I'll get scalded," she said.

Doc seized the copper water pipes, which would bend quite easily, and twisted them up so that the spouting streams of water were aimed at the doorway into the laundry room.

"Stay there," he told the girl.

He took a smoke grenade from his pocket, popped it on the floor. He popped two more—they sounded like ineffective firecrackers when they went off—out into the stairway and the other part of the basement.

Smoke came out of the grenades like fat, black animals that grew.

"Hey!" yelled a man. "Hey, what the hell is this?"

A gun emptied at least twelve consecutive shots into the basement, not a machine gun but an automatic with a special magazine, evidently. The bullets made big bumblebee-and-police-whistle noises, loud impacts.

Doc kept down in the smoke, let it spread and grow. He followed it toward the nearest window. The smoke climbed up and enveloped the window.

Doc, beside the window, said, "Here, try this way out." He said it very softly.

Someone outside the window heard him and began shooting. The man poured bullets into the window, emptied a revolver. "I'm getting him!" the man screamed. "Gimme another gun!" They evidently handed him another gun because he began shooting some more.

Doc waited until the man outside, in his excitement, got his arm and gun near enough to the window for Doc to reach. He could hardly see the gun flashes in the incredible blackness of the pall from the smoke grenades. But he could hear the blasting impacts of the weapon.

What Doc wanted most now was a prisoner, to be questioned.

He reached out and got the man's gun arm.

He pulled. The man squalled. Doc yanked furiously,

trying to get the fellow inside. But, outdoors, they thought fast and fell upon the man, grabbed his legs, hauled back.

"You're pullin' me apart!" the man screamed, and after that the shrieking was just agony.

They got him away from Doc. Skin came off the man's arm as if he had been scalded and he slid outside, safe.

Doc got away from the window, which was good, because now they emptied rifle, revolver and even shotgun charges in through the opening.

After that there was a shoot-at-the-next-sound silence, which the showgirl, Willie, broke by saying, "I'm O.K."

A man fired once, missed the sound of her voice by several feet.

The whole interior of the basement was now just a little less black than ebony.

Doc searched his pockets for an anaesthetic gas grenade.

He did not have any. He'd used them all earlier, at the railway station.

He had, however, an explosive grenade. He got one out, flicked up the little firing lever with a fingernail, tossed it out.

The explosion made the black air seem to become a sepia giant which slammed the bronze man against the basement wall. There were splinters, dust, masonry and profanity in the air.

"Hell, what're we up against?" a man yelled.

Another voice, the educated voice Doc had heard down the laundry chute, said, "It's got to be Savage. Stay with it, you guys."

But someone else lost his nerve and shrieked, "He'll get us all in this black stuff!"

"Gas!" bawled a third. "It's gas!"

That did it. They broke and ran, those in the basement. Someone screamed that the stairs had been blown away. His howl came from a part of the basement where there had never been stairs. The voice of Joe cursed him and said, "You're lost, you silly goon."

Doc made for the stairs himself. In the black pall they could not see him, and he was as safe with them as he was away from them.

Suddenly there was a fight, blows and profanity, a yell of agony.

"Joe, you knifed me!" a voice said.

Joe gasped, "I thought you were Savage."

The educated voice said, "Come here, come here! Come to me, all of you! And join hands! That way we can tell who is who."

Doc went over hastily, joined them, began pawing over them trying to find hands, and to get on the end of the line. He joined up with them, although he failed to get on the end of the line. He was in the middle of it somewhere.

"Now, up the stairs," said the educated voice. "And the minute anybody lets go your hand, shoot him."

The cavalcade got under way, moving with strained caution. Doc went along with them, aware that the situation under less deadly circumstances would have been thoroughly silly, and suddenly wondering why he had gotten into such a predicament. He should have seized a man, taking a chance on silencing the fellow quickly. Yet he had not, at any time during the asinine business of joining hands, gotten into a position where he felt that was safe.

The smoke from the grenades would have penetrated upstairs by now, too.

He would, at the top, pretend he was wounded, mutter something about having to drop out, and fall. As bothered as they were, they might not try to drag him out.

They climbed to the top of the stairs.

Doc opened his mouth to complain realistically about being unable to continue because of injuries.

The educated voice beat him to it, saying, "Joe, get the dog-carrying case."

Doc, immediately taking advantage of the order, freed himself from the men on either side of him. They wouldn't know where Joe was in the line.

But Joe, up ahead, said, "O.K., I'll get it. Wait for me."

"Here he is!" yelled one of the men Doc had just released. "Hell, he came up the stairs with us!"

Doc went down, to the side—and got his feet kicked from under him. He went down the stairs, heels over appetite as he expressed it later, disgustedly. He hit hard, got to his feet, went back up the stair again and fast.

Going up the stairs probably saved his life. Certainly if he had been at the bottom of the flight of steps, some of the storm of bullets they sent down would have hit him. As many men as could crowd into the head of the stairway did so and emptied guns downward.

Doc, crowding into them, snarled, "Watch out! Be careful!" He crawled through them, got behind them.

They stopped shooting.

"Joe, have you got that dog?" yelled the educated voice.

"Yeah," Joe said. "But I do not see what the hell—"

Doc went toward Joe. He located the man in the darkness, got what he thought was a wonderful break, spotted the man's jaw exactly and hit it a short, arching swing that should have submerged a whale.

Joe fell down.

Doc got the case. It was fairly heavy with an inanimate weight that was about the same as that of a dog.

They had heard the noise of Joe falling.

"What happened to you, Joe?" someone demanded.

Doc hastily imitated Joe's coarse voice, said, "Fell down. What you think?"

It was a good job of voice imitation. Under the breathless circumstances he thought it was excellent.

But a miracle happened, and Joe got up off the floor, yelling, "He hit me! Savage hit me!"

Doc had the dog case. He took cover. The room was suddenly full of crashing gun flame, and Doc found a door, got it open, leaped through, smashed into another wall. He had, like the burglar in the old joke, fled into a clothes closet by mistake.

Joe and the educated voice and the others fled out of the door.

Doc worked cautiously with the door. It had shut behind him and it had a spring lock. He did not dare take a chance on drawing attention to himself until the men were outside. Then he smashed the door open.

He heard at least two automobiles leaving with great haste.

The smoke cleared away after a while.

Willie came up the stairs cautiously. "War over?" she asked.

Doc Savage sat down in a chair and shrugged.

Willie frowned at him. "Where did they hit you?"

"They didn't," Doc admitted.

"You mean to tell me," said the girl, "that you came through that party without a scratch?"

Doc nodded.

"Then what makes your face long?"

"They got away," Doc said.

"Oh, is that all!"

"And that," Doc added, "is the most futile fight I have ever taken part in, I think."

"Futile?"

"No results."

"It sounded," said Willie, "like there was a heck of a lot of hither and yon."

"But no results. They got away. All of them."

"And you are disappointed?"

"Very," Doc agreed sourly.

"I will," said Willie, "be darned! I figured they'd scalped you at least six times. You should have heard it. Then I got the idea you had turned into ten men. I would even say ten wild men. Men howled and men screamed. Guns went off everywhere. The house is full of bullet holes. I happen to know there were over a dozen of them. You licked them. You chased them out. They were scared stiff. They ran like an alley cat that had just met six bulldogs. And you call *that* a failure!"

She fell into a chair.

"I give up," she said. "I came up here scared stiff and with every intention of fainting dead away. But you amaze me."

Doc Savage now took his mind off the fiasco which, in his opinion, the fight had turned out to be. He gave thought to the conversation he was having—he was talking. Usually he did not talk freely. And, in particular, he was not in the habit of talking easily to young women who looked as if they might have stepped out of a poster advertising the latest sensational movie. But he had been speaking freely, indeed slangily, with Willie. It was a little startling.

Suddenly, Willie shot to her feet.

"What"—she pointed—"is that?"

She had discovered the dog-carrying case.

"A dog case," Doc said.

"Is that the one they had? Did you take it away from them?"

"Yes."

Willie did a hop, skip and jump in her excitement.

"You," she said, "have solved the whole blamed mystery!"

The young woman started to open the carrying case, but Doc Savage put a hand on her arm. "Before we do that," he suggested, "suppose you tell your story."

"But, I—"

"Begin," Doc said, "at the beginning."

Willie scratched her head and looked longingly at the carrying case. "Well, O.K. Let's see, where was I when they busted—oh, yes! I was checking up on Tom Lewis."

"You had met him previously, I take it?" Doc inquired.

"Oh, you want it all?" She nodded vehemently. "Yes, I met him in St. Louis when I was working with the Municipal Opera. I told you I wasn't a burlesque gal, remember? Anyway, I met Tom in St. Louis. I guess his gift of gab fascinated me. You never saw such a guy for words. He was a salesman. With that line of patter he couldn't be anything else."

She paused, sighed, then laughed. "Tongue-tied in the middle and loose at both ends—that's Tom Lewis. I guess his words are what scared me. I got to thinking maybe he'd talked me into promising to marry him. It sort of bothered me."

Doc Savage listened patiently.

"My home town," she said, "happens to be the same one in which the Admiration Radio Cabinet Co. is located, and Tom Lewis travels for the Admiration concern, and lives in the same town. So, when I was home on vacation—which was the last two weeks—we saw a lot of each other."

She frowned darkly at the floor.

"We saw enough of each other," she continued, "for me to discover Tom Lewis wasn't a man whose mind was at ease. He was scared. I'm sure he is very scared—terrified."

She spread her hands. "You see what that did to me? It got me to wondering. First, I figured he was scared of me and trying to figure out a way of getting out of marrying me. Then I decided that wasn't it. So I thought—if he's scared, he maybe has done something."

Willie met Doc's eyes. "If he was a crook I wanted to know it in time."

"Go on."

"So I began keeping an eye on him. The more I watched

him the more certain I got that something was really wrong. And then I discovered men were following him and trying to get that thing."

Doc indicated the dog-carrying case. "This?"

"Yes."

"Who," Doc asked, "were the men following Tom Lewis?"

"The same gang you kissed good-by a minute ago."

"Where was this?"

"In the Ozarks. They're mountains in the Midwest, you know."

"And Tom Lewis had this dog-carrying case?"

"That's right."

"And they were after it?"

"You've got it. And Tom Lewis was plenty scared. I think he was scared of more than that they would get the case. I think he was afraid of himself. It looked to me like he was afraid of something they were going to do to him if they caught him."

"And then?"

"Tom Lewis lit out for New York," Willie explained. "The more I think about it the more I am convinced he had decided to come to New York to get your help. In fact I'm sure of that now."

Doc Savage asked, "How did you know all this?"

"Oh, Tom talked to me one night about you. He asked a lot of questions. I'd shown him those pictures of you I kept in my trunk before I met him, and that was why he asked me about you. When I told him about the pictures he thought it was funny. I guess it was. But when he talked to me about you that last time he didn't act like he thought it was funny at all. I know, now, that he was finding out all he could about you, so he could come and ask you for help."

"How did you get to New York?"

"Trailed him. That is, I trailed the gang who were trailing him. Tom got off the train somewhere en route to New York and I lost him. But I kept trailing the men and they led me here."

"When was that?"

"Only a few hours ago. This house seemed to belong to one of them. There was no one here but an old caretaker, and I don't know what became of him. I heard them quarreling with him."

Doc Savage was silent a moment. "Did you see Tom Lewis here?"

"No." Willie got a little pale. "Has he—"

"They captured him at the railway station in New York," Doc explained.

"That's tough." Willie sighed. "That's tough on Tom, but it relieves my mind. I was afraid, for a minute, you meant he'd thrown in with them. It'd be awful to think I'd been messing around with a guy who turned out to be a crook."

"They evidently sent him away before I reached here," Doc decided.

"Say, they *could* have done that! Come to think of it, I heard a car leave a little after that bunch got in from the city. They must have sent Tom away in that."

"That seems to bring us up to date," Doc said.

Willie asked eagerly, "Now, can I open this dog box?"

"There will," Doc said, "be nothing in it."

Willie hastily wrenched open the carrying case.

"You're right!" she exclaimed. "Nothing in here but some bricks!"

VIII

THE MUMBLING MAN

Doc Savage smashed the bricks to powder as a matter of precaution. But they were ordinary bricks of the type manufactured in New Jersey, and there was certainly no possibility of mystery about them.

The dog-carrying case also identified itself as having come from a Sixth Avenue luggage shop in Manhattan, and it was very new; and also the sales slip was inside, under the bricks, where the men had tossed it. The carrying case had cost eleven dollars and eighty-five cents, less tax.

Willie picked up the sales slip, said, "Look here, they bought this today."

Doc made no comment. He was acutely conscious that he had done more talking, and somewhat facetious conversation at that, than was his habit. This was evidently due to the influence of Willie, and he was somewhat disturbed.

He went through the house, searching. It was not a tidily kept place, although the furnishings had cost a considerable sum when they were new, which probably had been thirty years before in some of the rooms, no more than twelve or fifteen years in others. An effort had been made to cover and preserve the better stuff, but this work had been done by someone inexperienced, so that it had not been very effective. Clouds of moths flew up ahead of him from time to time.

Two rooms and a small servants' kitchen had been lived in, but that was all. The garments hanging in the closets here were those of a man.

Tom Lewis was not there.

Nowhere was there anything to show the identity of the man with the educated voice or Joe or the others.

Doc found Willie contemplating the dog-carrying case. Her face was long.

"I don't know," she said ruefully, "what to do now."

"Have you thought of doing the sensible thing?" Doc asked.

"Go back to St. Louis?" She shook her head. "Nothing doing. I started out to swim this puddle and I'm going to stay with it."

"What will be your next move?"

"I'm going," she said, "with you."

Looking alarmed, Doc said, "That will be too dangerous."

"Pfooey! Not as dangerous as stumbling around by myself, I betcha."

"I would much rather you did not."

Willie pointed a finger at him. "Now look, I was doing very well until you came along. All I wanted out of this was to find out if my intended was a crook. But you barged in and the lid flew off everything."

"But—"

"You messed up the playhouse," Willie said. "Therefore it is up to you to let me trail along until I'm satisfied."

"That," said Doc, "is a thin argument."

"I bet I make it stick, though."

They drove along a Westchester cross-county highway at a speed which kept them in the thin traffic stream and Doc switched on the directional radio-receiver and manipulated the dials. The tubes warmed up and he located the regularly spaced sound of the transmitter which he had fastened to the car driven by Tom Lewis' captors at the railway station. He identified the note by its resemblance to a mechanical interference.

Willie was interested. "Say, isn't that a radio direction-finder?"

"Yes."

"I thought so. My kid brother is a radio ham and I used to fool with the stuff myself. Where is the transmitter?"

"Fastened to the frame of a car which they rented."

"Oh!" Her eyes were wide. "That how you trailed them out here in the first place?"

"Yes."

Willie settled back in the seat and made small clucking sounds of approval. "You know, you may live up to your advance notices," she told Doc.

The trail left the main highway and headed more directly west, then northward through a section of dairy farms. It was evident that the men they were following had a definite destination but intended to get there without following the main highways.

"I'll bet," said Willie, "that they're driving at least one stolen car. That would explain why they are keeping off the trunk roads."

Doc made no comment.

Willie nudged him. "Hey, you never did tell me how you knew there wouldn't be anything in that dog-carrying case before I opened it."

Doc considered the point. "It did not feel as if there was a dog in it. The weight, I mean."

"Nonsense. The weight was just right. The weight wasn't alive, but then how did you know the dog wasn't dead?"

Doc made no reply.

Twenty minutes later, having evaded numerous questions put to him by Willie, he discovered that the direction-finder note was getting much louder. They were, in fact, rapidly approaching the transmitter.

A patch of woodland appeared. A lane turned off into this. In the lane—they would have missed it if they had not been looking for it—a car was parked.

"The rented sedan," Doc said.

He drove on, turned off the road, parked, said, "You stay here."

Willie sprang out after him.

"Nothing doing," she said. "I get scared when I'm alone."

"But I have to approach that car silently—"

"I'm going to surprise you," Willie told him. "I'm quite a woodsman. Daniel Boone didn't have a thing on me."

Doc, who was irritated, made the discovery that she had not exaggerated. Dancing and posture exercises had given the young woman a natural grace and certainty of foot, and she was almost as quiet as he was in traveling through the timber growth.

Frequent pauses to listen brought no suspicious sound to their ears. The woods were quiet, but not too quiet, for the birds were making their normal noises. There were no odors in the air that should not reasonably have been there.

They drew close to the car.

Doc gestured for Willie to stop.

She did so this time.

Doc then wasted enough time sneaking up on the car and going over it with care in search of wired bombs that he felt a little foolish when he discovered it was abandoned—and he turned around and saw Willie grinning at him.

There was a man in the machine.

He was tied hand and foot, making mumbling noises.

Doc hauled him out of the car.

"Not Tom Lewis," he said to Willie.

She shook her head.

"It's the caretaker of the house we just left," she explained. "Remember I told you they had a row with him? I guess they knocked him out and tossed him in the car here."

Doc looked at the car grimly. "In some way," he said, "they began to suspect this car was the means by which I trailed them. So they abandoned it."

Willie shook her head slowly. "If you ask me, that whips us."

IX

THE FRIGHTFUL DOG

Monk Mayfair and Ham Brooks were not in good humor. On top of their earlier difficulties with the campaign to stop their quarreling they had run into some plain-spoken policemen. The police department was shorthanded, short-tempered, and unfortunately they had encountered a cop who had once caught a fellow whom Ham had gotten off in court.

Finally, they had gotten the name and address of a taxi driver who owned a cab with the license number which Doc Savage had given them. The trip to the man's house had included a blow-out, running out of gas, a traffic jam with a military column. Then they arrived at the house and found the taxi driver was not home yet, and that his wife thought they were a pair of bill collectors.

The wife was very fat and death on bill collectors. She immediately showed them a beer bottle and threatened to alter the shape of their skulls with it. They retired to the sidewalk to wait. The wife stuck her head, and a kettle of boiling water, out of a window and threatened to scald them if they did not leave the neighborhood.

"Nobody loves us," Monk muttered.

"How could they?" asked Ham disagreeably. "With that face!"

"I thought," said Monk, "that we were going to call a stop to our private fussing until we figured out a way to put the quietus on this campaign Renny, Johnny and the others are conducting against us?"

"All right," said Ham, "since you ask it."

Monk didn't like his tone. "Listen, you overdressed shyster, you're not doing me any favors if I can help it."

"Look, tree boy," Ham said, "the favor they should have done you was pull you down off the chandelier a few minutes after you were born, and—"

They stared at the street.

"Oh, oh, our taxi driver!" Monk said.

They got up hastily and approached the hack pilot.

The taximan was a small, meek, henpecked fellow of the type who would have a wife such as Monk and Ham had just encountered, and who was still watching them from the upstairs window with her kettle of boiling water.

"Your name Gerald Deusen?" Ham asked.

"Look, mister, I'll pay you for the radio Monday sure," said the taxi driver. "Only, right now I'm as flat as anything. But by Monday—"

"We're not bill collectors," Monk told him.

This alarmed the cab driver. "Oh, damn me, you ain't my wife's two cousins, Fred and—"

"Heaven," said Monk, "forbid!"

Ham Brooks took charge of the conversation.

He hauled a ten-dollar bill from his pocket.

"Here," he said. "The redheaded man sent us."

The taxi driver immediately grinned. "Say, I'm glad to get rid of that," he said.

His cab had a trunk compartment at the rear and he went around, opened this. There was a dog-carrying case within and he picked it up, shook it, said, "The pooch seems to be all right." He handed the case over to Monk, whose mouth was open, then took the ten-dollar bill and pocketed it. "Glad to oblige you guys," he said.

Monk and Ham walked down the street self-consciously carrying the dog container, hardly able to credit their good fortune.

"Sure a lucky break!" Monk exclaimed.

"Break nothing," Ham told him. "Doc had it figured out that we would get the mysterious dog if we did it this way."

"Yeah?"

"You know what happened? It must have been this: At the railway station, Doc saw them switch dog cases. Or, rather, saw them give this one to the taxi driver and tell the driver they would pick it up later. Doc is good at reading lips, so he probably knew what instructions they'd given the driver."

"Why did they give it to a taxi driver?"

"Safest place. Suppose they had checked it in the baggage room in the station? A search would have turned it up. Suppose they had kept it? They might get caught and have it taken away from them."

"But they had a dog-carrying case with them."

"Fake, probably. Dead herring."

"The term," Ham said, "is red herring, not dead herring."

"Pardon me," said Monk, "but I happened to be looking at you while I was talking. I guess I was influenced."

Ham snorted. "Let's take a look at the thing."

"We better take it to headquarters, and—" Monk stopped, looked at Ham, grinned. "You know, it ain't too late to cut Renny and Johnny and Long Tom out of this thing. Doc, of course, outsmarted us."

Ham grinned back at Monk. "You got something there,' Ham said. "Let's turn into the park here."

They were passing a Brooklyn public park at the moment, and Monk nodded, headed down one of the walks. They strode along rapidly, but no secluded spots appeared.

"They sure designed this park," said Monk, "so a guy couldn't find a spot to neck his girl."

"I'll take the other side of the driveway," Ham offered. "If I find a place I'll holler. And if you find one, do the same."

"Sure."

They separated. Monk, who had the dog-carrying case, kept it with him. He walked along, swinging the case and grinning cheerfully. He could tell that there was a live dog in the case. The animal growled a time or two. "Bad-tempered pooch," Monk thought. "Now what the heck do you suppose a dog has got to do with all this?"

And almost immediately, Monk saw a little glade behind some bushes. Just the spot. There, they could open the case, look at the dog and see if they could tell what it was all about.

Monk opened his mouth to call to Ham. He closed it.

Monk was a double-crosser at heart where Ham was concerned. For years he had done everything possible to irritate and bedevil the dapper Ham Brooks, receiving in return—he maintained—more than he dished out.

"'Ah, ha,' said Desperate Desmond," Monk remarked to himself. "I'll just leave Ham out of this, too."

He opened the case and took a good look at what was inside.

Ham Brooks missed Monk Mayfair almost immediately, chancing to glance across the driveway, which was as wide as a street at this point, and noticing that Monk was not in sight.

"Monk!" Ham called.

He was not alarmed until he got no answer. Then, suddenly apprehensive, he dashed across the driveway, plowed into the bushes. "Monk!" he called. "Where are you?"

Thirty seconds or so and there was no answer.

Then there was a crashing of shrubbery—a large, animated object traveling full speed. This proved to be Monk. He came toward Ham.

"Monk!" Ham said. "You silly mutt, what is the idea of acting—hey! Hey! Monk, what on earth?"

Because Monk gave no slightest sign of seeing Ham,

knowing where he was, or knowing where he was going—
except that he wanted to get there fast.

"Monk!" Ham yelled.

Monk's mouth was open its very widest, with jaw and
cheek muscles straining as if he were trying to get it open
wider. His throat was a thick column of sinew, the way a
man's throat gets when he is strangling on his feelings.

"*Where's that dog case?*" Ham screamed at him.

Monk did not have the case.

All he had was an inarticulate spasm, paroxysm, fit or
whatever kind of a seizure it was, and an unearthly and
unbounded desire to get as far away from there as fast as mad
speed could do it.

Ham made a flying tackle.

He brought Monk down.

"Monk!" gasped Ham. "What happened? What on earth is
the matter? Where's the case?"

Wordless and frenzied, Monk tried to get up and escape.
Exasperated, Ham gave him a couple of wallops over the
head with his sword cane. "You haven't any brains, blast you!"
Ham said. "But I'll beat out the sawdust or whatever it is
you've got in place of them. What ails you, anyhow?"

This either stunned or sobered Monk because he stopped
struggling. He sat there for a moment, making visible efforts
to relax and to get his vocal cords to functioning. He made a
few croakings.

"I'll be superamalgamated!" he said.

"That's Johnny's word," Ham said disagreeably. "Come to
your senses, you accident of nature."

Monk swallowed a few times.

"Dog!" he gulped.

"What?"

"Dog."

Ham immediately hit Monk over the head with his
sword cane again. "You gossoon!" he said. "So you tried to
double-cross me, and took a look at the dog yourself. That
what happened?"

Monk nodded weakly.

"I wish I'd let you do it," Monk said with bitter feeling.

Ham's anger subsided as he inspected Monk. It was very
plain that something far out of the ordinary had happened to
the homely chemist.

"Where's the dog?" Ham demanded in alarm. "You let it get away."

"Box," Monk said.

"The dog is still in the box?"

"Y-yes."

"And where," asked Ham, "is the box?"

Monk looked around foolishly and pointed two or three different directions. Apparently he was confused as to just what direction he had been coming.

"I don't see what they gave you a head for," Ham said disgustedly. "Especially one that looks like that article you've got."

Ham hauled Monk to his feet and began hunting. He set out in the direction which Monk had been coming from when he first saw the stricken chemist, on the chance that Monk had not run in a circle, but in a straight line. This proved to be slightly faulty reasoning, but bushes were smashed down and flowers were trampled, so that Ham did not have the trouble he had anticipated in backtracking Monk.

"What ails you, anyway?" Ham demanded.

Monk mumbled something that was not understandable.

"There!" Ham barked. He dashed forward. He had found the dog-carrying case.

"This the same one?" Ham demanded.

"Uh-huh," Monk muttered. "I just ran off and left it."

"Why?"

Monk's answer was another unintelligible mumble.

"Oh, the devil!" Ham snapped. "What's hit you, anyway? I'll look in the case and see if the dog is there."

Ham started to open the case.

Monk grabbed his arm. "Wait!" Monk blurted. "Don't do that."

"Why not?"

"You better not," Monk said.

"Why—"

Monk made excited, worried gestures. "Look, take it to headquarters, and there we—well, it would be better if we all looked it over together."

"You're crazy," Ham assured him. "I'm opening it now."

Monk clutched his hand. "Wait a minute, hold on! I know how you feel. I felt the same way. But don't."

"You don't want me to open it now?"

"No, of course not."

"Why?"

"I don't want you to get the shock I got."

Ham snorted feelingly. "Why, you squeaking freak, you! What a lie! You don't give a whoop about me."

"Yes, I do."

"Never before," said Ham, "have you shown a disposition to keep me from getting a shock."

"But—"

"In fact," said Ham, "I can name times you've arranged trouble for me. I can name them so fast it'll make your head swim."

"But—"

"I'm going to open it."

Monk waved his arms frantically. "Wait a minute," he yelled. "At least let me prepare you for what you are going to find."

"Prepare me—"

"I'll tell you what you'll find in there," Monk said grimly. "Then you'll know, and you won't be shocked like I was—"

A man with a gun now came out of the nearby shrubbery. He was followed by three other men, also with weapons.

"I think," said the first man, "that this conversation has gone far enough."

X

THE RUSH WEST

Doc Savage and Willie Stevens drove into New York City with the caretaker who had been in charge of the country home of the man called Dirty Chin. The caretaker's name had proved to be Roy Chapman and he was convinced that he was badly injured, refusing to believe that a few bumps on the head and a gash in his shoulder would not prove fatal.

"Won't we ever get to the hospital?" he kept complaining.

When not squawking about that, he had complained that he had received a dirty deal at the hands of Dirty Chin, whose real name was T. G. S. Summers, alias several other names, probably.

"I knowed Summers was a crook," he said. "I knowed it all along. You could tell it by looking at him."

"Why," asked Willie, "did you stay on the job?"

"A man has gotta live."

"When I suspect there's a crook around," said Willie, "I look into it." She laughed ruefully. "Come to think of it, that's what got me into this."

The hospital came in sight.

Doc Savage asked the caretaker, "You are sure you cannot give us any information about the men who took over the house?"

"I've described them for you."

Willie said, "That was a great help. We had seen them all ourselves."

"What about Tom Lewis?" Doc asked.

"Yes," said Willie. "What about him? I have a personal interest in him. You are sure he was all in one piece?"

The caretaker asked, "That the young fellow you described, the tall one?"

"That's the one."

"Well, he had been bunged up some. They brought him to the place, then they put him in another car and four men took him away. I don't know where."

"When did they take him away?"

"Just before you folks started the big fight."

"Where did they take him?"

"I dunno. They had beat me and my head was ringin', and I was beginnin' to die—"

"We've heard about that," Willie said. "There's the hospital."

They parked the caretaker in the hospital, leaving him somewhat revived already by looking at the attractive nurses who were to take care of him.

Willie sighed as they drove on downtown. "Men are funny," she said. "Now there was one with a piece of spaghetti for a backbone."

Doc made no comment.

Willie eyed the bronze man speculatively. Doc's bronze size seemed to impress her. "Yep, there's sure some difference in men," she said.

Doc carefully avoided the subject.

Renny Renwick met them at headquarters. He was giving off excitement as if it were sparks.

"Monk and Ham are in trouble over in Brooklyn!" he roared. "Come on!"

They used a large sedan which would carry all of them and which had more complete equipment. It was one of several cars and trucks which Doc Savage and his associates had maintained for some time, keeping the vehicles in a private basement garage in the building which housed headquarters. The collection of cars, which had been extensive, was now considerably abbreviated—they had only two cars left in fact—because the other machines had been removed to defense plants, where their design could be studied and good features, or features suitable to military operations, adapted to war production.

Renny drove. The big-fisted engineer gave Willie a glance of admiration, said, "Holy cow! Wait until Ham or Monk sees you!" He turned the car on to one of the main traffic ways leading toward Brooklyn.

"Ham telephoned in," he explained. "It seems they got the carrying case with the dog in it. But they stopped off in a park and got into a little roundup."

"Who with?" Doc asked.

"Our friend, the redheaded man, I guess," Renny explained. "Holy cow! Ham sounded as excited as a tomcat with his tail on fire."

"But they had the dog?" Doc asked.

"Yes."

"Have they still got it?"

"I don't know."

Renny switched on a red light, a siren, and drove at a speed which was certainly not below thirty-five an hour. He paid attention to the driving, nothing else.

Willie watched the big-fisted engineer narrowly until she seemed satisfied that he was good enough a driver to warrant the speed he was making. Then she gave attention to Johnny and Long Tom. Long Tom's puny physique seemed to amaze her, and, being a young woman without inhibitions, she reached over and pinched to see if he had any biceps muscle.

"Kind of squirrelly," she said.

"Look, gorgeous," Long Tom said irritably. "You tinker with me and I'll backfire on you. Keep out of my way or you'll get run over."

"You must be the one who doesn't like women," Willie said.

She turned and inspected Johnny.

"Let's hear some of your words," she said to Johnny.

Johnny grinned foolishly.

Willie was a very attractive young woman.

"You should see your face now," Long Tom sneered at Johnny. "Just like somebody was tickling your toes with a feather. You stretched-out goon!"

Johnny sobered.

They pulled into a Brooklyn park, made a left turn, a right swing up a long driveway, and met Ham Brooks galloping down the street.

"They got Monk!" Ham yelled. "And they got the dog!"

The car in which Monk and the dog-carrying case had been taken away had gone due north over a boulevard route, Ham explained. They drove in that direction themselves, although it was an impossible hope, and they knew it.

While they drove, Ham explained what had happened.

"Four guys, altogether," he said. "One of them was red-headed. They were boys who knew their way around because they didn't waste any time and didn't make any mistakes."

Doc asked, "Were they watching the house of the taxi driver to whom they had given the dog?"

"They must have been, although we didn't see them doing that," Ham admitted. "We looked around while we were waiting at the taxi driver's house. The darned taxi driver's wife was threatening to throw scalding water on us because she thought we were bill collectors, and that might have distracted us."

He groaned miserably.

"I guess they trailed us into the park," he continued. "Anyway, they—but first I had better tell you about Monk and that dog."

He told them about Monk opening the dog case and how Monk had acted afterward, running through the park shrubbery.

"He was shocked silly," Ham said. "And for Monk, that is something. I've seen him get shocks before, and he's not one to be easily affected."

"What did he see when he opened the dog case?" Doc asked.

"That," Ham said, "was what he started to tell me when this gang jumped us."

"He did not tell you?"

"Not a word."

"Then you do not know what is in the dog-carrying case?"

Ham shook his head.

"But I would swear whatever is in the case is a dog," he said. "You could hear the animal move about and growl. It was an ill-tempered dog."

Willie stared at Ham.

"You didn't," she said, "learn anything?"

Ham shook his head. "They closed in on us. Monk had been about to tell me what he saw in the box and they heard that, so they concentrated on Monk. They wanted Monk because he knew what was in the box. Well, they got him. It was a heck of a fight but the best I could do was get away into the bushes. They got Monk to their car. There was another fellow in their car—"

Ham stopped, his mouth open.

"Well?" said Willie. "What did you forget and leave out?"

"The fellow in the car."

"Who was he?"

"What," Ham asked, "does this Tom Lewis look like?"

They described Tom Lewis to Ham and Ham nodded.

"Tom Lewis, all right," he said. "They had Tom Lewis in their car, a prisoner. They threw Monk in the machine, climbed in and took off. That's all there was to it. I got to a telephone and called you fellows."

There was a grim silence that continued for some minutes. Renny, driving their car, saw the futility of hoping to overtake Ham's captors and gave up the chase. He turned toward the Manhattan headquarters. The fact that the chase had to be given up did not contribute anything to the good spirits in the car.

Willie looked around at the long faces of Doc's aids and the expressionless features of the bronze man himself. They were not a gleeful lot.

"I must say," said Willie, "that I don't hear hope bubbling over."

"This is no time for sass," Long Tom muttered.

"Your faces are as long as beanpoles," said Willie. "Which

leads me to take it that you're up a stump, as we call it back in Missouri."

"That's right," Renny rumbled.

"Meaning," said Willie, "that you don't know where to turn next."

Long Tom scowled. "You ask too many questions," he said. "How would you like to become a girl standing beside the road trying to thumb a ride?"

"Throw me out," Willie told him. "I've been thrown out before." She inspected Long Tom and added, "Not, however, by a world-renowned electrical expert who acts like a kid who pulls little girls' pigtails."

Long Tom blinked and subsided.

Renny told Willie, "When you said we didn't know where to turn next you said a mouthful."

The car ran up the long, sloping ramp of Brooklyn Bridge, went over the hump and coasted down toward the packed thickness of Manhattan skyscrapers.

"Pessimism," said Willie, "is something they ought to shoot people for, like they shoot horses for broken legs."

"I suppose," said Renny indignantly, "you have an idea of what to do next?"

"No ideas," Willie told him. "Only a suggestion."

"And that would be?"

"Back home we've got a pesky shrub called buckbrush," said Willie. "It's a nuisance to get rid of in the pastures. And we've got a saying you can cut down a buckbrush, but there's always the roots."

"Meaning?"

"The roots of this thing are down in the Ozarks," said Willie. "Why don't you look there?"

They reached headquarters, left the car in the basement garage and rode the special high-speed elevator upstairs. Willie was not expecting the elevator to be the violent thing it was, and when it started there was inertia that made her go to her knees and yelp. Johnny and Ham collided with each other in their haste to help her up.

"Special elevator," Johnny explained.

Willie said ruefully, "I'm glad you told me. I might have thought it was a skyrocket."

They entered headquarters, found a pleasantly efficient young man waiting there.

"Hello, Frank," Renny greeted him.

The young man was Frank Burroughs, who had no connection with their organization except that he often furnished them with quick information. Frank Burroughs had what was by way of being one of the most efficient detective agencies in the country.

He said, "I have the information."

"What information?" Renny asked him, surprised.

"Mr. Savage asked for it," Frank Burroughs explained. "He wanted data on the Admiration Radio Cabinet Co., and on Admiration City, in the Ozarks. He wanted train, bus and plane schedules on the place. He wanted me to get plane tickets and priorities so they could be used immediately, and any other transportation necessary to reach Admiration City. Mr. Savage asked for this information several hours ago."

Willie looked at Doc Savage.

"I apologize," she said, "for being a little late with my crack about looking for the roots of this thing."

XI

SET-UP

The plane which Doc Savage flew to the Ozark country was large and fast, and when an inquisitive Army Aircobra came sliding up in the sky with the warning of a .37-millimeter cannon and a dozen .50-caliber machine guns in its wing and nose, and investigated them, they might have outrun the craft. Instead, they identified themselves and were politely shepherded off the military reservation over which they had wandered without clearance and permits. That was over lower Indiana.

Doc Savage turned the flying over to Renny, and got out a make-up kit.

He told Long Tom Roberts, "The next part of this job will be yours."

"Anything electrical about it?"

"Probably nothing electrifying except the performance you will be expected to give," Doc told him. "Here, let me start making over your face."

With dyes and chemicals he proceeded to change Long Tom's normal, pallid, mushroom-cellar complexion into a healthy outdoor leather. He made Long Tom's hair gray.

He sent Long Tom into the back of the plane to change clothes. When the electrical expert came out of the rear compartment he wore overalls and jumper, heavy shoes, battered hat, all of which were stained with the kind of stains a man working around a farm would collect.

"All I need now," he said, grinning, "is a straw to chew on."

From a luggage compartment, Doc removed a dog-carrying case. It was black leatherette, about the size to hold an Airedale. He removed the price tags from it, the labels, and gave it a scuffing. He opened a small packet which proved to contain ordinary dust and further soiled the dog case.

Doc sat down beside Long Tom.

"Here," said the bronze man, "is what you are to do."

He spoke rapidly, grouping his instructions so that each step was completely stated and clear, and repeating such points as might be doubtful, or giving alternate possibilities in cases where there might be a hitch.

Long Tom said he understood.

Willie hadn't heard the instructions and she looked at Doc Savage thoughtfully. "What goes on?"

"Just an idea."

"We have no idea whatever about what became of Tom Lewis or Monk Mayfair, or the mysterious dog, or what on earth is behind this mystery," Willie pointed out. "It looks to me as if we are going to have to do some tall fishing in order to get a clue."

"We are going to drop a baited hook in the water," Doc said, "and see what happens."

"But you don't even know what pond the fish is in."

"There are two kinds of bait for fish."

"How do you mean?"

"There is the bait the fish likes to eat, say a worm. And for game fish there is also the bait which makes the fish mad and arouses the desire to strike, like a casting plug."

"And we," said Willie, "are after game fish. That it?"

"Exactly."

Boone Shot, Missouri, was not much of a town, consisting of half a dozen log cabins and a ramshackle railroad depot. It was inhabited by picturesque and worthless natives for the most part, and times were hard. Back in the days when moonshining had been popular, and there had been wild turkeys in the surrounding hills, there had been a degree of prosperity. But Roosevelt had ruined the distilling business, and the dude hunters from St. Louis had slaughtered the turkeys.

Boone Shot had gotten its name, of course, from that grand old legend of the Indian-fighting pioneer days, Daniel Boone. Daniel was supposed to have shot the blue head off one of the local wild turkeys at a range of half a mile or so, or something like that. Nothing much else had ever happened around Boone Shot worth bragging about, probably.

Yet Boone Shot had gotten a good bit of publicity because the editor of the local paper happened to be a humorist, a publicist and a man with imagination.

The newspaper editor's name was Toot Alfred, and, of course, Boone Shot was not large enough to support a newspaper. It wouldn't support a filling station, for that matter, even before gasoline and rubber rationing. So Toot Alfred had to make a living by some other means, and he did it by corresponding for all the surrounding papers, including those in St. Louis and Kansas City.

Country correspondents for city newspapers ordinarily do not have incomes that would make movie stars envious, and Toot was no exception. But he did well. He paid enough income tax to make him turn pale on March 15th.

There was never any news around Boone Shot, but Toot Alfred didn't let this hamper him. If Farmer Hank's sow got her head caught in the lard bucket, Toot would do a story about it, and readers in St. Louis and Kansas City and points beyond would scream with laughter. Toot had the touch. Every speck of "news" that Toot sent out of Boone Shot got printed.

Given anything even slightly unusual, Toot could turn out a sensational item.

Toot was sitting on the porch of the general store, swapping lies with the locals when a car rattled up and stopped.

The man who got out was short, scrawny, weather-beaten and wore agricultural clothes, well-used.

The arrival put a foot on the store porch, took out a

jackknife, absentmindedly whittled a splinter off the porch post and began picking his teeth with it.

"Howdy," the stranger said, finally. "Nice day, ain't it? If it don't rain there ain't gonna be no watermelon crop."

No one said anything.

"I'm a stranger," the newcomer said. "Name's Hick Lewis."

There was another silence.

Toot asked, "Any kin to them Lewises over on West Fork?"

The stranger spat, "To them elm-peelers? I hope not!" he said.

The next silence was bitter. There were some representatives of the West Fork branch of the Lewis clan present.

The stranger added, "Got a cousin Tom Lewis, over in Admiration City. Travelin' salesman, he is. Fastest talker in the country."

After looking at them sleepily and chewing up part of his toothpick, the stranger asked, "Where's your depot around here? Should have me a express there. Got me a telegram from that Tom Lewis that said he was sending me an express."

"Depot's yonder," said Toot.

The stranger walked to the depot and disappeared inside.

What happened next probably exceeded even Daniel Boone's performance with the wild-turkey head.

The stranger howled three or four times inside the station. He burst out. He was carrying a leatherette-covered case of the type used for transporting dogs.

Howling at every jump, the stranger tore down the street.

He seemed to discover he had the dog case. He threw it away.

He ran fifty yards, stopped, looked at those on the porch of the general store. He pointed at the dog case. "That dog!" he bellowed. "That dog in there!"

He jumped up and down several times. Then he ran back and got the dog case. He picked it up as if it were a bomb.

"This dog!" he yelled. "You . . . you . . . never saw such a thing!"

He ran out of town at full speed, leaving his car abandoned in front of the general store.

He was never again seen in Boone Shot, Missouri.

* * *

Actually, the stranger slackened his speed when he was out of sight, caught his breath and walked three quarters of a mile up the side of a hill. Here he joined Doc Savage and the rest of Doc's party.

"Doc, how'd I do?" asked the stranger.

"Excellent, Long Tom," Doc told him.

"You saw the performance?"

"Yes. It was perfect."

Long Tom grinned. "You think something will come of it?"

"Cross your fingers," Doc said, "and wait."

Doc Savage had selected a small, natural cave, which they had chanced to find on the ridge, for a hiding place. Inside there was the remnant of a crude still, but there was no sign that the place had been used in years, or even visited by anyone.

Leaving the others concealed in the cave, Doc Savage made his way toward the village, climbed a tree and used a pair of strong binoculars.

From his perch it was possible to observe the entire town of Boone Shot, and activities there were simple enough that a watcher could get an excellent idea of what went on.

Toot Alfred was conspicuous in the group standing around looking at the ancient car the stranger had abandoned.

Then Toot left the group, went over and sat on the store porch. His attitude was that of a man thinking. He laughed to himself several times.

Suddenly, Toot made a dash for a small house which was evidently his home.

He was inside about an hour and came out carrying a sheet of paper.

The railway depot was also the local telegraph station, and Toot disappeared into this. He came out without the paper.

Doc was satisfied. He descended from the tree and joined the others in the cave.

Johnny had caught a rabbit and Willie was concocting a fine-smelling rabbit stew.

"I think my ancestors must have been hobos, the way I can make a rabbit mulligan," Willie said. "Have there been any results."

"It would appear," Doc told her, "that Toot Alfred filed a funny story about the incident on the telegraph wire."

"Sending it to the newspapers he corresponds for all over the state?"

"No doubt."

"Will they print it?"

"They print any and everything Toot sends them," Doc said. "The man has a reputation. Why, he is known all over the country, and New York syndicates have tried to get him to leave the backwoods and come to the city. Toot says he is too lazy."

Willie peered into the cooking kettle approvingly. "Now we wait, and hope the right people see that story."

Doc nodded. "And hope they react as we wish."

"They'll react," Willie predicted. "Some of them are sure to come charging down here to look into the dog mystery. They can't afford to pass it up."

The scheme got results in approximately sixteen hours, which was sooner than they had expected. Renny and Johnny were watching Boone Shot at the time, and Johnny arrived at the cave galloping and out of breath.

"The redheaded man himself!" he said.

Willie looked at Johnny in astonishment and said, "You *can* use small words, can't you? Well, what are we waiting on?"

Doc Savage said, "Willie, you and Ham and Long Tom break camp here, then stick by the portable radio receivers and wait for instructions."

"What instructions?" asked Willie. "Aren't you going to grab them?"

"No," Doc said. "You do as you are told for a change."

The bronze man ran toward Boone Shot with Johnny.

Willie put her fists on her hips and said, "How do you like that? Doesn't even explain what he is going to do!"

Ham grinned. "You don't seem to know it, but you get more conversation out of Doc than any two women I ever saw."

"I wouldn't call him any gale of words."

"You're doing all right."

Willie eyed Ham suspiciously to see if there was a double meaning to that. "Well, double meaning or not, you're wrong," she said. "What's the matter with him? I'm not exactly a Frankenstein product. But you'd think I was just something that had splashed on the wall."

Ham grinned.

"Don't grin, darn it!" Willie snapped. "I wish we could find Tom Lewis."

"Keep hold of your patience," Ham told her. "We are beginning to get somewhere and we'll find him if he can be found."

Willie sighed.

"I hope we find him quick," she said. "I want to take another look at him and see if he's the bundle of virtues I thought he was."

Ham laughed. "Doc has that effect on them."

"Oh, go run a rabbit!" Willie said.

XII

SAVING MONK

There was the redheaded man and two others. They were dressed well enough to command respect, but not too richly, and they were free with cigars and questions. Boone Shot was not a place where strangers learned much with questions, but the inhabitants were old American stock who did not have a contempt for pipsqueak government investigators; instead, had a great deal of awe for everyone connected with the government except "revenuers." So, when the redheaded man and the other pair casually flashed some cards which said they were agents of the F. B. I.—the cards said they were G-men, which alone would have proved them a fake to a knowing reader—they got results.

The exact story of what had happened when Long Tom Roberts visited the local depot came out. It was probably as truthful a story as had ever been told in Boone Shot, where lying was a practiced art and one of the main forms of amusement.

The redheaded man listened with attentive interest.

He thanked everybody.

"Come on, boys," he said.

They climbed in their car and drove down the road a piece and stopped in the shade to talk it over.

"Why the hell didn't somebody find out Tom Lewis had a cousin?" one of the men asked.

"What'll we do? Hire the local bumpkins to comb the woods for that dog case? Chances are, if this hick Lewis was as scared as they say, he threw the dog away somewhere."

"Or buried it," said another.

The redheaded man swore. "Are you guys crazy?"

"What you mean?"

"Suppose one of these brushhoppers would find that dog?"

"Ouch!"

They were silent and concerned with their troubles for a while.

"Then what'll we do about this?" one asked.

"Report it to the boss, I guess," the redheaded man said disgustedly. "Damn my soul! Who'd have thought there would be trouble every which way we jumped on this thing."

He started to get the car engine running, but one of the men reached over and stopped him.

"You know something?" said the man who had blocked his hand. "This thing is beginning to creep up on me."

"How you mean?"

"Well, in the beginning, it was all right. Good pay and all we had to do was act as guards and to grab this fellow Tom Lewis so the boss could use him."

The redheaded man frowned. "What's changed? It's still the same, ain't it? You left out part of what you were hired for in the beginning—you were to keep Tom Lewis grabbed, and that's all you've done. Tom Lewis got away and started to New York to get help from Doc Savage. Well, we stopped that. We had our troubles but we stopped it."

"Why," asked another of the men, "was that Monk Mayfair brought back here?"

"There," said the first, "is a question."

The redheaded man looked at them as if he wanted to use his fists on them.

"The boss wants to use Mayfair," he said.

"Same way as Tom Lewis?"

"That's right."

"I thought," said one, "that Tom Lewis was to be the only one."

"Monk Mayfair happened along," said the redheaded man, "and so he's going to be used, too."

"That's all?"

"Sure. Say, what's eating you, anyway?"

The other man scowled at the redheaded one. "Just this: You wouldn't be figuring on adding us to the list, would you?"

"*What?*"

"You heard me."

The redheaded man slapped his hands on his knees. He roared laughter. He acted as if he thought it was so funny he would have to get out and lie on the ground and roll around to enjoy it.

"What a silly idea!" he chortled.

"Just so it stays silly," said the other uneasily.

Doc Savage watched them roll away in the car, then in great haste packed the sensitive directional microphone and the amplifier with which he had been eavesdropping. The gadget was more sensitive than the human ear, and insects and birds had aggravated him, but he had heard most of the conversation held in the car. In addition he was an excellent lip reader, and he had missed very little.

He used the small portable "radio transceiver"—an outfit considerably more compact than the regular military "walkie-talkie"—and said, "Pick me up, Renny."

Renny arrived almost immediately in a car.

Into the radio, Doc said, "Long Tom, report. Also Ham."

"I'm all right," Long Tom replied.

"Here, too," Ham said.

"Both of you are ahead of the car they are using?"

"Yes."

Doc said, "Keep well ahead. In fact, drive fast enough that there will be no danger of them sighting you. When you get to an intersection, split if necessary in order to cover all possible roads leading toward Admiration City."

"Right."

Doc leaned back and relaxed.

Willie examined the bronze man thoughtfully. "The chase has started, I take it," she said. "That was a nice job of hooking the fish you did. I doubt if they have the least suspicion that they've been sucked in on anything."

Renny had been keeping a heavy foot on the accelerator. Now he caught sight of the car containing the redheaded man and the other two and slackened speed. After that he kept far enough behind them to trail the car, but not close enough to alarm them.

Later, after they came to a highway, Long Tom took over the job of keeping close track of the men. He alternated with Ham, who was using a different type of car in order not to arouse suspicion.

"They're heading for Admiration City, all right," Willie said excitedly.

The destination was not Admiration City. The car ahead turned off, began climbing a gravel road that snaked sharply up a ridge.

"Oh-oh, the lake!" Willie said. "The lake lies over this ridge—or one arm of it."

The ridge was a high one, bleak, gave a view of the country for miles.

Willie pointed out a cluster of neat, modern buildings in the distance. "The Admiration Radio Cabinet Co. plant," she said.

"Funny place," said Renny, "for a radio-cabinet plant. What was the idea of building it back here in the hills? Close to the supply of wood, or something?"

"Oh, no!" Willie told him. "Admiration makes practically no wooden radio cabinets. They are plastic. Some very new and unusual, types. Some of the minerals used in the cabinets and in getting the marvelous color effects in the cabinets are found here in the Ozarks. The plant was placed here partly for that reason. Also, it is close to the electric-power supply."

"Electric power used in making the plastics?" asked Renny, who was interested in any engineering matter.

"That's right."

"The plant," said Renny, "would still have been closer to its raw-material supply, and particularly to labor supply, if built in a city the size of St. Louis or Kansas City. Matter of fact, labor supply is usually the reason you find plants in cities."

Willie shrugged. "Mr. Walter Buxton."

"Who?"

"Walter J. Buxton. I think his middle initial stands for 'Jonas.'"

"Who is he?"

"General manager of the Admiration company," Willie

explained. "The plant started as a small concern in Jefferson City, and they built this plant here about ten years ago, just after the big dam was put in."

"I still do not see—"

"Oh, Mr. Buxton's home was down there where the plant is," Willie told Renny. "That was why he persuaded the Admiration company owners to build the plant here. Mr. Buxton is a very sentimental man."

"Friend of Tom Lewis, by any chance?"

Willie shook her head. "Not much. Mr. Buxton is a sensitive old gentleman, the kind of old fellow who follows a regular routine every day and likes to spend his spare time with his family. Such men don't like big talkers as a usual thing, and Tom Lewis talked as big as an elephant. Matter of fact, Mr. Buxton fired Tom once."

"Buxton fired Tom Lewis once, eh? Any hard feelings over that?"

"I don't think they ever got to kissing each other when they met," Willie said. "But Tom was too good a salesman to stay fired."

Doc Savage said, "Renny, stop the car."

The machine came to a stop. They listened. It was obvious that the car ahead had halted. They could see, through the trees, the pale-blue, crinkled sheet of the lake surface.

Willie frowned at Doc.

"Holy cow!" she said, borrowing Renny's pet expression. "Are we going to sit around and wait again?"

Doc pretended not to hear her. "Get in touch with Ham and Long Tom and Johnny," he said. "And be ready to move quick."

"All right," Renny asked, "if we move down toward the lake and keep an eye on what happens."

"As long as they do not discover you," Doc agreed.

He moved away from the car a few yards—and was suddenly not to be seen or heard.

Willie gasped. "Now there was a slick job of disappearing."

The bronze man went carefully and swiftly down the sharp slope toward the lake. He went fast because he was not sure that there was much time. The woodland was fairly open, the trees rather thick, but not much brush between them; enough, however, to offer cover. There were ledges of rocks here and there, large ledges which offered silent footing once Doc removed his shoes, which he did at once. The patch glimpses of the lake through the trees showed the water much nearer, and there was the smell of a fresh-water shore line.

There was, he discovered, no great hurry.

They were hiding their car. Beside the lake was twenty acres or so of flat ground and the hay had been cut off this and stacked. They were hiding the car in a haystack, shoveling hay around it with forks, and swearing at each other when the job looked like anything but a haystack.

The redheaded man was farther to the west, and he was gathering dry sticks and piling these on a tuft of grass. He struck a match and the grass and wood blazed up, sending aloft a wisp of blue smoke.

The man then poured a bottle of something, evidently crude oil, on the fire, and the smoke became very black.

He stook back and admired the smoke in a way that proved it was a signal.

"Get everybody together," he called.

"What's the idea?" someone shouted.

"We're all going in."

"Who told you—"

"Jim was waiting in the shack with a message," the redheaded man said angrily. "The boss is getting worried. He wants us all to come in. We're going to hole up until we see what goes on. Play safe. And, damn you, I'm getting tired of explaining every move to you."

The man who had asked the question scowled. "Listen, I don't like the smell of this."

"You've said that before," the redheaded man said contemptuously.

"Listen, I—"

"Shut up and go—"

"Lay off that stuff, Red. You keep telling people to shut up and somebody is going to do some dental work on you with a fist."

"Go on and—"

The other man walked forward, stiff-legged. "Red, let's settle something now," he said. "Why aren't the rest of the boys out here helping us?"

"The boss didn't think they—"

"Red, they got what Tom Lewis got, didn't they? Got what that Monk Mayfair is going to get? That right?"

"Hell, don't be silly," the redheaded man said, but there was suddenly no ring of truth behind his words.

The other stared at him fixedly. "So I was right."

"Keep still about it," the redheaded man growled. "What has been done has been done, and it's too late." He shrugged. "Anyway, you and I and the rest of us here are safe. He just needed half a dozen."

"Who needed half a dozen?"

"The boss. He's got them now. All the men he needs."

"How do I know—"

"Because I tell you," the redheaded man snapped. "Now go get the dog."

"Where is—"

"In the shack. Jim left him there. He's still in the same case."

"So Jim got in from New York all right with the dog?"

"He didn't have any trouble. We could have brought the dog with us for that matter. But it was better to split up and all take different routes back, in case something went wrong." The redheaded man jerked his head impatiently. "Go on and get the dog."

The man who had asked the questions walked toward a set of ramshackle outbuildings at the far end of the meadow. The structures were what remained of a farm, after house and barn had been torn down and removed. They looked as if they had stood abandoned for years.

Doc Savage, moving fast under cover in the woods, kept abreast of the man, then put on more speed and got ahead of the fellow.

The man walked around a shed that was more substantial than the other buildings. The shed was padlocked and he fooled with the lock awhile, then picked up a rock and smashed it off the door.

Doc Savage was very close to the shed then and he went forward fast, took the man by the neck. The man made a small, squawking noise, convulsive gestures of arms and legs. Doc got him back into the shed, down on the floor.

There were certain neck nerve centers which, if subjected to experienced pressure, produced a form of unconsciousness that was like a spell. Doc finally had to use a fist to get the man quiet enough to apply the pressure in the desired spots.*

After the man was limp Doc let him lie there.

The shack was empty except for the leatherette-covered dog-carrying case which stood in a corner.

Doc went to it.

XIII

SKELETONS

Doc Savage looked into the dog case for only an instant. He closed it quickly.

His face, ordinarily expressionless, was strange. The emotion on it was stark, incredulous, with a little of revulsion and much of horror.

He made, for a time, a small trilling note that was his unconscious habit in moments of mental stress. The sound, a low and exotic thing, might have been the product of a wind in a forest of arctic ice spires, or something as unreal. Certainly, it was more strange than human. It had a quality definitely ventriloquial, seeming to come from many places far away rather than any definite spot.

The bronze man realized he was making the sound and stopped it. He looked at the case.

He wheeled and went through the pockets of the man he had made unconscious, finding a gun, some paper money, cigarettes, pocketknife, racing form, two dice, folded typewriter paper that was blank, a mechanical pencil. He examined and identified all these objects by the sense of touch, except the paper, which he removed and inspected, together with the racing form and the pencil.

With the pencil he printed a note on the paper. The note said:

---

*This method of producing unconsciousness is not new. It has several forms, all of them dangerous if used by one without experience. As an example of the fatal consequences possible, some years ago, lifeguards on the beach at a New Jersey resort were causing unconsciousness by pressure on certain neck centers of "fun." They called it "hypnotizing," which it was not. One of their victims died, which caused an unpleasant furor.

I HAVE JUST REALIZED WHAT ALL THIS IS
GOING TO LEAD TO AND I CANNOT TAKE IT.
DIVIDE MY STUFF AMONG YOU IF YOU WANT
TO.

Doc did not sign the note—not knowing the man's
name—and did not print it too skillfully.

He left the shack, kept down, gained the wood. He ran
at full speed until he reached the car containing Renny and
Willie.

"The portable chemical laboratory," Doc said. "Quick!"

The imperative haste in his voice made Renny jump.
They got out the mobile lab, an affair contained in a pair of
metal equipment cases. Monk Mayfair had designed the
portable outfit and selected the basic chemicals which it
contained, intending that they should as nearly as possible fit
all emergencies connected with their work.

Doc dug out a pair of small phials.

"If you do not hear from me," he said, "do not try to
close in on the gang for a while. I have a plan that may
work."

He left them then, running back toward the shack on the
edge of the lake.

Willie looked after him uneasily. "What's he trying to
do?"

"Holy cow, your guess is as good as mine!" Renny said.
He sounded uneasy himself. "I think, from the way he
looked, that he's getting ready to take a heck of a chance."

Willie frowned, "I don't like that."

Renny looked at her sharply. "Don't," he said, "complicate
things now by falling for him."

"If that complicates it, consider it complicated," Willie
said slowly. She sighed. "Poor Tom Lewis," she added. "I
hope he's a guy who doesn't mind losing his girl."

Back at the shack, Doc Savage saw with much relief that
he seemed to have plenty of time. The redheaded man and
the others had finished hiding the car, and were standing
around the signal fire, fully two hundred yards from the
shack, watching the column of black smoke rise from the
burning crude oil, more of which they applied from time to
time, and looking up the lake. Apparently, they expected a
boat to be coming.

Doc Savage gave the unconscious man in the shack a hypodermic dosage of the chemical in the phial which he had just secured.

He applied local anaesthetic to a spot on the man's chest, over the heart, and another spot on his back. Doc then made small cuts, not deep enough to be harmful, at both points. He made them so they would resemble the point of entrance and point of exit of a bullet.

He broke open the man's gun, a revolver, took the lead from one of the cartridges, used a little of the powder it contained to make a powder burn around a hole which he punched in the man's coat and shirt. The powder, puffing up, made an odor of burned cordite in the shack.

Doc took another look at the men about the fire. They were still there.

Because he had the time, and because he was very interested, Doc Savage opened the dog-carrying case again.

He did not let the dog out.

The dog was a skeleton, and the skeleton was alive. The skeleton moved, growled, whimpered, snarled, made all the usual dog noises.

The light in the shack was not particularly good, and it was somewhat more gloomy in the dog case. Doc moved the case so that the light was a little better, but the dog was still only a skeleton that moved, growled, snarled.

"What's the matter, pup?" Doc asked.

The skeleton growled, but it was a more friendly kind of growl. Obviously the dog that was a skeleton had the emotions of an ordinary dog. It was somewhat bad-tempered, but it had been shut up in the case for sometime.

"Come on here, pup," Doc said quietly. "Why not be friends? You hungry? Nice dog!"

The skeleton was more docile and he put a hand slowly into the cage and found ears—not ears made of bone, either—and scratched and rubbed them. There was the feel of short, stiff and curly hair. He ran his hands over the animal and knew it was an Airedale dog with flesh that was translucent—not wholly invisible, he could tell now—and a skeleton that was quite real and probably slightly, very slightly, luminous in a radioactive way, so that it was more visible than an ordinary skeleton would have been in such dim light.

Doc struck a match.

By such light, the dog was not wholly a skeleton in

aspect, but a dog that had a dog's skeleton and a dog's body; but the body was a tough, leathery substance—as genuine to the touch as a real dog—that was as translucent as a clear, gelid substance, but not as transparent as glass or plastic of the Lucite type.

It was not an invisible dog except for the skeleton. Only in poor light did it appear to be so. But anyone opening the case and seeing the dog in the half light of the case interior might readily get the idea that the dog was nothing but a living skeleton.

Doc stared, frankly horrified and amazed, at the thing until the redheaded man shouted from the other end of the meadow.

"What the hell's keeping you with that dog?" he bellowed.

Doc picked up the unconscious man's gun, put it close to the hole he had powder-stained in the coat and fired a bullet into the earth floor.

He scuffed out the bullet hole in the dirt floor with a toe.

He put the gun in the man's limp hand.

Then Doc jumped, caught a rafter, swung up and lay on a rickety platform of loose poles and boards which formed a makeshift loft.

They heard the shot and came running, the redheaded man in the lead, and piled through the shed door. There they stopped.

"Hell, he shot himself!" gasped the redheaded man.

Another pointed. "Ain't that a note?"

The redheaded man jumped, got the note. He read it. His profane ejaculation was startled.

"What's it say?" asked one of the others. "What was wrong with him?"

The note, carefully folded, went into the redheaded man's pocket. "He killed himself all right," he said. "Just was feeling low."

"No other reason?"

"None."

The redheaded man then got to his knees and felt of the wrist of the prone man. Doc Savage, watching, became tense. This was the critical point.

The chemical, which he had administered with the hypodermic needle, was intended to slow pulse and drop body temperature, but it would not fool a doctor or even anyone who had taken a good first-aid course.

"Dead as a rock," the redheaded man said, and stood up. "We can't leave the body here, though. Have to take it along and get rid of it later." He gestured. "Four of you come and get it when the boat arrives."

He indicated the four men to do the job.

The four showed no enthusiasm.

"Wait a minute," one of them said. "We walk across that meadow carrying the body? We got to reach the lake, you know."

The redheaded man shrugged. "It's your worry."

"Hell, there's fishermen and squirrel hunters in these woods and along the lake shore. Chances are they're not blind."

Doc Savage waited patiently. This was the second crisis of his little plan, the most ticklish point. He watched them and nothing happened.

"Why not bury him under the floor here?" a man asked.

Doc was shocked. That wasn't what he wanted. It would ruin all his planning.

Hastily, he said in a low voice, using a ventriloquist's delivery so that the words would seem to come from one of the group below, "Why not wrap him up in those old sacks?"

It worked and the redheaded man growled, "There's an idea. Try those sacks."

The sacks, together with some old canvas, were stacked in a corner where they had been discarded. They dug into the pile. A man held up an enormous affair of burlap and said, "This is a hell of a big gunny sack."

"That's a wool sack, simpleton," he was told.

They rolled the body in canvas and burlap and put it in the wool sack.

"Now we can carry it without anybody telling what it is," one said.

"Hell, leave it here until the boat comes!"

None of them seemed to care to wait in the shack with the body. They went outdoors, stood around talking, but not too far away.

The sun was low and the evening was close, with the light an increasing redness. The dog in the case whimpered from time to time and its whimpering was weak, as if it had not been fed for a long period.

Doc got carefully out of the little makeshift loft. He took the unconscious man out of the bundle of canvas and burlap and placed him in the loft.

Doc took his place in the wool sack. He had some trouble wrapping the canvas and burlap around him so that it would cover him thoroughly, yet let him get out in a hurry—if that was necessary.

XIV

IMMEDIATE PROBLEM

The wait was nearly an hour, and not pleasant. The unconscious man on the makeshift loft floor snored softly, which was contrary to the rules. The drug which Doc had given him was supposed to be strong enough to keep his respiration not much beyond the point of necessity, but it was not functioning properly. Also, Doc had forgotten to place the man on his side or face, so that he would be less likely to snore. Only satisfactory thing about the snoring was that it was not loud.

The boat which came had a big motor, one that sounded like an airplane. They did not stop the motor and the men came running and got the dog-carrying case and the dog, and four of them picked up Doc Savage.

"Hell, he's made of iron!" a man complained, which was alarming to Doc, whose weight was probably close to twice that of the man they thought they were carrying.

They got him in the boat, however. Placed him over a coaming and lashed him there.

"Got an anchor?" a man asked. "Why not tie it to the body and drop it overboard?"

"You sink a body like that and they always come to the top, for some reason or other," said a man who evidently had experience along that line.

The boat stuck its nose in the air, made a great deal of noise and began hitting only the tops of the waves. It ran that way for a while, not as long as Doc had somehow expected, then slowed and turned and finally rubbed against a dock.

"O.K., tie her up," someone ordered, and the hollowness of the voice indicated they were in a boathouse.

Someone accidentally gunned the boat motor while they were tying up and the craft thumped into something. There was cursing.

"I'll go see what he wants to do with the body," a man said.

They waited. A man was telling someone what had happened during the afternoon—what had occurred in Boone Shot and thereafter.

The matter of how there could be a second dog was a great mystery, they agreed. Another point on which they thought the same was that Tom Lewis would be made to explain the second dog.

A man came back.

"He says to bring the body to the house," he reported, "and put it in the basement."

They gathered around Doc, untied him, carried him to the solid footing of land.

They dropped him. Hard.

There was silence.

"Who wants to unwrap him?" someone asked.

No one volunteered.

"Ted, you do it," said the voice.

The voice that was giving the orders was a new voice. The tone was that of an older man, the manner of delivery that of a man who had given many orders in his life.

The covering was removed carefully from Doc. He did not make any movements that were quick enough to persuade them to shoot. He counted six men, four with rifles, one with a light machine gun, the other with a pitchfork.

The six did not include the man who had given the orders—the new voice.

He wore a mask, a thing that was a hood of thin silk covering his whole head. Vision and speech and breathing was possible through the gossamery fabric, but its thinness concealed the man's features except for general contour.

"Sorry about the mask," he said in the same cultured tone. "I imagine some of my associates may suspect who I am by now, but it tickles my vanity not to give them the satisfaction of knowing they are right."

Doc examined the man's hands, such of his neck skin as was visible, and decided his age was somewhere around thirty, according to those clues. That was a little deceptive because the voice sounded older, more polished and trained, with the hoarser undertones in it that come with age.

"You see," said the man, "that you didn't fool us."

He seemed to expect an answer, got none, and scowled.

"They found the man you drugged lying in the loft of the shack," the man snapped. "Or are you curious about how you were discovered?"

Doc was silent.

In an increasingly irritated voice the man said, "Take his clothes. Then take him up to the house."

They removed Doc's garments—and the gadgets he always carried in them—and gave him a strip of canvas for clothing.

Then they moved up a hill, following a pleasant path through oak and elm trees on which wild grape vines entwined. The sun was behind the distant hills, and all the light that showed was very dull red. The twilight had been a very long one because of the height of the hills; the sun got behind the hills and then it was a long time until complete darkness.

This was an island. It was small, not more than three or four acres. It stood in the lake, which was not a natural lake, but one made by the construction of a hydroelectric dam. A strip of gravel that had once been a main road cut up over the side of the hump that was the island, and beside this, where it had been built thirty years or so ago, stood the house.

The house was a great old castle of an affair, made of wood and stone, forty or fifty rooms, a grand place with the splendor of the Gay Nineties still intact. It was preserved, for an old house; a show place built here in the hills, a family mansion left isolated on this island by the building of the lake, but kept in a state of good repair.

They went inside. The man with the thin silk sack over his head stepped to a shelf. He put his gun, a flat automatic, on the shelf.

"Leave your guns here. Leave any sizeable metal objects here," he told his men. "There is delicate electromagnetic apparatus in the laboratory which will be upset by any metal coming in its neighborhood. So leave your guns, please. There are enough of you to handle Savage barehanded."

The men weren't too happy about the order. There was some hesitating. "Go ahead!" the hooded man snapped. They complied then.

They walked through a small room, down a flight of stairs into a basement.

The basement was not a laboratory.

Half a dozen grotesque, unbelievable men with skull faces and revolvers stood in the room.

They pointed the guns at the new arrivals.

"All right," said the masked man to the newcomers. "Sorry to shock you boys, but you are going to join the experiment."

Shock and disbelief gripped the basement room in the shape of a frozen, unbreathing silence.

Doc Savage, standing motionless, watched the half dozen men who were like the dog. These men were dressed and all of them wore gloves or had cloth tied around their hands. The significance of the cloth and gloves was pitiful, frightening, for it showed a sickening wish not to see their own hands.

Two of them had bandaged their heads to hide the horror of the semitransparent, translucent flesh which actually let the bone structure show through. In the half light of the basement there seemed to be no flesh, only a cloudy substance around the bonework.

The degree of translucence which affected each man was not the same. Two of them were much less frightening than the others, one of these almost approaching normal. But whatever had happened to them it had happened to all six.

The redheaded man got words loose from his throat, said, "Join the experiment—what do you mean?"

The masked man had stepped back from them. He told the translucent men with the guns, "Watch them. If they make a move, shoot them!"

"What kind of a double cross is this?" screamed the redheaded man.

"I need more subjects for experiment," said the masked man grimly. "You are elected."

"You mean you're gonna try that stuff on me?"

"Right."

"But you said—"

"I said," snapped the other, his words blowing the thin silk out from his face explosively, "that I had hired you men to help in this. All right, you are going to help."

The redheaded man stepped forward. "You told me that I'd be an exception."

"I've changed my mind."

One of the redheaded man's crew now hit the red-headed man a fist blow into which he put everything he had. The victim's red hair flew up like grass from the impact and he fell stiffly, not making a sound during or after his fall. "Lousy two-face," said the man who had hit him, bitterly.

The man who wore the silk hood said, "If anyone else moves, shoot him."

No one stirred.

"Bring Savage," the man said, "into the living room."

The living room was a pleasant place furnished with the elaborate furniture of forty years or more ago. Doc revised his estimate of the age of the house a little. Probably it was fifty years old. Some of the furniture was that old as well, but wonderfully preserved.

He was placed in a straight-backed chair.

The man in the silk mask poured a glass of wine. "It is good wine," he said. "Not drugged, I assure you. Will you join me?"

Doc Savage said nothing.

The other shrugged. "I understand you are a man of resources," he said. "So I want to point out that you have a chance of coming out of this thing alive, and of also contributing a great service to mankind, if you do as you are told. The alternative, of course, is that you will become a strange-disappearance case. I believe I can hide your body so that it will not be found."

Doc watched him silently.

"I am going to give you," said the man, "the same explanation I have given the others."

"Why?" Doc asked bluntly.

The other shrugged. "Call it easing my conscience, if you wish."

He took a comfortable chair.

"The war," he said, "is responsible for this. The war has had a momentous and weird effect on many people, but probably it has affected no one more deeply than myself. It did a strange thing for me. It made me into a patriot of the most zealous order."

Doc said quietly, "It would be hard to find any patriotism in this thing so far."

"Before the war," the man continued, ignoring the remark,

"I was a placid, successful man with a family I loved. It was strange about my family. I didn't know how much I really loved them. I had two sons. My wife died several years ago, peacefully."

His hands tightened visibly on the chair arms. "Two sons. They were drafted. They were killed in action."

There was a tall grandfather clock, ticking rheumatically, between the two high windows. Beyond the windows, now, there was darkness.

"Killed in action," he said. "That was what the telegram said. And then the story came out. They had starved to death."

The man got up suddenly, walked to the window, jerked the curtains shut. He came back and sat down. During the whole move he had traveled at a near run without seeming to be aware that he was hurrying.

"Starvation is not a bad death, so they say," he continued. "Perhaps I would have been affected no more than any father who had lost his only two sons—but then, I saw the pictures."

His voice climbed shrilly. "Pictures of the bodies of my two sons, after they had starved. Pictures taken by a signal corps man and sent to me because the signal corps man had once worked for me and been fired, and hated me. I guess he sent the pictures for revenge. They were horrible. I remember that I looked at them, and looked at them, and then two days later I awakened and there were doctors there and they said I had suffered a terrible shock."

He was silent awhile, apparently controlling himself. He opened and closed his hands.

"Starvation," he said. "So I gave up everything, the presidency of my company, everything, to work out a means of making soldiers so they would not need food. I believed I could do this, and no more soldiers would starve, and the American army would be free of the enormous job of bringing supplies up to the front. But the main thing was that no more boys would starve."

Doc Savage's flake-gold eyes were expressionless, but he said, "A thing like that would take great technical and scientific experience."

"I had it."

"Enough?"

"You do not understand. I told you I was the president of

company. But I was more than that. I am a chemist specializing in plastics, and have been for many years. No one knows my ability, for a simple and mercenary reason."

He scowled. "My company," he said, "has the usual system of corporations—it lays claim to all patents and discoveries made by its employees while working for it. I did not own the company; I was only its president, at a salary.

"So I did what any human being would do—I did my research work under another name and sold my own discoveries to the company of which I was president. Perhaps that was crooked. I think not. I did the work in my spare time, paying for my own materials, and I think I was entitled to what I got. I certainly sold my discoveries in plastic cheap enough."

He looked at Doc Savage levelly.

"It is too bad you got into this," he said. "I perfected, or nearly perfected, my treatment to eliminate the need of food for a long interval of time. I made a test on a dog. It was successful. I needed a human being. So I selected a man I did not like, a salesman named Tom Lewis. I paid him a large sum of money and he agreed to be the human experimental subject. But Tom Lewis changed his mind."

The man spread his hands wearily. "Tom Lewis became scared of me—unnecessarily, I think, although I did fly into a great rage when he refused.

"Tom Lewis stole my experimental dog and headed for New York to get your help. That meant I had to stop him. So I hurriedly engaged a group of men whom I had contacted against such an emergency and sent them after him."

"The men in the basement?"

"Right. You know what happened after they started pursuing Tom Lewis to New York. They got him and they got the dog. But you got on their trail, and here you are."

Doc watched him for a moment.

"Plastics?" Doc asked.

"Yes, as I told you—"

"Plastics," Doc said, "are used in modern radio cabinets, are they not?"

"What you really mean: Is there a connection between the Admiration Radio Cabinet Co. and myself?"

"Is there?"

"I am Walter Buxton," the man said, "president of the Admiration concern."

*　　*　　*

The man stood up then and produced his gun. "Thi ends the explanation, and I think it is enough to take care c my conscience nicely."

"You are going to try your no-food stuff on me?"

"Exactly. On you and the others."

Doc Savage shook his head slowly, a gesture which ha more understanding than negative or protest meaning. "S the stuff is not successful."

"It will be," the other said grimly.

"With more than fifteen human subjects, I can work ou the bugs."

"You are going to make all of us like . . . like those mer with the guns in the basement?"

The other nodded. "Would you like to know why thos men with the guns are now helping me?"

"You evidently have a hold on them."

"That's right. Unless they play along with me they wil eventually die, or at least will not become normal. But I car make them normal. I am going to do it if they cooperate wit me. Otherwise"—he shrugged—"they will die or continue t look like skeletons."

"But—"

The man in the mask cocked his gun, the small automat ic hammer clicking audibly when he pulled it back.

"You will be the next subject for the material," he said "You will kindly walk ahead of me."

XV

THE SKELETON TREATMENT

Ham Brooks had been listening to a campaign con ducted by Willie. The campaign was to the effect tha they had better be doing something; that they had waite long enough. Ham privately agreed with her and he calle together Johnny, Long Tom and Renny, and they had conference.

"Nobody has seen a sign of Doc Savage," Willie pointe out, "since that shot was heard this afternoon. What kind of gang of assistants are you, anyway?"

Ham and the others, without saying so, had resented the waiting as much as anyone.

Long Tom asked Willie, "You going to take the responsibility of going ahead, when Doc's orders were not to interfere?"

"I'll take the blame, if any," Willie said promptly.

Renny told Long Tom, "If you think passing the buck to her will make it O. K. with Doc, if we bungle something, you've got another guess."

Long Tom grimaced.

"It gives us an excuse, anyway," he said. "Maybe we can make Doc think she vamped us, or something."

"I wouldn't waste time vamping you," Willie told Long Tom disagreeably. "You've been a sour pickle right from the beginning. What do you get out of life, anyway?"

"I get freedom from the worries women cause you," Long Tom told her. "Come on. Let's see what goes on."

They worked down to the shore of the lake, using care. They had seen the speedboat arrive and depart at dusk, but they had no means of telling whether all the gang had departed.

Eventually, they approached the old shack and the other outbuildings at the edge of the meadow. With much caution they investigated.

"Holy cow!" Renny rumbled suddenly. "Come here!"

The others hurried toward the astonished engineer's booming voice.

"Look," Renny said.

They stared at the forms on the floor of the shack.

"Four bodies," Ham said wonderingly. "Say, they're four of the gang who got Monk away from me in that Brooklyn park."

Willie had turned white.

"Are they dead?" she asked.

The bodies were sprawled in grotesque positions on the floor, but there was no blood and not much sign of death in their faces, something that Renny and the others overlooked in the excitement of the discovery.

The four bodies sat up and produced guns and said—one of them—in excited urgency, "Stand still or you'll get your heads blowed off!"

Long Tom, in a very disagreeable I-told-you-so voice, told Willie, "See what we get by following a woman's advice?"

* * *

Long Tom's disagreeable accusation directed at Willie
was not as misleading as he had hoped it would be because
when he simultaneously kicked at the gun arm of the nearest
enemy, the fellow had already dodged back. Long Tom missed
with his kick and was shot in the chest where, fortunately, his
bullet-proof vest offered the best protection.

The bullet force turned him over once, neatly, and
started him in a spell of coughing that did not stop until an
avalanche of men on his back jammed all the breath out of
him.

That was about all the resistance. Renny knocked a man
down and was knocked down instantly himself by a man with
a rifle who stepped out of the darkness behind them.

"All right, strip and use what's left of these gunny sacks
and canvas for clothes," someone said.

"Hey," Willie said, "there's a lady present!"

Someone laughed then took her outside.

Walking down to the lake shore, Ham and Johnny and
Long Tom and Renny felt ridiculous and futile in their skirts
of burlap or canvas.

Willie said, "You know, if it wasn't so darned serious I
could laugh until I fell over at you fellows."

Long Tom seemed to find this the first thing she had said
which did not offend him. He glanced at her admiringly, said,
"I hope you've got as much nerve as you act like."

"I told you I was in show business," Willie said.

"What's show business got to do with it?"

"It," said Willie, "is all nerve."

Their captors were using flashlights now. They signaled
for a while, got an answer from out on the lake. A boat came
in, moving rapidly, and swung in close to the beach but did
not ground.

Everyone waded out and climbed into the craft, which
was piloted by a young man in a sweater, who said, "This
about rounds it up, don't it?"

No one answered him. The boat got in motion. It was
fast, threw a considerable bone of spray, rocked and bounced.

They came to the island, after not more than two miles,
and swung into the boathouse. The crew tied up the boat, got
the prisoners out.

"How many?" asked a quiet, controlled voice.

"Four."

"That is good. That is all of them."

Of the voice, Ham muttered, "There is a guy who has done a lot of talking in his time."

They were marched up the hill, along the gravel road that had been a highway before the making of the lake, and into the tall, turreted, old-fashioned house.

"Take them downstairs," said the controlled voice. "But leave your guns on that shelf, so the steel will not affect the magnetic apparatus in the laboratory."

They could see the speaker, a tall, somber figure with his head incased in a silk bag.

The captors fell for the guns-on-the-shelf gag like, as Renny expressed it later, the pins in a bowling alley.

And then translucent men were suddenly around all of them with guns and menacing them.

Willie looked at the faces of the translucent men. She did what the others felt much like doing—screamed at the top of her voice and put both hands over her eyes.

The cellar room into which Willie, Ham, Long Tom, Johnny and Renny were crowded was utterly black and dank, smelled of confined air, and another odor definitely not pleasant. The place was dark, and light did not chance to get into the place as they were forced inside. The door, heavy and of wood, grunted shut behind them, and there was a rattling and thumping of the bar.

Johnny sank to a knee and felt of the soft stuff on the floor.

"A subterranean repertorium," he announced.

"This is no time," said Ham sourly, "for your words."

A strangled noise had come from a corner. It came again. It turned into words.

"Take away my head and call me speechless," it said.

"Monk!" Ham squalled.

Ham plunged around in the darkness and found Monk and began beating on him ecstatically.

Monk beat him back awhile, then said, "Watch out or you'll smash these half-rotten turnips. This place is a root cellar."

"Are you all right?" Ham demanded.

"Hell, no! We're locked up in here and they're going to give us—"

"Have they hurt you?"

"My feelings, plenty!" Monk said. "And some guy hit me

with a wagon spoke or something back in that park i
Brooklyn, and they've walked my frame a time or two sinc
then. How did you guys trail them back here? They figure
they had covered up everything."

Ham told him, "Doc invented another dog, let the new
get out, and they came to investigate. We got on their trail."

"Oh, you found out what that dog was?" Monk asked.

"No. What is it?"

"The head guy here," Monk explained, "thinks he i
right on the verge of inventing something to enable soldier
to do without food. He tried it out on the dog. It makes th
flesh get pale, and then lose all color, and then become kin
of translucent, like plastic or jelly or whatever you want t
call it. That's what ailed the dog."

Ham shuddered. "And those men we saw when we cam
here."

"That's right. How many men were that way?"

"About a half dozen."

"I gather," Monk said, "that they're all going to be mad
that way."

Willie, in a horrified voice, asked, "They will becom
that way willingly?"

Monk laughed grimly. "Not willingly."

"Then—"

"The first half dozen," Monk said, "were caught b
surprise, drugged and given the treatment. That was whil
the others were out investigating the false-dog alarm you
folks stirred up."

"But—"

"And now," Monk added, "the half dozen have to forc
the others to take it, or the head guy will refuse to give then
the treatment that will bring them back to normal. They're
going to do it to us—and to Doc."

Renny rumbled, "They've got Doc?"

"Sure have," Monk said. "I haven't seen him. But they've
got him."

Johnny Littlejohn had been moving around the dan
chamber, feeling of the walls. Now he stumbled over some
thing and fell into a soft mess of semidecayed vegetables up
to his elbows. "I'll be superamalgamated!" he gasped. "Ugh!"

Then Johnny roared, "Who's this? Here's somebody!"

The figure over which Johnny had stumbled groaned a
little. The groan was a man's voice.

"Oh, him," Monk said. "He's the chemist who worked out the no-food stuff in the first place."

Somewhere in the house a low rumbling started and became the noise of a heavy motor. As it accelerated there was a background of deep-throated whining that also increased.

"Diesel motor and generator," Monk explained. "That means they're warming up the apparatus that will turn us into translucent men. They use electricity and chemicals both in the treatment." He sighed. "I'd sure like to know more about the method. They produce an electro-chemical change in everything but the bony structure of the body."

"What," yelled Johnny, "about this man on the floor?"

"Oh, this house belongs to him," Monk explained. "He is a famous chemist. Been inventing plastics and selling them to the radio company of which he's president. Had two sons starve to death in the Aleutians in this war, and that got him unbalanced on this no-food thing."

"What's he doing here?" Johnny bellowed.

"He was," Monk explained, "robbed of his discovery by a very clever guy who saw the possibilities of the thing."

Willie spoke quietly, asking, "The guy with his head in the silk bag?"

"That's right."

Willie said nothing more.

The man on the floor said in a weak voice. "I must tell you people how it works. Some of you may escape and you can give the secret to scientists who can finish it out and make it practical."

He had trouble talking, had to catch his breath frequently.

"Human muscle," he continued, "is three-fourths water, as you know if you studied physiology at all. Its fiber contents are semifluid and can be forced out as muscle plasma by pressure, leaving a residue of sarcolemma, connective tissue, keratin, mucin, nuclein, and so on.

"You may also know that muscle in fatigue, or rigor, has turned acid, principally lactic acid. It was discovered by Fletcher and Hopkins as early as 1907 that the formation of lactic could be diminished or even prevented by sufficient oxygen. Later it was found that lactic is removed by resynthesis to a precursor, although not much is actually known about it. It is certain, though, that glycogen, a carbohydrate, is necessary for the restoration of activity to a fatigued muscle.

"What I did was affect a chemical substitute for glycogen, combined with a method of creating a static condition in the tissue which is unsympathetic to the formation of toxic lactic, the accumulation of which is fatigue. Now, listen closely and memorize these formulas."

He gave them complicated chemical terms, repeating each several times.*

Willie spoke in the darkness. "I think I have met you," she said.

The man on the floor asked, "You are Miss Stevens, are you not? I do not forget people."

"That's right, but call me Willie," Willie said. "This is a terrible thing to happen to you, Mr. Buxton."

"Buxton!" Johnny barked.

"Walter Buxton, president of the Admiration Radio Cabinet Co.," Monk told them.

"Who in blazes," demanded Renny, "is the guy with the silk sack over his head?"

A voice from the door told them, "Quit worrying about little things, you guys, and come out of there. We're going to give you the treatment now. Get moving."

XVI

FROM BEHIND SILK

The laboratory was a big room made more cavernlike by the lighting system, which was seven sputtering, wavering candles stuck in their own wax on pieces of furniture here and there.

"Keep the electric lights off," said the man with the silk

---

*It has long been the policy of the author not to give exact chemical formulae which might be dangerous in unskilled use. The complexity of modern chemical science is such that it has become like a loaded machine gun—nothing to fool around with unless you know what you are doing. However, much scientific work has been done along these lines, and marvelous progress has been made in the field of blood plasma. It has been discovered that blood plasma—the fluid that carries the blood cells through the body—can be preserved for years, then injected into the blood streams of wounded or injured persons with excellent effect. These are the "blood banks" so widely mentioned during the current war.—Author.

bag over his head. "We need all the current and no magnetic interference from the house wiring."

The prisoners stared at the apparatus, and they were a little disappointed. There was nothing but a tank, a glass tank, full of sour-looking green liquid and a few electrodes. Nearby was a table on which chemicals stood, but these looked no more impressive than an amateur photographer's darkroom array.

They had rigged a strait jacket out of a two-by-twelve-inch plank and some rope. That was for the unwilling victims while they were being treated.

There were nine men with translucent faces and gloves. Over half of them had small machine guns and the others had revolvers and pistols.

Those who were to get the treatment made up fully as large a crowd and no one looked happy.

Doc Savage was not in evidence.

The man in the silk hood stood before them.

"I want to make a little speech," he said.

Nobody getting ready to make a speech ever got more silence or more attention.

"I want," he said, "to point out a fact. I want to point it out so that every one of you will get it in his head and understand just what it means."

He stood in the darker end of the room and his voice was deeply timbred, but somehow artificial-sounding.

"There is no sense in going into an elaborate, scientific explanation of what happens to your bodies when you get this treatment. It is a system for the prevention of fatigue, which is chemically the formation of lactic acid. The preventing is done by introducing into your muscular tissue a substitute for glycogen, a carbohydrate which affects the restoration of activity to fatigued muscles, and also producing a static status of tissue which is unsympathetic to the formation of any fatigue toxic."

He let them listen with bated breath for a while.

"The fact," he said, "is that none of you will recover, or will live very long if I am killed."

He let that soak in.

"Important fact, isn't it?" he said dryly. "Good life insurance for me, wouldn't you say?"

"The scientific reason for this, in broad terms which you will understand, is simple. First, you would not be happy as you are. You are not exactly running skeletons, but you are pretty sickening sights. That is the first reason. The second one is that nature is a strict mistress. You do not upset the balance of nature without paying for it. There are simple laws. Anything that goes up must come down—as simple as that. What this no-food treatment does to your bodies is against all the laws of nature. Everything gets tired. That is a natural law. But you do not get tired, so there is a penalty. The penalty in your case happens to be death."

Again he waited.

"I can give you treatment," he said, "that will make your bodies normal."

Someone's teeth clattered audibly.

"Remember—I can keep you alive," he repeated.

He stepped over into better light.

"I am going to unmask," he said. "I want you to stand and look at me, every one of you, for thirty seconds. Understand! Look at me thirty seconds, and think about the consequences before you do a thing. In that thirty seconds remember I, alone, can keep you alive."

He gave them plenty of time to comprehend that and mull it over.

He pulled the sack mask off his head and showed them that he was Doc Savage.

They stood there awhile—but not thirty seconds. Shock held all of them for a moment. Then they reacted as differently as any undisciplined group which had lost all leadership.

Monk and Ham and Renny came out of it first because they had half known, in the last minute or two, that this must be Doc. They started walking toward the translucent men who had the guns, going slowly but purposefully.

Then a man—not a translucent man—made a break for the door.

One of the translucent men switched a machine gun toward him, but came down on the firing lever of the weapon too quick. The gun ripped at everyone's eardrums with its clamor, took great gouts of plaster and lath out of the ceiling.

What happened then was entirely a product of strain and collapsed horror.

The room was suddenly a fighting mêlée. Some tried to get at the translucent men. The latter fought for their lives. Others just tried to flee, and men tried to stop them.

Two machine guns blasted out. Doc got to one of them, stopped it. Ham and Monk had hold of the other one and got it; and somehow did not recognize each other and struggled for the weapon, kicking and yelling. They got each other down on the floor before recognition and sense came to them; after which they just sat there and looked at each other foolishly, as if hypnotized.

The man who had broken for the door was down, ripped badly by the first machine gun that had started.

Doc waded through the translucent men, grabbing weapons, shouting orders to stop fighting, but even his powerful voice had no effect on the uproar.

A tall man took out across the room at full speed and ran through the window without even a falter in stride. The glass and wooden parts of the window sash showered down.

Wind came in through the smashed window and blew out the candles, making the place completely black.

Doc Savage spoke in Mayan, a little-known language which he and his aids used when they did not wish to be understood by others.

"Just lie down on the floor," he said, "and let them get it out of their systems."

"What," asked Monk in Mayan, "about the boats? Can't they escape from the island in them?"

"I disabled the boats," Doc said.

"Did you," asked Monk, still in Mayan, "disable the guy who was wearing the silk sack in the first place?"

"Only temporarily," Doc explained. "He is upstairs in the attic, and in fairly good shape, providing none of these machine-gun bullets have gone through the ceilings and hit him."

Eventually, there was peace.

Doc went out into the night and did some shouting. He came back into the house and said, "Come daylight and we will get them all rounded up without trouble. The translucent men are going to help."

Renny asked, "Can you cure them of what ails them?"

"Yes. It should be simple," Doc said.

"Sure?"

"I have conducted experiments with this stuff myself," Doc told him. "That was about a year ago."

Renny thought that over.

"Holy cow!" he said. "That means it won't work, huh? Buxton's stuff won't substitute for food and eliminate fatigue?"

"Not successfully," Doc said. "That is going to be quite a shock to him. His motives in this thing were good, you know. Nothing like this would have happened if he had not revealed the secret to a man he thought was honest, but who turned out to be a crook."

"Meaning the guy in the attic?"

"Yes."

Willie said in a voice remarkably subdued for her, "I guess my hunch about Tom Lewis being a crook at heart was right."

No one said anything.

"Tom Lewis is the man upstairs, isn't he?" Willie asked.

"Yes," Doc said.

"Look, don't get any long faces over me," she said. "Remember those pictures I told you I used to stick on my wall? Well, I can put them back up again."

Which made Doc feel somewhat alarmed.

THE ANGRY CANARY

I

The cage was there on one of the shelves in the package check-room at four o'clock when the two men on the night shift came to work.

It did not at that time bear much resemblance to a canary cage, because it was wrapped in coarse brown paper and tied around with string. Some expertness with knots had gone into the way the string was tied. That is, the knots were not conventional granny knots.

The two check-room attendants were pleasant fellows. Fred Lill, fiftyish, lived in Brooklyn and had a son studying at Columbia to become a doctor. Jim Presse, younger, unmarried, had grown up on an Iowa farm. Actually, though, the only important part Fred and Jim took in the matter was when Fred tore a bit of the paper loose from the cage. He did this as an act of misguided kindness.

This happened after six. The hours of four to six were peak rush for the check-room, as steel-souled Manhattan hurriedly emptied itself of office workers, and quite a few of these picked up packages or week-end or overnight cases. About six, the pressure eased, both men fired up cigarettes, and Fred walked back along Tier Seven and cocked his head at the paper-wrapped cage. Fred's interest was bird-like. Owlish, because he was a fat man.

"Hell of a lot of scratching around going on in there," Fred remarked.

"Canary cage, isn't it?" Jim wasn't too interested.

"Guess so. Looks like it." Fred frowned, and added, "Poor birds are probably smothering in there. Some people are sure careless." And on impulse, he poked a finger against the paper, broke it, and peeled a piece loose.

Jim asked, "What'd you do that for? Now somebody'll complain about the paper being torn." He came over and glanced at the cage, but with no interest. "There was probably holes in the bottom for ventilation." He bent down and looked. "Sure. A couple of holes."

"Black paper under the brown," Fred said, pointing. He was surprised. "Why wrap it in black paper, then put brown over that?"

Jim shrugged. "I don't know nothing about canaries. Maybe they're like chickens. Sit still and roost when they're in the dark. Or is it canaries in there?"

A shrill tittering came from the cage.

"I never heard a canary make a noise like that," Fred muttered. He leaned down and put an eye to the hole he'd made. "Yeah, canaries. Two of them—" He stopped on a rather shocked note.

"Sounded like the canary giggled," Jim remarked. "But like I said, what I don't know about the things is plenty, and anyway it's none of our business—say, what's the matter with you?"

Fred was distressed. "They're fighting!"

"Yeah?"

Slapping a hand against the cage, Fred said, "Here, here, stop that!" He jiggled the cage around. "They won't stop!"

"Aw, the cage was probably wrapped that way to keep it dark so they wouldn't scrap," said Jim indifferently. "Cover up the hole, and they'll be all right. They'll settle down."

Fred followed the suggestion quickly. He was upset. "I never saw anything like that—such hate. Such viciousness." He stepped back from the cage. "I wish to God I hadn't messed with it."

Jim laughed. "Why get worked up about a couple of birds pecking each other a time or two?"

But Fred was distressed and puzzled. "We keep three canaries at home," he muttered. "They never act like that." He shook his head, adding, "It isn't a natural way to act."

"I can say the same thing about some people," Jim said.

Both check-room attendants noticed the man named Plott before he indicated any intention of approaching the checking concession. He was not anyone they had seen before, and they came to know him as Plott only because that was the name he presently gave them.

"Hey, Fred," Jim said.

"Eh?"

"Day in and day out, a lot of funny-looking people pass here," said Jim softly. "But take a look at that skeezicks yonder. The one over by the newsstand."

Fred studied the individual. "I see what you mean." Then he added, "He seems to be heading this way."

The man was of average height, but there his claim to the average began and ended. He had perfectly white hair which seemed to grow forward-pointing on his head instead of backward, his skin was the rich hue of diluted gold, or of knotty pine, and he was thinner than a healthy man had a right to be. His eyes were large, bulbous and almost transparent. Should these oddities escape note, he wore a green suit of a shade hitherto unheard of, and a yellow shirt about equally as preposterous.

"Wow! And I thought fire engines were gaudy," Jim whispered. He sauntered over to the counter, asking the man, "What'll it be, pal?"

The man spoke English so precise it couldn't be his mother-tongue.

"I deposited a package for safekeeping earlier in the day," he said. "Unfortunately, I seem to have mislaid the small ticket which I am supposed to present to reclaim my property. I should like to obtain the article, however."

"Sorry." Jim shook his head. "You'll have to have your claim-check to do business here, mister."

The man looked at them. His eyes were like glass bulbs containing slightly soiled water. "Oh, luckily, I can perfectly describe package and contents. That should serve, shouldn't it?"

"No tickee, no washee," said Jim.

"I beg pardon?"

"Just an old American catch phrase, like showing your claim-check if you want your package," Jim told him curtly.

The man looked at Jim in a way that gave the latter a somewhat creepy sensation. "But I can tell you my name. It is Plott. Mr. Plott." He did not smile. As a matter of fact he did not smile at any time, as if he was physically incapable of doing so. "My item of property consists of a canary cage. I can, if you insist, describe the birds inside, even to their age and sex."

Jim felt a strong urge to be rid of the fellow, and he said,

"Look, to save a long argument, I can tell you that you won't get to first base with us. We have rules to follow. If you want your package without a claim-check, you'll have to see the boss-man about it."

"Boss-man? You mean someone of higher authority?"

"Yeah. Buck Fineberg. See him. He's in the main check-stand on the upper level, north end. Go see Buck, and he'll take care of it."

The odd man had been kneading his thin hands together during the discussion, and now there was a greenback in his facile fingers. Mysteriously, too; where it had come from would be hard to say.

"Conceivably, there could be an alternative?" he asked.

Jim looked at the bill.

"Inconceivable!" he said curtly.

The odd man bent his head slightly. "Then I shall consult with your Mr. Buck Fineberg." He turned and went away.

Fred moved up beside Jim and breathed hoarsely. "Didn't you notice he had a double sawbuck?"

"Jobs these days," said Jim angrily, "are worth more than twenty bucks."

Fred grinned and said, "That's right, boy. That's sure right." He went back and stood looking at the canary cage and listening.

Jim called, "Them birds still going at it?"

"I'm afraid so," Fred said. "I can't understand it, either."

The second one who didn't have a claim-check was a girl. Not a gloriously lovely girl, and not a homely one either, although there was some reason to believe she might have taken pains to make herself non-distinctive. Her dull grey coat was shapeless, but she clearly wasn't, and her seal-brown hair drawn back from her forehead as straight as strings didn't have the aspect of always being worn that way. No rouge, no powder, nothing extra at the eyes. And she, too, wanted the canaries.

She smiled a nice enough smile. "I know people who've mislaid their claim-checks must be an awful nuisance, but I haven't mine. I have a package here, though. Now, how do I go about getting it?"

Jim liked this one, and he said temporizingly, "Well, now, that's a tough break, isn't it?"

Fred happened to have overheard. "No check, no package," he said bluntly.

Jim wheeled and frowned at him, so Fred shrugged and moved away. Jim grinned at the girl. "Fred's an old grouch. A nice guy, but an old-timer who's heaved too many satchels around in here." He leaned forward confidentially. "I'd sure like to help you, Miss—"

"Meg," said the girl promptly. "Margaret, I mean. Miss Margaret Prince. And I would certainly like to pick up my package without causing a lot of bother."

"I'd like to have your address, too, for our files," Jim said cunningly. "And your telephone number."

Margaret Prince hesitated. "Well, all right. It's East Barent Avenue. 1233 East Barent. The telephone is Barentwood 9-7600."

"Fine, fine. Now could you describe your package?" Jim asked. And his eyes bugged slightly as he listened to the girl say, "Yes, of course. It's a canary cage wrapped in brown paper and tied around with string. There are two canaries inside. They are named Jim and Joe."

Jim grinned foolishly. "Well, my name's Jim, too," he said. After a moment of confusion, he asserted, "I'll go back and have a look for it." He sauntered to the rear, found Fred, and told him, "This one's after the canaries too."

Fred scowled. "Going to give them to her?"

"I'd rather she had them than old queer-eyes," said Jim dryly. "But the answer is, hell no."

The girl listened to Jim with a little frown of disappointment when he came back. She said, "You say I'm to see a Mr. Buck Fineberg? Very well. But I did hope it wouldn't be necessary to bother a lot of people, just because I lost my claim-check."

Jim looked at her steadily, and told her a lie. "I think Buck was on duty here this morning when you probably left the package," he said.

"Oh, good! Maybe he'll remember me, and that will save a lot of explaining," she said happily.

Jim was nonplussed, a little ashamed of himself, and he passed the buck to Fred, saying, "I'd let you have it, only old sourpuss"—he jerked his head toward the rear, where Fred was—"doesn't like the idea. You know how it is. I gotta get along with the guy."

"I understand," said Miss Margaret Prince, and she walked away.

"Between the two," Jim told Fred, "I think the babe was straight goods. She looked all right to me."

"They mostly all do—to you," said Fred.

"Hell, I lied and said Buck was in here when she left the package, just to see what her reaction would be. And she seemed pleased, and hoped he'd remember her. Does that sound like she's a sharper?"

"It sounds," said the more experienced Fred, "about like a woman would sound when she was making a fool out of a guy with a bushy tail like yours."

"Yah. Nuts." Jim jerked his head. "How the canaries getting along?"

"They're still fighting."

"In the dark."

"Yes, in the dark. They haven't let up an instant. It's incredible."

"What's so incredible about a fight? I mean, almost everybody and everything is equipped to do a little fighting. That's why moose have horns."

"I don't think canaries ever fight in the dark," Fred said. "Mine never have, anyway. And I've never seen anything like this hate, unadulterated hate, which these birds manifest."

"The way you're talking, I'm beginning to feel funny about this," Jim said.

"I feel that way when I look at those hate-crazed birds."

Jim went into the back, picked up the telephone and got himself connected with the larger check-room on the upper level of Grand Central, where supervisor Buck Fineberg presided. Jim spoke with Buck for a few minutes, then hung up. "Hey, Fred, old scare-face never showed up to ask Buck for the package. What do you think of that?"

"I'm not surprised."

"Nor the girl either."

"I'm still not surprised."

Grabbing up the telephone again, Jim dialed the number which Margaret Prince had given him as her own. Upon receiving an answer, he asked boldly for Miss Prince, and the reply he received made an interesting study on his face for Fred to watch.

"Well?" asked Fred.

"It was the precinct Police Station," said Jim sheepishly. "They don't know any Miss Prince."

Twenty minutes later, Fred called thickly, "Jim, come here."

Jim hurried to Fred's side. "What's the matter now?" He saw that Fred was staring at the canary cage sickly.

"One bird is dead," Fred said.

"Huh?"

"Dead. The other bird killed it."

Jim shrugged. "Yeah? Well, that ought to quiet things down on the old homestead."

Grimacing, Fred said, "Oh, don't be so cold-blooded. If you had seen the poor little things showing such malevolent hate, you wouldn't be so smart about it."

But the other man was getting tired of the whole subject of canaries. He spoke his mind on the matter. "Oh hell, get it off your mind. Two birds get to fighting in a cage, and there's a winner. So what? So if you don't blatt out that you opened up the paper in the first place so they could get a look at each other and start operations, there's nothing to it. Forget the whole thing."

Fred was peering into the cage. "Hate," he murmured. "I never saw such anger and hate in a bird. I didn't know a canary could show such a thing."

"Oh, shut up," said Jim. "You and your angry canary!"

II

The possession of a reputation had long ago saddled Doc Savage with a few handicaps. Out of somewhere near a hundred and forty million U. S. inhabitants, not each one had heard of Doc Savage, but the percentage who had was respectable. Impressive, too, considering the care which Doc had taken to avoid publicity, or at least notoriety. Since the scientific genius of the man, his startling physical ability, and his unusual Galahad-like occupation of righting wrongs and punishing evildoers, was not unknown in quite a few odd corners of the world, perhaps the total terrestrial population of around two billion two hundred million should be consid-

ered in the percentage table. The point was, that out of a
number like that, there were sure to be screwballs to make
life irritating.

Doc Savage's work, the righting of wrongs and punishing
of evildoers whom the normal fingers of law enforcement did
not seem to be able to grasp and crush, was itself enough
out of place in a currently war-cynical and distrustful civiliza-
tion to make it a subject of disbelief, and on the tongues of
the ignorant or disillusioned, of ridicule. That sort of thing
perhaps had been believable in the days of Galahad, but it
had become as unfashionable as tin pants, rescuing damsels
in distress, and knighthood in general.

In plain words, the gag had been worked to death.
Charlatans had used it. Too many politicians had instigated
wars to save humanity, until it was becoming pretty clear that
what the world needed was saving from the leaders who were
continually getting control of the masses. The world was
getting wiser, or at least more cynical, about the whole saving
business with its iron curtains and goose-stepping. Do-gooding
was out of style these days. A guy was supposed to have an
angle. And if the angle wasn't at once apparent, the thing to
do was be disbelieving and hold an air of ridicule.

Doc Savage's "angle" wasn't apparent, and for a pretty
good reason. He didn't have one. He did good, righted
wrongs, punished evildoers, did scientific work so completely
for the benefit of humanity as a whole that money-minded
corporations, or publicity-minded "foundations" wouldn't fi-
nance it, and the only return he received was inner satisfaction. It was well that he expected no other return, too.
Satisfaction was frequently all he got.

Doc Savage was a man of fantastic feats and good deeds
and taking return only in satisfaction had not made him a
meek nor an impoverished man. He was a spectacular person. Physically, a giant bronze man with hair a little darker
bronze and strange flake-gold eyes that could be sympathetic,
firm, or scare the hell out of a wrongdoer, he could do things
with sinew that were not quite believable. Mentally, he was a
phenomenon that a biographer would find hard to make convincing. A man simply didn't accomplish such scientific or
psychological feats. It was a difficult fact to sell.

But the point was that there was enough percentage of
zanies on the planet, two billion two hundred odd million to

make some isolation desirable. So, while Doc Savage's headquarters occupied as conspicuous a place as there was in New York City, the eighty-sixth floor of one of the city's tallest buildings, and there were forty or fifty elevators operating in the vertical arteries inside, getting to see Doc Savage personally was a matter that took doing. More specifically, it took a crime. A fantastic one, of one that the law didn't seem to be able to touch. Even then, there was a certain screening routine.

Lieutenant Colonel Andrew Blodgett "Monk" Mayfair, who looked like a reasonably pleasant ape, was one of the screens. Monk had approximately seven-eighths-inch of forehead, and was one of the world's great chemists, when anybody could get him to work at it.

From the private detective agency downstairs, which sifted the inflow for cranks and chaff, Monk received a parcel-room claim-check.

"It came in the mail," he was told.

Not much impressed, Monk asked, "No note with it, or anything?"

"Just this." He was handed a bit of colored paper with one torn edge.

"Blazes!"

"It impressed me, too," said the private detective whose office force did nothing but screen and investigate the people who wished to see Doc Savage.

Monk took off his hat, which looked as if it had been used to dust off his shoes, and scratched around in some bristling rusty shingle-nails that served him as hair. "Doc won't care for this much. He doesn't like something to start out smelling of money, particularly big money, as payment for his services."

"Then you're not interested?"

"In one-half of a thousand-dollar bill? Hell yes, I am," said Monk. "But the question is, will Doc be? What else was there with this?"

"Just that. The claim-check. The half a thousand-buck bill."

"Hmmmm. Well, I'll take it upstairs and see what the master says."

Monk took the private elevator to the eighty-sixth floor, and in the reception room, a large place with comfortable chairs and a ghastly old-fashioned steel safe of tremendous size, and an inlaid table that was a priceless Oriental piece, he found Attorney Theodore Marley Brooks. He paused to speak unpleasantly to Ham Brooks. "Hello, shyster," Monk said. "I've warned you before, and I'm going to do it again. But this is the last time, savvy?"

Ham Brooks, a very dapperly dressed man, sneered.

"Well, well, it breathes, it walks on its hind legs, it looks like the missing link," he remarked. "What can it be? Not a certain lout of a chemist who has been molesting my girlfriend?"

"Yours? *Your* girlfriend! Hell's bells!" Monk turned purple, waved both arms and screamed, "Molesting! Where do you get that stuff, you miserable flea on the reputation of Blackstone? Audrey was, and is, my girlfriend."

Ham smirked. "Is, you say?"

"Yeah, even if you did have her out last night," Monk bellowed. "And I'm telling you, you tort, if you mess around with Audrey once more, you'll be asking, 'Where's my arms and legs?' I don't mean maybe."

Ham leaped to his feet, seized the slender black cane which he habitually carried, and screeched, "Don't you threaten me, you physical freak!"

"Threaten you?" Monk howled. "I won't say a word. I'll just—"

A buzzer somewhere in the room made several irritated beeping sounds. It ended the dispute temporarily, because it was a signal from Doc Savage.

Monk found Doc Savage in the laboratory, which was the largest room, composing over two-thirds of the skyscraper's eighty-sixth floor, that lay behind a library containing Doc's amazing collection of scientific tomes. Monk asked uneasily, "Our little fuss bothering you?"

"It was shaking the whole neighborhood," Doc Savage said briefly. "Female trouble again?"

"Yeah," Monk admitted sheepishly.

"Which one?"

"Audrey," Monk muttered.

Doc Savage's metallic bronze features remained expressionless, and he said thoughtfully, "Do you fellows know what is going to happen to you sometime? You're going to get so interested in one of these competitions that some blond fluff with dark blue eyes is going to ring one of your fingers."

"How'd you know she had dark blue eyes? You never met Audrey," Monk demanded.

"They go with peroxide, don't they?"

"I think I should resent that," Monk said. "What makes you think we might get hooked?"

"Because you'll be so busy watching each other, you'll forget to watch the girl."

"You mean shot with a marriage license when we're not looking, eh?" Monk snorted. "Fat chance. Ham and I are wary old wolves. We love 'em and leave 'em. There's nothing to it." Monk fished around in his pocket and brought out the claim-check and the half of a thousand-dollar bill. He presented these to Doc Savage. "Interesting trivia from the afternoon mail," he remarked.

Doc looked at the items, but did not take them until he had pulled on rubber gloves. "You'd better be more careful with odd stuff through the mail," he said. "Science has been doing some hair-raising things with killing germs lately."

"You must be getting jumpy."

Doc Savage said nothing, but carried the check and the greenback fragment over to a microscope and took a look at them. He was a giant of a man, and it was impossible for a casual air and normal mannerisms to conceal the fact of his fabulous physique. Monk, watching him, was impressed, and Monk had known Doc for quite a few years, and he was not easily impressed. Doc was more than a physical giant. He was a trained symphony in sinew and coordination, the product of a childhood devoted entirely to rigorous training at the hands of experts who had been hired by the man's father and given one instruction: If interminable training will develop a superman, produce one. There are probably limitations to what consistent practice and self-development over a period of years can accomplish, but sometimes Monk wondered.

"No germs, eh?" Monk remarked.

"Apparently not." Doc took the two articles to another contrivance, a device of his own development for measuring radiant emission which was considerably more sensitive than the Geiger counter and its successor, the one which utilized certain properties of diamonds.

Monk was amused at the giant bronze man's precautions. "If they should be radioactive, so what? They wouldn't likely be charged enough to harm a man."

"The claim-check is for a package at the stand on the lower level at Grand Central Station," Doc Savage said. "The package could be a bomb, triggered for detonation by the presence of a radiant nearby."

Monk nodded. "But that would take imagination and some scientific skill."

"Decency has no corner on imagination, unfortunately," Doc said. He seemed satisfied with his examination. "They seem to be clean. What do you make of it?"

"I don't know what to figure." Monk shook his head. "The two things just came in the mail. Postmarked a little after noon." He hesitated, then added, "The half of a thousand-dollar bill gives it some bite. The bill's genuine, I think."

"Yes, seems to be."

"You going to pick up the package and see what gives?"

Doc looked at Monk thoughtfully. "You might wish you'd done that yourself, in case acquiring the package should lead to a contact with the owner later."

"Yeah? How you figure?"

"A female."

"Eh?"

"The package seems to have been checked by a brown-haired, brown-eyed girl who is rather exotic, probably about twenty-four years old, smokes long gold-tipped cigarettes, and is quite a traveler. Sound interesting?"

Monk blinked a couple of times. "Sounds more like you're running a whizzer on me."

"The brand of cigarettes she likes is named Trieens, and her most recent trip was to India."

"How you figure that?" Monk asked. "And don't tell me it simple, dear Watson. . . . Or is it?"

"I'm afraid it is." Doc indicated the microscope. "Put the things under the glass and see for yourself."

Monk grunted, and followed instructions, but the examination did not fully convince him. He said, "I see the flecks of face powder, and tobacco, but danged if it means that much to me."

Doc said pleasantly, "If you had been doing research recently into allergies as related to cosmetics and tobacco, as I have, it would be clear enough. First, the powder: Face powder, a shade used by medium-complexioned girls but shunned by blondes and deep brunettes. Second, the tobacco, from an exotic cigarette, Trieens, made in India and not shipped abroad at all because of government monopoly regulations. They're long and gold-tipped, and since they're sold nowhere but in India, perhaps she bought them there. And there's a trace of perfume about the claim-check, a rather rash scent affected by younger women."

Monk grinned. "I missed the perfume, but she sounds interesting. Shall I take this up and see what it draws?"

"If you wish."

"Okay."

Monk collected Ham Brooks, and they caught a cab uptown. Monk did not tell Ham about Doc Savage's theory that a girl was involved; as a matter of fact, Monk invited Ham along only because the girl, if any, might pay the headquarters a visit during their absence and if Ham was there, and if the girl was promising, that would give Ham the inside track. Ham probably suspected chicanery, because he thought Monk had brought him along merely for the pleasure of renewing their quarrel about the blonde, Audrey, whereas it developed Monk was unusually quiet. Monk, for his part, was absorbed by amazement at Doc's deductive performance with the claim-check and thinking about it admiringly. But Ham was alarmed.

"What snide deal are you pulling on me?" Ham demanded.

"What? Oh calm down, you're not in the company of another lawyer, so nobody is going to steal your shirt. . . . Somebody checked something at Grand Central and sent Doc Savage the check, along with half a thousand-dollar bill, and we're going after it."

Ham was interested. "We're going after the other half of the bill, I hope you mean."

"The package."

"That's an impractical approach. The thousand-dollar bill is the thing," Ham said.

It was dark, a little after nine o'clock, and the midtown traffic was catching its breath after the theater rush, so that their cab was able to enter the drop-off at Grand Central without delay. They strolled inside, descended the steps, made the proper turns, went down the ramps to the lower level and located the check-room.

Fred Lill looked down at the check when Monk dropped

it on the scuffed and shiny sheet metal counter-top, and Fred stiffened instantly. He had recognized the number on the claim-check as matching the stub on the canary cage.

"Are you the party who checked this?" Fred asked suspiciously.

"We got the claim-check, ain't we?" Monk countered. "Trot it out."

Fred hesitated. There had been enough mystery surrounding the canary cage to upset him, and while he would be glad enough to be rid of the thing, he didn't wish to invite more trouble. He said, "Will you give me your name, Mister?"

"Listen," said Monk. "I've been checking packages in depots since I was a runny-nosed little stinker so-high to a poodle, and I never had to give my name before. What are you getting up, a Christmas card list?"

Fred scowled. "Did Mr. Plott send you for the package?"

"Who's Mr. Plott?"

"Then it was Miss Margaret Prince?" Fred suggested.

"Who's she?"

"You don't know either one of those people?" Fred asked pointedly.

"Can't say I do," said Monk. "Can't say I understand why you're galloping around bushes, either. Would you care to trot out whatever this claim-check calls for, or would you care for a little trouble?"

Fred stiffened. "You can't scare me. I don't like your manner."

"You won't get the package?"

Fred shrugged. "Sorry. I can't. It's not in my section. If you could describe the package, which I don't imagine you can, or identify yourselves as honest citizens, I might help you. But the attendant of the other section, Jim Presse, is out to lunch. He will be back presently, if you care to wait. In fact, he's due back now."

This was half-truth to the extent that Jim Presse was indeed out to lunch, but for the rest, Fred wanted to wait until Jim returned and consult him about procedure.

"Honest citizens, he says," Monk growled.

Ham eyed Monk in exasperation, remarking, "That comes of letting you do the talking. That face of yours has upset the man. One look at that sub-human visage, and it's Katie bar the door."

Monk ignored this and asked Fred Lill, "Who are these people, Mr. Plott and Margaret Prince?"

"Two who tried to get the canary cage," said Fred triumphantly.

"The what? Canary cage?" demanded Monk.

That had slipped out, and Fred winced. "Wait until Jim gets—oh, yonder he comes now." Fred sighed with relief, and called, "Hey, Jim, here are two more guys after that cage. What'll we—"

The other man in the check-room attendant's uniform stalked past, swung a leg over the counter, slid across it, muttering as he did so, "Back in a minute. Feel kinda sick." He hurried into the rear, between the long aisles of shelf-racks.

Fred was shocked. "That isn't like Jim. He didn't look at all right—" He scowled nervously at Monk and Ham. "Just a minute, you guys. I want to see what ails Jim." He turned and hastened after the other man.

Monk glanced at Ham, and the latter was saying, "If you ask me, there is something odd—" when Fred Lill's whoop of terror reached them from the rear. "Help! This ain't Jim." Fred shrieked. "Help! He's got the cage!"

Ham finished his speech with, "Take the left aisle, Monk. I'll go right." And they were both across the metal-topped counter instantly and lunging to the attendant's aid. But Monk was just as quickly back in view. His homely face was distorted, his hurry wild. The reason was promptly self-evident when a clap of gunsound exhaled from the rear. Monk yelled, "He's in this aisle. He's got a gun." Ham said, "Well, go in and get him." Monk's reply was pained. "I'm not bulletproofed today," he said, and this was not in any sense intended to be smart-aleck; what he meant was that he wasn't wearing a bulletproof undershirt of chain mail which Doc's aides often wore.

The sequence of the next twenty seconds of action they mostly reconstructed later. The invader, who was not Jim the attendant—they later found the genuine Jim unconscious in his underwear in a men's room booth—had knocked Fred Lill down and taken the canary cage. He was, as Monk had called, coming up the other aisle, and he knew Ham was in the adjoining one and moving fast, because he gave packages on one of the shelves a shove and these toppled through and made an excited mound on the floor before Ham, who stumbled over them and went down. Scrambling up, Ham spoke his mind in Harvard accents, but not Harvard words. Meantime, the intruder went on with the canary cage, and passed Monk, who was flat at the end of the aisle, waiting, full of anticipation.

Monk made his pounce as the man went past. Monk's object was to do a judo disarmament, a spectacular feat, but not a difficult one if the armed man is close enough. Monk knew, as do most men who teach judo tactics to the police, that it is perfectly safe to start taking the gun away from anybody fool enough to jam the muzzle against any part of the body, and that it can be done in practically every case before the trigger can possibly be pulled. This wasn't quite that simple, but nearly.

And Monk was wonderfully successful. A flash of movement, and he had the gun. He didn't have the man, though.

The two things that happened next were right in the tempo of action. First, Monk found out why the man had fired only one shot earlier. The gun was jammed. It was a cheap foreign automatic, and the new shell hadn't fed. It was useless to Monk. Second, the man had another gun.

Monk's immediate desire was to be elsewhere. He dived backward wildly, hit the floor, which was dusty and littered with torn claim-checks. Two or three bullets went into the steel shelves, broke up the contents of some packages and suitcases, and from a hole in a traveling bag a trickle of bourbon came, contributing the unnecessary aroma of a brewery.

The intruder left with the canary cage.

The man ran headlong for fifty feet and reached a ramp leading up into the station. Then, prudently, he slowed his pace. He turned right, then left, heading for the spot where the crowds were thickest. Grand Central Terminal is a monstrous tabernacle dedicated to haste and it is generally not possible to hear the arrival of incoming trains, and trains are not as quiet as mice. The shots, while they had made a hell of an outlay of sound in the vicinity of the check-stand, had contributed minutely to the overall noise of the station.

Crowds are also the boon, temporarily at least, of a

fugitive who keeps his head, wears a casual look, and doesn't stay in any one place too long.

The man had the canary cage, which was conspicuous, and would mark him instantly once the police had spread fully an alarm. He debated what to do with it. Check it at another stand? He was almost tempted. It would be bold enough, surely. But he didn't have quite that much faith in the ability of the normal to escape notice when men were searching for the unnatural. So he kept the cage with him.

In the end, he concluded to walk out of the station right now, before the word became general. He wondered how much time had elapsed. It was hard to tell, and he wasn't sure what facilities for a quick broadcast of a description the police had in the station.

The latter question was answered rapidly, for the station loudspeaker began to boom out his description.

He was already at the entrance, however. He walked out casually. No one stopped him. He looked for a taxi, found one that was emptying itself at the ramp, and shoved inside. He settled back calmly, saying, "Penn Station, and in a hurry if you will. I want to catch another train."

The driver grunted. "Cab ahead has gotta move out of the way first."

Two or three seconds later, the cab door was opened casually, and a man got inside. A large man with rather unusual bronze features and strange flake-gold eyes.

"Hey, this cab's occupied," objected the man who had acquired the canary cage.

"So are you," Doc Savage told him.

III

"The thing I object to," Monk Mayfair remarked disgustedly, "is not that Doc made a grab and saved the bacon. That was all right, because I know he doesn't think we're a couple of saps. But what I resent is that we made of ourselves, voluntarily and with only mild urging, a pair of saps. That guy with the canary cage walked through us as if we were duck-pins."

"Oh, shut up," Ham said. He told Fred Lill, "Not you, Mr. Lill. Go right ahead. You thought the man was your co-worker, Jim Presse, and you walked back to see what made him seem different. Then what?"

Fred Lill was speaking uncomfortably into a wire-recorder. "He hit me," he said. "And that's all I knew for a while. In fact, that's all I know."

"Do you know why all this rumpus is being made about a cage with two canaries in it?" Ham asked.

"No, sir. I don't know from nothing, and I'd like to forget all about it," Fred Lill said.

"Okay, thanks, Lill." Ham closed the machine, and he and Monk went to the first-aid room in the station, where Jim Presse was being treated for a scalp cut and a headache.

They recorded Jim's account, which seemed to add nothing to the general picture.

Riding downtown, Ham remarked, "This is an odd one, isn't it? Somebody wants Doc to have the canaries, and somebody else is all against it."

"Yeah, the girl was sure anxious for Doc to have them," Monk agreed.

"What girl?" Ham scowled. "You've been holding out on me, you baboon." They quarreled during the rest of the ride over the girl from India who smoked exotic cigarettes.

Doc Savage was seated in the reception room at headquarters. The canary cage reposed on the inlaid table nearby. Across from Doc sat a slender young man with a wiry body, a hard brown face, rather thick lips, and a manner that was not otherwise stupid.

"He given out anything yet?" Monk asked, indicating the stranger.

"Silence, exclusively," Doc Savage replied. "Let's hear the recordings." He arose, adding, "We'll listen in the other room, however. Monk, will you keep an eye on our speechless friend here."

Monk strode over to the stranger, said, "Go on, make a break for it. Go ahead, pal. Let's see if your footwork is as good as it was." But the young man merely scowled.

In the library, with the doors closed, Doc Savage and Ham Brooks listened to the recorder play-back.

"Doesn't clear up much, does it?" Ham asked, when that was finished. Doc Savage looked thoughtfully at the machine.

He said, "Both check-room attendants state there were two canary birds, which fought until one was killed." Ham nodded and explained, "That's right."

"There is only one bird in the cage," Doc told him.

Ham was startled. "One! But I don't get that. Both men said the cage held two birds. I think they both actually saw two birds in the cage."

"Nevertheless, there was only one bird when I took possession."

"Which bird is in the cage? The winner, or the loser?"

"The loser. The dead one," Doc said.

The stranger with the hard brown face sat in the reception room and the only indication of inner tension was the claw-like hold his hands kept on the arms of his chair. Monk Mayfair raked a finger around in the small litter that the stuff they had taken from the man's pockets made on the table.

"Not a thing here to give him a name or a home. That in itself is pretty near evidence against a man, come to think of it," Monk remarked. He watched Doc Savage slide an ampoule of chemical into a hypodermic, and laughed. "You want to bet your big silence lasts much longer?" he asked the man.

The man stared with wordless intensity at the needle. He watched Doc Savage show him the label on the container which had held the ampoule, and a thin mist appeared as by magic on his upper lip. "You can't shoot that stuff into me! It's illegal!" he blurted, using a voice considerably more high-pitched than the one in which he'd last spoken nearly an hour ago.

"It's illegal, he says," Monk remarked. "Now that's reasoning for you. He only shot at me a couple of times."

"I think he knows what it is," Ham remarked. "I suppose he should, at that. A couple of national magazines have carried stories about its hypnotic qualities on the human mind."

Monk went over and stood behind the man, remarking, "It may be illegal, you potlapper, but you're going to talk your head off in a minute or two." Suddenly he seized the man from the rear, pinioning his arms, clamping him to the chair. The man screamed. "That stuff's dangerous!" he shrieked. "I read where—oh my God, no! Don't!" Doc Savage had his left arm now, and Ham his legs, and the man's howling clawed at the busy silence in the room for a few moments longer, then began to change in quality. The drug was quick, and would produce fairly complete anaesthesia in hardly more than twenty seconds. But it was not anaesthesia Doc wanted, so he checked the flow carefully. He glanced at Ham, said, "Begin feeding him questions. You've done it before, and know about the results to expect." And to Monk: "Set up the wire recorder, in case there is something that might interest the police."

The following half-hour was a monotonous matter of applied effort, livened only occasionally by a gem of pertinent information. Since the man talked in a twilight state, his mind free of conscious control, there was dullness spotted with bursts of hysteria, and the whole was incoherent as to form. Only Ham's steadily repeated questions gave it a plan and progress.

In summary, they learned: The man's name was Clinton Williams and he had been born to a mother who had waited only until he was old enough to leave with his father, then she had disappeared. His career consisted of grade-school, one hitch in the reform school, different penitentiaries, two hitches, the army two years, kicked out, and a series of odd jobs and minor criminal activities which had resulted in late months in an association with a gang of thugs headquartering in Jersey City, and headed by one named A. C. Black.

Black was known, naturally, as Blackie, and a few days ago he'd hired himself, Clinton Williams and the whole gang of bruisers out to a Mr. Plott, a foreign gentleman. The remuneration was handsome, their duties negligible, consisting of trying to find a young lady named Miss Meg Prince. Or Margaret Prince, really.

Mr. Plott furnished the information that Miss Prince had arrived by plane from India via Cairo, London and La Guardia Airport, with Mr. Plott hot on her heels, whereupon she'd given Mr. Plott the slip. The gang did the rest. Included in the coterie was a private detective who'd had his license lifted, and it was through his management that they located Miss Prince living in a discreet hotel in the fifties off Madison Avenue.

Profusely delighted with their services, Mr. Plott assigned them the next part of the job—Miss Prince had two canaries, and he wanted them. He wouldn't mind, either, if he got

Miss Prince also. The canary birds first. Then Miss Prince. Mr. Plott wouldn't mind if the canary birds were dead, but he wanted the bodies. As for Miss Prince, preferably she should be alive in condition to talk.

But Miss Prince had been wary, had discovered they'd found her about the time it happened, and without delay she had left her tiny hotel carrying what was clearly a canary cage enclosed in paper. She'd checked this at Grand Central, then mailed the claim-check to someone, although first visiting a bank and exchanging a number of traveler's checks for a single bill of large denomination.

Clinton Williams had been assigned the job of getting the birds by force after Mr. Plott had failed in a peaceful attempt. In the meantime, others of the gang were going to see what could be done about removing Miss Prince from circulation.

"Two birds?" Doc said.

Yes, there were supposed to be two birds in the cage, the man said.

"There was only one bird, and it was dead," Doc said.

That confused Clinton Williams, because his mind in the drugged state was incapable of rationalizing to any degree. He began to mumble, and Doc listened carefully and wonderingly, gathering that Mr. Plott had felt that one canary, or either canary singly, was of no value in the scheme of things. Both canaries were needed.

"Why were the canaries angry?" Doc asked.

The man didn't know that. He had no idea why they were valuable. In fact, he did not know anything more of pertinence.

"Monk and Ham," Doc said, "you get up to that girl's hotel, find her, and bring her in. I'd like to know why she wanted me to have two angry canary birds."

Monk put on his hat, remarking, "Miss Prince is the girl who called at the check-room in an effort to get the birds back. The check-room attendants gave a pretty good description of her, and I guess we can recognize her from that. It should be simple."

"To insure it being simple," Doc warned him, "you'd better be careful. According to this fellow, the rest of his gang is hunting her."

Ham said, "This seems screwy to me. Why would Mr.

Plott pursue Miss Prince all the way from India to get a
couple of angry canary birds?"

"Your guess is as good as mine," Doc said. "And you two
had better get going."

When Monk and Ham had gone, Doc took a pair of
handcuffs from the desk and manacled Clinton Williams to
the heavy chair in which he sat, fastening the man's ankle to
the lower part of the chair, so that it would be impossible for
the fellow to walk away carrying the chair.

Obtaining a pair of tweezers, Doc extracted the dead
body of the canary from the cage, carried both bird and cage
into the laboratory, and began running tests.

He checked the paper cage wrappings, both brown
paper and black paper, for writing, visible and secret. There
seemed to be none. The black paper was not American made,
and was quite worn, as if it had been used to wrap the cage a
number of times. It was completely light-proof.

He noted one significant thing about the cage. It was, or
had been, divided into two compartments by a wire partition,
and the small door in this had in some fashion come open,
allowing the two canaries to get together, whereupon one had
killed the other.

As he prepared to inspect the canary itself, the radio
receiver emitted a hissing sound at one side of the room,
then Monk's voice, saying: "We're almost at Miss Prince's
hotel, Doc. Nothing unusual yet."

Doc Savage picked up the push-to-talk microphone.
"Report at five-minute intervals. And don't walk into any
traps."

IV

Ham Brooks, glancing sidewise at Monk Mayfair, remarked
uneasily, "You didn't mention our guest." He watched Monk's
face, and saw the homely chemist wince, a sight that would
ordinarily have pleased him, but which gave him little satisfaction under the present circumstances. Ham concluded that
Monk was harassed by a feeling of guilt, and he knew he had
the same misgivings himself. He noticed that Monk gave the

en an angry poke with his thumb, a gesture that was
necessary, and he felt some sympathy for Monk as well as
himself, a sort of we're-in-the-same-boat complex.

"One would think," stated the spectacular, if somewhat
mished, blonde riding with them, "that I'm not very
lcome."

She was Audrey, the belle they had been besieging, and
e sounded near tears. And Audrey near tears was like a
ten drowning.

"Now, my dear, you mustn't get that idea," said Ham
stily. "It's perfectly lovely having you along. Perfectly."
m remembered to add, "It's Monk who doesn't want you
ound."

"That's a damned lie," Monk muttered, which was an-
er lie.

Audrey looked daintily hurt. "I don't care, neither of you
re a bit nice." She pouted. "You're not being nice now,
her."

"Baby, you've got it all wrong." Monk was glancing at the
crophone, wondering how Doc Savage would react if he
ew he and Ham had a lady friend around their necks.
aby, I was just surprised to see you, that's all."

"You certainly seemed surprised," Audrey snapped.

"Yeah, I was bowled over—with pleasure, I mean,"
onk assured her. "What gets me is this: How'd you happen
be waiting there in the lobby of the building at just that
ne?"

Audrey favored Monk with a frown. She also moved a
tle closer to Ham, coyly. "I'll bet you don't know," she said,
hat time it was."

"Why, about three minutes after nine o'clock," Monk
id, after glancing at his watch.

"I thought so," Audrey said.

"Huh?"

"We had a date for eight o'clock." Audrey sounded near
ars again. It was both puppies and kittens drowning. "I
ood around a whole hour, waiting. And you'd forgotten."

"No, baby! No, never!" Monk proclaimed loudly, also
ondering how he'd happened to forget it. "You see, Audrey,
've been busy on a big case and—" He noticed Ham's free
nd giving Audrey's shoulder comforting pats and scowled.

"You just passed the street the Prince dame's hotel on," Ham volunteered. "You taking a tour, or something?"

"Stop pawing my girl," Monk said.

"Who's your girl?" said Audrey. "And who is this Prince person?"

"Oh, some babe Monk's interested in," said Ham helpfull

Glaring, Monk said, "Aw, she has canary birds." Th didn't sound like much of an explanation, but it was the be he could produce. He U-turned the car angrily in the traff blowing his horn, and drawing irate blasts from other moto ists, an uproar that was promptly joined by the twitter of traffic cop's whistle. The cop, brawny and red-faced and she of temper, came over, fisted his hands on his hips an listened to Monk's statement that they were Doc Sava aides, replied with the classic understatement, "That's fine haven't given an assistant celebrity a ticket in a week." H wrote out and presented a traffic summons.

Monk then drove on and yanked the car to the curb front of the Prince girl's hotel.

Audrey giggled. "I thought Mr. Savage was such important person. I'm surprised they'd dare give you ticket."

"It's this shyster lawyer we've got along," Monk growle "They probably know him for what he is, and that handica an honest man."

Audrey noted their preparations to enter the hote "You're not going to leave little Audrey alone in this dar lonesome street?" she asked anxiously.

Monk groaned inwardly, and looked hard at Ham order to hang the responsibility for an answer on him.

"I'd be simply terrified. Simply petrified," Audrey bleate

"We wouldn't think of petrifying you," Ham said uneas ly. "So come along."

The hotel lobby gave them a genteel air of honesty an quiet, and the middle-aged clerk surprised them with th information that they were expected. "Miss Prince? Yes i deed," he said. "You say you are associated with a M Savage? Then you are to go right up. Five-fourteen."

They traveled over a well-trod taupe carpet and stoppe on a rubber mat in front of the elevators to wait for a cage appear. Monk drew Ham aside and muttered, "I don't lik

e idea of hauling Audrey around with us. There may be
eworks."

"You had the date with Audrey, so get rid of her your-
lf," Ham retorted. "If this Prince character is expecting us,
w come she didn't contact Doc Savage directly? And how'd
e know we would show up?"

"Secrets?" Audrey's pert little face was beside them. "I
ve secrets."

Monk contemplated Audrey's rather plump throat, and it
curred to him that his fingers would fit around it very
cely, and willingly, too. An elevator came, though, and they
tered. "Five," Ham said.

"Canary birds? So you're going to see the lady about
nary birds?" said Audrey, simpering. "I think that's just too
veet for anything, but I don't believe a word of it."

"Shush, baby," Monk muttered. "It's supposed to be
pt quiet."

"Oh, a mystery!" shrieked Audrey. "I do love mysteries!"

Extremely irritated with Audrey, Monk examined the
onde to learn what he had just found that he had missed
fore. He saw a very cute number, strictly jewelry-case, the
ual quota of baby blue eyes, cupid-mouth—the model
me fully equipped, he had to say that. Brains? Who bothered
out brains? He hadn't noticed, and he imagined Ham
dn't either. Which led him to recall Doc Savage's remark
at sometime the two of them, Ham and himself, would get
running competition so hard that one would likely get
rmanently hooked. Oh brother! Not if he could duck.

"What did you say?" inquired Audrey, dragging her
gertips over his arm.

The door was no different from the door of a room in any
her hotel that had been built perhaps twenty years ago,
cept that possibly this one gave back more silence.

"Knock again," Ham said. "The desk clerk downstairs
emed to think she was in."

Monk flattened his knuckles on the door again, got more
lence from that point, and a rather pleasant-voiced, "Good
rening, gentlemen," from behind them. They whirled as if a
ake had hissed at their heels.

Here was a silent man. That was the first—and lasting—
pression Monk got of the fellow, and it dealt in no way with
s voice, which was mellifluous, resonant, free-flowing and

confidence-inspiring. Otherwise he was tall, slightly sof
looking and handsome in a very careful way. "I trust I'm n
making a mistake," he added.

"What kind of a mistake would you make?" Ham Brool
asked him.

"My name is Kelvin," the man said, smiling pleasantl
He opened his right hand and there was a piece of paper
it. "I have the answer to a question written here," he adde
"Will you tell me who you are, or rather who you represen
They will be identical, I hope."

"Doc Savage," Ham said. "And I don't get this."

"Oh, excellent." The man who had given himself th
name Kelvin presented the bit of paper. On it was writte
Since you are from Doc Savage, I am at your service.

"What kind of service," Monk asked suspiciously.

"Guide, you might call it."

"Yeah?"

Kelvin beamed pleasantly. "Bear with me for a bri
explanation. The hotel is my residence—this is my roo
behind me, as a matter of fact—and a few days ago
managed to make the acquaintance of a very attractive an
interesting young lady, by name Meg Prince. Margaret Princ
We had dinner and did a few theaters, with the result that
was totally fascinated, and when Meg asked me to do a favo
for her that seemed somewhat bizarre, I'm afraid I consente
with unseemly enthusiasm."

"Oh, you know Miss Prince?" Ham said.

"I just said so, perhaps with too many words."

"What do you know about her?"

"Charming. Mysterious. And frightened."

"Frightened of what?"

Kelvin shrugged. "I have no idea. The mysterious qual
ties I mentioned add to the young lady's fascination."

"Canary birds?"

Surprise arched Kelvin's eyebrows. "She has two,
believe. She kept them always in a cage which had tw
compartments, and it was always darkened."

Monk said, "Let's get around to the favor you mentioned.

"Certainly. Meg asked me to accost anyone who knocke
on her door, ascertain whether they represented Doc Savag
or included Doc Savage, and then I was to guide them
her."

"Okay, pal," said Monk curtly. "Where is she? Just tell us that. We don't need any seeing-eye help."

Kelvin's head bent apologetically. "I'm supposed to show, not tell, you."

"Yeah?" said Monk suspiciously. "Brother, the story sounds thin to me, and if you think—"

Audrey stamped her foot. "Oh, tush!" she said. "I think Mr. Kelvin is being nice and gallant, and you're acting nasty to him."

"Shut up," Monk said.

Audrey gasped. "Oh, you big baboon!" she cried. She shrank back against Ham Brooks for protection, wailing, "He told me to shut up!" Ham stroked her shoulder comfortingly, telling her, "He's a baboon, all right, and I'm glad you're finding it out."

Monk said, "Hell!" disgustedly. "Oh, all right, let's go along with this guy like sheep," he added. He looked thoughtfully at the door of Miss Prince's room. "But first let's take a look in here."

The door was locked, and Monk bent down to examine the lock, then drew out his pocket-knife, opened the large blade, and shoved it against the narrow strip of wood which served as a buffer for the door. He pried and the strip came up easily—suspiciously easy. He hesitated, sure the lock had been picked recently the way he was going to pick it now, wondering whether he should mention the fact. Then, without speaking, he took the card-case from his purse and shoved one of the celluloid card-protectors into the slit he had made. After a bit of maneuvering and pressing, he felt the bolt slide back. He pushed the door open.

Inside there was just a hotel room with the things in it that hotel rooms have—when they're ready for a guest, but before a guest checks in, or more exactly, after a check-out. There were no clothes, no bags, no article of personal nature whatever. Two used towels in the basket in the bathroom, cigarette ashes but no stub in one of the trays.

Monk looked at Kelvin. "Got any remarks you want to make about this?"

Kelvin shrugged. "Only that I imagine Meg moved to another address to which she wishes me to bring you."

"Okay. Let's get there."

The elevator operator was sleepy and he looked at them

once, but not again, and the cage took a long tired time getting them down to the lobby. They walked silently to the revolving door and it let them out on to the street one at a time, along with gulps of warm air that smelled faintly of cleaning-fluid.

"Better check in with Doc on the radio," Ham told Monk, when they were in the car. And Monk took up the microphone, switching on the transmitter and receiver so that it would warm. Thirty seconds was about right for the filaments to heat, and after that had passed, he pressed the push-to-talk button. But no response came—the audible one should have been a muting of the receiver while the transmitter was on the air. There was none.

"Transmitter's on the blink," Monk muttered. "It won't work."

Kelvin seemed both interested and surprised. "You mean to say you fellows use two-way radio, like the police?"

Monk looked at him narrowly. "It's nothing new. It wouldn't be very original either if somebody fixed the thing so we couldn't use it to report where we're going."

Kelvin's eyes narrowed. "Does that remark have a personal touch?"

Audrey said disgustedly, "What crude manners you have, Monk! You're behaving utterly stupidly."

"I hope no more than my manners are stupid," Monk said darkly.

V

His name was Caspell. He had once been high brass in the army—Brigadier General C. E. Caspell. The man was not a has-been by any means, and probably threw more weight than he ever had as an army man, officially. He was, by inclination, a scientist, and by profession, a watchdog on the progress of science as it related to the unholy practice of war. Caspell was a product of the era; war had turned scientific, and the advent of the atom bomb had been a sort of presentation of diploma to show the graduation of the laboratory into the realm of death and destruction. Caspell belonged to an unsung section of the government intelligence that applied itself to the ferreting out of any new discoveries that might be dangerous to the safety of the nation. He did not head the department, but he was second in charge, stationed in New York, and he was a brilliant man.

"I don't want to seem to exaggerate," Doc Savage said to Caspell. "But I feel it is fortunate that you were in New York and immediately available."

"I take it this is important?"

"My guess would be so."

"How important?"

"It will take a little peering through the microscope and looking at analysis results," Doc said. "But you might start holding on to your hair now."

Caspell was scientist enough to follow his nose through the information Doc had assembled, which meant that he was quite some scientist indeed. The stuff was complex. Not only the physiological side of it, which any top-ranking brain surgeon would not have found too complicated, but the psychological, or neurological aspects, tying one into the other, as they did, made it something strictly not for junior-grade dabblers in—even the word applied to the study was not exactly simple—neurenergenics.

"I don't believe it!" Caspell said. He didn't speak as a man who didn't believe, though. He sank in a chair, a straight and hard chair and he sat there in a straight and hard way, mopping his face with a handkerchief. "My God! Of course it's possible—I mean, there's a reason for everything. . . . You say this canary came from where?"

"The girl came from India. Presumably she brought the canary birds." Doc had given Caspell a general picture of the situation. "She came, as nearly as we can gather, in fear, and she was pursued by this Mr. Plott character."

"Reading between the lines, that would indicate she was coming to you with this ghastly thing in hopes you could stop it," Caspell said.

"That seems far-fetched. India is a long way off—"

"Not to me. You underestimate your repute in faraway places, Savage."

"Nevertheless—"

"She brought two angry canary birds, didn't she?" Caspell demanded. "Samples. The two birds were samples. Why else would she bring samples, if not to show them to you to prove her story."

Doc was wary. "Let's not jump to conclusions. The infernal thing may not be perfected. Perhaps it will work only on canary birds, and they hoped by some trick to get me to continue development."

Caspell jumped up suddenly. "Savage, you really think a thing like that is possible?" He sounded more than a little wild.

"Certainly."

"No! Oh Lord, no!"

Doc shrugged. "Why not? The medical dictionaries even have a word for it—neurenergen. Meaning a substance supposed to furnish the energy of the neurosis. Medically, a neurosis is a nervous disease, especially a functional disease. A functional disease is one that affects the functions of the body but not its structure. You see, it can even be reduced to small words."

Caspell leveled an arm at the dissected fragments of the canary bird. "You've just shown me a change in the structure of that canary—"

"Not bodily—"

"Now wait, the brain is part of the body, isn't it? The brain of that bird—"

Doc Savage interrupted gravely. "Tell me this, Caspell. As far back as two years ago, or even six months ago for that matter, would cerebrology have offered enough knowledge to indicate that the abnormal condition of that particular part of a canary bird's brain meant that the bird was incapable of doing anything but hating and being angry?"

Caspell shuddered. "Stop it! You're scaring the hell out of me. This is shadowy stuff from the unknown, and I don't like thinking about it."

"The thing I want to know is this: Did the canary hate one thing? Was it angry only, for instance, at the other canary?" Doc said.

"You can't tell that. It's dead now—"

"There were two angry birds. The other one disappeared. If we could get it, and if it is alive, and could be observed—"

"Dammit, let me back away from this for a minute!" Caspell gasped. "I tell you, it frightens me more than the damned bomb ever did." He went to the window, stood scowling outward, and his hands moved uneasily, unable to find a place, in his pockets or elsewhere, where they felt safe. "You know this trouble in India," he said grimly.

Doc looked at him sharply. "India has had nothing but trouble for months," he said. "What trouble? Be specific."

"I can't be—not too specific." And in a moment, Caspell added bitterly, "My God, we discussed it down in Washington the other day, and somebody said, 'They must be brewing some new drink over there that makes them hate each other.' Or something like that. Just a remark that looked dumb at the time." He wheeled. He licked dry lips. "How would it be done? Something in the food? A secret ray? Ultra-high-frequency magnetic field?"

"That's what we've got to find out."

"How?"

"Monk and Ham have gone after the Prince girl." Doc threw an uneasy glance at the radio. "They're not reporting in, though, and it's beginning to worry me."

"What do you want me to do?" Caspell asked.

"You saw that fellow tied up in the outer office? He's a hired thug, Clinton Williams by name, member of a gang employed by Plott to stop the girl and the canary birds from reaching me. We shot him full of hypnotic, so his story is probably square. I want you to take him off my hands—the police would do it, of course, but their imaginations are a little too self-respecting for a thing like this."

Caspell nodded. "I could do without my imagination right now, too. We'll take Mr. Clinton Williams. We'll ply him with a few questions."

Doc gave Caspell a spool of recorder wire. "Here's his story, recorded as he told it. It should help."

"It will," said Caspell ominously. "What else can we do?"

"Nothing I can think of right now," Doc told him.

Caspell seemed puzzled. "I appreciate your handing this Williams bird over to us—but is that why you called me in? It doesn't seem too important, measured alongside the other."

"It isn't," Doc told him frankly. "As a matter of fact, I'm doing something I've never done before, probably because it never seemed so urgent to take such a precaution. . . . Frankly, I wanted you to know, or the proper agencies of this government to know—it amounts to the same thing—that there is a ghastly probability that someone has discovered a means, chemically, electrically or otherwise, of altering the minds of human beings so that they are consumed by anger and hate. I particularly wanted the information, because it is obviously far-fetched and astoundingly unbelievable, to get into the hands of a man of sufficient mental breadth to understand that such a grim thing is possible. In fact, that it seems preposterous is only because the structure of the mind is the least-understood of all things in the human body. I didn't want it laughed at, or passed up as silly. . . . In case, as you've guessed by now, I should have the bad luck to lose out with this fellow Plott. By losing out, I mean getting killed."

Caspell nodded. "I understand."

"Good." Doc hesitated. "Would you mind sticking around here a while." He showed Caspell how to operate the radio transceiver. "If Monk and Ham call in, tell them I've gone looking for the other angry canary."

"All right, I'll stay here and tell them that," Caspell said, nodding.

Fred Lill's tired roundish face became flat-looking with surprise, and he said, "Oh, you again! Well, come in." He wore no shirt, had a glass of milk in his hand, as he stepped backward opening the door. "I was just having a snack before I piled into the hay."

"This won't take long, probably," Doc Savage said, entering a three-room flat which was obviously kept by Mrs. Lill with great care on the small salary that Fred earned at the check-room. An elevated train, outward bound through Brooklyn, made a long clanging bedlam through which Doc Savage waited patiently. "It's about the missing canary," Doc added.

Fred Lill bobbed his head. "Yes, I guessed that. . . . You're Doc Savage, aren't you? I talked to my wife about it after I got home from work, and she knew about you. You're a famous man."

Doc looked at Lill thoughtfully. "That isn't what is making you nervous, is it?"

Lill winced. "No. . . . You're pretty sharp, aren't you? To see that I'm nervous, I mean."

"Do you have the missing canary?" Doc asked.

Fred Lill registered indecision and reluctance, all the while shaking his head. "No, I don't have the bird." He hesitated, then blurted, "Damn it, I'm not going to get in a lot of trouble over it. Jim is a young fool in some ways, although a nice boy, and one you wouldn't suspect of feeling tenderhearted about a bird."

"Jim? You mean the fellow who works with you in the check-room?"

"Yes. . . . Jim has the canary. He took it out of the cage because he was sorry for the poor thing. And then, after all the rumpus over the birds and the cage, he was afraid to tell anyone what he'd done."

"Where is the canary now?"

"Jim took it home with him. I have Jim's address." Fred Lill went to a table, seized pencil and paper and wrote for a moment. "Here's the address," he said.

"Thanks, Lill. You should have told this sooner." Doc pocketed the paper, after glancing at it. "One thing more. Did you see Jim Presse take the canary out of the cage?"

"Well, yes," Fred said uneasily.

"Don't be alarmed. This was the canary that killed the other bird? The victor?"

"Yes."

"How did the canary act toward Jim?"

"Why, just kind of scared, was all." Fred Lill was puzzled. "Like any bird would toward a stranger who was handling it, I would say."

"The bird didn't seem to hate Jim?"

"That would be kind of funny, wouldn't it, for a canary to hate a man?"

"Just answer the question."

"No. I didn't notice anything I would call hate."

"The canary was in a good humor?"

"It was scared," said Fred Lill.

"But it didn't act as it had toward the other canary?"

"Oh, no. No indeed."

"How did the canary act toward the other bird?"

"Hateful and angry," Fred Lill said grimly. "I never saw such hate and ferocity. Never."

"All right, thanks," Doc told him. "I'm going to see Jim Presse about the surviving canary, but don't telephone Jim about my coming. In fact, keep this under your hat."

"All right," said Fred Lill, nodding. "But what do I say to your man if he calls again?"

Doc Savage, moving toward the door, whirled sharply. "What man? Did someone telephone you, saying he was one of my associates?"

Fred Lill stared. "Yes. Didn't—"

"When was this?" Doc demanded.

"Why, about an hour and a half ago—"

"You didn't tell him Jim Presse had the canary?"

"Well, yes. Did I do wrong?"

"You probably saved your own life," Doc said grimly. "But how Jim Presse came out is another matter."

At between fifty and seventy miles an hour, using the siren and the red lights continually, Doc Savage made the trip back from Brooklyn in record time. He used outlying streets, the ones normally employed by trucks, because it was not yet late enough in the night for truck traffic to begin appearing. On Thirty-eighth Street, he shut off the siren and doused the red lights, but kept rolling fast. The car was his own, outwardly not an unusual looking machine, but equipped with the scientific gadgets he liked to use, and the development of which were a hobby with him.

There were only three cars parked in the block between Third and Lexington on Thirty-eighth. He decreased speed, and as a matter of course, used one of his gadgets, pressing a control button as he passed each of the three parked machines. The small hissing that resulted in each case was not particularly noticeable.

Doc drove on, completed half a circle of the block, and stopped on Thirty-seventh. He had, in passing, noted that Jim Presse's address was a building of small apartments, a tobacco-colored brick structure three stories taller than the surrounding brownstones. An innocent-looking place, but he took a lot of trouble to get into it by the back way, first entering an apartment house on Thirty-seventh and pressing all the buttons in sight until someone buzzed and let him in the door. He walked upstairs through the smell of last evening's dinners, and twice he mumbled, "Excuse me, I rang the wrong bell. Wanted Mr. Glickens." Glickens was a top-floor name he had noticed. On the top floor, he found the way to the roof. The hatch was padlocked, but that held him up not much more than a minute. He had a kit of useful tools that he used on it.

The way across the rooftops was easy, and there was no alley, so presently he stood beside Jim Presse's apartment house. The windows that could be conveniently reached from the roof all showed him distrustful teeth of painted iron bars. So he used a little steel grapple-hook on the end of a knotted silk cord, and presently—it had not been difficult for him, since his physical strength was close to abnormal—he sat on the windowsill of a hall window one story up. He used the kit again—glasscutter, a quick cut in a circle, then a bit of stickum to hold the glass from falling when he tapped it sharply and it opened where he had scratched. He unlocked the window and went in, being once more met by last night's dinner odors. Jim Presse's apartment was five-one-three.

That was one floor up, and he met a man. The man was coming down the stairs, lightly, turned a little sidewise, whistling softly. It was not an American tune he was whistling, and the man's clothing wasn't American, nor was, less noticeably, his face. His voice was. He said, "Hi, pal." And went on.

Doc had been making no sound, and he continued to make none, and the man didn't either, presently. When Doc noticed that, he leaned over the well the zig-zagging stairs made, and looked down. The man had his shoes off, was carrying them, and making terrific time down the steps.

Moving fast now, checking, Doc reached Jim Presse's door. It was a metal door, but not too impregnable if one knew where to hit them with a foot, and he knew. He went in, and found Jim Presse at once, not a difficult discovery, because the man was spread out on the floor pretty much as he'd stopped moving, if he'd moved much after the knife had done its work on his throat. The cut somehow looked as if the hand with the knife had just reached around from behind, and yanked. It was a messy murder.

Ten seconds later, Doc Savage was taking the third flight of stairs down, and he made just as good time to the lobby, which was empty. The man, the man who had nothing American about him but the two words, "Hi, pal," was not there. Neither was one of the three cars that had been parked in the street.

Doc went outside, crowded both elbows against his ribs, and sprinted around the block for his car.

Since the advent of atomic fission and the resultant

interest in locating radiant materials, a number of detectors have been developed which make the Geiger counter—itself not the original instrument for such a purpose, but probably still the best-known to the public—seem as cold-nosed in comparison as a Pekingese lapdog staked out against a bloodhound. The one Doc had in his car was phenomenally sensitive, so much so that he had trouble with it. The thing worked, all right, but directionally it indicated his own car.

He worried with it for a while. The tank of radiant spray, a quick-drying adhesive charged with enough radioactive substance to make it quite dangerous if a person's clothing got a full squirt of the stuff—was shielded fully, and the indicator shouldn't be nosing out the tank, instead of the car in which the killer had fled. Doc finally figured it out. There had been enough breeze in the street to blow some of the vapor back on his own car, where it had settled and hardened. The stuff wasn't something one just wiped off.

So he changed to a cab. A taxi came along, fortunately. He climbed in the back seat with his contraption, which was rather bulky.

"Head over toward Fifth Avenue," he told the driver. "I'll tell you where to go then."

The driver got the cab moving. "What the hell've you got there, Joe?" he wanted to know.

"An invention we're testing," Doc said. And when they came to Fifth, "Try going north for a while." He had picked up no indication as yet, except the two cars left behind, which proved it was working.

"Damned world's getting full of inventions," offered the cab driver. "One thing wrong with the world, if you ask me, Joe."

"Could be." Doc watched the indicator intently, and decided he had an indication. "Keep going north," he said. It could be that he was nosing out the office safe of some doctor who used radiants for treating cancer or some other malignancy. He silently condemned himself for depending on such a dubious contrivance in a city where there were so many possible false scents. "Keep north. Step on it," he said. And then later, "Head east at the next block."

"This leads towards Queensborough Bridge," the driver said. It did, and they took the sweep of ramp and rolled between the dark leaning girders, and the river was a thing below them, shining faintly in mist like a snake's back. Doc gave directions. Right. Then right again.

"You goin' to the airport with that thing?" demanded the driver.

It was a good guess.

VI

Somewhere in the half-moist and half-black night, an aircraft engine was running steadily and monotonously and with a certain oddness about its sound that, to the knowing, explained why it ran on and on that way. It was an engine getting a run-in after an overhaul. What it did to the airport, to the whole mass of darkness around the airport, was lend a sense of poised urgency. Doc Savage stood for a long time looking at the car, the one that had been parked in the street before Jim Presse's apartment house, and he found himself doing what anyone else with a moment of spare time must be doing—waiting unconsciously for the drumming engine to increase speed, slow down, miss a single beat. Anything to break the voodoo-like drumming.

"Want me to wait?" the cab driver asked. He was looking at Doc's gadget with wonder.

"No, thanks."

"What is this gimmick, anyway? You acted, coming out here, like it was some kind of direction-finder."

Doc said, "It is," and walked away from the cab, and away from the car, which was empty. Parked, too, near the terminal building itself. He stopped in the shadows, and used his pocket radio in an effort to raise Monk or Ham, but there was no response. Bothered now, more wrapped with the grim feeling that things weren't going well, he scowled at the terminal. What had he overlooked that he should reasonably have done? The canary that Jim Presse had taken? He might have searched for it. But he was still certain, as sure as he'd been back in Jim Presse's room, that the canary was in the possession of the man he had met on the steps.

He walked into the terminal, entering by a side door, moving unobtrusively, and giving the occupants of the big waiting-room a careful inspection. The drowsy faces—sleep rode anyone at this time of the morning—were as uninteresting to him as they were to themselves. There was somehow the dry dull taste of fatigue in the air and a kind of subtle disgust with life for having such a thing as four o'clock in the morning to offer.

Then he saw Monk and Ham. Just like that. They walked in much as anyone else would walk in, by the entrance from the taxicab ramp, which was also the way from the parking lot.

Doc took just about half a step toward them, then stopped. Monk and Ham had company. Two people. The blonde seemed familiar although there was not any single feature about her that he recalled, and he concluded that it was the assemblage—a flashy, doll-faced blonde—that he recognized. Automatically and immediately he placed the blonde as Monk and Ham's current goal, yet knowing she was not really their type. She was just what they liked to pretend was their type.

The man was a different proposition. He had too much assurance, packed too much confidence, along with a hand under a topcoat that he carried over his arm. The hand might or might not contain a gun. He walked always slightly behind Monk and Ham.

They went straight to a loading gate that was open and lighted, and the confident man, without taking his one hand from under the topcoat, used the other hand to display four airline tickets. Trans-Atlantic tickets, Doc saw.

Then they passed on through the gate, and Doc moved quickly, urgently, and saw them, still a compact party of four, get aboard a four-motored passenger ship. Doc hailed a porter. "What destination?" He indicated the big plane.

"London, Cairo and Calcutta."

"What is the departure time?"

The porter consulted the clock. "Due out in about thirty seconds."

Doc moved swiftly, and had a pass-case out when he reached the loading gate. The attendant there stared in surprise. "Yes, of course, Mr. Savage," he said hastily. "Are you going over on—"

"I want that plane held," Doc said. "Get on the phone to the tower. Tell them not to issue taxiing clearance to the ship."

The gate attendant, slack-jawed with surprise, wheeled and began fumbling for the telephone on his desk.

Doc Savage did not walk directly to the passenger roll-steps. He walked, instead, a bit to the left, which put him almost at once under the gleaming wingtip of the ship, cut off from view of some of the cabin windows. Two men were at the engines with fire-extinguisher carts, and one of these started toward him angrily. Doc ignored him, cut right, kept close to the hull, under it in fact, and then whipped around the stairs and up them.

"Keep the door open," he told a startled stewardess. "The ship isn't moving just yet."

"Who do you think you are?" she demanded.

"The last four passengers aboard—where did they go?"

The girl stared at him. "I don't believe you have any authority to—" She went silent, flushed, and then gasped, "Oh, I'm sorry. I didn't realize who you were.... The last four? Compartment fourteen."

"Fourteen is in the back?"

"That is right, Mr. Savage. Is there anything I can do—"

"Keep the door open, so the pilot won't get a green light from it. As long as the ship isn't buttoned up, he won't start the engines.... And listen—if there is trouble, or anything that looks like trouble, don't start investigating. Leave the plane at once and summon the police."

Doc went inside, warily, using his eyes. The plane was a new type—there were, Doc understood, about twenty of them in service, all on trans-oceanic work. They were land-planes, four-engined, with double-decked fuselage arrangements. That is, the public rooms, the lounge, the bar, were topside, while the lower deck was divided, in the fashion of continental railway trains, into a series of four-passenger compartments with individual doors opening off a single aisle down the starboard side of the ship. The seats in these compartments were readily convertible to berths, pullman fashion. These were the deluxe accommodations for long-flight passengers. Aloft, on the recreation deck, there were individual seats that were sold, club-car fashion, to short-trippers, individuals traveling, for instance, between London and Paris, or Paris and Rome.

Touched by the pleasant compact modernity of the great

ship, but not letting it divert him, Doc moved aft. Fourteen would be well to the rear, as the stewardess had said.

There was music above, small seductive strains that was more a mood than sound. The compartments had plastic doors, solid panels of lightweight stuff that looked like weighty glass doors but probably weighed a couple of pounds apiece. He gave each little room a sharp glance as he passed. He saw no one he knew. Nobody seemed scared by him. Neither fact meant anything.

Monk, Ham and the varnished blonde were in Fourteen. They sat three in a row on a seat intended for two, and they were held there by an ample number of handcuffs. Five sets.

Reaching for the door, Doc saw Monk's lips moving, and on Monk's face was the look of a man with a snake in his hands. The chemist's moving lips said, "—gone forward—watch out—saw you in the station—" The cabins were soundproofed expertly and it did a weird job of muffling and de-terrorizing Monk's voice of excitement, which was always a surprisingly tiny voice for such a violent-looking man.

The soundproofing did nicely with the shot sound that now came. It made it round, full-toned, a handsome loud thing without the loud nasty squawk of labored gases and tortured lead. Almost a nice sound, and the bullet was in Doc's back before the sound got there.

Doc landed on one knee and one elbow in the compartment, and because of the ghastly feeling in his back, he rolled completely over. There was no sensible reason, other than pain, for rolling. That, and the absurd notion that he hadn't put on the chain mesh undergarment that he'd learned to wear almost day and night.

Two other nice bullet noises arrived while he was on the floor. One slug made a rather respectable rip in the compartment bulkhead on the aisle side. It was a mystery where the other went.

"The plane's crammed with them," Ham Brooks said. "They're all over the ship."

Doc rolled over again, still in considerable agony, and then looked blankly at a generally shapeless and abused chunk of lead on the carpeting. It was, probably, the bullet that had hit him. Further inspection indicated it was likely a .45-caliber, and it went through his mind that the slug packed a little over four hundred foot-pounds energy, according to ballistics tables. Not helpful thoughts, but they fitted well with the way his back felt.

He said, "You fellows know too much about handcuff locks to just sit there. What are you waiting for?"

Monk grimaced. "For them to come along and put something besides combination locks on the cuffs, I guess."

"Sorry." Combination locks, the sort which opened by twirling a little numbered button, were tough. Doc added, "Get down on the floor as much as you can. The seats will stop handgun bullets." He rolled over once more, and laid hold of the handcuff links which fastened Monk's wrist to the seat armrest. "Let's see how good stuff they put in the chain."

The blonde, Audrey, said thinly and shrilly, "You can't break those in a million years. Monk tried."

"Thanks, baby," Monk said. "But I'm just an ordinary strongboy. I need two hands to straighten out a horseshoe. Now watch the real thing."

Everybody was speaking with the casual air of the fellow in the dentist chair asking, "Is it going to hurt, Doc?" But even that sort of composure was unexpected from a baby-faced blonde, so Doc filed a fact for future guidance. Audrey, in a crisis, became about as soft as one of the diamonds she wore.

Doc set himself against the chain. He had good purchase for pulling, except that one foot presently went through the rear bulkhead. Then the seat armrest gave. It came out, literally, by the roots.

"I don't believe it," Audrey said, wide-eyed with amazement. "A ten-ton truck couldn't have done that."

As time is related to the endless wheeling of a second-hand on a watch, none of this had taken long. But there had been an interval, and the enemy had been using it to make developments. A voice was shouting, and it seemed to be urging the passengers to get off the plane.

Now the same voice screamed at them. "If you don't want a lot of innocent passengers hurt, lie low until we get them off," it said.

"Know that voice?" Doc asked.

Monk agreed, unpleasantly, that he did. "Yeah, that's Kelvin," he said.

"And who would Kelvin be?"

"The guy whose face I hope to use for a little dancing," said Monk bitterly. "Foxy. Convincing voice. And a quick hand with a gun. Also, he told us he was taking us to Miss Prince, and we fell for it."

"Savage, you hear me?" Kelvin yelled.

"Yes," Doc called.

"I'll be damned—you must be bulletproof," Kelvin said disgustedly. "I'd swear I shot you through the heart. Okay, what about letting the passengers leave? Or do you want to include them in the party?"

"Get them off the plane," Doc said. "But don't try any tricks."

Ham growled, "That's like telling a goat not to smell. They're pulling something."

"No doubt," Doc agreed. "But if he's willing to let the innocents off the ship, it's worth the chance. How many men have they got on board, anyway?"

"Ten," Ham said.

"How do you know?"

"I don't. I'm taking Kelvin's word for it. He said ten."

"He might have dropped a word of truth," Doc said. "We'll take it seriously."

"What about these handcuffs?"

Doc picked two buttons off his coat. He added a third button, this one from a hip trouser-pocket flap. "Try these," he said. "One at a time, though. Better still, half a button."

There was a shot. Not from the plane. Doc lifted up to look through the window. A uniformed policeman stood just outside the loading-gate, holding a revolver which he had fired in the air.

"Come out of that airplane with your hands in the air," the officer shouted.

A single shot answered, and the policeman fell. He lay perfectly motionless for a moment, then one leg began to move. Scratching and grating against the black pavement, the one moving leg slowly propelled the officer out of sight, a stomach-wrenching thing to watch. Where the policeman had been, there was the beginning of a smeared wetness, and his revolver.

"That was cold-blooded," Doc said grimly. "It's not the safety of the passengers they're worried about. But I wonder what?"

Monk had carefully broken a button in half. He placed this, balanced carefully, on a link of the handcuff chain, after first wrapping his own handkerchief and Ham's around the adjacent wrists for shields. Now he moistened the other button, the one that was different, and applied it quickly to the first one. The result, a moment later, was a hissing and eye-hurting blue light such as comes from an arc-welder. Monk jerked, and the cuff links separated. He and Ham both whipped their arms around, attempting to cool the metal that the special Thermit had melted.

Kelvin had seen the glare. He yelled, "You guys set this ship on fire, and we'll shoot you down when you come out!" He sounded alarmed and puzzled.

"Just let us know when the passengers are all out," Doc called.

Kelvin cursed at him. And the man's enraged voice was suddenly half-lost in the drumming, deep-throated and at first troubled; that meant one of the engines had started. A second engine took hold immediately. Then the other two.

"Why are they starting the engines?" Audrey asked uneasily.

"Probably want a private party," Monk said. "Maybe they'll taxi to the other end of the field, then light their firecrackers." The plane gave a lurch. "We're moving!"

"Are we in danger?" Audrey demanded.

"I've felt safer," Monk told her.

"They're missing a fine chance," Ham said, "if they don't jam the throttles wide open, jump off, and hope we'll crash into the bay at the end of the runway."

Doc Savage had thought of that. He lunged to the window, reasonably sure he would not be shot from the outside, now that they were moving. He watched the runway, the pattern of marker-lights, and noted that the plane was being guided from the flight compartment. "There's a pilot at the controls," he said. And a bit later, "They're taxiing to a runway."

"If they're going to take off," said Ham, "I sure wish they'd warm the engines a little more."

"Why? Is that dangerous?" Audrey asked, sounding suddenly alarmed.

"La Guardia Airport," Ham reminded her, "is filled-in ground with water on three sides."

"This much airplane," Monk contributed, "makes a big splash."

"Shut up! You're scaring me!" Audrey wailed.

"Only now? Personally, I've been white-faced for twenty minutes," Monk muttered.

"I can't swim!" Audrey yelled in terror. "Do something!"

"I am," Monk said. "I'm shaking like hell."

The bawling of the engines increased, and they could feel the vibration shaking the rear section of the fuselage which housed the compartment. It was increasingly difficult to maintain balance, for the plane was accelerating speed. They crouched, faces strained, looking at each other in growing apprehension. Doc Savage suddenly went to the door, knocked it open and ducked his head out, then back. This drew a shot.

"That," croaked Monk, "is the first time I was ever glad to see you shot at. It means they're on board."

The quality of the plane's labor changed somewhat—as if the big craft had finally entered an element in which it was more at home.

"We're airborne," Doc said.

"Is that good?" Monk muttered.

VII

"As I remember the way these ships are designed," Doc Savage said, "the upper deck ends right above this compartment."

He moved to the rear bulkhead, and inspected the rent where his foot had gone through while he was straining to snap the handcuff linkage. He began kicking at the torn section, which split wider.

"I see your point," Ham Brooks told him. "They can shoot down through the floor above. But if we can get farther aft, they still can, only we mightn't mind as much."

"Doc, how many compartments aft of this one?" Monk demanded.

"One, I think."

"Will we be safe there, like Ham says?"

"I don't know how safe," Doc said. "But they can't riddle us from above."

Doc continued to kick at the thin bulkhead skin, pausing to drag out the insulating material and expose the other wall. He broke through that, peered cautiously into the rearmost compartment, then began widening the opening.

"Anybody in there?" Ham asked.

"Yes. A girl."

Ham said bitterly, "Oh, fine. Some dame who was too hysterical to get off with the other passengers."

Doc crawled through the hole he had made. A moment later, his head reappeared. "Better join me," he said.

Monk pushed Audrey through the aperture, ignoring Audrey's terrified, "Do the engines sound as if they're likely to stop?" Monk and Ham followed through the hole.

They examined the figure of the young woman in the compartment. She did not return the inspection. Her eyes were closed.

"She looks," said Ham, "like somebody who has been described to us."

"She does, and she doesn't," Monk agreed. "Didn't the check-room guys describe the girl who tried to get the canary birds as a dull number. No zip?"

"They must have been blind. Look at those legs. This one's got glamour," Ham said.

"It's Miss Prince, I think." Doc, on his knees, laid two fingers against the girl's throat. In a moment, he moved the fingers slightly, then rolled the girl's eyelids back. Monk, looking over his shoulder, remarked, "She's nice-looking, too."

"So is a cobra," said Audrey bitterly, "if you don't happen to know what a cobra is."

"Speaking," asked Monk, "from a knowledge of facts? Or just speaking?"

Audrey shrugged. "Just speaking. She's the one who got you into this mess, isn't she?"

Doc Savage completed his examination. "I'm not sure about the drug. But that's what they've done to her." Ham had been searching the compartment, and he reported, "No purse, no baggage of any kind. Too bad. I was hoping there'd be a gun lying around somewhere."

"Speaking of guns," Audrey said grimly. "Don't you think you might do a little shooting yourselves. To let them know we're not pushovers."

"With what?" Ham asked wryly.

"What? You mean you haven't got a gun? Oh, Kelvin searched you, didn't he? Well, hasn't Doc Savage—"

Monk shook his head gloomily. "Doc has never carried a gun that I know of."

Audrey flopped angrily into a chair. "A fine predicament we're in! Cornered in an airplane flown by a lot of crazy killers." She compressed her lips and glared. "A fine thing." She pointed at Monk and yelled, "And you promised me a nice quiet date for tonight, you homely baboon!"

They were being left alone, and it worried Doc. He made a precautionary move against surprise by smashing a small mirror which was part of the compartment equipment, then tossing a seat cushion out into the corridor, and flipping another cushion so that it landed at an angle of about forty-five degrees. On this, he pitched the mirror fragment that was the largest in size. It gave them a periscope view of the passageway.

They saw immediately that Kelvin stood at the far forward end of the passage. He held an automatic pistol, quite a handful of gun, which he aimed deliberately at the mirror. However, instead of firing, he grinned and lowered the gun, calling over his shoulder to someone.

Another man now appeared beside Kelvin, a grotesque figure of an old man, bone-thin, lemon-skinned, with a snatch of forward-protruding white hair. His green suit was an outstandingly ugly shade.

"Wearing a carnival-barker suit like that, he walked right under the noses of the police who had his description," Doc said gloomily. "That's the fellow who also tried to get the canary birds out of the check-room."

"Who gave his description to the police?" Monk demanded.

"Caspell undoubtedly did that first thing."

"Caspell? You mean the big shot in the new department

the government set up for science espionage?" Monk was puzzled. "Who rang him in?"

"I did, and gave our prisoner Clinton Williams to him," Doc explained.

"You mean," asked Monk, "that there's an angle to this that is up Caspell's alley?"

"Seems so."

"Caspell's field is atoms, germ-weapons and such gimcracks. I don't see where canary birds connect up."

"The connection," Doc said, "will curl your hair."

Kelvin and the bizarre old man—Mr. Plott, according to the name he'd given the check-room men—had been watching the mirror. They seemed cold-bloodedly amused. Both turned away, and their place was taken by another man, a complete stranger, who kept a spike-nosed automatic pistol in his hands and settled down to watch.

"They seem damned self-satisfied," said Ham nervously. "Somehow that doesn't cheer me up any."

Audrey had been peering out of the window. She got their attention. "There's an awful lot of water down below," she said.

Monk went over and looked out gloomily. "There generally is, of the Atlantic Ocean," he said.

The plane had lined out in a course more northerly than easterly, which indicated the destination might be Europe, a premise that seemed almost too fantastic. True, they could not keep an accurate check, because within about an hour, the ship entered an overcast, a great area of stratus cloud evidently two or three thousand feet in thickness, and they flew through this for some hours. Doc expressed the opinion that they were making the Atlantic passage, but somewhat south of the Great Circle route. Heading, conceivably, for the Mediterranean section.

"You mean," said Ham, "that they've stolen one of the biggest passenger airliners, and us with it, and are heading across the Atlantic Ocean?" He grinned foolishly. "A fiction writer would really need a hole in his head to dream that one up."

"Oh, I don't know," said Monk. Monk's nerves had stopped twanging sufficiently to allow him to assume his normal position contrary-wise to anything Ham had to offer "The plane flies the Atlantic on regular service, doesn't it?"

They received some attention from forward. A coffee cup, hurled from up ahead, landed against the cushion which pillowed the mirror. There was a note tied to the cup handle, and they raked it inside cautiously with a loop made in the end of Monk's belt.

Your compartment has window. Better use it and jump You'll enjoy it more.

"They've got a humorist in the crowd," Monk muttered.

A few seconds later, there was a series of loud reports shots, accompanied by the vibration of bullets tearing through the floor from the upper deck. Doc put his head into the compartment they'd left earlier, and noted the ragged hole in the ceiling. He paid some attention to the pattern of the shots.

"They were pretty careful," he remarked, "not to send any bullets near the control cables, which run along the keel of the ship." He glanced sharply at Monk, and suddenly went to work on the floor, ripping up the carpeting.

They discovered, gratefully, that there was a hatch in the floor, equipped with simple lock-fasteners that could be released by using a half-dollar as a screwdriver. Lifting the hatch aside, they found they had access to the long tunnel like conduit through which the control cables for elevators and rudders, and the controls for the trim tabs, passed.

"Let's have your shoelaces," Doc said. "Also anything else in the way of cords."

Highly interested, Monk, Ham and Audrey watched him rig a purchase on two of the control cables. This wasn't simple, because the cables didn't offer much of a grip. Miss Prince, while still unconscious from the drug she'd been given, was beginning to stir and moan.

Doc was studying the rearmost parts of the plane. "We might," he said, "get clear aft."

"One man back there," said Monk, "could make some body nervous."

Doc indicated the bulkhead. "Go to work on it. See what can be done."

Monk and Ham took turns kicking. They were not successful. "This one," said Monk, "is thicker." He frowned at the sheet of metal. "Now, if I was an aeronautical engineer, I'd know what to do with that one button I have left."

Doc Savage gave the matter thought, pounding on the bulkhead with his fist to locate the hollow-sounding spots. "Try here," he said. "Half a button, only."

Monk prepared carefully, borrowing some chewing gum from Audrey to hold the button in place. "All set? Here goes." He applied the ignition charge, stepped back, and there was a display of heat and blue glare as the Thermit ignited, liquified and slid downward, cutting a slit nearly three feet long. Monk gave the metal a kick while the edges were still hot, and it started to tear. He continued kicking.

Several shots were fired into the compartment immediately ahead, coming from the upper deck.

Doc instantly dropped into the floor opening, seized the cords he'd attached to the control wires, and yanked. The plane gave a sickening vault upward, then, as Doc changed pressures, it toppled off on one wingtip. In a moment, however, the astonished pilot began to use his strength on the control wheel and rudders, and the ship shakily found an even keel. Doc tried two or three more yanks. There was not much response.

Audrey had watched, first in fright, and then with some contempt. "Didn't you waste that?"

"Ham, crawl back in the stern," Doc said. "Figure out how to put leverages on the controls. We can partly handle the ship from there, in a pinch."

Monk grinned. "They won't know. They'll think they can outpull us on the control cables. They'll be cocky."

"That's the idea," Doc agreed.

Miss Prince opened her eyes, looked around carefully, then stared fixedly at the floor. She said, "This isn't my hotel room?" in a confused voice.

"You bet it isn't your hotel, toots," Audrey said. "You're a long way from anybody's hotel."

After a vague glance at Audrey, one that held no recognition for the blonde, Miss Prince resumed staring at the floor. She wrinkled her forehead repeatedly. Then she lay back, determined to wait for her mind to clear.

"Good idea. Wait until your head stops ringing," Doc said.

"It isn't ringing," said Miss Prince dully. "It's full of fog, or mud, or something."

"You're on a plane. A big one. A Trans-Atlantic airliner. We're cornered in the rear part of the ship. A number of men, including a Kelvin and a Mr. Plott, control the rest of the ship and are flying it. Likewise, they are trying to kill us."

Miss Prince closed her eyes again for a moment. "I don't," she murmured, "think I like the joke."

"It's true, anyway. The stocky man is Monk Mayfair, a chemist. The slender one is Ham Brooks, an attorney. Both men are associated with me. The lady is Audrey, who came along for the ride."

"The ride," said Audrey bitterly, "is one I won't forget for a day or two."

Miss Prince stared at Doc, her dark eyes open wide. "You wouldn't be Doc Savage?" she asked wonderingly.

"Good guess."

Miss Prince frowned. "You're Doc Savage? And you're cornered in the rear of an airplane? You're in trouble? But I understood you were supposed to be rather invincible."

Audrey laughed wryly. "Invincible? What's dat?"

"Baby," said Monk to the blonde, "you're beginning to develop a personality like a rock in a shoe."

Miss Prince took her head in her hands. "Let me think," she mumbled. "This is awfully confusing."

"I'd call it scary," said Audrey coldly. "Anybody with brains, and I'm beginning to think that lets out present company, would be frightened out of their wits."

"Like you are, for instance?" Monk suggested pointedly.

"Exactly."

"You don't act it," said Monk. "You seem cool as icicles."

"Wait," said Audrey, "until I begin to melt. Just wait."

With visible effort, Miss Prince had been thinking. "There is a gap," she said. "I remember my hotel room. I came in, looked under the bed, in the bathroom, and locked the door. Then I looked in the clothes closet, which was the wrong time. I should have done that before I locked the door, because they were there. Two men. I couldn't get the door open, because I'd locked it. One held me. The other jabbed something sharp into my arm. The gap begins there. It ends here. What happened?"

Doc said, "We can fill it with a guess—they got you out of the hotel and aboard the plane."

"That seems impossible."

Doc shrugged. "So does kidnapping an airliner, and us in it."

"Yes, I guess so."

"Is that," Doc asked, "the only gap?"

Miss Prince frowned thoughtfully. "I see what you mean," she said.

Monk dropped down into the opening in the floor, and gave the control cables a hard jerk. This caused the plane to give a short goat-like buck, but the pilot retained control. There were, however, loud frightening curses from the forward part of the ship. Monk grinned. "Sounds as if we've distributed a little unhappiness," he remarked.

"It won't be funny," said Audrey, "if they get unhappy enough to rush us."

"Suit me fine," Monk told her.

"But you haven't a single gun. You're unarmed," Audrey reminded contemptuously.

Monk grinned fiercely. "Unarmed wasn't the word used," he said.

Monk started to get in the hole again, but Doc stopped him. "The middle of the Atlantic Ocean," Doc said, "is a poor place to hurry things. Let's ride along. They'll probably leave us alone for a while." He turned to Miss Prince, adding, "Also, if I get killed, I'd hate for it to happen in a state of ignorance. Have you got a story to tell us, Miss Prince?"

Miss Prince nodded quickly. "Yes. Yes, I certainly have. But I don't know which end to begin."

"The canary birds?" Doc suggested.

"Well, all right, but that will mean telling it backwards," she said. "I was stuck with the birds. I wanted you to have them. But I was being watched. I was mighty frightened, too. You see, it had been a long race to New York, and I'd thought I'd be safe when I got there. But I could see I wasn't. It was disconcerting."

"Who was watching you?" Doc asked.

"Plott, for one. Not that he was alone. Only I didn't know the others by sight. That was no help, either."

"Who is Plott?"

"The one who killed Reverend Lauterbach," Miss Prince said, and suddenly looked shaken.

"When did that happen?"

"In Cairo, while we were en route from India. They poisoned him. An Egyptian dish called *lahmquishtah*. The Reverend loved it. I detested it.... After that, I made a run for New York, knowing that's what the Reverend would have wanted." She frowned. "No, that's taking the story the wrong direction. It's awkward, backtracking."

"You were chased from India?" Doc asked.

"Yes. We didn't know it, though, until Cairo. Then it was too late."

"How had you left India?"

"From Karachi? By plane. Before that, from Apozai, by one way and another. Whatever was secret. We thought we were doing a good job of skedaddling." She paused and compressed her lips. "I guess not."

Doc Savage said thoughtfully, "Apozai? That is up near Afghanistan. Pretty far from the beginning of any thing."

Miss Prince shuddered.

"But close," she said, "to the beginning of the end. Likely as not."

"Is around Apozia where it developed?" Doc asked.

She nodded. "That's the snake's nest."

A single shot sounded. A single desolate bullet passed in the corridor, striking the cushions, shattering the mirror, and doing no harm. Monk grunted, and tossed out another bit of mirror, so that it landed in a position to show them the forward portion of the corridor. He waited expectantly for it also to be smashed by a bullet, but nothing happened. "Guess they were just venting spite," he remarked.

"Plott," said Doc, looking at Miss Prince narrowly, "seems a likely type. Half of something or other, isn't he?"

"Half Tibetan," she agreed. "And I hope a Tibetan never hears me say so. He'd be insulted. The other half of Plott is something with the white skin, I'd guess."

"But hardly a white soul," Doc suggested. "Father evidently had money, though. The man, to get the kind of a scientific education he needs for such a thing, went to a lot of schools. Advanced ones."

"You're not," said Miss Prince, "as much in the dark as I thought. Or am I wrong?"

Doc asked, "Who was Reverend Lauterbach?"

"My uncle. Mother's brother. Missionary. Loved the far and the odd places of the earth. But a curious man, too. Spent a good part of his life, when he wasn't converting, satisfying his curiosity. Reverend would hear that a tribe of natives in Borneo stood on their heads whenever they saw a full moon, and he wouldn't rest until he got to Borneo and found out why. Curious. A seeker of answers to riddles. He died of it."

"And so," Doc said grimly, "could a lot of others."

She nodded. "You seem to know. Did you read it in a book somewhere?"

"Not in a book—in the brain of a canary."

She stared at him. "You mean it showed. There were physical traces?"

"An aberration of that type, and as intense as that one was, shows in changed formation of the brain."

"A canary's brain," said Miss Prince, "can't be very big. You're not stretching truth?"

"I take it the canary was a laboratory case. Overdosed." Doc looked at her thoughtfully. "Did I miss on that?"

"You hit it on the nose."

"You'd better put a few words around the canary. I don't know everything about any of it, and practically nothing about the part we've reached," Doc told her.

"Let me get myself in India in the first place," she said. "It was a rather ordinary way to get there—I finished business college and applied to the mission service for a job, requesting foreign service. Well, they knew I was Reverend Lauterbach's niece, and so they assigned me to him. I thought they were just being nice to me because of Uncle, but I found out otherwise. The Reverend was a tough one to work for, and I suppose they were doing him a dirty trick when they sent me. Anyway, I wound up in India, first at Karachi, then farther north near the Afghanistan border. We were there about a year before the British got out of India, and the civil uprisings started." She looked at them grimly, and put a question. "Did the internal troubles in India get much publicity in the States?"

*   *   *

"Nearly all printed media—newspapers, magazines, and so forth—carried fact stories on the strife that followed the setting up of self-government in India," Doc told her. "It was a pretty gory affair."

Margaret Prince shuddered. "The stories couldn't have been half as bloody as the facts. Believe me, they weren't exaggerated. It was ghastly. It seemed impossible to conceive such bloodthirsty, murderous hate in human beings, particularly those who incited the violence. And that is the thing that aroused Uncle's interest."

Doc Savage's attention was sharp. "The leadership in the rioting and wholesale murdering—it didn't seem to be organized." He sounded shocked.

"Organization," said the girl, "is having a plan."

Doc nodded. "That's what fooled me."

"Oh!" She stared at him. "You noticed an oddness about the trouble in northern India, too?"

"Everyone who was in touch with the situation was unpleasantly surprised," Doc said. "But they looked for organized effort—communist, fascist, or some other totalitarian master-minding. I know that's what I looked for. I didn't see much of it, and that seems to be where I missed the boat."

She nodded. "The Reverend was more fortunate—or unfortunate—maybe. Anyway, he traced the source of the crazed leaders. He couldn't trace them to men who were influencing them. But he traced them to a *place*."

"Where?"

"Near Apozai. Near the place I mentioned."

Monk and Ham were staring. Audrey, her blonde head tilted, seemed interested in a skeptical way.

"Now let's get this straight," Doc said. "Massacres and violence in a part of India was being stirred up by men. These men were influenced into doing what they were doing. Influenced by a *place*?"

"Yes."

"Are you sure you mean a place? Don't you mean other men in a place?"

"I—yes."

"Yes what?"

"I mean," said Margaret Prince, "that men have found out how to make other men *hate*."

"How do you mean?"

"I mean mechanically—that is, it may be electrically, or sonically. Let's put it this way: By some scientific discovery, the human mind can be thrown out of kilter and the part of it that hates developed out of all proportion."

"Your uncle, the Reverend Lauterbach, discovered this thing?"

"Yes."

"Was your uncle a psychophysicist?"

"I don't know what the word means. I guess he wasn't." She frowned, and added sharply, "Oh, I see what you're driving at. Well, let me tell you this: Reverend Lauterbach knew enough to find out what was going on. You don't have to know what causes influenza, to be able to see when someone's got it."

"He didn't discover how it was being done, then?"

"Why do you think we were coming to New York with the two canary birds?"

"Where did you get the canary birds?"

"I don't know. The Reverend got them. He went away from camp one night, and came back frightened and in a desperate hurry, and we lit out for New York at once. He told me he was going to get the canary birds to you to prove that his theory wasn't crazy, and that you were a man who could stop the devilish thing if anyone could."

Audrey sniffed, shaking her blond hair back over her shoulders.

"I wish somebody'd stop it," she said.

Presently Doc Savage produced a pocket knife, slit the seat coverings, shaped out swatches of fabric, and began fashioning a pair of moccasins. They were of quite small size, and he worked idly but with care, paying no attention to the curious stares.

"What," demanded Audrey, "do you think you're doing?"

"Making moccasins."

"What?"

"Moccasins. Indians used to wear them." He glanced judiciously at Audrey's shapely foot. "They should about fit you, if you'd care for a souvenir."

Audrey sniffed.

"If I get out of this mess with my life," she said, "that'll be souvenir enough for me."

VIII

Monk Mayfair and Ham Brooks, after several years' association with Doc Savage, had become rather experienced with trouble. At least, they had learned to pretend some degree of unconcern. Familiarity with danger, they had discovered, does not breed contempt, or not more than once, anyway. Because a man contemptuous of danger is a man soon dead. Pretending they weren't terrified took a lot of effort, and they never managed to be as calm as Doc Savage seemed to be, and it unnerved them.

Doc had been sleeping four hours. Monk and Ham were wide-awake and jumpy as cats.

"You'd almost think," Monk complained, "that Doc is sure those guys aren't going to rush us."

"Why would he think that?" demanded Audrey.

"Search me," said Monk. "I sure don't share the belief, either."

"If you were rushed," Audrey asked thoughtfully, "what would you do?"

Monk grinned, but with no pleasure. He showed her a couple of small metal pellets. "Doc gave me these. They're grenades. Explosive. They'd blow half the front end of this airplane to pieces."

Audrey paled. "You wouldn't be crazy enough to use those things?"

"If they're crazy enough to rush me, I would be," Monk said.

Audrey jumped up and, before anyone could stop her, shoved her head out of the compartment and screamed, "Don't rush us! They've got bombs here! They'll blow the ship apart!"

Monk and Ham seized Audrey and dragged her back. "You baby-faced dope!" Ham yelled. "Why'd you do that?"

"You think I want to be in an airplane when its blown apart over the Atlantic Ocean?" Audrey screeched. She was shaking, showing signs of hysterics.

Doc Savage had awakened, and was watching placidly. "I

lon't think she did us any harm," he said. "As a matter of fact, ve might all get some sleep now."

"Sleep!" said Audrey bitterly. "I doubt if I will ever sleep again."

There was land below. At first, it had been a long way below, fully twenty thousand feet down, so that there had not been much detail. Doc, however, after watching the terrain or a time, said, "I think we're well south in Africa, crossing eastward over a deserted part of the Sahara."

Twenty thousand feet was a lot of altitude, and now the ship began to gather more. Simultaneously, they noticed that the cabin pressure started dropping.

"Trying to get high enough to knock us out," Doc said. Took their time getting the idea. Ham, crawl back in the tail section. Set the elevator trim-tab for full nose-down. You can do that, because of the way the trim-tab is connected, without their being able to tell exactly what is wrong, can't you?"

"I think so," Ham said. He scrambled through the hole they had opened into the tail section.

Margaret Prince was staring anxiously. "High enough to knock us out? You mean lack of oxygen?"

Doc nodded. "Yes. They've blocked the forward section off, and opened a window in our part of the plane."

"Are we in danger?"

Doc hesitated. "Well, it's hard to say. The ceiling of this ship is enough to get up where there isn't enough oxygen. But I think the trim-tab, plus Ham's weight back there, will keep the ship from doing its best. As a last resort, we can force the elevator main control into diving position."

"Why not do that at once?"

"They don't know we can partly control the ship. We may need to surprise them later." Doc gestured at the seats. Stretch out and relax as much as you can. Don't get panicky. hey can't get above twenty-five thousand, and the pressure altitude inside won't reach that."

Regardless of Doc's assurance, what followed wasn't pleasant. The symptoms of anoxia, or oxygen want, began to appear. They were, characteristically, greatly at variance with individuals. Monk, for no reason at all, began to giggle. Just stare at the ceiling and giggle at intervals. Audrey was the only one who became hysterical, and she did it in a ghastly restrained fashion, glaring at them all with intense hate.

"The ship's not getting any higher," Doc said quietly. He was watching the mirror arrangement on the pillows, their periscope for inspecting the forward part of the plane.

Suddenly Doc whipped to the door. He had, in one hand, a slab of mirror glass, and he whipped this back and threw it forward into the passage. A howl of agony was the immediate result. The mirror on the cushion showed him a man, one he had not seen before, staggering backward with a badly cut face. The man disappeared.

The plane began to descend.

"They've given that up," Doc said calmly.

Ham joined them presently. "Man, that was rough," he muttered. "But I don't think they caught on about the trim-tab. I reconnected the thing, anyway."

The ship continued to drop, and presently it leaned over in a lazy turn. Monk jumped to the window. "There's an airport down there! We're going to land."

Their compartment was, fortunately, on the starboard side of the ship, which was the inside of all regulation traffic pattern turns, so they were able to get a full look at the airport. Doc Savage recognized it immediately, said, "The place is south of Barca, in Libya. Bomber base first established by the Nazis, later developed by the Allies. I was in here a couple of times during the war." He pondered for a moment, added, "As far as I know, the field is still maintained as an auxiliary for heavy ships. Rarely used, though."

"Rarely used or not," Monk said, "you can't tell me there's an airport too remote to have heard of the theft of a plane this size, and be on the lookout for it."

"It looks to me as if they're calmly going to land," Ham remarked.

"That," said Monk, "would worry my insurance company if they knew about it."

The plan of landing became evident at once. The ship was going to use the north-south runway, whereas the administration buildings, a far from impressive cluster of ramshackle structures that had survived from the war which had long ago touched this part of the north African coast, were at one end of the east-west runway. Coming in slowly, with a little wider pattern than was necessary—a hint the pilot was unfa niliar with this type ship to some degree—the plane leveled out on the final approach. The landing was good enough. The ship stopped at the end of the field farthest from the buildings.

Immediately, the engines were killed. They could hear rucks approaching.

From forward, a voice hailed them. "We're going to efuel. If you stick your heads out, or start yelling, you'll be hot. Otherwise, you will not be harmed."

Doc listened to the yelling between the truck drivers and the plane crew. There was an angry dispute, clearly between the truck drivers and two men who had hired them to fuel the plane. The drivers had recognized this as the tolen ship. As soon as that became clear, the fuss ended. Doc took a cautious look. Both drivers had been knocked unconscious.

The refueling proceeded. Both tank trucks were enormous affairs, and one went to work on each wing-tank.

A battered jeep started to approach from the hangars. There were a few shots. The jeep turned and pulled a fast cloud of dust after itself in flight.

Refueling done, the tank trucks were driven aside, the two men who'd hired them climbed aboard with the others, the engines started, and presently they were in the air again.

"Our friends," said Monk gloomily, "are used to organizing."

"That's not all they're used to," Margaret Prince assured him. "They're experts at handling undesired guests. And we qualify."

Monk nodded. "They radioed ahead from New York for their pals to be ready with gas, probably."

"Radio," said Margaret Prince, "works both ways."

"Yeah, you mean they've probably arranged a reception committee at our destination."

"Wouldn't you imagine?" she asked.

"I've been," said Monk, "trying to stuff my imagination in a hole and keep it there. Don't drag it out."

After more endless hours of flying, during which nothing violent happened, Doc Savage concluded they must be over northeastern India or southern Afghanistan. In either case, it was a wild-looking country.

"They know where they're heading," Doc remarked.

"And if they're smart, they've arranged an ambuscade at the landing-place. We'd better get on our toes."

A half hour later, Margaret Prince said, "That mountain off yonder looks familiar. Unless I miss my guess, we're near Apozai."

"I wonder," Doc said, "if you've flown over southern Nevada?"

"Flown? No. I've driven. Should I have remembered something?"

"The mud lakes."

"What? Oh—oh, I see. . . . I think you've got something."

"I'd be satisfied," complained Audrey bitterly, "if half your talk made sense. Just half."

"A mud lake," Doc explained patiently, "is not really mud, but is the bed of a lake that is flooded during the rainy season, and the rest of the years is as flat as a floor and baked hard as pavement. Most desert countries have them. There are a few, a very few, in this part of the world. One might be handy for a landing-field."

Ham had been watching from the window. "Nice predicting," he called. "Yonder's our lake bed."

The big plane sank lower, and passed over the expanse of dried mud, which did not look any too large, and which was surrounded by low brush-covered hills.

With no difficulty, they saw a group of some dozen horsemen clustered near the downwind end of the lake bed. These gentlemen, some of whom wore turbans, waved rifles in the air.

"Reception committee," Ham said.

The plane began a slow swing to the right, then a steeper turn to the left.

"Pilot's going to drag the place downwind to look it over," Ham decided.

"Ham," Doc demanded. "Can you do business with the elevator controls?"

"Sure. The rudder, too, if I had some help."

"The elevator will be enough. Get set. Monk, you park at the hole so you can relay instructions to Ham." Doc hesitated, and added a word of possibly unneeded caution. "This wouldn't be a good time for you fellows to have an argument."

Ham grinned thinly. "We'll call a truce."

Doc issued a few instructions. "It may be messy," he finished. "And it's not going to do the airplane any good. If anybody has a better idea, let's hear it."

"Sounds fine to me," Monk said. "How about the rest of you?"

Audrey shuddered violently. "I vote awful. We could all be killed."

"Could," said Monk, "is half a word."

The pilot, as Doc had surmised, intended to make a very low pass at the mud lake so that he could satisfy himself the area was smooth enough for a landing. Doc, having looked it over on the first trip across, thought is was satisfactory. Also, his plan wouldn't pay off so well if they made a conventional into-the-wind landing, which would mean the plane rolling to a halt near the horsemen.

He watched the scrubby, brownish, hump-like hills swell upward. The pilot was coming in very low. They heard a whining noise.

Monk, crouched at the torn gap in the bulkhead, ready to relay to Ham, laughed. "Getting the gear down," he said. "That's a favor for us, I'd say."

"Get set," Doc said.

They neared the lake.

"Down elevator!" Doc said sharply.

"Down elevator!" Monk roared.

The plane seemed to drop from under their feet. Doc, at the window, watched carefully.

"This," he remarked, "is an awkward place from which to land an airplane." He waited a moment. "Elevator up slightly!"

"Elevator up slightly!" Monk howled.

Monk was perspiring. Forward, a man was screaming profanity.

The plane, diving, had narrowly missed the last hill-crest. It was still headed down. The horsemen, alarmed, some of them almost in the path of the ship, spurred their mounts wildly.

"Up elevator a shade!" Doc shouted.

Monk relayed, and almost instantly, which was somewhat quicker than Doc intended, the wheels hit the lake surface. It was, as landings went, a ghastly experience. The ship gave two terrific bounces, seemed inclined to stick with the baked mud surfaces, which wasn't too smooth after all. "Elevator full down," Doc ordered.

The plane had simply been forced down until its wheels touched the ground. The full-down elevator would keep it from rising. The rest was up to the pilot. He couldn't take off again, and future developments depended on how soon he realized this.

"Get set for a crash," Doc said.

The tires were shrieking now as brakes were applied. With a ghastly dipping, like a fowl trying to get a grain of corn off the earth, the ship rocked forward on the nose wheel and back as the pilot tried to jump it off.

Doc held his breath, waiting. If the pilot had thought quickly enough—and had the nerve to carry out his convictions—he'd simply have slammed the throttles wide open and let the plane keep going at the better than a hundred mile an hour at which they'd slammed it on the flat expanse of dry mud. The man should reasonably know that Doc's group wouldn't hold the ship down long enough to insure a crash at high speed.

But the pilot was stopping. With a final howl of tires, a great jolting, the ship climbed up into the rough ground at the edge of the lake, slewed partly around, halted.

Doc, having waited for the plane to halt, struck hard at the window escape-hatch mechanism. The panel could then be opened, and he leaned out, picked his target—the wing area near the root on that side—and threw one of the explosive grenades.

The explosion, considering the miniature size of the explosive charge, was impressive. The whole plane flinched sidewise, the wing collapsed slowly, and the plane sagged down on that side. Lazily, which was fortunate, because the tricycle gear held the fuselage more than a dozen feet off the ground. Puncturing the groaning of tearing metal, hardly louder, there was a great mushy cough as the gasoline in that wing-tank took flame.

Doc wheeled. "Is Ham trapped back in the tail?"

"No. He's coming," said Monk, "like a scalded cat."

"Out," Doc said. He seized the magazine rack above the window, swung out feetfirst, turned and dropped to the ground. "Pass the women out."

Margaret Prince was beside him almost at once. He gave
er a shove toward the shrubbery and boulders that littered
he hillside.

"Run," he said, "but not too far. We hope to join you."

Inside, Audrey started to argue. An instant later, Audrey
came flying out, argument and all. Monk had tossed her.

Flames had blanketed the entire forward section of the
plane on this side. Plott, Kelvin, the pilot, the others, could
be heard leaving on the opposite side. None of the sounds
hey made were happy.

Doc wheeled, searching for the group of horsemen.
They were, he discovered, out of view. The plane, in twisting
partially around, had died so as to conceal this side of the
raft from sight. That was more luck than Doc had expected.

Monk was now out of the ship. Ham, also, in a moment.

"We've got fifteen or twenty seconds," Doc said urgently,
for traveling."

IX

They ran a few yards, and the tangled undergrowth of
he *cchota puhar*, the Himalayan subhill country, was around
hem. The lava outcroppings, the thin eroded gullies and
vadis, were at the same time sanctuary and difficulty. Doc
avage, even with death milling around in confusion back
here by the burning plane, was impressed with the oddness
of sudden transition into a foreign scene. It was a thing that
ong-distance air travelers almost always feel, he knew, but he
vas upset by the strangeness anyway. He saw the same sense
of unreality on Margaret Prince's face when they found her. It
vas there as much as danger was. And even her incredulous,
They didn't see you, either?" didn't dispel it.

"We got a break. The way the plane careened broadside
nto the hill was luck."

"Some," she said, "was managing."

"Get down," Doc said. "Let's try this gully."

They slid into a wadi, trying to make no noise, clinging
o the roots of scrub *ballut* for purchase. Doc studied the
ormation of the gulch as they advanced, and when the

footing changed suddenly from coarse sand to lava, he said "All right, we'll split here. The rest of you keep together—"

Monk, jaw sagging in alarm, blurted, "Hey, now, wait minute—"

"Keep together," Doc said. "Take your time, and leav no footprints. Stay out of sight."

"I take it," said Monk uneasily, "that you're going to dra a herring."

"Let's hope so." Doc examined the footgear of the tw women. "Could I borrow your footgear, Audrey?"

"My shoes, you mean? You expect me to walk barefoote over these rocks? What for?"

"For herring-tracks," Doc said, smiling. "I'll bring th shoes back."

"You hope." Audrey hesitated, then said angrily, "Oh, a right. At least I can die with my shoes off."

Doc produced the moccasins he'd made quite a b earlier. "You won't need to go barefoot, after all. You can wea these. Lucky I made them to fit you."

Audrey looked stunned.

"Luck," she said, "that was manufactured well ahead time, I'd say."

Monk took her arm. "Doc is full of that kind of luck Let's get going."

When they had disappeared around a turn in the twistin little canyon, Doc Savage took a course at right angles, an made plenty of tracks as he went, leaning over to dig th heels of Audrey's sharply fashionable slippers into the earth When he had worked his way well up, he quickened h pace, using care to keep hidden from the burning plane, no marked by a column of dark smoke. And shortly he reached spot where he could get a view of the excitement at the ship

What he saw brought, at first, surprised disbelief. Th horsemen, Plott, the others, were ringed in a big circ around the flaming airliner. Guns ready, they were watching

In a moment, it became clear why. Down there, the still supposed Doc and the others were in the plane. Th reason? He saw that also. Ham, the last one out of the ship had had presence of mind to close the window. There was n clear evidence that the occupants of the rearmost compart ment had escaped.

He waited and watched, and they did the same, intently

rimly, poised to murder. And then he turned and began to
limb, going slowly, leaving plenty of tracks. He chose now,
vhenever possible, going that would trouble the horses, so
ough that they would have to dismount and lead the ani-
aals. He left fewer tracks now, but enough. Those were
ugged, fierce hillmen of Pakistan down there, the horses
idicated that, and the turbans, the *topis,* the baggy *putloons,*
aarked the men. Violent *darinda* tribesmen, from the
orthwest.

Shots came abruptly. He crawled to an eminence to
vatch again. They were firing into the rear section of the
hip. Suspicious finally. Puzzled by the lack of life in the
lazing plane.

He could distinguish the howled orders of the *Wali,* the
eader. An old man, but with a scraping banshee voice.

"*Kya hoo's?*" the old voice squalled.

So now you want to know what happened, you old devil,
Doc thought grimly. Well, you'll find out presently, the worse
ack. The aft section of the plane isn't going to burn.

Doc located the *Wali,* a scrawny jackanapes in rags on a
ne Arabian horse. A scarecrow on a living throne of beauty.
lott stood near him. The old brigand brandished a very
aodern submachine gun. "*Undhur jao!*" he squawked.
Khabardar raho!" And his ragtag following, obedient to his
owling, approached the flaming wreck warily.

Waiting now only to count the men in European garb,
Doc numbered them nine. They would be the ones who'd
aken over the ship in New York, plus the pair who'd ar-
anged the refueling. Nine. The odds hadn't been pleasant.
Jor were they even that pleasant now.

Climbing again, Doc glanced frequently into the west,
neasuring the sun for time. An hour, he decided, would see
he death of the day. And a fairly dark death, too. There were
uite a few clouds.

High on the side of a hill, where he could watch the
razily gutted courses of the wadis, he waited again. This
ime, for pursuit. He could still hear, faintly, the shouts that
ame up from the rim of the mud lake. Distance lent a novel
uality to the cries, like coyote yappings in Montana. The
orsemen, galloping about in search of footprints, seemed
rimly playful. Illusion only, which suddenly lost its dream-

like air when a robe-flapping Pakistan hillman found the tra
His shrieked, *"Age-barho! Age-barho!"* had had a biti
ugliness on the evening air, even before the old chief took
the cry.

They were wild riders, but cautious. Half a dozen swarme
up the gully. The others rode wide, taking rough goin
punishing their horses with spurs.

In a space of time so short that Doc could feel it in t
pit of his stomach, they came to the point where Doc ha
separated from the others. They over-rode the trail ther
shouting, and gave Doc a ghastly few minutes when
imagined his side-trail hadn't diverted them. Then they bobbe
into sight, fanned out again, riding hard, following Doc
phony trail. He waited long enough to count them. The
were all on the false scent. Excepting, of course, those wl
didn't have mounts, and who had remained where the pla
was now a darkened carcass that leaked smoke.

Doc took flight now. He was calculating about it, howe
er. He left fewer clues, but not too few.

Deliberately, he left one of Audrey's shoes wedged in
crack in the rock in which he jammed it.

A couple of hundred yards beyond where he left tl
blonde's slipper, Doc noted den sign, spoor that indicated tl
lair of some animal nearby. He investigated, came shortly to
hole of some size, large enough to show him that it must l
the home of some *richh, bhalu,* a common sloth or blac
bear.

He crawled back into the den a few yards, waril
because the animals were dangerous and this one might be
home. Far enough, only, to make tracks, and then he witl
drew, with the hair-raising conviction that there was actual
a bear in there. It made no difference about the bea
personally. He only wanted the pursuers to think they ha
been fools enough to hide there.

Going on, he left no tracks now. He took infinite pai
about that. And, half a mile away, he crawled up the side of
crag and stretched out to watch.

It was cool. The air had a slight bite, like spiced win
because of the odor of *phul,* an aromatically noisy littl
mountain flower that was rampant at this season. This w
high country. The Indus plain lay to the south and east, th

Helmand Desert was to the west, and not very far west, either. At this season, at this altitude, the desert didn't mean heat. He studied the country, trying to figure their probable whereabouts, other than the general fact that they were in northwestern India, the outlands of Pakistan. Near Apozai, Margaret Prince had said. The word "near" was relative, didn't mean much. He had, frankly, no idea where they were.

The hillmen were following his trail. He could see Plott, on a horse, with them. They were having slow, noisy going.

He watched Plott, wondering if the man was the mind behind this unpleasant and improbable thing, and he concluded presently that Plott was. The conviction, held back half-formed in his mind for some time, loosened and stood full-bodied, an ugly thing. He regretted bitterly the fiasco in New York. It was preposterous to be trapped in the cabin of a plane and hauled off to India, and do nothing to prevent it. He believed he saw, looking back, two or three possible moves they might have made, either toward escape or aggression. He had thought of these at the time in each case, but they looked a great deal more workable now than they had then. Probably lying here alone in the dusk with trouble all about had something to do with the hindsight optimism.

He began to worry. The laboratory where the thing had been developed might not be here. This was an improbable country for it. They would need apparatus, special apparatus and a lot of it built to specifications. Pakistan was not a place where you got delicate special equipment for supersonics, or UHF electrical frequencies, or however they were doing it. Pakistan was a dazed little nation just born, one that hadn't quite learned what to do with itself.

On the other hand, Pakistan was logical too. Here they were Moslems, and the fanatic Moslem zeal had sprayed itself bloodily over a good part of northwestern India. Raids and bloodshed against the neighboring Kashmir state, violence directed at Hindu India, a little senseless to the distant world of newspaper readers and maneuvering United Nations diplomats, a bright outer world where there were foes as clean-cut as communism and freedom, Democrats and Republicans, Joe Louis and Jersey Joe Walcott. The violence of religious conflict was a strange violence, and so a good backdrop for manufactured hate. If they wished to test it. And of course they would want to test it. You had to test a thing that preposterous. It began to look logical to him again, and he liked it better. Too, it occurred to him that he was worrying, so he stopped that. To flatly say, *All right, stop worrying*, and make it stick—that was one of his better abilities.

Now they came to the hole in the ground. There was some laughter. A few shots went into the hole.

The old *Wali* raised a voice as shrill as a ten-cent whistle. He wanted to know if, down there at the carcass of the plane, they had any hand grenades. They hadn't.

So a man crawled back into the hole in the hill. He didn't come out, and it was evident that something of interest happened in the hole. A second man was elected to crawl in. He did so unhappily. The first had gone in willingly. That one did not come out either. Nor did the first. But a large sloth bear did, full of rage.

The bear made a good show. It caused three horses to bolt, riderless. The men scattered. Then someone shot the bear.

It was getting dark.

Doc Savage stalked the horses that had bolted, but gave it up presently. They were wary nags, and took out and kept going in three assorted directions, showing no communal instinct.

Doc threw away Audrey's other shoe.

His traveling had purpose and urgency now. There would be no more trailing tonight, unless they had manhunting dogs, which was not an impossibility. The night came, black but not utterly, enabling him to move freely, although it hid some of the footing.

Finally in the gulch where he'd left Monk, Ham, Audrey and Margaret Prince, he used his flashlight. Except for a switch to turn it off and on, it was in no ordinary sense a flashlight, not even one of those which have a small hand-operated generator. This one had such a generator, but intricately made and with a great deal of power built into it.

The gadget had many purposes. It could, in a strong man's hands, power a fair-sized radio transmitter, do anything else that electric current of considerable voltage and some amperage could do. It could shock a man painfully. Set off explosive charges with the proper electric detonators.

It also could, and did, activate a cell that produced

more ultra-violet light, outside the visible spectrum, than seemed quite logical. Ultra-violet rays having a rather odd, but not at all uncommon, effect on striking certain substances. Fluorescence.

Doc searched, and presently picked up the footprints left by the treated soles of the moccasins he'd given Audrey. The fluorescence was distinctive, a particularly malevolent greenish, like the crushed eyes of a cat.

He began to climb. The ultra-violet made other sporadic displays of odd-looking light as it struck various mineral outcroppings. But the footprints led on, not much more difficult to follow than the reflectors that warn of turns on highways.

Monk and the others had parked for the night in a particularly rugged spot where there were plenty of rocks and gullies at hand for cover.

Doc approached quite near the camp, but did not enter. He became immobile, a shadow that was part of shadow, and waited. That in itself was not the safest of things to do, in case Monk or Ham came on him unawares. Monk had a habit of immediate violence.

X

The combination of skunk-black night, danger, and empty stomachs had brought out Monk Mayfair's primitive nature, he claimed. He mentioned it. He explained that the thing they should do, lying there in the bitterly cold darkness, was to listen for sounds at odds with the general theme of the night—the chirp of a disturbed bird, the stilling of night insects. He spoke softly, and one began to suspect, to cheer himself as much as anyone.

"What I like," Ham Brooks told him, "is that ring of confidence in your voice. Solid and confident, like a piece of spaghetti on a vest."

"Okay, so I can hang a hat on my goose bumps," Monk muttered. "You think they couldn't get Doc?"

"Of course not."

"Thanks. But I heard a lot of yelling and shooting back there."

There was quite a silence.

"I don't think they did, either," said Margaret Prince softly.

"What," demanded Audrey, "convinces you?"

"I just know they didn't."

Audrey sniffed. "Those guys in nightgowns and long underwear didn't look very comic opera to me." She shuddered. "I never heard a bullet before. I thought they whined. They don't. They—it's like something torn out of your brain. I didn't like it."

"None of us liked it," Margaret Prince said gently.

Audrey stirred angrily. "Well, don't be so calm about it!" She was silent for a moment, then demanded disagreeably, "I thought you'd been in this neck of the woods, so how come you don't know where we are?"

"Because," said Margaret Prince patiently, "I don't recognize anything but those two flat-topped mountains off to the east. They were east of our camp when I was here with my uncle, Reverend Lauterbach."

"That's swell. That tells us a lot," said Audrey. "The mountains are all of fifty miles away."

"Indeed?" Margaret Prince said. "They look nearer ten miles. How did you guess?"

"Baby, I've seen mountains before," Audrey snapped. "They fool you."

"Like," said Margaret, "people?"

"Huh? What do you mean by that crack?" Audrey demanded unpleasantly. "And never mind what you meant. You're right. Me, I just dressed up and left my apartment in New York for a date with a sucker, and look where I am? Sitting on a hill on the other side of the world, scared stiff."

"Sucker?" said Monk. "I sorta resent that."

"Go ahead and resent, you baboon," said Audrey. "The next time I date a guy, I'm going to make darned sure he's somebody with a comparatively unexciting occupation, like a bank bandit."

Monk chuckled. "Blondie, there's times when I think you're enjoying it."

"That," said Audrey, "I resent."

They had spoken in very low voices, and now for a time they were silent. They were paying close attention to the night, and it had a subtle quality of change when it was observed intently. Small sounds of the wind, the popping of a rock somewhere as the bitter night cold shrank it, the discontented clutter of a bird, became charged with possible meaning.

And at length Monk asked Margaret Prince gloomily, "You have no idea exactly where we are, in relation to where Reverend Lauterbach found those canary birds?"

"No. I wish I did have."

"But you think their laboratory, or whatever layout they used to develop this hate thing, is near?"

"I'm sure it is."

"Why?"

She was still a moment. "Well, Reverend Lauterbach got the canary birds from their lab. And we'd found the region by tracing back on a couple of fanatics."

"By fanatics, you mean men who were clearly distorted by hate?"

"Yes."

"Who," Monk asked, "did these guys hate?"

Her voice was quiet and weary in the darkness. "The Hindus. It was the old Moslem against Hindu religious strife that you've read about. It isn't new. Even its bloody violence isn't new. But these men—they were different. Their hate was completely unnatural."

"Many of them loose around India?"

"The Reverend wondered, and hoped not many. We hoped perhaps only a few, and rather believed so."

"Why?"

"Well, it was the two we found. One was in Karachi, and the Reverend investigated him long and patiently. You understand, the hate applied only to Hindus. On other subjects, even another religion—Christianity in Reverend Lauterbach's case—they weren't normal, but they weren't violent either. They did have sort of a distorted animal-like cleverness....The man in Lahore was like the one in Karachi. And Lahore is a long distance from Karachi. It was the fact that both fanatics had visited a month in the same house, but at different times—"

Monk's interest sharpened. "Hey, this I hadn't heard. Same house?"

"Same house. Different times."

"They were," Monk asked, "visitors in this place? Or guinea pigs?"

"Guests." She hesitated. "Both, I guess. They thought

they were guests. Really, they were guinea pigs. Here is how it happened. It was almost the same in each case. The victims met a man who was very friendly and congenial, an older man with white hair that seemed to grow forward instead of backward, and who had large bulbous eyes—"

"That," said Monk, "would be Plott."

"Yes, so it would seem. Plott invited these men to be his guests, and they visited him a month—in each case, it was a month to the day. The guests ate, as nearly as Reverend Lauterbach was able to ascertain, about the same diets, did about the same things, slept in the same rooms."

"Plott," said Monk, "must be the mainspring, the big wheel, the guy that pulls the trigger. I'm glad to know that. I might meet him again."

Margaret Prince asked grimly, "Would you like to know a little more about how the guests were treated by Plott?"

"Sure. Let's have it."

"This," she told him, "might mean something to a psychiatrist. Reverend Lauterbach seemed to think it did. First, the guests were placed in a frame of mind as near complete relaxation, except in one respect, as was conveniently possible. That is, they were well-fed, well-entertained, and their worries about the future were somewhat dissipated by Plott's assurance that he had excellent jobs to offer them, beginning in a few weeks. That was one status of the treatment."

She frowned. "The other side of it is more sinister. Mr. Plott was a Hindu-hater. He bore on this fact—the enmity for the Hindus, the need for their extermination—rather persistently. Both guests indicated that they acquired their hate for the Hindu at this time, although they didn't call it that. They called it getting an 'understanding' of the need for annihilating the Hindus."

Monk grunted, said, "What was happening seems pretty clear. They were getting the treatment, and exposed to the hate they were supposed to soak up. It doesn't take a psychiatrist to see that."

"These men weren't just sold on an idea," Margaret Prince said sharply. "They were fanatics. Absolutely crazy in their cunning hatred of the Hindus."

"Like each canary hated the other canary?"

"Exactly.... One more thing finishes my story about Plott's unfortunate guests. Their dismissal as guests. He told them the Hindus had destroyed the factory in eastern India o which he had intended to send them as superintendents, and so he had no jobs. He was so sorry. The final touch, you see."

Presently Monk began to talk, seemingly at first only reciting a little of Doc Savage's past history, which seemed unnecessary and depressing under the circumstances. Then Margaret Prince suddenly saw that Monk was making a point.

Monk was telling her about a system that Doc Savage had used for a long time in dealing with criminals. Doc, Monk explained, maintained a rather grim institution in the wilder section of upstate New York—it was surprising how primitive some sections of New York State were, if one only knew it—which was both "hospital" and "school." Doc sent his criminals here, where they underwent a brain operation which wiped out all knowledge of the past—not a wondrous thing these days, but quite a novelty when Doc developed it, and still a fantastically skilled operation the way his trainees did it. Following the operation, the former crooks were trained to hate crime, lead normal lives, and were taught a trade or profession. In other words, Monk pointed out, another part of their brain took over and handled the functions eliminated by the operations which blocked or cut off the hitherto active brain tissue areas.

"This Plott," Monk remarked, "has probably found a way of accomplishing the same thing, but differently and without surgery. The same general idea, anyway."

"I guess so. Yes, it seems logical."

Audrey made an angry sound. "Yak-yak-yak," she said.

"Now," said Ham, "what's eating you."

"Nothing but yak-yak-yak," Audrey complained. "We're in deadly danger, and you sit here and gab."

"Can you think of anything safer?" Ham demanded. "We don't know this country. We go gallivanting around in the dark, and no telling where we'll wind up. We're supposed to wait for Doc, anyway."

Audrey made another disgusted noise. "The great Doc Savage," she said, "is probably cold meat right now.... And I'm not going to stay awake over it, either." She jumped to her feet.

"Hey, where you going?" Ham demanded.

"Over yonder where I can't hear this yak-yakking," Audrey snapped. "And where I can listen for our would-be hosts in the nightshirts and long-handled underwear."

She flounced away. Alarmed, Ham arose and followed her, but he was reassured when Audrey scraped some sand into a shape to somewhat fit her curves, and settled down.

"You stick around," Ham warned. "Don't go gallivanting."

"What kind of fool do you take me for?" Audrey retorted.

It was perhaps an hour later—past midnight—when Monk sat up abruptly. He had been lying on his side, ear against a peg which he had forced into a crack in the stone, an old trick he'd heard somewhere helped you catch the vibration of any footsteps that approached. What he'd heard was not footsteps, but a softly whistled birdcall. He waited for it to come again. It did. He reached over and touched Ham. "Hear it?" he asked.

"Yes, but what's the idea?" Ham whispered. "Why doesn't he just walk in?"

Monk said, "I'll find out."

He crawled away in the darkness, moving quietly, and presently he tried the bird imitation himself. Just once. It didn't come out too well. But good enough, it developed, to guide Doc Savage to him.

"Man, you've had us worried," Monk muttered. "Where you been?"

"Right here, for quite a while," Doc said.

"Huh? And you didn't let us know? I don't get it."

"You were all right," Doc said. "There was nothing I could do, except for your peace of mind."

"You put a low value on the latter, I take it," Monk grumbled. "Well, I'll tell Ham and the others—"

"No. Better wait a few minutes."

"Why?"

"We might be heard."

"By who?"

"The viper," Doc said, "that we've been nursing along."

Five minutes later, they eased back and crouched beside Ham Brooks. He in turn informed Margaret Prince that Doc had shown up. She was startled. "But I hadn't heard a thing unusual." She sounded frightened. "Why, they could be right on us and we wouldn't hear them!"

Ham chuckled. "I wouldn't say so. Doc has a way of getting around."

"Let's tell Audrey," Margaret Prince said. "I'm beginning not to like her, but she should know."

Doc started to make some comment, but held it, and they moved silently to the spot to which Audrey had withdrawn. She wasn't there.

"Good God!" Ham gasped. "She was here. I left her here. The little fool has wandered off!"

"Wander," Doc said, "might not be the word."

"What do you mean?" Ham blurted. "Hey, you knew she was gone! When did she leave?"

"About fifteen minutes ago," Doc said. "Miss Prince, you haven't loaned out your shoes, I hope?"

"My shoes? Of course not. But why—"

Doc turned the ultra-violet projector on the hard-bitten earth. In a moment, he had found Audrey's footprints. The fluorescence was not as pronounced as in the beginning, but still quite detectable.

"Viper?" Monk said softly. "How the hell do you recognize a viper, when it's wearing an evening dress and its hair is blonde?"

"They don't," Doc said, "get scared enough at the right places."

"Oh. On the plane, you mean?"

"Yes. She wasn't afraid of the real danger—which was from Plott. But little things, like the motors maybe failing on take-off, scared her pink."

"By golly, I did notice that," Monk muttered.

Ham said disgustedly, "You never noticed any such damn thing. You goggle-eyed ape, a fine girlfriend you rung in on us!"

"I rung in!" Monk bleated. "Hell, you were dating her too, you shyster lawyer."

"I'd suggest," Doc said, "that you two work that out later."

XI

The harridan hills swept down abruptly to the little valley, and the valley was lovely, a delightful smile as it were, on the ugly visage of the Pakistan *chota pahar* country. In width about a Bengal *kos*, the rough equivalent of two miles, it was perhaps twice as long, and it existed, and was beautiful, because of the water. Fine sweet springs fed it, not only a small stream, but also moistened the subsurface so that here in the vicious hills there was a bit of paradise.

The house stood well to the southward where the sun was most kind. A stone house, it had considerable size, although the thickness of the walls made it a little deceptive in proportions from a distance. It had been built by a former *Wali* who'd been to England to school and had seen a medieval castle. But this wasn't a castle. It was just a house. But a large house.

Two hundred yards down the lane, there was a guard, a man so well hidden that no one would have detected him had they not known he was stationed there.

Audrey hailed the man. She spoke poor Hindustani.

"Idhar ao!" she said. She had trouble with the vowels, which were more like German than English in Hindustani. But the guard understood. He also recognized her voice.

She was expected, he told her, also in Hindustani. Then he added that it wasn't a good idea to speak Hindustani here in the Pakistan countryside, where Moslem didn't love Hindu.

"Oh, shut up. I can't speak anything but Hindustani," Audrey snapped. "You'd better get me into the house. My husband may be nervous."

The master was a little nervous, indeed he was, the guard confessed. And he went with Audrey, passed a word, and she was admitted into the house.

Plott was upset, all right. He glared at Audrey.

"What, no kiss?" Audrey asked coldly. "No wifely greeting at all?"

Plott, in the beautifully chiseled English that marked him as not born to the tongue, described several varieties of stupidity, attributing them all to her.

"Stop it!" Audrey snapped. "I've had it rough the last two days."

"Rough?" Plott sneered. "It seemed to me you were well-cared for. You and your two gentlemen admirers."

Audrey laughed angrily in her husband's face. "Was I?

While you sat up forward in that plane, all the way from New York, and shook in your boots. A fine active villain you turned out to be."

The carefully neat and almost continuously silent Kelvin stood there. He was smiling slightly.

Audrey included Kelvin in her rage, yelling, "And you were a fine flop, too! You were going to decoy them into a trap in New York!"

Kelvin's smile widened, got a little frost.

Plott muttered, "We're wasting time. Where are they?"

Audrey told her husband angrily, "Where do you suppose? Parked out in the hills, about two miles from here."

Plott winced. "They're durable."

"They're dangerous, too," Audrey assured him. "That may have soaked into you by now. They're old operators, and they're quick with a dodge. That Doc Savage, in particular, seems almost abnormal."

"You can lead my men to them?"

"My men?" His wife smiled contemptuously. "You mean you're afraid to venture near them?"

Plott winced. "Not at all," he denied. "I shall go along."

"You're damned right you will, if you expect me to go near them again," Audrey snapped.

The house was in a state of siege anyway, so assembling a foray party was no more than a ten-minute job. Plott, irritated by his wife's contempt, made a harsh business of ascertaining if each man had firearms, ammunition and grenades.

Doc Savage, from the darkness fifty yards beyond the doorway, watched the door open and the party begin filing out.

"Monk," Doc said softly, "is the guard unconscious still? We don't want him waking up just now."

Monk whispered, "I'll work on his neck a little."

The guard was sprawled beside the homely chemist in the darkness, and he found the proper spot near each of the man's ears, and exerted a pressure which, properly applied, induces unconsciousness. Rather dangerous, but effective when knowingly done.

"Get in the house," Doc said. "All of you. If it goes right they'll be coming back in a hurry. So be ready for that."

"When?"

"Start now."

Doc parted company from them, and moving rapidly traveling a course he'd previously explored for obstacles, he reached a point where the guard had been stationed earlier.

Raising his voice, speaking excellent hill dialect, Doc said, "Master, they are very close to Doc Savage."

Plott's party halted. Plott cursed. "Where in the Prophet's beard did you find that news, and why delay it?" he snarled.

"There was a man here a moment ago," Doc said calmly. He was standing behind a boulder. "He has gone."

"Why did he go?"

"To help with Savage, I'm sure. Help is needed, Master. It is suggested that you go to their aid."

Plott swore violently. He had not, apparently, decided there was anything odd about the guard's voice. The reason—he didn't speak the hill dialect too well himself. That became clear when one of the other men, a native, said something excitedly.

"Come here, you!" Plott yelled in Doc's direction.

Disgusted because he had been hoping to split the party, Doc drew back and let fly with one of the little explosive grenades. It landed, as he intended, slightly beyond the group.

Before the explosion came, ear-splitting, he was headed back and running for the house. It was a good move. Where he had been, three hand grenades let loose almost simultaneously.

Monk had the door open.

"Nice delaying tactics," Monk said. "We found the supply of guns."

"Any grenades?"

"About half a case."

"All right, they'll be back," Doc said. "The path is narrow, and so is the door, and they'll come in one at a time. Let's personally accommodate the first ones. Then shut the door and see what we can do with the others as they try to break in."

Ham joined them. He carried three light hand machine guns in his arms.

"I ran across what seems to be a hell of a well-equipped electrical lab," he said. "I think we've found the nest."

Monk, at the door, said, "Here they come. In kind of a hurry, too."

Plott, running wildly, was first through the door, and Monk struck him hard. The man dropped. The next one inside stumbled over Plott's form, went down. Doc clubbed him. Audrey followed, saw what was happening, wrenched back flat against the wall, and began screaming. They got another man. No more came in.

"Hell, that was a short go," Monk said. "They're wise."

"Get the door shut," Doc said. He helped with that himself, slamming the heavy panel, dropping the bar in place. "Ham, try for the roof. Heave a few grenades over the neighborhood. And let's get away from the door."

He reached out then, seized Audrey by the arm. She stopped screaming, but still went through the motions, able to manage nothing but an exaggerated asthmatic outpouring of one breath after another. Doc tugged. She came along, loosely as if tied together by strings, but not tied very tightly.

They were well back from the door, and around a corner, when the door caved in, the heavy planks driven deafeningly by an exploding grenade. Two more grenades followed, opened themselves in the hallway where Plott and the other two lay unconscious. Audrey gave up a great gasp, apparently all of her breath.

"She hit?" Margaret Prince asked anxiously.

"I think not," Doc said. "She probably thought of Plott there by the door."

Monk threw two grenades through the door, winding up like a baseball pitcher. The house thumped in all its stones from the impact as they let go. No more eggs came in the shattered door.

A moment later, a fresh salvo of blasts sounded outdoors. They had the typically nasty quality of grenades. Ham had found a way to the roof.

There were a few erratic rifle shots.

Silence.

"You don't reckon," Monk said wonderingly, "that this is all of it."

The sun, when it came, lowered a widening wedge of hot light into the valley, and a thin ground-fog that lay along the stream like the breath of ghosts, held out stubbornly for not more than an hour. After that, the valley lay clear and sun-swept, and there was no movement at all for a long time.

"Kind of a pretty place," Monk remarked. "You see any sign of our playmates?"

They lay on the roof, carefully concealed behind the thick stone parapet that must have been erected with exactly such a purpose in mind.

"I think they cleared out," Ham said.

"Want to shove your head up and find out?"

"Not me."

"Match you," Monk said, "to see who goes down and has breakfast."

"Throw it on the roof, you crook," Ham said. But he lost anyway.

Monk found Margaret Prince in the big hall downstairs, and asked, "How's your patient?"

"Audrey? She's a mess." Margaret shook her head sadly. "I guess Plott meant something to her. Money, anyway. And probably, she imagined, a great deal of power later on. She's really a cheap sort. She's an American who followed her G.I. husband over here, deserted and divorced him, and married Plott."

"She took up with Ham and me before you even got to New York," Monk said. "She explained how that happened?"

Margaret nodded. "It was simple enough. She was visiting in New York—buying clothes. Plott got in touch with her by radiophone, told her to strike up an acquaintance with either you or Ham Brooks. Plott knew, of course, that Reverend Lauterbach and I were going to Doc Savage with the canary birds."

"Doc in the lab?"

"Yes."

Doc Savage was sprawled in a chair in the laboratory, a room of considerable size, crowded with instruments and mechanisms for experimental work in UHF electrical frequencies, as well as supersonics.

"Any sign of an attack?" Doc asked.

"No sign of nothing," Monk assured him.

"Well, don't take any chances." Doc waved at another room. "There's a radio transmitter in there, a pretty good outfit. I got hold of the Pakistan Army station at Karachi, and they're going to get a party of soldiers in here by plane. They'll land on that mud lake, so they'll be here by this afternoon."

"I won't," said Monk, "be sorry to see them."

"We're probably safe enough until they get here. In other words, it's all over."

Monk indicated the apparatus in the room. "You figured out how the dirty work was being done?"

Doc Savage did not answer immediately. He leaned back in the chair, frowning, and presently he shook his head, saying, "Not the details—which are all that is important, really. But, generally speaking, we had it about right. A combination of supersonics—the kind of sound waves that drive small animals insane, kill insects, do all sorts of odd things to the makeup of atomic structure—a combination of that, and high-frequency electrical fields."

"The room where the so-called guests slept—is it fixed up for the treatment?"

Doc waved a hand. "You can see for yourself. In there."

Monk wandered into the other room, but was not much wiser for the trip. He emerged presently.

"Man, that thing's complicated," he remarked. "More little tubes and wires and big tubes and pipes and things. . . . What are you going to do with it?"

Doc looked up. He seemed surprised.

"Destroy it, of course," he said. "The human race has enough to worry about, as it is."

Monk went down to the kitchen. Margaret Prince was preparing breakfast. "What is he going to do with Plott's devilish outfit?" she wanted to know.

Monk told her.

"Yes, Reverend Lauterbach intended to do it that way, too," she said softly. "He'll be pleased."

THE SWOONING LADY

I

She used a way of walking, arms held rigidly down and a little out from her body, shoulder blades twisted back, that made it seem she might be impaled on something. Impaled, meaning the way a butterfly would be on the point of a needle.

Nice-looking. Undeniably nice-looking, not flashily dressed and not cheaply either. A trifle over average height, generally sweet honey in coloring, and, as to figure, the very best of everything in the right places.

She walked like that for a few yards, then went a little faster and got up on tiptoes in an unsteady way, and it seemed a very fortunate thing the lamppost stood just there, where she needed it.

Mr. Monk Mayfair's interest was, by this time, well stirred.

A fine morning for it, too. At this late June season, springtime was very full-bosomed in New York's Central Park. And this morning hour of ten o'clock was filled with splintering sunshine and the singing of birds. Mr. Mayfair's headache, a trivial affair that had resulted from absent-mindedly sniffing the wrong test tube in the laboratory yesterday, was more irksome to him because it carried no pleasant memories of a night out on the town, than for any other reason.

He noted the way her fingers were biting at the shiny green metal of the lamppost.

"Lady," he said. "Lady, may I be of assistance?"

She looked at him. Lovely eyes. Beautiful distressed eyes. His toes tried out the tips of his shoes for room.

"I'm afraid—I don't—oh, thank you—" A special voice, too. The sound of a harp over a lake. Then she added, "Why, aren't you Roxy?"

"Who?" Monk said. "Me? Roxy?"

She looked at him. She seemed to get stronger. "Aren'
you Mr. Roxborough?"

"Me?" said Monk. "Well, I'm afraid not—"

She got a lot stronger indeed. "You're not?"

"Well, no—"

"Pass on, you baboon," she said. "Take a walk. Scram
Make tracks."

"But I—"

"Just charge it up to experience," she said. The voice
was still nice, but she was putting something in it that could
be used for varnish-remover. "Get along, little missing-link
Beat it."

"I resent the *little* part," Monk said. "I weigh two
hundred and thirteen pounds without my fountain pen. What
if I am five foot five? You think it worries me?"

"Go away."

"You," Monk said, "made a damned quick recovery."

"Are you leaving?"

"Not until I—hey! Ouch! Awk!" He was wearing his
usual ghastly yellow necktie. She jerked this tight, flipped a
knot into it—he couldn't breathe. He was wearing his favorite hat, the one which looked as if it had been used frequently to fight bumblebees. She yanked this down over his eyes.

Presently he recovered from everything except indigna-
tion. But by that time, she was nowhere to be seen.

In order to ease the strain on his dignity—Central Park
on a ten o'clock June morning with the sun shining is
invariably a populous place, so several spectators were staring, and some of them were laughing—Mr. Mayfair took
himself away from there. He walked rapidly, turned left,
walked rapidly a bit farther, turned off on the turf with a
scowl at a KEEP OFF THE GRASS sign, and climbed up an
easy slope of rocks. Here there were no gigglers, grinners or
laughers. Monk sat down.

"Sir Galahad," he said wryly, "you shoulda stood on your
horse."

He noted that by accident he had chosen a cooling-off
spot from which he could look out across some shrubbery and
over the path which had been the scene of his recent
embarrassment. It did not seem important at the moment.

he path at that point was near an entrance to the park from entral Park West, which was an avenue walled with apartent houses where the rent for two rooms was five hundred ollars a month and up.

Mr. Mayfair tried laughing. He managed, but not happi-. The sound was a little chipmunkish, he decided. He vore, and this at least had fervor.

"Of all the damn things!" he remarked. And presently he mpered this with, "Not a bad-looking babe, either. Spirit-d, too."

This about concluded the talking-to-himself stage of his motional subsidence, and it was followed by a thought not elated at all to the swoon-and-quick-recovery damosel. *I'm ternally damned glad Doc Savage and Ham Brooks, and in articular Ham Brooks, didn't see that little happening*, he nought fervently.

He could produce in his mind a clear picture of what)oc Savage's reaction would have been, in view of a recent arning by Doc that he, Monk, was a pushover for almost nything in skirts that was blonde and glittered, and while ere might be enjoyable things to be said about being a ushover, it could be overdone. This speech, one of the sort)oc Savage did not make often, had followed an episode in hich such a blonde had nearly been the finish of all of them.

Monk clearly recalled what he had said. "I've learned. I m going to be very hard to get," he had said. "I understand at your unusual occupation, which is righting wrongs and unishing evildoers who are outside the law in the far corners f the earth, in which I am associated with you, becomes angerous at times. I shall henceforth treat all blondes with isdain."

"Disdain?" Doc said.

"Exactly."

"Never mind attempting the impossible," Doc said dry-. "And our profession sounds a little corny, the way you just ated it."

Monk looked out across the park and shuddered. Then e stared. Disbelieving, he shaded his eyes with a hand. He as inspecting the part of the path where he had recently eceived discomfiture.

"For God's sake," he muttered. "She's at it again."

* * *

Doc Savage headquartered on the eighty-sixth floor of midtown Manhattan skyscraper. He owned the building, b inhabited only the spacious eighty-sixth floor with an arrange ment of laboratory, library and reception room, and maintaine also a smaller suite of two rooms on a lower floor, the latte occupied by a private detective agency which did nothing b screen would-be visitors, weeding out the cranks and curiosity lookers. The sleuth agency was one of the lesser expenses fame.

Monk Mayfair entered the reception room which co tained comfortable chairs, an odd and wondrous inlaid Orie tal table, a huge and ugly safe, and Brigadier General Theodor Marley "Ham" Brooks, an attorney.

"Good morning, stupid," said Ham Brooks.

"How did you know, you shyster?" Monk asked sourly.

Ham laughed. "That's a nice knot you've got in you necktie."

"This?" Monk glared and fingered the knot, which he' been able to loosen somewhat, but not untie. "A dame trie to choke me."

"An improvement over the knots you usually tie—" Ha paused, looking interested. "What was that? A dame trie to—"

"Never mind."

"It looks as if you finally met an intelligent lady, I woul say," said Ham cheerfully. "Sought to strangle you, eh? Quit a worthy project."

"Nuts to you, Blackstone. Is Doc around here?"

Ham tilted his head toward the laboratory. "How did thi happen? This garroting—"

Monk walked into the laboratory. Doc Savage was work ing with a wire recorder, doing voice imitations, runnin scales, imitating sounds, then playing the exercises back an listening to them disapprovingly. Monk listened for a fe moments. The range, power and flexibility of Doc's voice wa still a source of astonishment to Monk, although he had bee associated with the giant bronze man for several years, an was fully acquainted with the freakish background that ha made Doc Savage into the package of marvels—physica mental, and scientific—that Doc was.

Doc Savage was living proof of the argument that if yo begin early enough, and train hard enough, you can d

most anything. Monk knew that Doc Savage had been
placed, at cradle age, in the hands of a succession of scientists, physical culture fiends, psychologists—even a genuine
yogi or two—and had received a training which probably no
other human being had ever undergone. The result was more
than just a giant bronzed man with visual signs of unusual
strength, a man with hair a little darker bronze than his skin,
and rather hypnotic flake gold eyes—the result was Doc
Savage, physical marvel, mental wizard, scientific genius, and
withal not quite as freakish as he could have been.

"Doc, I had a funny thing happen to me," Monk said. "I
mean, I don't think it was so funny, so I guess it was funny."

Doc Savage shut off the recorder. "Not another blonde
lady?"

"That won't pass as mind-reading, but I resent it anyway," Monk said. He grinned. "But this is an odd one. A
babe is swooning for guys in brown tweed suits up in Central
Park."

"Let's do that slowly again," Doc suggested. "A babe
—"

"A beautiful honey-colored young lady. Gorgeous. I tell
you, such a charm bundle I haven't seen in—"

"Swooning?"

"In Central Park. About Seventy-second Street where
that path turns south—"

"And for . . . ?"

"Guys in brown tweed suits. Beat-up grey hats, too.
Here's how I know—I watched her. She did it twice. Each
time it was for a good-sized man in a brown tweed suit and a
grey hat, and that's how I figured out why I got the treatment. I'm wearing a brown tweed suit and grey hat."

Ham Brooks had come in to listen, and he remarked,
"You flatter that burlap bag you're wearing by calling it a
tweed suit. You say this swooner is a dish?"

"I say you can keep out of this, you disaster-to-the-law-
profession," Monk snapped.

Doc looked pained. "Let's not start that now," he said.
"Monk, what do you think this girl is trying to do?"

Monk shrugged. "Swoon for Roxy, I guess."

"Who?"

"Roxy. Or Roxborough." Monk frowned, and added,

"The way it looked to me, she lost interest in me when sh found out I wasn't named Roxborough."

Doc looked at Monk thoughtfully. "I take it you wish investigate this swooning lady further," he said. "But wh gets me is this: What on earth has happened to you to ma you come around asking permission to get embroiled with blonde?"

"I've reformed," Monk explained proudly.

"And he wanted to come in and shave and fix his neck before resuming operations," Ham said.

"Yeah. I wanted to spruce up—why, I never said a such thing," Monk declared indignantly.

Doc asked, "But you would like to investigate further

Monk nodded. "But only because of the mysterious a inexplicable behavior of this babe."

"Oh, then blonde-chasing is farthest from your mind Doc inquired.

"The very farthest."

"Good," Doc said. "But you had better take Ham Broo along for a chaperon."

Monk staggered. "That," he yelled indignantly, "is th dirtiest trick this day will see."

II

The balmy June day, as such June days will be, had turn into a stinker. Up out of the southwest, pushing against th soft warmth, a thunderstorm came whooping and gobblin and gnashing fangs of lightning. It fell upon Central Park wi a rush of wind, flying leaves, swirling dust that was nasty the way that only New York dust can be, and then came pelting rain.

The swooning lady was fortunate. Rescue in the shape a taxicab was managed, but Monk Mayfair, watching from h vantage point on top of the rocky knoll, was not as lucky. I the time he reached his car where it was parked, he w soaked. He climbed in, blew the rain off the end of his nos switched on the radio and as soon as it was warm, demand of the microphone, "All right, fancy-pants, did you lose her

There was no answer.

"Don't be coy, Ham," Monk said. "Did you or didn't you ee her hop into a cab when it began to rain?"

The radio receiver returned a hissing silence for a few econds, and then a voice, Doc Savage's pleasantly timbrous one, saying, "Ham probably finds it awkward to report to ou just now, Monk."

"If he lost her, I'll make him awkward—"

"Ham is driving the cab in which she is riding."

"Oh!" Monk said, and presently added, "The double-rosser!" This last was quite bitter.

"What do you mean?"

"We matched," said Monk, "to see who would get to trike up an acquaintance with her when it came time for hat, and Ham lost." He glared at the microphone.

"She will think Ham only a cab driver. You can hardly all that an acquaintance."

"You're talking to a guy who knows Ham Brooks. . . . And y the way, where in the heck are you, Doc."

"Riding along about two blocks behind Ham's cab."

"Huh? You're uptown here?" Monk was dumbfounded. What's the idea?"

"Things were slow, and this seemed interesting," Doc xplained.

"Oh, you got a look at the babe too, did you?"

Doc said dryly, "We're turning east on Fifty-ninth Street, you care to join the procession."

The girl told her cab driver to drop her off at the Park egis Hotel, and Ham Brooks thought she sounded a little ngry. He also reflected that, if she was an inhabitant of the 'ark Regis, she was well supplied with green material. It equired plenty of greeners to put up at the Park Regis. The inimum rate was around twenty a day, Ham understood. Iam, having been too busy for some time associating himself ith the adventures of Doc Savage, and neglecting the law usiness as a consequence, was short enough of funds to be oney-conscious.

"The Park Regis, Miss," he said, swinging the cab to the irb, "is about half a block down the street."

"Thank you. What is the fare? Wait, you say half a lock—"

"Meter reads sixty-five, Miss," Ham said, smiling apolo getically. "Yes, half a block. I'm awfully sorry. I have a fla tire. Too bad, raining like it is."

"All right, I suppose you can't help a flat tire," she sai curtly. She paid him, and added a quarter tip. She prepare to alight.

"Here, Miss, take this umbrella," Ham said.

She hesitated. The rain was pelting down. She eyed th umbrella, a rather ample one with a heavy and ornate handle "You're offering me an umbrella?"

"Sure, why not," Ham said offhandedly. "Some guy le it in the hack a couple of hours ago."

"Aren't you supposed to turn in lost property?"

"Yep, and I will, too. I'll just come by and pick it u when you're through with it. You live at the Park Regis Okay, I'll stop in for it."

She nodded. "Well, thanks. I'll leave it with the doorman.

Ham found the answer not entirely satisfactory; part this finagling was designed to learn whether she resided a the hotel, and the reply left him in doubt. Ask her again she was a guest there? Better not.

"Huh? What's that?" he said.

It was another half-dollar for his kindness with th umbrella. He grinned foolishly and guiltily.

He did notice, though, that she glanced at the tire when she was on the sidewalk. She needn't have bothered that was all taken care of. One tire was flat. This taxicab wa part of Doc Savage's working equipment, and a very specia job. You could punch a button and flatten a tire any ol time—inflate it almost as quickly, if that was necessary.

Ham watched the way her legs swung. He whistle silently. Very nice. He shut off the engine, leaned back an turned up the volume on their UHF radio frequency.

With interest, Ham listened to the sounds that now came from the radio, these consisting of swishings, clickings bangings, crashings, and once a thunderous female voic saying, "Damn the rain, and damn several other things! Ham laughed; he liked a lady with spirit. He switched on th windshield wiper and through the space that was cleared saw the young lady take a seat at one of the small tables under th awning of the Park Regis' nationally known sidewalk cafe. A

at point, Doc Savage and Monk Mayfair climbed into the
b with him.

"Judas!" Monk said, looking at Ham.

Ham turned up the radio volume a bit more. They
tened to the sounds, which were now of different quality,
ss violent, the scuffings and thumpings somewhat different,
d presently there was a measured series of loud bumps,
en a voice, clearly a waiter's voice, saying, "You wish to
der, Mademoiselle?" And a girl's voice, the swooner's voice,
plying, "Yes, thanks. Bring me a shrimp cocktail, the soup,
e Kansas City steak, the gooey dessert I like, and coffee."

"Nice appetite," Ham remarked.

"She's hungry," Monk muttered. "She's had a hard day
ooning."

"She called for the dessert she likes," Doc Savage remarked.
hat means she eats there regularly. Does she live there?"

"You couldn't prove it by me," Ham admitted. "I didn't
t that one over."

Monk pointed at the radio. "You got the gain turned up
high on that transmitter in the umbrella handle. Don't
ed that much pickup."

"How did I know," Ham retorted, "that she wouldn't
nd the umbrella in a corner or in a closet somewhere? And
e extra pickup will do no harm."

They were two gentle-looking men. Brothers, it could
, except for the difference in their voices, but even that
s a negative quality, the lack of something that you reason-
ly expected. The lack of any difference, really. They were
o peas in a pod. One took the stage, spoke; the other
pplanted him, and there was little to tell which was one
d which was the other.

"Good afternoon," the voice of one said.

"Good afternoon," the other said. And then he added,
iss Morgan."

"Miss Dannie Morgan," added the first.

Miss Dannie Morgan looked at them. She was well into
e Kansas City steak, and she chewed and swallowed the
ece she was currently working on. She did it gracefully, and
was done along with some rage, so it was doubly graceful.

"The little Sir Echo brothers," she said unpleasantly. "Sit
wn, boys. Get ready for some bad news."

They stared at her, their polite small smiles sligh[t]
shaken.

She gestured impatiently. "Pull up chairs, Juan, Joll[a]
think I'm going to tender my resignation."

They gasped in astonishment, together. They whipp[ed]
out chairs and sat down. They began to talk. Each one wo[uld]
take a deep breath and expend it all in a spurt of words;
other would be ready when he ran down. The gist of it w[as]
that they couldn't understand what possessed her—wasn'[t it]
congenial employment, and at good wages too, forty dolla[rs a]
day, and didn't she enjoy being an actress? After they had s[aid]
that three or four times in three or four different wa[ys]
Dannie Morgan broke in and told them what she though[t of]
it. It wasn't much.

In the meantime Ham Brooks, in the taxicab with D[oc]
Savage and Monk Mayfair, burst out laughing.

"You know what they remind me of?" Ham said. "T[wo]
brown seals balancing balls of butter on their noses. Don't [ask]
me why."

"Forty bucks a day," Monk said. Monk's financial sta[te]
was currently similar to that of Ham, so forty a day impres[sed]
him. "The swooning business is profitable."

Doc Savage listened to the radio, picking up from [the]
little transmitter in the umbrella handle. One of the po[lice]
men—he had not yet distinguished Juan from Jolla—[was]
saying that it was of course only a joke they were preparing [to]
perpetrate on their friend Mr. Roxborough, but they h[ad]
gone this far and spent so much money, a hundred a[nd]
twenty dollars including today, that it would be a shame [to]
disappoint them now, wouldn't it?

Doc Savage frowned.

"Joke?" he said, giving his opinion. "At forty dollar[s a]
day? Three days, a hundred and twenty dollars? I doubt i[t."]

Miss Morgan had the same feeling.

"You boys," she told the pair, "are a couple of sucke[rs,]
but you seem to be nice boys—polite ones anyway—and I [do]
feel a little guilty about letting you down."

"You mustn't," Jolla said.

"Mustn't let us down now, that is," said Juan.

There was more argument in which she said they we[re]
wasting their money, and they assured her they should be t[he]

idge of that; it was a wonderful joke, very wonderful indeed, hat they were trying to play on Mr. Roxborough.

"All right, all right," said Miss Morgan impatiently, urrendering. "But on one condition. I'm getting tired of wooning for wrong men. Either produce a better description f Roxborough, or I do quit."

The two men glowed. "Better than a description," one aid, and the other said, "We have a picture. Finally we have picture."

Doc Savage whipped up, stared in the direction of the idewalk cafe, not too distinguishable through the rain. He ecided that Miss Morgan was holding the photograph, a mall affair about three by four inches, and examining it.

"Get us a shot of that picture if you can, Ham," he said uickly. He whipped open the dash compartment. "Where is he miniature camera that's supposed to be in here? I hope— ere it is."

Ham said, "I hope this works," took the camera, and got ut into the rain. He trotted toward the cafe.

"What," demanded Monk Mayfair, "will he use for an xcuse? If he says he came back for the umbrella, that's not oing to be so hot."

Doc was bothered about that too. "Better she kept the mbrella than we get a copy of the photograph," he agreed. But Ham may work out a quickie."

Ham did. He approached the table under the canopy. Because of the sound of rain on the canvas, and her interest 1 the picture, Miss Morgan did not immediately note his rrival.

"Oh! The nice cab driver!" She looked up, placing the hotograph on the table. "You came back for your umbrella?" he asked.

"No, not for the umbrella, Miss." Ham dangled a five- ollar bill before her. "Did you lose this, Miss? I found it in 1y cab."

Miss Morgan eyed the greenback speculatively, then hook her head.

"Well, I found it and thought maybe it was yours," Ham aid. He grinned. "You seem to be an honest customer, Miss. 'ou'd be surprised how few of them I meet . . . I keep a file of

unusual or interesting customers." Ham whipped out th
camera. "Could I have your photograph?"

He had evidently prefocused the lens by guess, becaus
he lost very little time. There was a wink of white light as th
flashbulb went.

"*Por Dios!*" gasped one polite man.

"By God!" said the other, as if the exclamation neede
translating.

"Thank you, Miss. Thank you very much," Ham sai
pocketing the camera again. "Thanks for the picture. And ye
just keep the umbrella and use it until you are through wit
it."

Ham backed away rapidly. The girl called something an
it was not understandable because she was moving the um
brella around the table at the time, the resultant jarring ‹
the microphone drowning her words. If it was an offer t
return the umbrella to Ham right now, which was probabl‹
Ham pretended not to understand. He waved. A few m‹
ments later, and he was approaching the cab.

"Thank heavens," Monk remarked, "for New York beir
full of cab drivers who are characters. Any place else, i
would look screwy—"

Doc lifted a hand for silence. He was listening to th
radio. The two amiable men were discussing, in rapid Spanis‹
this precise point; a moment later they reached Monk
conclusion—there were a lot of uninhibited hack drivers i
New York. Who could tell what those guys would do?

Ham climbed in with them. "If there was film in th
camera, and if the usual twenty other things didn't go wron‹
I got a picture."

"What did the man in the photograph—Roxborough-
look like?" Doc demanded.

"I didn't have much of a chance for a close look. Just
big rugged intelligent-looking guy."

"But you got the photograph in the picture you took?"

"Yes."

"What about the two polite *caballeros?*"

"Them, too," Ham said. "They may be a little out ‹
focus, although I had the lens stopped down as much as
dared to get depth of field."

Doc held out a hand for the camera. "I'll develop an

nlarge the shot, and see what can be done with it. Monk,
ou might try trailing the two men when they leave her."

Monk nodded, but pointed at the radio speaker. Miss
Morgan's nice voice, diverting for peals of laughter, was
elling about her experiences swooning for men in brown
weed suits and grey hats. "But the funniest one of all," she
aid presently, "was a short homely fellow who looked like the
rother, or the first cousin at least, of a baboon. You should
ave seen his face!" Her mirth became uncontrollable.

"At least," Monk said bitterly, "I made an impression."

Doc Savage put the film through a fine-grain develop-
ent at headquarters, fixed and dried it, then clipped it into
n enlarger and made a print, blowing it up to the greatest
imensions possible without too much loss of detail.

Examining the result, he found that as Ham had said,
oxborough seemed to be a burly Anglo-Saxon type. In the
hotograph, Roxborough was looking directly at the camera,
nd wore a small but distinctive one-sided smile. Taking into
onsideration the facial characteristics, Doc decided the man's
air was rather sandy, the eyes a dark blue, the complexion
untanned. There was one gold tooth shown by the small
mile.

Making four more copies of the print and drying them,
Doc dropped in at the nearest precinct police station and
astituted a routine gallery check to see whether any of the
ur individuals shown had a police record. Since he fre-
uently worked with the police, too many explanations were
ot demanded of him.

En route back to headquarters, he used the radio to learn
vhat progress Monk and Ham were making.

Ham Brooks said, "The conference broke up without
nything more being said that was interesting. I'd say it was
his way: This girl is someone the two men hired for the
wooning job. An actress, probably."

"Is she staying at the Park Regis?"

"Yes. Registered under the name they called her, except
hat her first name is Daniella. Daniella Morgan."

"That hotel," Doc suggested, "charges stiff rates. Rather
igh living for an actress who would be needy enough to
ccept employment as queer as this."

Ham probably winced over that. At least there was a

pause before he said, "Acting is a little like cab driving—y
don't have to be screwy to do the job, but it helps."

"Well, don't enthrone the young lady too firmly until y
know a little more about what goes on," Doc suggested.

Presently Monk Mayfair reported in. He had trailed th
two men to a hotel on Seventh Avenue not far from Tim
Square.

"Been registered about a week," Monk said. "Names a
Juan Leon Schaefero, and—this will stop you—Jolla O'Sulliva
The Irish get into the damnedest places."

"Where did they register as being from?"

"Miami, Florida," Monk said. "I was coming to tha
Both gave the same address. One zero zero seven Sprin
Street, Miami."

"There is no such address in Miami," Doc said instantl

Not too surprised, Monk said, "I wouldn't argue wi
your memory for things like that, having seen it work. I gue
they're a couple of crooks as far back as last week when the
registered, eh?"

Thirty minutes later, Doc Savage was back on the rad
and in contact with Monk again. "I must have a hole in m
head today," Doc said bitterly.

"Yeah? You mean we're overlooking something?"

"The most obvious thing of all—the particular locati
which has been chosen for the swooning," Doc told him.

"In the park, you mean?"

"Yes, but specially the fact that it is near the point whe
a path leaves the park. A footpath. That suggests th
Roxborough frequently uses that path. It follows that he liv
in the neighborhood, and since there are apartment hous
directly across Central Park West from that point, we've bee
overlooking something."

"You want," Monk said, "me to start inquiring at th
apartment houses for Roxborough?"

"Exactly."

"That," said Monk, "is a good job for Ham. He has a gl
tongue."

"The girl has had a good look at you, so you can't ver
well take over the job of trailing her," Doc pointed out. "Sh
would recognize you instantly."

"I was afraid you'd think of that," Monk said bitterly.

"Drop past here," Doc said unfeelingly, "and pick up one of these pictures of Roxborough."

III

"Roxborough!" exploded Ham Brooks. "Hey, fellow, isn't your name Roxborough?"

Now, at five fifteen in the afternoon, the June sky stood out a clear cyanite blue, stripped of clouds, and the air had a rain-washed freshness that it had lacked that morning. There was in fact little evidence of the noontime rain other than the clean bite to the air, together with a few pools of rainwater standing mirrored in depressions in the blacktop footpaths and park drives. Nursemaids were abroad with their charges in carriages. Dog-walkers were plentiful, and pigeons and squirrels were getting their usual quota of peanuts and popcorn.

"Oh!" said Ham Brooks. "What the hell!"

Doc Savage was pleased. "I look a little like Roxborough's picture in this getup, do I?"

"Quite a lot," Ham admitted. "For about two seconds, you had me fooled. . . . But what's the idea? You Sherlock Holmes, or somebody?"

Doc smiled unhappily. "Of all the causes for a man making a fool of himself, impatience is probably one of the first. Let's grant that. I was impatient. In short, why not learn what is supposed to happen when Miss Morgan swoons for Roxborough."

Ham stared at Doc Savage, then laughed heartily. "This I want to see. When do you make this test, Mr. Roxborough?"

"Is the young lady at her stand?"

"Yes."

"Has she swooned for anyone recently?"

Ham shook his head. "The photograph of Roxborough seems to have reduced her percentage of error."

Doc nodded. "I might as well try it now. You'd better be in the neighborhood, but out of sight. Incidentally, don't show yourself unless the situation seems desperate."

"Fine, and I know I'm going to enjoy the bandstand seat," Ham said cheerfully. "By the way, that's the new type

of contact lens you are wearing to change the color of you
eyes. How do they work? Do they have the drawback of th
old ones, the pigment in the plastic cutting down visio
efficiency too much?"

"They're not too much improvement," Doc confesse
"All right, I'll give you five minutes to get set, then go aroun
and enter the park. We'll see what happens."

The thing nearly fell through at the beginning becaus
Miss Morgan had bought a nickel sack of peanuts and wa
making friends with two perfectly willing squirrels and
score of beady-eyed pigeons. When she glimpsed Doc Sav
age, she started violently and seemed uncertain about wha
to do. Doc cooperated by pretending not to have noticed her
and turned to the path railing, where he paused to mak
clucking sounds at another squirrel. He was aware that Mis
Morgan was moving away hastily. He gave her time to mak
her pitch.

A few minutes later, when he resumed his stroll dow
the path, he saw that she was prepared. She did it well, too
As a doctor, which was his most specialized training, he coul
pick certain flaws in the performance, but as a whole she gav
an excellent delineation of a young lady about to collapse.

He came in on cue, as she was collapsing against th
lamppost.

"My dear young lady," he said anxiously. "Are you ill?
there some way I can be of assistance?"

"I'm afraid I—I don't—Oh, thank you—" She looked
him, and her eyes widened in a very passable imitation
recognition. "Why, aren't you Roxy?"

Doc hoped he seemed enough taken by surprise.

"Why, how did you know that?"

"You're Roxborough, aren't you?"

"How did you know? I don't believe I've met you." H
took her arm helpfully. "You seem ill. Is there something—

She threw both her arms about him. Not fondly, h
realized. And she screamed. There were no words in th
scream, just sound.

Twenty feet distant, behind a bush, there was move
ment. One of the polite men came into view. Juan, Do
thought. He still wasn't sure which was which.

"Dannie!" screamed Juan. "My dear sister! My darling sister!"

He howled this while bounding toward Doc and the girl, which somehow kept it from being comical.

"You beast! You damned beast!" This was directed at Doc Savage, at closer range. Juan stared at the girl. "Dannie! Good God, what has he done to you?" Back went Juan's head, and he began to bawl, "Police! Help! I want a policeman!"

Doc was puzzled, though the girl looked puzzled also, and he demanded, "What's the idea? Who are you, fellow?"

"You've abducted and drugged my sister!" Juan screamed at him.

"Did I?" Doc said ominously.

"I want a policeman!" Juan screeched in a voice that made the pigeons leave in hasty clouds.

Ham Brooks, evidently thinking the whole thing was quite funny, stepped from behind a shrub about thirty feet distant and called his own idea of humor. "You first dial 0 for Operator, fellow."

Ham later tried to explain that the remark was a display of genuine wit, recognizable as such by anyone who had been in a New York telephone booth and noted the printed instructions on how to get a policeman: *Dial 0 for Operator and say: I want a policeman*.

The point, however, was that he was felled by a blow from behind, delivered by a blackjack, before he witnessed any audience reaction to the bit of great wit. Ham pitched forward on his face.

Jolla waved the shot-filled leather persuader with which he had dropped Ham, and yelled, "Juan! Is wrong—something! This *hombre*—I recognize heem. Is cab driver—is helper *El Hombre De Bronce*—to Doc Savage, thees guy belong."

A little scrambled, English and Spanish and accent mixed together, but he got it out.

It meant something to Juan, too. Instantly—and right here Doc Savage began to have a low opinion of the efficiency of the contact lenses, deeply blue in coloration to disguise the spectacular gold flake of his eyes—Juan had a blackjack of his own in hand. He swung it with skill and speed. The left side of Doc's head seemed to depart with a crash; he was vaguely aware of the hard dark feeling of the path pavement against his hands.

"He is not Roxborough," Jolla's voice said.

"I know that, you fool," said Juan. "I knew it all along."

"Then why did you not stop her—"

"How was I to know he would say he was Roxborough?"

"Who is he? Hit him again," Jolla said.

"I have hit him once," said Juan confidently. "He is as good as dead."

Doc, on his knees, mentally damned the new type of contact lenses which had hampered his vision. He would have to make the best of it; to remove the things, you needed the little rubber vacuum cup device.

Doc reached, got Juan's ankle, jerked—intending to get on and lay his hands on Jolla, a perfectly feasible campaign that should not have been beyond his ability. It did not however, work out. He had made a further error in misjudging the capabilities of the pair.

The next few seconds—it might have been two seconds or fifteen—came near being as brisk an interval as he ever experienced. The two were judo men. The worst kind of judo, and wizards at it. It was his agonized impression that not one clean blow was struck; there wasn't even anything as decent as merely trying to break his arms.

"He is good!" Juan blurted.

"Too good," agreed Jolla. "Let us leave here."

"Take the girl?"

"Oh, sure."

The conversation was particularly irritating to Doc Savage because it was carried on during the climax of as vicious a hand-to-hand encounter as he had ever experienced. Not that they had damaged him greatly. But it is almost impossible, as he had known, for one good big judo man to do anything with two good little ones. The whack on the side of the head was no help, either.

He knew that footsteps had left rapidly. Miss Morgan in flight.

Then Juan and Jolla took off, in the direction the girl had gone.

Doc Savage lost no time, but lunged to the right—he had, luckily, kept his sense of direction—and scrambled over the low stone wall that bordered the path at this point, then

opped into its shelter. That was a good idea, too. There
ere two shots, one bullet chipping stone off the wall, the
ther ricochetting and climbing off into the sky with the
ound of a sick violin.

Now Doc removed the contact lenses. He threw them,
ith a rare venting of sheer impotent rage, as far as he could.
Nearly trapped by one of his own gadgets, he thought
itterly. Then he crawled a few feet, got behind a tree, and
ook a chance on a look around.

The scene of the late fight on the path was impressive.
arious bits of clothing, some of it his own, were strewn
bout. He was somewhat surprised to see no loose arms or
egs.

Nearly two hundred feet distant, Juan and Jolla were just
vertaking Miss Morgan. They seized her. She kicked, bit,
creamed. Juan placed his hands on her, did a couple of
hings with them, her screaming changed to ghastly shrieking,
nd then she was loose and still. Juan then shouldered her
imp figure. For a smallish man, he seemed to do it very
asily. They sauntered away with the girl.

A policeman came into view, running, the usual big
oliceman with a red face and high-pitched shouting voice.
uan and Jolla faced the oncoming officer; they seemed to
tudy him with deliberation. Then Jolla raised a hand; fire
nd noise came out of the hand, and the officer veered lazily
ff the path and went headlong and blindly and still running
nto a thicket of brush. He made a considerable thrashing
ound in there and the sound remained exactly where it was.

Juan and Jolla wandered off into the shrubbery with Miss
Morgan. From the first about their movements there had
een, or had seemed to be, a careless ease and no hurry at
ll.

Ham Brooks, lying on the grass a short distance from the
ath, decided to get up. He seemed to make the decision
ery carefully, then placed both hands on his head, lifted the
ead with some difficulty until his face was off the turf, and
ith more of the same care, endeavored to rise. The downfall
f the project came when he thought it necessary to release
is head in order to convert the use of his hands to getting
imself erect; when he did that, the weight of his head jerked
im back to earth.

Doc Savage got up and set out after the two polite—and

capable—men and the girl. Passing the thicket where the policeman had gone, he saw the officer sitting there, service revolver in hand.

"Hey, you!" the officer yelled. "Stop!"

Doc said, "Take it easy, Grant," and then when the officer raised his gun, added, "Grant! Detective Squad, the Twentieth Precinct. Don't be a fool!" The gun lowered a trifle then, and a moment later Doc was out of sight.

Head back, stretching out, Doc ran, veering a little to the right, now leaving the path, guessing on the route the two men would take—it was clear they had cased this part of the park thoroughly and knew the lay of the ground—and hoping to intercept them, or at least keep track of them. He was successful in only the last part.

They were, when he saw them again, climbing over the breast-high wall that bounded the park on the west. They draped the girl on the wall like a sack, vaulted over, picked up the girl, and trotted across the wide thoroughfare, Central Park West, apparently blissfully unaware of screaming brakes, wildly dodging automobiles and angry howls from drivers. Their destination—a small grey sedan parked across the street.

They made it, too. Piled in and the car got moving.

Self-disgust had now built up into quite a lump inside Doc Savage; it was unpleasantly in his face that there had been too much bad luck in the last few minutes. Tough breaks did not come that many to a package. This was the kind of thing earned you by stupidity, poor planning and overeagerness.

He went over the park wall and into the street in a bitter mood, and spotting parked a half block to the north the taxicab that Ham Brooks had used that morning, he made for it, further disrupting the Central Park West traffic—at least a dozen car horns were hooting and farther off a policeman's whistle was twittering—and piled into the cab. The key was not in the lock. More nice breaking of luck. He leaned down, head under the dash, jerking out ignition wires and tying them together, and while he was doing that, there was a loud whacking of a nightstick on the window—he looked up and there was an angry police face there.

"You got a moxie," said the angry voice of officialdom. "You think you steal a cab this easy? You think that?"

Stevenson, this officer's name was. There were quite a few thousand policemen in New York, and Doc Savage did not know all of them by name by any means, phenomenally developed though his memory was, but he did know this one was Stevenson, Archie Stevenson, and the one in the park with the bullet somewhere in him had been Grant.

"Hello, Stevenson," Doc said. "Doc Savage, remember?"

"Now that's pretty good, Johnny, but I'll tell one," Stevenson said. He hit the window a harder rap. "You think I don't know Doc Savage? You think not?"

Doc sat up and pressed the starter and the engine began turning over. He looked at the policeman; the latter wrenched angrily at the door, which wouldn't open, then gave the window a blow that should have shattered it but didn't. Doc said wearily, "You think I got time to argue, Stevenson? You think that?"

He drove away, and Patrolman Stevenson took a gun out of his pocket and aimed carefully at the back of the cab for a while, but finally put the weapon away without firing and began to run for a callbox.

There was some guesswork in the first part of the chase southward, but not too much because for more than a dozen blocks there was no turn-off eastward from the street—Central Park was on that side—and Doc had watched the right-hand streets for half a dozen blocks, and seen no sign of the grey sedan. He was fairly sure the car was still headed south on Central Park West. He got in the center of the thoroughfare, pushed in the siren button and locked it, and was doing better than sixty by the end of the first block.

The men in the grey car heard him. There was no reason why they shouldn't, nor did he particularly care. It was not, normally, his practice to pile headlong into something and try to bull through in a hurry, but then nothing was going right anyway. So, when he caught sight of the grey car, he made up his mind to overtake it, crowd it, ram it, anything to stop it.

It was easy. A little noisy and rough, but easy. The two polite men could not drive a car the way they handled themselves in a hand-to-hand fight. Consequently, they were slow taking a right turn to get off the straightaway of Central Park West, which speaking in a traffic sense was about as near being wide open spaces as anything in midtown New York

City. Doc Savage, actually, was not more than a hundred feet back when they took the corner; his calculation rounding the corner after them was a lot better, hence his loss of speed less. The die was cast then. They knew it. Halfway along the block, they cut their engine, threw on full brakes, and took to the sidewalk. Destination, the front of a store. They must have seen the thing done in a movie sometime; there was that unnaturally spectacular air about it.

The car struck, they had the door open, and while glass was crashing and the street full of noise, they were out and trying to remove Miss Morgan. They looked up, saw Doc, gave up the girl. Back into the store they went.

Somewhere toward the rear of the store, it occurred to them that they might as well shoot the girl. But by that time, Doc had thought of that; he had seized her ankle, was dragging her back out of view. Three bullets came, two in the car and one that took a bit more glass out of the store front.

Presently Doc got up and ran back through the store— ran as much as was possible while still keeping behind objects which he hoped would dissuade a pistol bullet. *Let there be no back door to this place,* he thought. It was one of those novelty shops with a lot of crockery, antique glassware, plaster statues, a place that would certainly show the effects of a fight. But it had a back door into an alley courtyard.

The alley-court had the typical inhabited tomb smell of such places in New York; naked brick and grime and festooned clotheslines, too much of all of it, including nearly a dozen open windows and at least three open doorways.

He never did find what door or window the two soft-voiced little men had used. Neither did the police, later.

Miss Morgan contributed nothing at this point. She was gone when Doc got back to the grey car piled against the shop door. Just stood up, brushed herself off and walked away, a bystander said.

IV

"The police," said Ham Brooks, "seem to feel there was an undue amount of hell raised for the results achieved."

Doc Savage looked at the blank wall of the Twentieth Precinct Police Station. "What results?" he said bitterly.

A police captain named Scoffield came in. He wore a wryly dissatisfied look—five minutes ago when he'd left he'd been mumbling something about jailing them—and he stood in front of Doc Savage for a moment without speaking. Then he said politely, "I have instructions from the brass to turn you loose, and to present you with the keys to my precinct. That's fine." His voice went up several notes and he added, "All but the keys! The hell with that—I don't like civil wars in my precinct!"

"We're not happy about it either," Doc said.

Captain Scoffield held one, then two, then three fingers in front of Doc Savage's face, shouting, "A policeman shot in the shoulder, the park filled with loose bullets, the front end knocked out of a store! . . . You know what the brass downtown said? 'Scoffield,' he said, 'Scoffield, Doc Savage is one of the most effective enemies of crime and criminals in the world today, and you damn well better give him every assistance.' Okay, that's what the brass said. Now, you know what I've got personally to say?"

"Oh, skip it, copper," Ham said disagreeably. "You weren't out there in the park being knocked over the head and shot at." Ham stood up, put on his hat, winced violently, took off the hat, and said, "We'll see you again, I hope not."

As they were leaving, a police lieutenant named Croll hailed them. Croll was getting out of a department car. "Hello, Savage," he said. "They sent me up here about some pictures you asked the Department to check on earlier in the day."

Croll produced a print of the photograph Ham had taken at the Park Regis Hotel sidewalk cafe and indicated the faces of the two gentlemen, which had been ringed with a pencil. "Rough boys," he said.

"We found that out," Doc said dryly. "You mean they have police records?"

Croll nodded. "Like reading an encyclopedia on crime," he declared. "South Americans. Not any special republic down there—mostly Venezuela, Brazil and Argentina, though. They've splattered over into Spain and Mexico a few times. We have nothing to show where they were born, but they first showed, eight years ago, as rival wrestling champions of

South America—the rivalry was a phony, and they were jailed for going into the tank for each other. The South Americans take their wrestling more seriously than we do, I guess. They broke jail, killing a guard, and in the next three years at least seven murders were chalked up to their credit. With that practice behind them, they haven't been spotted as often, although they've sure been active."

Croll scowled at the photograph, shaking his head. "The damnedest aspect is the variety of jobs they're suspected for. Confidence swindles, narcotics, bank jackings, jewel thefts—more jewel work than anything else—and about anything you want to name in the way of violence and deviltry." He moved the point of the pencil over until it rested on the girl. "Who's the sugar-bun, besides using a name like Daniella Morgan? Pretty, isn't she?"

"We have no idea," Doc admitted. "Any special reason for asking?"

"Well, we already put a phone call through to Buenos Aires," Croll said. "They tell us there's some feeling down here two *Padres Feliz*—what the hell does that mean? In Spanish, I mean. *Padres Feliz?*"

"Happy fathers, or something like that."

"Well, that's what they're called down there. Happy fathers, eh?... Well, from Buenos Aires we hear it's suspected they got a brain. A mastermind. Somebody who does their planning." He stared at Miss Morgan's likeness. "Man, she would be quite an ornament across a breakfast table, wouldn't she? You suppose she's their sparkplug?"

Ham Brooks said, "Of course not!" He seemed to have more on the subject, but glanced at Doc Savage and flushed.

Doc said, "We don't know a thing about her, really."

"Well, you want to be careful of those lads," Croll said.

Monk Mayfair, feet on the inlaid desk at Doc Savage's headquarters, looked up from the ghastly crimson necktie he was admiring. He held the tie aloft for their approval. "Bought it just before the stores closed. Pretty sharp, eh?"

"Utilitarian, anyway," said Ham.

"What's that mean?" Monk asked suspiciously.

"Well, if you get your throat cut, it's certain no one would notice any difference."

Monk grinned. "You're usually funnier than that. Say, I

hear there was a rumpus uptown. Maybe it had something to do with the swooning babe. Think I should investigate?"

Stunned, Ham looked at Monk. "You mean you just vaguely heard about something?"

"Yeah," Monk admitted. "Something about a cop getting shot, some bird getting knocked cold, a car crashing into a store. Think it was around the part of the park where—" He peered at Ham Brooks. "You look kinda—you hurt somewhere?"

Ham was speechless.

Doc said, "Monk, I thought you were supposed to be working the apartment houses across the street from the park in search of Roxborough."

Monk shrugged. "That didn't take long."

Doc looked incredulous. "You mean you found him?"

"Oh, sure. Third place I asked," said Monk airily. "I tried to raise you guys on the radio to let you know, but you were off enjoying yourselves somewhere. So I came down here to give myself a little spit and polish." He leered at them. "I might meet Miss Morgan again, you know."

"You missing-link!" Ham yelled. "You sit down here smirking at a god-awful necktie like that while we're getting ourselves massacred—"

Monk was not too impressed, although interested. "Anybody who massacres you two will know he has been to a party. . . . Hey, you mean the rumpus in the park—"

When Ham ran out of words and fell to hissing and waving his arms, Doc finished the story of their doings and undoings. "This stuff you see covering us isn't exactly glory," he finished. "Now, Roxborough? Who and what?"

"Damn, I'm sorry I missed the entertainment," Monk said. He grinned at Ham. "Particularly when our law-book friend here acquired the knot on his head."

"What about Roxborough?"

"We might as well go up and ask him," Monk said.

The apartment door was made of prima vera mahogany, not the bleached imitation stuff but the genuine Honduran mahogany cut at the right season of the year to get the exquisite coloring, and it was at the end of a sixteenth floor hall in an apartment on Central Park West a couple of blocks south of the American Museum of Natural History. Solid gold doorknobs would have gone well with the rest of the hall fittings, without making anything look any richer.

Doc pressed a pearl button set in the edge of the door; there was no sound anywhere, but presently the door was opened, also without sound, by a man as tall as Doc Savage and somewhat thinner, a rangy man with eyes like the glass corks in the blue perfume bottles that come from France, a jaw made for breaking things against, and the most remarkable weather-beaten suntan on his face. The face had the coloring and texture, or marring, of a cordovan boot that had been worn too hard and too long over too rocky country. This was Roxborough.

He said otherwise. "Richardson. Charles Richardson. And I believe you've made a mistake, because I don't know you," he said.

"Savage. Doc Savage," Doc said. "No, we haven't met. But there is no error, either. Only a lie somewhere."

Roxborough examined them. "Indeed? I have heard of Doc Savage. . . . Do you mind my doubting your statement, however?"

Doc shook his head. "That makes us even. I doubt one of yours."

"Yes?"

"Yes, Roxborough, I do."

The man was wearing a long alpaca robe, a sheath of a robe with pockets, and his hand started for one of the pockets. Started, and made four or five inches of the journey, and Doc Savage had the wrist and had stopped it and was bending it up and back.

"Here we go again," Ham complained. "And with this headache I've got!"

Roxborough's free hand, a fist, started up and around. Doc caught it in his palm with a cap-pistol smack, and now the two men stood close together, silently. Two or three times violent shaking effort went through Roxborough's body, and sweat made a rather magical appearance on his forehead. Then he said, thickly, "There is nothing in the pocket."

Monk went over and felt of the robe pocket. "He's right." He slapped his hand over the rest of the man. "None of the usual pistols and daggers on him, apparently."

Doc released Roxborough. The man stepped back. They followed him inside.

Ham made a quick tour of the apartment and came back and said, "I don't find anything but a mighty elegant decoratng job." He looked at Roxborough. "Nice taste you have—in ecorations."

"Thank you."

Doc asked, "Your name is Roxborough?"

The man hesitated. "I've gone to a lot of trouble not to et it be known," he said bitterly.

"Why?"

The man turned and went to a chair and sat down. He rranged the robe over his knees. "You can go to any part of ades you choose," he said.

Doc Savage asked Monk Mayfair, "How did you find his partment?"

"Why, by showing the doorman that picture." Monk was urprised.

"The doorman know him as Roxborough?"

"No, the doorman only knew him as the tenant of ixteen J."

"Take a look around the apartment," Doc said. "Papers, etters, or anything—"

"Search warrant?" Roxborough asked angrily.

"The police could get one here pretty quick, I imagine,")oc said. "Does that interest you?"

Roxborough grinned thinly. "I had always heard you vere a man of great culture, a scientist, a mental wizard, Mr. avage. The impression I have now is that of a common thug.)oes that interest *you*?"

"Not," Doc said, "as much as your unwillingness to have he police present."

Presently Monk, from another room, called, "By golly, he guy does his bookkeeping at home." There was a silence nixed with rustling of papers, two whistles from Monk, both mpressed, the second more so than the first. Then Monk aid, "Our boy gets around. Mining properties. Canada, ;old; Mexico, silver; Brazil, diamonds; Africa, diamonds." He ustled some more papers. "Heck, no bank statements.... Well, e seems to be incorporated as Roxborough Associates, a Aaryland corporation with offices in New York."

Doc Savage was watching Roxborough's face, and he had een something. "New York company, eh?" Doc said. And ow he was sure of it—the man didn't like being connected /ith New York. "Check on it," Doc told Monk.

"Check on—"

Doc glanced at the pattern of black night sprinkled wit[h] city lights beyond the window. "There will probably be n[o] one at the company offices this time of night, but see if yo[u] can run down one of the officers by telephone."

Roxborough's face had lost color.

"Would you do me the favor of not doing that?" he aske[d] thickly.

"Why not?" Doc asked him.

The man winced. "I would much rather you didn't."

"You'll have to give a reason, fellow," Doc said.

Roxborough was silent.

"Monk, call one of the company officials," Doc ordere[d]

Monk nodded. "Okay. I know a fellow named Jenkste[r] who is up on the mining business. Maybe he knows who ru[ns] the outfit." Monk telephoned his friend, discussed some gi[rl] called Candy with him, then got the desired information. H[e] dialed a number, presently said, "Mr. Kineberg? This is M[r.] Mayfair of the Doc Savage organization calling. I believe yo[u] are an officer in a mining concern headed by a Mr. Roxborough[.] Can you tell me—says what?... The devil you say! When di[d] that happen?... Three months ago? Why, yes, I remember [a] newspaper story about the incident. No trace, eh?... Oh, [it] was? Well, I didn't notice anything in the newspapers abou[t] that. What about the bodies?... Yes, that would be a di[s]agreeable thing, and it could happen down there in th[e] jungles. Yes, I can understand.... Well, I'll tell you wha[t,] Mr. Kineberg, this news puts a different angle on my propos[i]tion, so I'd better call you back later. Thank you, an[d] goodbye."

Monk hung up, turned and looked wonderingly [at] Roxborough. "That was Mr. Kineberg," Monk said dryly.

Roxborough scowled.

"Kineberg," he said, "is probably a slick crook!"

"You think so?" said Monk.

"I do!"

"He didn't sound very dishonest to me," Monk said.

"I don't give a damn how Kineberg sounded," Roxboroug[h] snapped. "You couldn't tell anyway. The man is a smoothie.["]

"You're sure of that?"

"Yes—" Roxborough hesitated, glowering. "That is, [I] think so. I'm hoping to find out."

"How?"

"By giving the so-and-so a chance to show his true colors," said Roxborough bitterly.

"Then what will you do?"

"Do? Do?" Roxborough's head came up; his eyes flashed glassy rage. "I'll have the law on him, that's what I'll do."

"Oh," said Monk.

"What do you mean—oh?" the other man shouted.

"I thought you might haunt him?"

"Haunt him?"

"Sure. You're dead, aren't you?" said Monk.

V

Without warning, it started to rain again, and after the raindrops had washed violently against the windowpanes for a few moments, there was a whacking burst of thunder and two great winkings of lightning, then a burst of wind through a partly opened window that made the curtains spring outward and curl upward almost to the valance-boards. Monk went over and closed the window. Then he resumed his speech.

"This guy"—Monk pointed at Roxborough—"is either Roxborough, or he isn't Roxborough. But as far as the officers of the Roxborough mining corporation think, Roxborough is dead. He died on a plane that crashed in the Colombian jungle three months ago. I don't know whether the rest of you remember that plane crash, but—"

"The Carib-Caracas-Lima Airways ship?" Doc Savage asked.

Monk nodded. "That's the one. Went down in the jungle. They found the wreck three weeks later, and it was a mess. It happened in some of the nastiest jungle in the world, and the ship was torn wide open. All they found was what the jungle animals had left of the bodies." He glanced meaningfully at Roxborough. "You—or Roxborough—was listed as a passenger on that plane," he said.

Roxborough scowled angrily. "I'm not denying it, am I?"

Doc Savage took the stage, saying sharply, "You were on the plane when it crashed?"

"Certainly I was on it!" Roxborough snapped.

"You weren't killed?"

The man sneered. "Do I look dead?"

"You'd better," Doc said ominously, "take a more civil and cooperative attitude."

"I'll take any damned attitude I want to," Roxborough said angrily. "I was on the plane. It crashed. I wasn't killed. Those are the facts."

"How many others weren't killed?"

"None."

"You were the only survivor?"

"I was the only survivor."

"It must have been a bad crash."

Roxborough nodded. "It *was* a bad crash."

"What caused it?"

"It was caused by the plane hitting the ground in the jungle."

"That," said Doc, "doesn't answer my question, and you know it."

"I'm no aeronaut," said Roxborough violently. "How do I know what went wrong? One motor tore itself out of the plane without any warning at all, and probably messed up some of the controls doing it. The plane came down in a long dive, and it hit damned hard."

Doc Savage eyed the man narrowly. "As I recall, it was a two-engined ship?"

"So what? It crashed anyway."

"And both motors were in the wreckage, as I also recall, when the searchers located the plane remains."

"I didn't say one engine fell off. I said it tore itself out of—well, it tore itself up, but it didn't fall out."

"And there were no other survivors?"

"No."

"You got out?"

"Yes."

"Was it a tough trip?"

"You're damned right it was a tough trip," said Roxborough roughly. "You've probably seen that jungle. You know what it must have been like. I can tell you one thing—if I hadn't knocked around in jungles plenty, I wouldn't have made it. That's how tough it was. There are head-hunters in that jungle."

"You were scared?"

"I knew what I was up against."

"Did you," Doc Savage asked dryly, "have amnesia or
me other loss of memory that caused you to come to New
»rk and forget you were Roxborough?"

The man snorted. "My memory," he said, "has never
·en impaired for one minute."

"Indeed?"

"I told you why I came to New York incognito," said
»xborough violently. "It was to watch my partners in the
·ining business. I suspected them of being a bunch of
·mned crooks, and I wanted to catch them robbing the
·mpany blind after they thought I was dead."

"And have you caught them?"

"Not yet, but by God I will—" He paused, stared at Doc
·vage and the others, and regained control of himself. "You
·ys," he said, "are getting me excited, so I'll talk too
·uch.... Now suppose you do some talking. Just why are
·u bothering me?"

"Not," Doc admitted, "an unreasonable question."

"Care to answer it?"

"I don't see why not."

Roxborough listened to Doc Savage's story of what had
·ppened—Monk's experience with the swooning girl, the
·vestigation they had started making for no other reason
·cept that they were curious, and the culmination in violence—
·d hardly changed expression. The man had a poker face.
·e casually lit a cigar, and when Doc was sketching the
·olent latter part of the recital, Roxborough grinned. Doc
·ished: "The two professional South American crooks are
·ing hunted by the police, and the girl Daniella Morgan is
·so being sought. But one thing is sure, the polite pair do not
·ve the girl—unless they've caught her since." He glanced
· Roxborough. "Now, does that jolt anything loose?"

"No, and why should it?" Roxborough countered.

"They were setting some kind of a trap in the park for
·u, whereby they were going to accuse you of abduction.
·at's the way it seemed, anyway," Doc said. "I thought that
·ight jog your memory."

Roxborough sneered and waved his cigar. "You just let
·ur feelings of self-importance get away with you, Savage. In

other words, you stuck your schnozzola into something a
got it soundly biffed for your pains. Let that be a lesson—
The cigar stopped in midair, hung poised. The man's mou
closed, then opened again, and he said, "Maybe—why, t
story of yours might be true!"

"You're making a mistake if you don't think it is tru
Doc said.

Roxborough sprang to his feet. "For crying out loud!"
hurled the cigar at the fireplace. "That's the kind of a di
trick my partners would pull!"

"What do you mean?" Doc asked patiently.

Roxborough stamped to the window, wheeled and ca
back, and said, "Don't think I'm letting you bluff me in
telling you anything I don't wish to tell. I'm not a man w
can be bluffed. But this just came to my mind—I'm suppos
to have a visitor from South America, a Senorita Lea Blan
Ramero Oristezza, and this screwy stuff may have somethi
to do with that."

"In what way?"

"Senorita Oristezza," said Roxborough, "cabled me t
she would be in New York the day after tomorrow, a
wished to see me."

"About what?"

"I don't know that," said Roxborough. "But I can gue
it's about mining properties. The Senorita is a businesswo
an, a go-getter, and she owns commercial diamond mines
Brazil and is interested in the African diamond pictu
although to what extent I don't know. I do know sh
aggressive, a ball of fire in a country where women a
supposed to wear veils and sit on balconies and only go o
with chaperons. The Senorita Oristezza doesn't comply wi
convention, but she's a stickler for morals. She heads
temperance drive down there, is active in demanding poli
cal reforms, and I hear she's very narrow-minded about t
little pecadillos of the people she deals with."

Monk said, "Sounds sort of stuffy to me."

"You're damned right she's stuffy," said Roxboroug
"And you see what that means? She's a narrow-minded pu
tan. Suppose she came up here and found me in jail charg
with kidnapping and drugging a girl? What do you think s
would do with her business—not give it to me, that's sure
He threw both hands in the air and swore violently. "Tha

It's a trick by my stinking partners to get me in dutch with
is woman, who could throw a lot of business my way if she
anted to. And damn near ruin me if she wished, also."

"You're supposed to be dead," Doc said.

"Huh?"

"How," Doc asked, "did Senorita Lea Blanca Ramero
ristezza learn otherwise?"

The question did not bother Roxborough as far as could
e noticed. "Oh, that," he said. "I should have brought that
. There's one man who knows about my escape from the
ane crash. He's a man I trust. Bill Crater, down in Lima,
eru. Bill is my right hand down there, and not like these
inkers I've gotten mixed up with here in New York."

"The Senorita learned of your continued existence from
ur friend Bill Crater in South America?"

"That's right. Bill phoned me about it."

"Do your partners here in New York know you are
ive?"

"I didn't think so," said Roxborough bitterly. "But judg-
g from the signs, they must."

"Providing," Doc pointed out, "they were responsible
r the stuff that began with the swooning girl."

"Oh, they were."

"You're not sure, though?"

"In my own mind, I'm positive."

"Could you prove it?"

Roxborough shrugged. "Probably not right now."

"Just what," Doc asked persistently, "have they been
ing that leads you to suspect them?"

"Different things," said Roxborough impatiently. "You
st forget about me and my partners, Savage. I'll take care of
at. Chuck Roxborough can wash his own linen."

"Give me an example," Doc urged.

"An example of what?"

"Of the different things your partners have done that
ve aroused your suspicions."

Roxborough scowled. "Stop pinning me down on intangi-
es. If I could prove anything, I wouldn't have come up here
ter escaping from that crash without telling anyone I was
ive." He pondered, pocketing his hands, and looking angri-
at the floor. "It's little things, mostly. Funny business
ound the office. Documents disappearing. Not as much

profit showing on the books as should be. Odd and unexplain
trips the partners have been making to various compa
properties. Things like that. Nothing I can hang 'em for, b
plenty I can suspect 'em for."

"Nothing you can put your finger on?"

"That's it. Nothing my finger can hit on."

"But not imagination on your part?"

"No, sir!" Roxborough raised a fist. "I'm not a fool! I'
been around businessmen long enough to be able to sense–
The telephone started ringing, and he held his fist alo
looking surprised.

"Your telephone is ringing," Doc said.

"I'm not deaf. . . . It couldn't be anyone phoning me.
must be for you fellows."

"We told no one we were coming here," Doc sai
"However, Monk, you answer the phone."

Roxborough looked startled, yelled, "Wait a minute! I
answer—"

But Monk Mayfair had already scooped up the instr
ment, and was saying, "Hello? . . . Yes, Mr. Roxboroug
apartment. This is his serving-man speaking. . . . Very well
will see if he is in." Monk covered the mouthpiece, turned
them, and announced, "A lady to see Mr. Roxborough."

"Lady!" Roxborough exploded.

"She seemed to know Mr. Roxborough lived here
Monk said.

"I don't see how the hell that could be!" Roxborou
exclaimed angrily. "Ask her who she is, and what she wants

Monk grinned. "She explained that. She is Senorita L
Blanca Ramero Oristezza, and she had a business appoi
ment with you for day after tomorrow. She wishes to advan
the time to right now."

Roxborough gulped. "Holy smoke! Tell her to come rig
up."

Monk returned his attention to the telephone, a
Roxborough took out a handkerchief, mopped his face, a
remarked to Doc Savage, "You know, I probably owe y
fellows a debt of gratitude at that. The Senorita is a very pri
person from what I've heard, and if I had been in jail f
abducting and drugging a girl, my goose would have be
cooked. Much as I dislike people interfering in my affairs,
must say thanks for—"

"The Senorita," Monk announced, turning from the telephone, "says it is preposterous to think she will visit a gentleman's apartment unchaperoned. She will wait for you in the lobby downstairs."

"Good God, tell her I'll be right down!" exclaimed Roxborough.

Monk conveyed the information, then hung up. "It's a deal. She'll wait."

The handkerchief traveled over Roxborough's rugged, leather-beaten face again. "Would you like to come down and meet the Senorita?" he asked, suddenly pleasant. He saw the expression on Doc's face, laughed, shrugged, and admitted, "Oh, all right—I did realize that she must have heard of the great Doc Savage, and would be favorably impressed by finding him in my company." Then he shrugged. "Okay, if you don't want to meet her, that's all right too."

Monk Mayfair caught Doc's eye. "Personally, I'd love meeting a Senorita," the homely chemist said emphatically.

"All right," Doc said.

Roxborough's scowl became a grin. "Fine. With a dame as straightlaced and puritanical as the Senorita Oristezza, a character witness never does any harm." He whipped off his robe, hurried into the bedroom, and reappeared presently wearing a coat and slicking down his hair. There were indications that he had given himself a squirt of perfume. He hurried over to an arrangement of flowers by the window and selected an appropriate bloom for his lapel.

Monk came close to Doc Savage. "This should be right interesting," he whispered.

"You think so?" Doc asked, puzzled.

Monk nodded. "If my memory for voices hasn't taken a vacation," he said, "the Senorita Oristezza is our pal, the swooning girl."

VI

There were muddy footprints, the indirect result of the flurry of rain outdoors, on the elevator floor, and a porter was on his knees going after them with a damp cloth. After

Roxborough had stepped into the cage, he scowled at t
porter, and said, "Get out of here, fellow!" in a harsh voic
The startled porter stepped into the hall and they left h
behind as the cage descended. Roxborough glanced at D
Savage, and added curtly, "I don't want any dirty port
slopping around in here when we step out to meet t
Senorita Oristezza. Call it snobbery if you want to."

Doc Savage said nothing in a disapproving way, and t
cage completed its silent trip to the lobby. The doors whisper
open, and they stepped out into the impressive lobby.

The fainting-lady-Miss-Senorita Oristezza stood well ov
in the discreetly lighted portion of the lobby where the
were pieces of furniture in the extreme modern motif. S
did not turn at the sound of the elevator. She was indifferen
itself.

And very agreeable to look upon. Doc Savage was forc
to concede. She had changed her appearance considerabl
and the theme of her personality was now high Castilian; t
effect of acres of rich lace, mantilla and flashing fan w
predominant without these articles of apparel actually bei
worn.

"Senorita Oristezza?" said Roxborough in what was
far the most polite tone any of them had heard him use
date.

The Senorita turned—languidly, still indifferently; s
was getting a lot of effect into it—and got a good look at D
Savage, then changed her mind about the whole thing. T
Miss Morgan of the doings in the park had been a very se
possessed young lady who would not have screamed even o
little scream at sight of a roomful of mice—the Senorita d
almost as well. Just a little yelp. Then she took off for t
door, her high heels making hurried whettings on the floc
She was fast. She was through the door almost immediatel

"What the devil!" Roxborough roared in astonishment

"Stay with him and explain it to him," Doc Savage to
Monk and Ham.

The door was a revolving one, because the lobby w
air-conditioned, and it had stopped turning by the time D
Savage reached it. Stopped rather abruptly. The reason: Sl
had wedged a high-heeled slipper into it. Doc Savage had
little trouble with the mechanism that in theory prevent
the door from turning backward, but finally shook the slipp

e, and got outside. The other slipper was on the sidewalk.
vidently she felt she ran best barefooted.

He saw her now. The logic of her flight was apparent; she
d parked her car, a rich cream roadster with the top down,
most directly in front of the door. She was already in it, had
arted the engine, and was pushing at the gear-shift lever.

Doc Savage sprang forward. He saw he was not going to
t to the car door in time; the machine was moving now. He
anged his course, stepped on to the rear bumper, and
aning forward, seized the back of the boot which enclosed
e lowered top. This act, purely by chance, was almost
ithout noise, and she did not look around, and apparently
d no idea he was there.

She drove a block, took the first street to the right, still
ithout turning her head.

"It is doubtful," Doc remarked, "that you could throw
e off by turning again."

She lifted, from surprise, quite visibly on the seat. And
e tried an expedient instantly—stamped the brake, shifted
a lower gear, and gave full throttle so that the car leaped.
oc kept his grip. She looked back.

"Pull over to the curb," he said.

Her response was to seize a small pistol, evidently lying
the seat beside her, and point it at his chest. "Get off!" she
id. "Get off right now!"

He said, "I'm going to climb up there in the seat with
u. And incidentally, would you mind watching where you
e driving?"

"I'll shoot," she threatened.

"If you feel that's the thing to do, go ahead," he said.

And he climbed into the front seat. She did not shoot.
e slid over far to the left, and kept the gun pointed at his
idriff, however. And presently she added, "You have more
rve than good judgment."

"Not at all," Doc said pleasantly. "I'm simply wearing a
illetproof vest, and you've been very painstakingly aiming
my stomach."

"Darn!" she said.

He noted that it was a drive-yourself car. Rental job.
he small label in the lower right-hand corner of the wind-
ield told him.

"You speak a nice Yankee grade of English, Senorita," h
said.

She reached the next corner, turned, began looking fo
an empty curb space, found one, pulled into it and shut o
the engine. "You know, I have just concluded you are De
Savage after all," she said. "You were the man in the par
when all the trouble started, weren't you?" Dressed differen
ly, and with something that changed the color of your eyes?

"Yes."

"You *are* Doc Savage?"

"That's right."

"I think I'll check it, though," she said, and he suddenl
understood why she had chosen to park. Halfway down th
block there was a police patrolman approaching, saunterin
idly, and she leaned out and called, "Officer! Could I troubl
you a moment?"

As the policeman approached, she slid her pistol under
fold of skirt. "Yes, Miss?" inquired the officer, beaming at he
prettiness. "Something I can do?" He looked across, discovere
Doc Savage, and touched his hat. "Good evening, Mr. Savage.

The girl leaned back. She laughed. "I had a questio
but you answered it," she told the officer. "Thanks a lot.
won't bother you any more."

The policeman touched his hat and sauntered away. An
Doc asked her pleasantly, "What do I call you? Senorit
Oristezza? Dannie Morgan? Or what?"

She said, "I made up the name Dannie, and I like i
Let's use that one. However—" She opened her purse, fishe
out a passport and laid it in his hands, then switched on th
dash light so he could examine the document. "If you insist, i
could be Senorita Oristezza, you notice," she said presently

He nodded. The passport identified her as Senorita Le
Blanca Ramero Oristezza. "Dannie, if you wish," he said
"But it's strictly a Yank name."

"Why not? I think I've spent approximately half my lif
up here in schools."

He looked at her, suddenly having difficulty restraining
smile, and she noticed the amusement, demanded, "Well
what is funny?"

"Roxborough," he said, "characterized you as th
puritanical severe Senorita Oristezza. Not once but severa

mes, he emphasized your primness, straightlaced ideas and
nder sensibilities."

She hesitated, and then shrugged. "The Senorita Oristezza
somewhat of that character, and I am afraid I let the
annie person run away with me. A vacation from myself,
?" Then she frowned. "But this Roxborough, he is not
stified in outlining my character to anyone."

"Not justified in what way?"

"In no way—the man doesn't know me personally."

"He did not give the impression he did."

"He does not." The frown was still in place, and it
owed no indication of leaving her forehead. "But the man
ew a great deal about me, did he? That bears out the
ought I've had."

"What thought was that?" Doc Savage asked.

Her small hand made an angry gesture. "Did you know I
n in the mining business—and specifically, in the diamond
ining business?"

Doc Savage nodded. "Roxborough told us that. He says
is in the same business."

"The man Roxborough," she said, "has been recently
vestigating my mining interests with the intention of buying—
s own intention only, I might add. I have no wish of selling,
d have said nothing of selling."

"What," Doc asked, "is unusual about that?"

She gestured impatiently. "I am, in business, what you
ould call a complete operation. The diamond business I am
eaking about. I have the mines where the stones are produced,
en I have the cutting firms where they are prepared for
arket—both commercial stones which are used for cutting
rfaces in machine tools, and the white and blue-white
ms, which are cut for jewelry purposes—and I also have a
arketing organization. You understand me? My business is
ding diamonds in the earth, preparing them for market,
d selling them. That is how I happened to have somewhat
ore than two million dollars worth of diamonds on the plane
hich crashed.

Doc looked at her sharply.

"You mean," he said, "that you had two million in
ones on the plane which crashed with Roxborough the only
rvivor?"

"Exactly."

"And when the plane wreckage was found later—"

"My diamonds weren't," she said vehemently.

Doc Savage looked at the Senorita Oristezza intently
then found he could concentrate better if he turned an
gazed at the unprepossessing buildings along this part o
Columbus Avenue. Now, he reflected, had come to light
factor that the situation had needed. "A motive, a reason fo
the shenanigans," he remarked. "Two million in diamonds coul
do nicely. For a lot of men, that's enough to shake the world.

"You sound," said Senorita Oristezza, glancing at hi
sharply, "somewhat disappointed?"

"Somewhat," he admitted.

"I suppose two million dollars of my money is beneat
your dignity!" she snapped.

"No, don't get me wrong," he said quickly. "It's just thi
Normally, my associates and myself steer clear of involvemen
in matters concerning theft of money or jewels."

Her eyes flashed angrily. "Oh, is that so? And here I ha
been hearing that you were a sort of Galahad who made
career of righting wrongs and punishing evildoers whom th
law can't handle."

"That's right," he said briefly. "The police usually han
dle theft nicely." He looked at her intently and added, "Whe
the wrong parties have the good judgment to ask the polic
for help, that is."

She bristled. "Meaning I should have run to the police
Is that it?"

"Why didn't you?"

She pointed a finger at him. "Listen, you!" She poke
him wrathfully with the finger. "What do you know about th
diamond business? Don't tell me what to do!... Oh, I'
answer your question—first, the diamond shipment on th
plane was a secret. For security reasons—to avoid the ver
thing that seems to have happened. Theft. I am not sure ou
police would be certain there was two millions in stone
aboard just because I said there was. Secondly, I had nothin
but vague suspicions. The police are not lovers of vagu
suspicions, I assure you, in investigating myself."

"Nevertheless," he said, "you should have notified th
police."

She sniffed. "I have as much right as you have," she said, "to hunt crooks!"

He grinned. "What steps have you taken?"

"The first one was finding out that Roxborough really hadn't perished in the plane wreck," she said rather proudly. "I did that by checking closely on a man named Bill Crater. Bill Crater lives in Lima, Peru, is honest—even if he is a friend of Roxborough's—and when I went to him and asked him if Roxborough was alive, he admitted it. . . . Well, I did give him the idea I knew Roxborough hadn't died in the plane wreck—I was only guessing there—and so I said I wanted to do business with Roxborough about a mine, and I came to—"

Doc held up a hand. "Wait a minute. Why single out Roxborough for suspicion? There were eleven other people on the lost plane, as I recall."

"Roxborough," she said, "was the only one remotely connected with the diamond business. I figured, since my diamonds had disappeared, Roxborough was the man to investigate."

"So you came to New York?"

"Exactly. And found two of the most notorious criminals in South America skulking around his apartment—you probably know them by now as Juan Schaefero and Jolla O'Sullivan."

"Skulking?"

"Yes. Shadowing Roxborough. I did a little shadowing of Roxborough myself at first, and that's how I found out I had company."

"Then what?"

"I struck up an acquaintance with Juan and Jolla," she said calmly. "I knew they were big-time crooks. I wanted to know what was going on."

"That," Doc suggested, "was a little like climbing into the tiger cage to look for the wristwatch, wasn't it?"

Her eyes flashed wrathfully. "Until you bungled it, everything went well. I pretended to be a show-girl out of work. Not too honest. I was intrigued when they hired me to swoon for Roxborough—I couldn't figure out why."

"Do you know why now?" Doc asked curiously.

"I guessed. It was to get Roxborough in trouble and disgrace him in the eyes of the Senorita Oristezza."

"They knew you were coming?"

She nodded. "I can't guess how. Roxborough obviousl
didn't tell them—they being his enemies."

"That makes Roxborough appear honest, doesn't it?
Doc inquired. "Juan and Jolla being his opponents."

She waved her arms.

"At this point," she confessed, "I am confused. I do n
know what goes which way."

"But you are sure the diamonds are involved?"

"Two million in unset diamonds do not just walk off,
she said pointedly. "Juan and Jolla, on the other hand, hav
assisted other jewels to walk away from their owners."

Doc looked at her thoughtfully. "You have any objection
to discussing all this with Roxborough?"

"I should like to do that," she said.

He nodded. "Then we will."

This was a small dapper little man who, like a to
general in some imaginary army, was crisp and gaudy an
spectacular in the improbable uniform of dove grey with gol
trouser piping and an overdoing of gold epaulets and che
bric-a-brac. He even looked neat and imaginary lying ther
on the floor on his back, just inside the revolving door wher
Doc Savage came upon him. Doc went down on a knee
partly to take the small man's wrist and partly to get behin
the large chair that was nearby, overturned.

"Get back," Doc said to Dannie. "Something has happene
here."

Other than the overturned chair, and the little man i
the doorman's uniform, there was gentle peace in the lobby
Roxborough's apartment building. . . . Pulse in the little doo
man's wrist; he was only knocked out. . . . None of this coul
have happened many moments ago.

"Monk! . . . Ham!" Doc called sharply, and the soft peac
in the place absorbed the rapping anxiety in his voice an
gave back nothing. He could hear the girl behind him; sh
had not gone outside as he had ordered—at least by "back
he had meant the sidewalk outdoors. She had not gone, bu
probably it was all right because there might be as muc
danger outside as in here. He turned his head very briefly
She was behind a large urn which contained some grotesqu
plant, and out of the anxiety striking at all sides of his mind

e said, "If you can't follow any other instructions, at least
ay there!" He said it angrily.

And now out of the rear, but seeming out of the whole
obby because of the way it tore silence apart, came a single
ot. The tall urn fell apart, splitting first in the middle, the
arts falling inward upon themselves with a noise like the
ocking of wood blocks, and the girl stood exposed in the
reckage. Not standing, exactly—crouched back in the litter,
m-fingered hands played up in front of her face in terror,
aiting for another leisurely bullet, waiting to die.

In the rear, a laugh. Jolla. Doc had tagged the two men
ith their proper voices now, yet so identical were the two in
eir ways that he could apply no special characteristic to one
at would not fit the other. The laugh had a high wild
ntemptuous ring to it.

Doc seized the overturned chair now—he had kept low
hind it—and scuttled with the chair as a shield, pushing
e chair ahead of him, until he had collided with another
air, and then a third, picking them up stacked ahead of
m. One chair was no real protection against a bullet, three
ot much more actually, and so he skidded the whole thing
ward one of the ceiling pillars. In the meantime, the lobby
led twice with earsplitting sound. Both times the bullets
mmed into the chairs. He looked back. She was still there.
er hands were still up in front of her in ghastly expectation.
e Senorita Lea Blanca Ramero Oristezza was conceivably
ishing she had followed his suggestion to go outside, he
flected without satisfaction.

He began to hear Monk Mayfair somewhere, and had
fficulty at first telling whether the sound meant rage, pain
terror. Monk's natural speaking voice was the small squeaky
ie of a gravel-tonsiled child, but the voices of Monk's
notions were tremendous and varied—foghorns, calliopes,
histles, French horns. Monk in a tizzy was apt to sound
actly like Monk in terror. But presently he classified the
roar to mean thwarted rage. It was either far off or there
ere many walls between the voice and where Doc crouched.

In the rear somewhere, Jolla's voice said calmly, *"Bueno."*
Another speaker asked, "What's the gorilla upset about?"
Jolla laughed. "He is saddened. I backed the car on to

the sidewalk manhole by which he intended to exit from t
basement and assail our rear."

"We had better get out of here."

"I think so," Jolla said. "There is a buzzard of bad lu
flying tonight."

Doc Savage listened very carefully—they could ha
made the speech about leaving as bait to draw him into t
open. He strained ears, eyes, for a long time, maybe
minute! They had really gone. Through a back door.

He went with headlong speed to the door, but first int
corridor, naked stone and mortar and one bleak electric bu
for illumination, and then to the door. A service entrance.
steel door. Locked. It was a spring lock, and they h
knocked off the knob by which it could be opened from t
inside.

He saw what they had done before he reached the do
a hand dived into his clothing while he was trying the pan
and the same hand came out of his clothing with a phial-
little bottle, thin-walled, plastic, in two compartments. I
crushed this against the door at the lock, smashed it ha
with the heel of his hand. It split and the contents, rath
gooey, stuck there like pale tar.

Counting—fifteen seconds was supposed to be the ti
ing when the stuff was used like this—he wheeled and g
away from the door. The explosive was not particularly ne
only a little more developed than the similar material th
had been used for sabotage and demolition during the wa
The detonating medium was his own development, a chem
cal in the smaller compartment of the plastic container th
would touch it off, taking, in the quantity used here, abo
fifteen seconds to do the job. . . . He got to sixteen, sevente
and eighteen—he must have hurried it a little.

The fire was deep green. It came as a sheet that cover
the door almost completely. Not much of it seemed to co
back through the starkly naked stone service passage; but t
rush of air did, enough of it to knock Doc off balance, ma
him wonder about the future condition of his eardrum
although he was using the old under-shell fire trick of a wi
open mouth and feigned scream to lessen the chances
damage. Like all explosions, there was a vacuum effect aft
this one, and that snapped the door open, what was left of

He went out on to the sidewalk.

The car was going away. Four or five cars were moving
the street, none of them close. He had, at first, no idea
hich was the one, then dashed out into the street and was
ot at from far away, near the end of the block. That
entified the machine—a coach, a late model, blue. New
rsey license plates, and he got the number.

A sidewalk manhole, inlet for fuel oil into the apartment
use basement, lifted, rocked, fell and clanged. Monk wedged
beside the fuel oil inlet pipes and thrust his head out.

"How many?" Doc asked.

"Four, I think," Monk said. "No, five. One would have
en in the car. They weren't laying for us in the lobby. They
me in the back way, so I thought if I got into the basement
d came out this way, I'd be behind them—" He went
ent, had about ten seconds of paralyzed horror. "Ham!...
xborough...?"

"I saw no sign of either one," Doc said.

"Then they took them."

Doc said grimly, "We'll look and make sure!" He wheeled
d swung into the service hall, then into the lobby, where
met the Senorita Oristezza. She was walking toward them,
e trance-like step after another, arms held rigidly down and
ghtly away from her body and with her shoulders twisted
ck as if impaled, much as she had been walking when
onk first saw her out there in Central Park this morning,
eparing to swoon for him. Only this time there was not
uch pretense about it.

"It has temporarily let up," Doc told her. "So turn loose
d faint if you wish to."

"I wish I could!" she said thinly.

VII

At first there seemed to be no one in the ornate small
che which held the telephone switchboard, the PBX board.
ut when Doc leaned over the black counter with its edging
lucite, he frowned, then asked quietly, "You called the
lice?" She nodded up at him. "Yes," she said. "Yes, I
ve—the police—I think they're still on the wire—" A small

voice that came from somewhere else, apparently. She wa
least fifty and a ghastly example of what peroxide and cosm
ics will do when mixed with terror.

Doc stretched out an arm, took the headset and lifted
transmitter. "Twentieth Precinct?... Who?... Davis. W
Davis, this is Doc Savage. There were five of them, we thi
the two South Americans and three helpers. They abducte
man named Roxborough and my aide, Ham Brooks. Here
description of the car." He gave the general information ab
the machine and the license number, added the direction
departure. He listened to questions. "No one killed, app
ently. Some shooting. The doorman knocked unconscious

He turned then and went to Dannie. "Easy, Dannie,"
said quietly. "Easy, and you last longer." His words seem
not to have much effect; she looked at him with eyes too w
and hands tied desperately together. "Did they follow
here?" she gasped. "Was it because of me they trapped—

The telephone operator made a hissing sound. Th
wheeled. She was trying to speak. Doc watched her, and s
said with her lips only, "A call for you, Mr. Savage—one
those men—"

"Put it on the house phone," Doc said. "And plug in
another wire to telephone the police to trace the call." Wh
she only stared at him wordlessly, he told Dannie, "Sh
excited. You make the call. Get Detective Davis, communi
tions at the Twentieth Precinct, and tell him what y
want—this call traced."

He reached over himself and studied the board a m
ment, then plugged the call into the house phone.
crossed over to the instrument.

His, "Savage speaking," got one of the voices he w
expecting. Juan's.

"Need I identify myself?" Juan asked.

"It's not necessary," Doc said grimly. "And let me t
you something, fellow: If my friend Ham Brooks is harme
you and the rest of your outfit are going to regret it right i
eternity. And don't underestimate that threat just becau
you seem to have been rather successful in South America—

"I'll do the talking—"

"And you'll do the paying if Ham is harmed," D
snapped. "I make a threat very rarely, about once a year a
rule—"

Juan laughed angrily. "Really, Mr. Savage, you're more wordy than I had heard—"

"What about Ham Brooks? Is he—"

Juan swore, an anxious surprised sound. "Time to trace this call, eh? That is why you keep interrupting—Senor Savage, you molest us further and your friend Ham Brooks will circulate no more. You understand the word *morte?* That is what I mean. Goodbye."

When Doc Savage turned, Monk was standing there. He had gone out to their car and returned with an electrical apparatus having vague resemblance to a serviceman's test oscilloscope. Pale-faced, dry-lipped, Monk asked, "Is Ham okay?"

"The implication seemed to be that he was," Doc said. "But I'm not too sure."

"They took him along to... ?"

"That's right. The old thing all over again—they'll kill him if we don't leave them alone."

"They will, too," Monk said thickly.

"And will anyway, if we stand here," Doc said, and turned back to the switchboard.

Dannie shook her head at him wordlessly. "I don't think they've traced the call yet." She handed him the telephone, and he listened to the voice of the policeman named Davis shouting angry demands for haste, then to Davis saying, "Savage?... A booth in a drugstore on Broadway—relay me a description of the guy. We have a prowl car on the way over there now. Go ahead with the description and give me time to repeat it into the other microphone."

Doc Savage began to describe Juan in short takes, the outstanding characteristics first—not that the police didn't already have a description of the man, but freshening it wouldn't hurt—and once he turned to ask Monk exactly how Juan had been dressed. A different suit, Monk said. A hard-finished light tan cloth, a dark brown hat. Monk was by the door, tinkering with his contraption.

It continued, the describing, the waiting for the police car to reach the drug store, and Doc waited with poorly restrained impatience. He was aware that Dannie watched him woodenly, without visible signs of breathing.

Monk, scowling at his device, said something angry and

discontented. He picked the thing up and went outdoors wit
it.

From the telephone: "Savage?"

"Yes?"

"He got out of the drugstore. Our men are there. We'v
got half a dozen other cars piling into the neighborhood."

"I'm going over that way," Doc said. "If there is anythin
more, we will listen on the police radio and answer on th
same frequency."

He took Dannie's arm. "We'll find a safe place for yo
later. Right now, I'd like you to go alone and answer questions.

"Of course," she said, nodding. "But what kind
questions?"

"Juan and Jolla. . . . You might have picked up, durin
your meetings with them, something that would help."

"I don't know what it would be."

"Neither do I, until we dig for it."

In the night, hulking and silent, Monk Mayfair leane
against the hood of their car, which was the same machine
the trick taxicab, and fingered the dials of his piece
electronic apparatus.

Dannie touched Doc's arm, whispering, "What is h
doing?"

Doc Savage, plagued by anxiety about Ham Brook
welfare and the fate of Roxborough, answered almost curtly
"We've found it helpful," he said, "to provide various meth
ods of keeping track of one another under trying conditions.
He decided that sounded pedantic, a little too pat, a stuffed
shirt sort of an answer. He could not think of anything better
pointed to Monk's apparatus and added, "That is one of ou
devices."

Monk looked around. "I've got this thing fired up all it'
take, and don't get a thing except ourselves."

Dannie stared, not comprehending.

Doc said, "We can leave our shoes here. That migh
help." He took off his own shoes, Monk did the same, an
Doc carried them back into the apartment building and le
them with the astonished telephone operator. There wer
police in the lobby now, and a few spectators. Doc answere
the fewest possible number of questions and returned to th
car.

"A drugstore on Broadway," he told Monk, and gave the address. "Juan phoned from there. The police got on the spot in practically nothing flat, but he was gone. Let's get up there."

They climbed into the cab, Monk driving, his gadget on the front seat beside him. Doc and Dannie rode in the rear, and presently she said, "What did you mean—I might have picked up something that would help now?"

"I meant just that."

"I can't think of a thing," she said grimly. "Oh, I know where I telephoned them. Maybe that would help. It was Strickland 9-7070."

"That's the telephone number of their hotel, and the police know about that."

"I can't think of anything else."

"Let's fish around," Doc said. "Juan and Jolla are professional criminals, and their success indicates they have developed formula for their actions. Most criminals do, and one important item in the master plan is what we call an out. A route of escape if things go wrong. Usually they have more than one. . . . Well, Juan and Jolla have taken flight, and the way they've done it indicates an advance plan. Now what we've got to do is try to recall something you may have noticed that might give a hint."

She nodded. "I see. It wouldn't necessarily have had to seem important at the time, would it?"

"You've got the idea," Doc told her. "Suppose you start talking, and we may come across something."

Dannie shuddered. "I just can't think of a thing that night—well, I won't try. I'll just tell all the little things about them I noticed. I did observe them closely, believe me, because I was going to turn them in to the police after I found my diamonds. Let's see, they drank their coffee black. They both liked thick steaks, and usually, in fact always, they would order the same things to eat. They dressed similarly, too; not exactly alike, but if one was wearing tweeds, so would the other. And if one wore brown shoes, so would the other—no, wait. Twice I noticed Jolla wearing canvas sneakers when Juan wore regular shoes. They even kept their fingernails about the same length, and spotlessly clean. I remember how Juan, meeting us late at dinner, eyed Jolla's spotless fingernails, then began cleaning his own with a knife.

They were soiled, some tarry substance under them that h
dug out and raked off on a napkin, almost destroying m
appetite. I don't think they went to shows. Jolla read books i
English, though—I saw one in his coat pocket once, only
part of the title. *West Indies* something or other. That was a
I could read—"

Doc held up a hand. "Hold it. I think we've got a patter
here."

She shook her head, puzzled. "I don't see where I'v
shown anything except that they're so very much alike—"

"Sneakers—tar under the fingernails—a dark blue boo
with the first two words of the title *West Indies*—the boo
was dark blue, wasn't it?"

Dannie gasped in surprise. "Good Lord, yes!"

"The *West Indies Pilot*," Doc said. "A handbook put ou
by the government for shipmasters and pilots in the Caribbe
an. Sneakers are worn on boats. You find tar around boats
particularly seagoing sailboats."

Monk grunted explosively. "A boat! That's it! They've go
a sailboat for their get-away."

Dannie thought for a moment. "The ocean," she said, "i
fairish-sized. I don't see that this helps us so much."

"It's a lot better," Doc said, "than nothing."

On the block before they reached the drugstore, the
passed two police cars in motion, and there was a third at th
drugstore. A fourth arrived while they were parking, and ou
of that one climbed the ill-tempered Captain Scoffield. H
saw Doc and advanced growling, "I told you to take you
wild-west show out of my precinct, and I meant—" He sa
Dannie, flushed, bent to look inside, discovered that she wa
very pretty and grudgingly took off his heat. "Sorry, lady
Does your insurance company know you're going around i
Savage's company? It's a good way to shorten your lif
expectancy."

"It hasn't shortened it so far, Captain," Dannie sai
smilingly. "In fact, I suspect I am four or five hours olde
right now than I would have been except for Doc Savage.'

Captain Scoffield grunted. "They catch these guys wh
have been running you all over town?" he asked Doc.

"We might go in and find out," Doc said.

Before they reached the interior of the drugstore, how

er, a patrolman arrived breathlessly with the information: 'wo blocks over—they found the car."

It was a parking lot. A police car was cocked across the ιe entrance, and two officers, guns in hand, were carefully arching among the cars parked in the steel-wire fenced ιclosure. A sergeant saluted Captain Scoffield, explaining, don't think it's going to get us anything. They just changed rs here. They had another machine planted for the skip."

"Get a description of it on the air!" Captain Scoffield ιapped.

"We ain't got much of a one—"

"Get it from the parking lot attendant, then!"

The patrolman turned and shouted, "Come over here, u! Guglimo, or whatever your handle is!" A dark-faced ιuat man brought over an insolent manner and began :manding who the hell the police thought they were, shoving κpayers around. "Shut up!" the patrolman interrupted him. ιnd tell the Captain here how come you haven't got the :ense number of that car on your records like you're sup->sed to have."

The man scowled. "They take da page from da book," he owled.

Captain Scoffield swore, shoved his angry red face close › the lot owner's dark one, and bellowed questions. What ιnd of a car was it, how long had it been there, when did ιey take it away, and what was this about no license num->r? To this he got insolent answers: The car had been there week, it was a black sedan but he didn't recall what make, ιe men had come for it about fifteen minutes ago and left ιother car, that blue one, in its place, and as for the license ιumber, he had put that down in his book as usual, but the ιge was torn out of the book, as they could see if they would ›ok, and if they could read. Now, who did these cops think ιey were, Dick Tracy or somebody?

Captain Scoffield had an answer. "Take this guy down ιd book him for investigation, and if he stays snooty, lock ιm up as a material witness."

Mr. Guglimo was shocked.

In the meantime, Doc Savage had gone to the blue :dan in which Ham Brooks and Roxborough had been ιuled away from the apartment house. In the rear seat, on ιe floorboards, he had found two rubber heels—actually two

thick plates of a metal resembling lead, with a covering
rubber to make them resemble heels.

Doc showed the finds to Monk.

"Oh, brother!" Monk said excitedly. "Now we can go
town."

Captain Scoffield came over angrily. "Picking up e
dence and packing it off, are you!" He snatched the disguis
heels out of Monk's hand, stared at them without compreh
sion, feigned a full understanding of the things, and wrapp
them in his handkerchief. "Savage," he said, "I've told you
take your trouble-making out of my precinct. I'm telling y
again. Beat it. You hear me?"

Monk extended a hand. "Could we have those?"

"Certainly not!" Scoffield snapped. "They're evidence.
clue."

"A clue to what?" Monk asked innocently.

"You get out of here," Captain Scoffield said wrathful
"I'll figure it out."

"Want to bet?"

The Captain came over and poked Monk in the ch
with a thick finger. "Do *you* want to bet that, if I hear o
more remark out of you, I don't take you down and lock y
up for investigation yourself?"

"Cut it out, Monk," Doc said quietly. "You're getti
nowhere, and the Captain is right—we've been stirring
trouble in his bailiwick, and since we've accomplished prac
cally nothing, he has a right to resent it."

"Nothing!" Monk blurted indignantly. "Why, hell, n
we've got the lead that will take us—"

"The Captain isn't interested!" Doc said sharply. "Come
We've been ordered away from here, you may have noticed

Monk walked to their car, mumbling under his breat
"The Captain," he said, "could use a thirty-eight to blow t
wax out of his ears, and not notice any difference afterwards

VIII

By ten o'clock, they had finished a circuit of Manhatt
Island, first down the elevated highway on the Hudson Riv

le, then up the waterfront street on the East River, then
e boulevards, and near the Triborough Bridge. Doc Savage
id, "It's picking up a little. East of us somewhere."

Monk, driving, asked, "Which side of the Sound? Long
land, or the Bronx and Connecticut?"

"Long Island," Doc said. "We can cross over at Whitestone
it seems advisable."

Monk turned to the right, taking the long swinging
pproach of the Triborough Bridge; there was the vague sensa-
n of rising, the cab ran silently and hard. The lights of Manhat-
n spread out behind them, and ahead they could see
e measured flash of the airways beacon at La Guardia
ield.

"You understand how the gadget works?" Monk asked
annie.

"Not too well," she confessed. "Like a radio direction-
nder, you mean?"

"It's not the same thing at all, but the general idea is
milar," Monk explained. "The bait we're hunting is in the
eels of the shoes Ham Brooks is wearing. A radiant substance—
erely a couple of small pieces of the proper metal that have
en placed in an atomic pile and energized. Radium would
ave the same effect. Give off emanations. In the heels of
am's shoes, as I said. The stuff is dangerous—the radia-
ons, that strong, can give a severe burn if exposure is over
appreciable interval. For protection, the energized bits are
nclosed in metal shields—not lead, but a more effective
ielding alloy which Doc and I developed about a year ago.
he rubber heels—really metal with a coating of rubber—
ere the caps Ham wore for safety. He'd managed to tear
em off. I knew that when I found them in the car they
andoned. And that was why, earlier, I couldn't pick up
ything on the machine—Ham hadn't gotten the caps off
et."

Monk drew her attention to the electronic contrivance,
hich Doc was now manipulating.

"We're proud of that gadget," he told Dannie. "Doc
orked it out for the army. They're going to use it for
etecting dangerous radiations in case of an atomic war. It's
e best thing in the way of sensitivity that anyone has
eveloped so far. The best, because it's more directional."

"Then you can find Mr. Brooks with the device?" Danni̶
inquired anxiously.

"We can find his shoes, anyway," Monk told her.

They lay beside the car, in the weeds—half-hidden s̶
that Monk stepped on one of them and turned his ankle an̶
gasped in pain. Then he kneeled and explored with h̶
hands. There was not much light; no moon, the sky full ̶
cloud formation, another spring thunderstorm thumping an̶
winking redly in the southwest.

"Ham's shoes!" Monk's voice had a fringe of horror. ̶
was afraid for a minute he might be in them."

"Keep your voice down," Doc warned. He was goin̶
through the car, searching mostly with his fingertips. H̶
found articles of clothing—everything that Ham Brooks ha̶
been wearing, apparently. "They stripped him," Doc said̶
"Taking no chances on stuff in his clothing."

Monk said gloomily, "They must have heard abou̶
us. . . . You suppose their boat is around here?"

"That," Doc whispered, "is what we're going to try t̶
find out." He touched Dannie's arm, adding, "Get back i̶
our car, Dannie. The body is armor-plate, the windows ar̶
bullet-resistant glass, so you'll be—"

"You expect me to wait in the taxicab?" she demanded̶

"Yes. You should be safe—"

"Hold it!" she exclaimed. "It's not that I don't want to b̶
safe, but if you think I'm going to sit here in that cab, just o̶
your assurance they couldn't get at me if they came back—
nothing doing."

"But you will be safe."

"The safest place I can think of," she said grimly, "i̶
right at your elbow. And that's where I'm staying."

Doc gripped her arm. "Don't be a fool, Senorita Oristezza̶
The way things have been going, with those fellows runnin̶
over us at will—"

"You," she said firmly, "haven't done so bad. You starte̶
from nothing—at least with a fool girl swooning in th̶
park—and you've got the two most dangerous criminals i̶
South America, and their gang, on the run."

"I'm not going to argue. You stay in the car, Dannie."

"I go with you. And I'll not argue either."

"Listen!" Monk exploded. "Off to the left, toward the
\)y—"

The night possessed a damply sodden quality that blunted
\ounds, but they could catch faintly a thin squeaking. Short
\ duration, it ended in a muffled thump. Doc Savage, whose
\earing was sharper, said, "The rollers on a gaff squeaking."

"A what?" Dannie breathed.

"A gaff, one of the spars holding a sail. It slides up the
\ast as the sail is raised. That sound was someone hauling up
\ gaff a short distance, to make sure it was free-running, and
\tting it drop back. In other words, someone is preparing
\ e sails of a boat for hoisting." He moved away. "Over this
\rection."

Monk told Dannie uneasily, "You'd better stay here. This
\ likely to get rough."

"Frankly," she whispered back, "I wouldn't miss it for
\ything."

The hills swelled up to the east, stubby dark hills that
\ust be like sleeping animals out there in the night, and the
\ad threaded crazily where the hills dropped down into the
\a, or more properly Long Island Sound. Between road and
\lt water there was comparatively level ground sometimes
\o hundred yards wide and sometimes fifty feet. Being not
\o far from residential New York City, it was a popular
\ction for middle-class yachtsmen, the fellows with the
\e-to-twelve-thousand-dollar boats. Their yacht clubs were
\attered along the shore, and there was occasionally a small
\mmercial dock and a struggling boatyard. Out on the water,
\ere would be a flaking of small craft. All of it, of course,
\w pretty indistinguishable in the darkness.

The going would not have been bad, except that they
\ere barefooted, which was all right for silence, but several
\mes Doc heard the girl's breathing stop painfully as she
\epped on stones.

They made out presently the fact that they must be near
\e water. But the night was black, completely black, and Doc
\ached out and stopped Monk and Dannie. For Dannie's
\enefit, he whispered, "I have a projector that uses black
\ght. With special goggles, we can give a fair imitation of
\eing in the darkness."

Irked, she said, "So that's why you haven't been steppin
on rocks and bumping into things."

He said, "We haven't used it yet. We will now."

He had, as a matter of fact, only one projector and on
pair of the complex goggles necessary for use of the thing
The contrivance was not new; he had used it over a period c
years in progressively improved forms, and this one was eve
more developed as to compactness and efficiency than th
similar apparatus which had been used during the war.

Doc donned the goggles, switched on the projector, an
made an adjustment of the scanning device—utilizing th
principle of black light fluorescence on a sensitive screen, an
not simple as to construction.

The contrivance, in portable form, had one drawbac
which Doc and other scientists had not been able to overcome—
there was no depth perception. There was simply a fla
picture; distance could be judged if there were enoug
objects of known relative size in the scene, and a man coul
aim and fire a rifle accurately in the blackest night, bu
walking around with them was another matter.

He saw the boat now. A schooner, gaff-rigged, two masts
the hull about seventy feet on the waterline, undoubtedl
with an auxiliary engine that could flog the old hull along a
five or six knots. A beamy craft, quite a lot of freeboard,
semi-clipper bow, and the whole thing not yachty or slat
ternly enough to attract much attention. There were boat
like her all up and down the coast. She would even escap
special notice in the Caribbean, being not too different i
appearance from the interisland trading schooners seen there

They had removed the sail-covers. The sail-tops too, th
short lines that were used to tie the sails in neat furls on th
spars, and the sails lay loose and ready in the lazy-jacks
Forward, a pair of men were taking stops off the stays'
Another man came up from below carrying oil-burning run
ning lights, and began clipping them to the lightboards an
safety-lashing them there.

"Take a look," Doc said, and transferred the scannin
device to Monk.

Monk muttered, a moment later, "That's the outfit. I'n
sure the guy tying on the light was at Roxborough's apar
ment house during the excitement." He shifted the device t
Senorita Oristezza, and she gasped with surprise at the clarit

of the image. "It has an awfully odd color," she whispered. And then she asked, "What are we going to do?"

"Not to give a facetious answer," Doc said. "The best we can."

"Shouldn't we telephone the police?" she demanded.

He said quietly, "I'd like you to go back to the car and do that." He knew she was looking at his face through the scanning gadget, and grinned wryly. "If we can ask you to do it without giving you the idea we're trying to get you out of danger."

"Aren't you?"

"Some," he admitted. "But somebody should get the police. And quick, too. Those fellows are going to sail any minute."

"All right, I'll do it," she agreed. "What do I do? I mean, how do you work the radio—"

"I left it switched on, and set up on the police channel. Merely pick up the microphone, press the button you'll feel on the side, and start talking. They'll come back when you release the button. You can hear them on the receiver, although the volume is low."

"All right."

"Be careful," he said. "We don't know they're all on the boat."

She moved away in the darkness, after returning the black-light apparatus to Doc. She took much the route by which they had come, which was a path, then the waterline highway, and made fairly good time, breathing through her teeth each time her bare feet found sharp stone or stubbed against an obstruction. Her silk hose were a ruin; they were no protection anyway.

Suddenly she saw a car coming toward her along the highway. Because she was very scared, the car seemed an odd thing, a reeling scouring blaze of white light pursued by a mechanical moaning. She debated briefly waving her arms, trying to stop the machine, then dismissed the notion in a hurry—on the schooner, they would notice a thing like that. She wondered if the *Padres Feliz*, the Happy Fathers, had a guard posted. She shuddered. The name *Padres Feliz* when applied to Juan and Jolla had an ugly macabre quality like the laughter of skeletons. She slipped off the road, wanting to fall because of the way the stones hurt her feet. She crouched there and let the car go past with a sound like a long heavy cough.

Madre Dios, I'm scared, I'm terrified, she thought. The feeling, she knew, was quite simply arrived at. She was growing more frightened proportionately as she left the neighborhood of Doc Savage. That surprised her. The man grew in stature with distance, particularly in a devilish situation like this. Doc was a giant bronze man, rather handsome—now he seemed the superlative of both these things. She had imagined herself not greatly impressed with his gadgets—now, contrarily, she saw him as a wizard, a genie of protection. She grimaced at herself; one exaggeration was as annoying as the other. But she wished she was back there at the schooner with him. *Why, I felt safer walking into possible ambush with him,* she reflected, *than I feel walking toward safety now, alone.* She hurried out on to the road again.

Presently, limping, she reached the taxicab and tugged at the door.

It was now that Jolla came softly from the darkness, softly and unheard. Without speech or other preliminary, he whipped the side of her head twice with the blackjack, which he handled adeptly.

It was a very quiet unconsciousness. Jolla kneeled beside her and took her skull between his fingers the way one would test a football for air pressure, and felt for crushed bones.

"A hard head," he remarked, "in every sense of the word."

Doc Savage told Monk Mayfair, "I don't think it's safe to leave the goose out of the oven any longer. The Senorita Oristezza, if she should happen to get hold of a thick-headed cop, may not work this instantly. We can't afford to wait. From all signs, they're about ready to shove off, and with Ham as hostage, we don't want to risk a running fight at sea—"

"Put with fewer words," Monk said, "you think we'd better light our match."

"That's it." Doc gave Monk the black light device. "Move in closer, keep your eye on things, and if you see I need help, step in with an offering."

Monk's voice was uneasy in the darkness. "You going to work around to their rear?"

"Going to try to."

"You," said Monk, "are going to need luck. I'll bow to the east."

"Do that."

Monk was silent for a few moments, then whispered, "I'll keep my fingers crossed, too. I think there's more than five of those guys—" He paused, listening, said softly, "Doc...?" There was no answer. The bronze man had moved away without sound. Not too surprised, Monk himself began to work toward the schooner.

Doc Savage had taken a course somewhat to the right, and for a reason. The tide at this hour would be flowing out, and he had no intention of swimming against the tide when it was unnecessary. He intended to use the water, try to board the schooner from the seaward side.

Silence was not too difficult. The spot was being used daytimes by boatmen, so there were no large weeds, not too many twigs that offered danger of snapping underfoot. His bare feet found these trouble spots easily. He found, by the sense of touch, two hauled-out dories, a pile of lumber, the greasy track of a marine railway—he followed the latter down to the water edge and, crouching there, studied the schooner.

He saw something new. They had hung hooded lanterns off bow and stern, dangling a few inches above the water, and looking more closely, he saw why. Lying in the roll of sail that was the jib, well out on the bowsprit, was a man. A watcher. There would be another at the stern, no doubt.

Seeing this, realizing they were alarmed and on guard, he had a bitterly cold sensation of moves too recklessly made. One in particular—he should not have sent the Senorita Oristezza back to the car. If these fellows were on guard so carefully ...

He eased into the water, cautiously, a few inches at a time, not wading but crawling out on hands and knees. The tide flow began to push against him. There was five or six feet rise and fall of tide here, so the movement of water was considerable.

He had taken off no clothing—this for a reason also. His clothing was his armament, his gadgets. An example was a pencil which he now used. It was a pencil, all right, but also other things, including, when he stripped the sections out to full length, a telescoping tube. He was going to use it for breathing underwater, and proceeded to do so. It had other purposes—a mirror would clip in the end periscope-wise; it was not a bad blowgun. But now he breathed through it only.

He moved, underwater, slowly toward the schooner, letting the tide carry him.

Monk saw Jolla bring the Senorita Oristezza to the schooner. Jolla walked rapidly and easily, the girl across his shoulder. He gave from a distance the whistling call of some nightbird, and it was then that Monk turned the black light scanner in that direction. Monk stiffened and had threads of frost for nerves.

There was nothing he could do—that is, it wasn't the time for doing. He realized that only when he had stood and taken a step forward. Monk sank back behind a pile of scrap lumber, but it was a difficult thing to do. Particularly for Monk to do. Monk was no exponent of caution, of letting a plan get ripe. He crouched there, the palms of his hands getting moist.

Not thirty feet from the schooner, Monk could hear what was said. Juan came on deck. He flashed a light briefly.

"Where did you collect her?" Juan asked softly in Spanish.

Jolla told him. "Back on the road. I thought I heard a car. It took time to find it, and then she came."

"Savage is here?"

"I would say so."

"That isn't good," Juan muttered, and wheeled to one of the crew. "There is scrap iron in the bilge for ballast. Bring a good-sized piece." To another man, he said, "Rope."

Jolla said dryly, "Have I not heard you say you would never kill a woman, my friend?"

Juan snorted. "I did not think I would like to remember the look in the eyes of a woman when she died." He bent over the Senorita Oristezza. "This is different. This one is unconscious. Unconscious with her eyes closed, I am glad to say." He straightened, adding, "However, if you will loan me your handkerchief to cover the upper part of her face, I would appreciate that."

"You will use a knife?"

"Why not? A knife is the best death."

The man with the rope started with lashing the girl's arms, but Juan laughed at him, said, "She will be dead, you fool. Tie it around her waist. She has a slim waist." When the man staggered up from below with a slab of ballast iron that had a hole in it through which they could lash the rope, Juan personally took over the job of binding.

"If they're around here—Savage and that baboon—they may be seeing this," Jolla said uneasily.

"So what? If we kill them, they will not care then. If we do not, then they will take us. Savage is a man who either dies or wins. I have heard that of him. In the latter case, will we care? To be tried for one more murder. What difference?"

Juan straightened. "The handkerchief," he said.

Monk Mayfair had not quite stood it this far. He was easing forward a step at a time. What had happened to Doc? Damn it, they couldn't stand by and let the girl be killed.

Juan spread the handkerchief over Dannie's face. She had not moved except when they jerked her limp form about. The knife came into Juan's hand. Long of blade. Juan balanced it speculatively, and remarked coldly, "There is an art to this. The art is not to make it gory. The spine, not the jugular, just a careful severance of the white cord there, a simple surgical operation—"

Monk yelled then. He always yelled when he went into a fight, and he howled now. He began it with words. "Doc! They're killing Dannie!" And after that he made sound, just sound, a frenzied roaring that was more product of the primitive than normalcy, heavy-throated like the anger of the jungle.

The noise did not dull his awareness. So he understood that three or four men were converging on him from the sides, not men from the schooner, but men who had been lying concealed in the vicinity, under innocent-looking piles of trash.

There was no shooting. Monk did not have a gun. One of the assailants was armed with a revolver, but he did not fire, merely stood back and waited, ready to use the gun if Monk managed to whip, single-handed, a half-dozen assailants.

Monk very nearly did that. He veered left, his arms opened and took in two assailants together; he fell with them, deliberately, and they began to shriek. The others piled into the struggle.

Juan, for the first time a thin whistle of terror going out with his words, said, "They were closer than I thought!" He jumped ashore and ran and stood by the melee, occasionally launching a kick into the ball of bodies.

Out of the fight on the ground: curses, gasps, bones breaking, dust and two hats. Then a shoe. These and hands and feet which were quickly jerked from sight again.

Juan kicked once more. Solidly. He leaned over the melee with a flashlight.

"We've got him," he said angrily. "Stop fighting each other."

He seized Monk by one leg and began dragging him toward the schooner.

"That is two?" Jolla called.

"Yes, two."

From the stern of the schooner, where he had lain across the rail watching the water intently all during the fracas ashore, a lookout spoke.

"Someone hand me a grenade," he said, "and I think I can make it three."

Jolla lunged to the man's side. "In the water?" he demanded.

"Yes." The watcher's voice was ghost-thin with terror. "I think I saw a face look up at me. It rose from the water—sank again—"

"When?" Juan wheeled. "Savage is in the water! Under the boat! Use the hand grenades, you fools! On all sides of the boat, all at once! Not too close, not close enough to smash the hull—"

"How close would that be?" someone wailed.

Juan cursed. "Never mind! Get them in the water. Let the boat sink if—"

The first hand grenade let loose underwater. Not an impressive explosion, seemingly; yet the ship jumped slightly. The others followed; spouts of water climbed violently, a few times with kernels of flame. Nine blasts in all.

"Keep throwing them in!" Juan screamed.

"That's all. There are no more."

They blazed flashlights at the water, watching and waiting, and if anyone breathed, it was not audibly. The water boiled for a while, mud came up in clouds and streaks,

atching the surface with blackness. The tide carried the mud
way.

A man whimpered in pain. A puppy-like sound, but
ud. They all jumped. Monk had broken the man's arm.
nother sat down sickly, white-faced, and began trying to get
is arm back into joint at the elbow. Monk's work also.

"*Dios!*" Jolla pointed. "Bubbles!"

He seized a rifle, the only rifle in the crowd, and aimed
t the spot. With a soft cough, another bubble broke at the
irface. There were two more in quick succession. Jolla
ocked the rifle deliberately.

Juan muttered, "I would not be too sure the bubbles
iean anything. They could be the result of the explosions
nderwater—"

"A hand!" a man screamed. Simultaneously, Jolla's rifle
nashed. And as the shot echoes came caving back on them
om the nearby hills, Jolla shrieked almost with a madness.
I missed the hand. But it was a hand. Savage is out there."

Now all the lights centered on the spot astern. Juan
wore suddenly, seized a life preserver and heaved it as far as
e could astern. It floated slowly away. "To judge how fast the
de will carry a body—"

Again he did not finish, because Juan's rifle was jarring,
ne muzzle laying out sheets of flame. An object had rolled
artially into view above the surface, a thing that could be
othing but Savage's body. It was his coat; Juan began
hrieking that it was Savage's coat, the same color, the same
esign, which was a little preposterous because the distance
as too great for that. All the time Jolla was firing; he
mptied the clip, and screeched for another, pumped that
ito the object, which now sank from sight.

Jolla continued to fire, clip after clip, until Juan seized
im and shook him repeatedly.

"That is three," Juan told him. "There are no more."

IX

The gentleness came back to the one who had used the
ifle, and with it a weakness of the legs that became a complete

inability to stand, so that he folded down and sat, foolisl
staring at the rifle, on the deck. Alarmed, Juan demande
"You have been hit? A piece of a grenade perhaps—"

Jolla looked up at the other man. "I am sick with t
sweetest sickness I ever had. I think I have been dying
night from thinking about this Doc Savage. I think tl
sickness is life. Get below and see whether the explosio
started the hull leaking."

Juan laughed. He swung over and dropped down t
companionway, glancing forward to make sure Ham Brooks
lashed to the mainmast where it passed down through t
cabin—and Roxborough—trussed up more comfortably (
the floor—were there and helpless. They were. Ham gagge
could say nothing, but Roxborough demanded, "Wh
happened?"

"A bon voyage party," Juan told him, laughing again
he went over to peer down into the bilge. The man who h
gotten the scrap iron had lifted aside a section of flooring (
the purpose, and not replaced it. Juan used a flashlight;
tossed a match on to the water that is always to be found
the bilge of a sailboat, and watched it to see whether the
was a flow from any direction.

He returned to the hatch, called, "She's making prac
cally no water. Cast off and get the sails up. We'll use tl
engine after we're outside."

Someone pushed the girl down the hatch, saying, "Catch
"Is it necessary?"

Jolla's voice, still faint with the sickness he had calle
good, replied, "Of course it is, stupid. One body floati
around the harbor is enough."

Juan caught the Senorita Oristezza, carried her over ai
dumped her on the bunk opposite where Roxborough lay. I
stepped back, looked at the girl's legs, and began to appro
of the idea. "No, that body wouldn't be suitable in a harbor.

The schooner heeled as the wind caught the one sail th
was up, and there was a chorus of mouse squeakings as th
other sails were hoisted, fores'l and then mains'l.

On deck, forward near the forecastle hatch, a man fe
heavily.

"What happened?" Jolla yelled.

"There is a wet slippery place here on the deck," th
man complained.

Jolla laughed. "The grenades splashed water on deck," e said happily. "And presently we shall be at sea, and there vill be waves breaking aboard. The weather forecast is for loudiness and storms. Bad weather for any planes which aight seek us." He sounded happy about it.

When Monk Mayfair regained consciousness, his imme- iate feeling about the world was that he wanted none of it, ae Indians could have it. He spent a few seconds trying to lentify various portions of his body—teeth, eyes, ears, square aches of skin, in different places—a sort of mental roll call to ee how much of him was still left together. The overall icture was not encouraging, although he could find nothing nportant missing. And now suddenly, it having taken all this me to make mental connections, he realized that he was ed and in a boat with Ham Brooks, Roxborough and the enorita Oristezza.

Monk stared at them. They all seemed to need repairing a one spot or another. Monk opened his mouth, intending to peak loudly and clearly; after trying, he sat there rather olishly. The voice must have been his own, but it seemed usty and under the floor somewhere.

He was sitting against the mast. He peered at his xtended ankles, noting they were roped. He tried his wrists ehind him, and they were tied also, on the other side of the aast. It was a thick mast, and his arms were in an agonizing ramp.

Monk tried again. "Where's Doc?" he asked.

The others—Ham, Roxborough, Dannie—had been ordless; they remained wordless now, but in a different way. Ionk peered at their speechless faces and began to wish, vish with a ghastly dull endlessness, that he had not asked aat question. Unasked, his imagination would have had full rild play, but its worst could not have been like this. He did ot say anything more, and they remained there each in a ersonalized pool of horror, until Juan and Jolla came down om deck.

Juan and Jolla came together, which was appropriate; aey were polite and smiling, and gently complimenting each ther in speech again; in other words, back in form.

"We have a short speech to make," Juan said.

"Short, but you should listen," added Jolla.

There was now hardly a trace of the accent of *Espanol*
their voices. They had changed clothing and wore seagoi
garb, yachtsmen's garb that enhanced their illusion of sam
ness, although the clothing itself was not identical.

"You understand, I believe, what caused the who
thing," said Juan.

Jolla watched their faces. "Diamonds. Raw diamon
from the Senorita Oristezza's lease in Southwest Africa ne
Luderitz, and from Brazil. The value of two million dolla
and a bit over in American money."

"*Pesos del Estados Unidos*," said Juan.

"Yes, United States dollars."

Juan nodded. "They were on a plane which crashed a
Mr. Roxborough was on the same plane and escaped. Th
wreckage of the plane was found and the diamonds were n
there."

"The connection between Roxborough and diamon
seemed obvious to us," said Jolla.

"And unfortunate."

"Unfortunate, yes. It misled us—"

"We think—"

"Yes, we think—"

Ham Brooks raised his head—there was no gag in h
mouth now—and said, "Oh, for God's sake, what's the idea
the vaudeville act? Or does it have an idea?"

Juan grinned. "The idea, as well as any other ideas, w
be of very brief interest to you."

"Brief!" said Jolla.

Monk moved impatiently; he almost yelled from th
cramping pain in his arms. The general idea was that Jua
and Jolla had decided, or were saying they had decided, th
Roxborough had not made off with the diamonds. They ha
come to New York to take the diamonds from Roxboroug
which they had concluded was a bad move. That was wh
they were saying. What they meant might be almost anythi
else.

Monk said painfully, "If you figure Roxborough didn't g
the diamonds, where'd the stones go?"

Juan smiled, pointed at himself and his associate. "N
we," he said.

"Then who?"

"The jungle where the plane crashed is quite primitive,
not uninhabited. There are aborigines. Indians. They go
d and use blowguns, but they are not without some
act with the world—enough contact, we are afraid, that
might have recognized the diamonds for what they
."

That was a long speech and Ham, his head cocked up,
led at Jolla, waiting for him to attach a statement of some
but Jolla was silent. Ham sneered. "That's a fine picture
nocence you draw. It would look better in a comic strip."

Juan shrugged. "It is of very temporary importance what
think."

"Then why make it?"

Juan nodded at Dannie and then at Roxborough. "The
anation is for them. They are not going to die, unless
are particular fools."

Ham looked at the man intently. He let his head back
fully on the bunk covering. "That's pretty good," he said.
t's half of a loaf. Now what's the catch?"

"No catch."

Ham's lips twisted sourly.

"No, I am sincere," Juan assured him. "What would
death gain us? Oh, they can report to the police that we
criminals and murderers?" He laughed unpleasantly. "Is
news to the police? I think not."

"What will you do with them?"

"Do? Leave them on an island someplace, I suppose.
n we get south, of course, in the Caribbean."

Roxborough lifted his head and looked at Dannie. He
ed pleased at the prospect.

Juan produced his knife. "There is no foolishness this
, as there was on the deck with the girl earlier."

Monk sneered at the man from the floor, where he
ched beside the mast. "Afraid to let us go, eh?"

"Exactly," Juan agreed. "We have quite an opinion of
ability. Perhaps you are not the remarkable sort that
Savage was, but I don't believe we would sleep well with
free. I suspect that, if it took years, it would still be a
of you dying or ourselves. So why take a chance?"

"You've got something," Monk admitted sourly.

"You take it calmly."

"Try cutting me loose," Monk said, "and we'll r[e] that."

Juan looked at the homely chemist, contemptuous[ly] the beginning, then with growing unease that he soug[ht] throw off with a curt shoulder movement. "My ugly fri[end] the day of your miracles is past, now that Savage is de[ad]

"You think so?" Monk, a little blind with rage, a [little] incoherent from the pain in his bound arms, shoved his [head] forward and yelled, "How would you like for me to produ[ce a] little miracle, friend? How would you like that? Just w[atch] me and—"

A man fell through the skylight.

Nothing could have been more perfectly timed. M[onk,] like an angry dragon prophesying disaster, had reached thre[e] screaming climax—and *crash!* A shower of glass, glitterin[g in] the cabin light. The man did not fall completely through [the] skylight, which was in the center of the cabin roof at [this] point, just forward of the mast, and crossed with a d[ozen] brass bars. But the man hit hard, hard enough to bend [the] bars and break the glass. Looking up, they could see [the] utterly blank face and wide motionless eyes staring dow[n at] them. He was one of the crew.

"You fool!" Juan screamed. He had been badly sha[ken.] He leaped to the galley, seized a frying pan, and came [back] and smashed it up against the skylight bars, striking the [man] ineffectually in the face, shrieking, "Pick such a time to [fall] into the skylight, will you—"

He stopped. He had the frying pan drawn back [for] another blow; it hung in his hand, stiffly; the hand and [the] arm loosened and it seemed that the pan was going to [pull] him over backward; his eyes grew big and bug-like as [he] ogled the face of the man.

"He is dead!" he said.

This was an error. The man breathed. Blood filled [the] creases of his lips from the damage done by the frying [pan,] and this became crimson bubbles.

Somewhere on deck there was a stumbling sound— [a] stumbling, except that no steps and no profanity followe[d.]

"That sounded like a man stumbling," Juan said. "[Will] you look? What the hell is going on up there?" He said th[is]

of the crew. There were three crew members below
·k.

The man took the required number of steps up the
1panionway ladder, three, to permit him to gaze out on
·k.

He said, "Someone did stumble..." For a three-word
ement, his voice did a lot of trailing off.

"What is it?" Juan asked hollowly.

The man in the companionway said, "They seem to be
·ping." He said it oddly, not with any particular disbelief,
contrarily as if he believed it very much and didn't
lerstand it. "They are lying there—" He stopped, blinked.
1ey are lying—" His face was dulling; puzzlement, which
st have been a terrific emotion within him, barely stirred
shape of his face. He said, "I feel—sleepy—" And with
classic, he laid down on the floor at the foot of the ladder.

Monk, held tightly jammed to the mainmast, felt a slight
against his back; he heard the chug of a sound that
ompanied it. They all must have heard. Monk brought his
1s around in front of his face, rolled over and seized the
1d-axe which had sliced the ropes and buried half an inch
the mastwood. He loosened the axe, which was sharp,
hed through his ankle bindings, stood up, lunged to Ham
·oks—Ham had his wrists over the bunk edge, ready for
operation—and chopped through Ham's wrist cords.

"Operations are underway," Monk said. "Doc, be care-
There were eleven of them aboard, all told."

Doc Savage came in from the forecastle. He said, "The
·k has been taken care of. Get ready for it to happen here."

Juan had been having a ghastly time trying to decide
ich way his knife should go; now he turned, ogling Doc
·age, and suddenly threw the knife. He used the under-
1d delivery best for short range; the knife did not turn over
the air, but traveled point-first and sliced through the
nze man's clothing, hit the bulletproof mesh undergar-
nt Doc was wearing, and bounced visibly.

Monk struck Juan then. Juan rolled with the blow but
1t down with wiry deception, trying—and succeeding—to
e Monk the idea he was badly dazed. Monk lunged for
. Doc Savage yelled, "Look out, Monk, he's a judo
ard—" But by that time Monk had hold of Juan, and

began learning the fact for himself. It became a no
enlightenment.

Short-lived, though. Because presently Monk look
down foolishly at Juan, who seemed to be sleeping; he peer
at Juan with a sort of all-out idiocy of expression, th
continued in character and bent from the waist and laid
hands on the floor, held that position briefly, then stretch
out on the floor.

Doc Savage and Ham Brooks waited silently, flat-cheeke
tight-lipped. Ham, to make doubly sure, clamped a ha
over his mouth and closed his nostrils with thumb a
forefinger. Even then, he had difficulty not breathing, b
cause the coming of the gas had caught him very short
breath.

In not much longer than a minute, Doc Savage and H
were the only ones consciously able to move.

X

A single splinter of lightning arose briefly off the sou
ern horizon and stood there quivering.

Dannie, looking forward, distinguished Doc Savag
form.

"He's tying up the last one now, isn't he?" she demand
nervously.

Ham Brooks took the occasion to squeeze her ha
comfortingly.

"You're all right. Everything is perfectly all right,"
assured her. "You understand about the gas, don't you? I
anaesthetic only, odorless, colorless, and has the unus
quality of quick oxidation when exposed to the air, t
oxidation rendering it harmless. By that I mean that if o
manages to hold their breath for about a minute or a min
and a half, the effects can be escaped. That is what Doc an
did. It is what Monk would have done if he had been be
with any sense."

"Yes, I understand that now."

"It's absolutely harmless," said Ham. "Please be assur
of that. It won't hurt you, because I've been knocked out
that stuff dozens of times—"

Monk, from the companionway, said unpleasantly, "Y
think you're a good example?"

"I didn't," Ham told him, "forget to hold my breath
the gas wouldn't take."

"You didn't," Monk told him, "have hold of the character an." Monk explained to the Senorita Oristezza, "Ham is ght about the anaesthetic gas producing no ill effects erward—except that sometimes you do wonder what the ckens happened." Monk chuckled. "If you want to see mething funny, take a couple of the grenades to a dull party metime and drop them in somebody's pocket. They're very in-walled glass capsules, crush easily, and you should see e uproar when everyone goes sound asleep for about fifteen inutes, then wakes up and tries to explain it."

Roxborough, sitting in the cockpit, growled, "That's all ry cute. I'm impressed. My neck is also saved, and I'm ateful for that. But when do we head for shore?"

"We'll get around to that," Monk said.

"Well, I can use a night's sleep," said Roxborough.

Doc Savage came back from the bow in time to hear the t remark, and agreed, "We all can. A night's sleep I mean."

Roxborough stirred impatiently. "How'd you get away m them when they thought they'd shot you underwater, d how'd you get aboard? I missed out on that."

"That was just some hard swimming underwater, plus e fact I had a tube by which I could get an occasional eath of air without surfacing," Doc explained. "When the ht broke out on shore with Monk, I tried to come in on —and surfaced directly under the nose of a lookout. You ow what happened then. The grenades weren't too bad, t they weren't good, either—I swam astern, shoved up a nd, blew a few bubbles after drawing the air through the be, then stripped off my coat and tied it in a knot and rned it loose underwater. Monk tells me that when the coat rfaced, they shot it to pieces and figured they had finished ."

"While you were doing that," Roxborough said, "you mbed aboard?"

"That's it. By the bow—the bobstay chain and the bow-rit and then down into the forecastle. Later, someone pped and fell on the wet spot where my clothing had ipped, bothering me for a minute."

"They were a pack of fools," Roxborough said curtly. most as big fools as you fellows were to let it get this far ng."

"You think so?" Monk asked belligerently.

Doc said, "Easy does it, Monk."

"I don't like this guy's manner," Monk said indignantl▍ "And I never have. If he's such a hot-rock—"

"Cut it out," Doc said.

"Let him shoot his mouth," said Roxborough. "I think can handle him."

"You're getting cabin fever," Doc said impatiently. "Sto fussing. Here, Roxborough, here's a loaded revolver. Will yo go forward and guard the prisoners. Someone should sit u there near the forecastle with them, in case they work the bonds loose. Here's a flashlight. You can use it occasionally

Roxborough hesitated, then growled, "Okay. Maybe if did something useful it would improve my temper."

Monk listened to Roxborough moving forward to the bo area, where the prisoners had been assembled on the dec bound hand and foot. It was dark, intensely dark, and Mor leaned over and laid a hand on Doc's arm, whispered, " found them, Doc. I guess they're diamonds—"

"My diamonds!" Dannie gasped.

"Sh-h-h-h," Monk admonished. "Yeah, I think so. I` sure."

Dannie blurted. "But how—"

Ham whispered, "It was a collaboration job. I notice that Juan and Jolla both seemed a little too interested in th bilge—remember when the floorboard was up so the fello could get the slab of iron? Well, Jolla closed the floor ve carefully, went out of his way to do it, when there we plenty of other things more urgent. And when one of them, forget which one it was, looked in the bilge to see how hig the water was—whether the grenades had opened leaks—h sort of reached up under the planks to ascertain that som thing was still there."

They were quite silent for a while. Dannie was evident thinking—suddenly her breathing stopped, then she made long gasping sound of surprise. "But they said they did have the diamonds. . . ."

"Shush! Quiet!" Doc urged.

"That was some kind of a trick!" she blurted. "If they ha the stones, why pretend—they said they were going to tur Roxborough and me loose—"

"Will you," said Doc bitterly, "keep it a little lower."

She gripped his hand. "Why all this furtive quiet—"

"You," Doc told her in a low voice, "were going to be —eed—as a witness."

"Witness of what?"

"Of Roxborough's innocence, where the diamonds were oncerned."

"Then he's not—?"

"We hope to know in a minute."

She dragged in breath heavily. "I can hardly believe —after all, they did hire me to play that trick on Rox-orough—"

"What," Doc asked, "could have done more to convince ou Roxborough was the innocent victim?"

"You could be right . . ."

"We'll know in a minute," Doc said again. "Monk is vearing the black light gimmick, watching Roxborough, up orward there guarding the prisoners—"

"With a loaded gun!" she breathed. "My God, you veren't fool enough to give him a loaded gun when you uspected—"

Doc chuckled reassuringly. "Loaded with blanks," he aid. "The thing we're fairly sure Roxborough will do—if he's uilty—is untie Jolla and Juan and the others and attempt a reak. On the other hand, if he doesn't—"

"The other hand," said Monk softly, "won't be needed. Roxborough is cutting Juan loose now."

Doc stood up silently, went forward along the deck, uite soundless in the darkness until he was close behind Roxborough, and there he thumbed on a flashlight beam and plattered the glare over the two men.

"Open packages?" he inquired.

Look for four more
Doc Savage adventures
in

The Doc Savage
Omnibus #2

Coming in January 1987
from Bantam Books

Special Offer
Buy a Bantam Book
for only 50¢.

Now you can have an up-to-date listing of Bantam
hundreds of titles plus take advantage of our uniqu
and exciting bonus book offer. A special offer whic
gives you the opportunity to purchase a Banta.
book for only 50¢. Here's how!

By ordering any five books at the regular price p
order, you can also choose any other single boo
listed (up to a $4.95 value) for just 50¢. Some restri
tions do apply, but for further details why not ser
for Bantam's listing of titles today!

Just send us your name and address and we w.
send you a catalog!